CW01497153

THE HEIR APPARENT

Rebecca Armitage is a journalist with the Australian Broadcasting Corporation, who likes to write about royals. She has written stories about the death of Queen Elizabeth II, the coronation of King Charles III, the exile of Prince Harry and Duchess Meghan, and the abdication of Denmark's Queen Margrethe. As digital editor for the ABC's International news team, she has covered several US elections and travelled to Israel to cover the war in Gaza. She lives in Hobart, Tasmania, with her husband and a poorly behaved German Shorthaired Pointer named Chino. *The Heir Apparent* is her first novel.

THE HEIR APPARENT

REBECCA ARMITAGE

ONE PLACE. MANY STORIES

HQ
An imprint of HarperCollins*Publishers* Ltd
1 London Bridge Street
London SE1 9GF

www.harpercollins.co.uk

HarperCollins*Publishers*
Macken House, 39/40 Mayor Street Upper
Dublin 1, D01 C9W8, Ireland

This edition 2025

1

First published in Great Britain by HQ,
an imprint of HarperCollins*Publishers* Ltd 2025

Copyright © Rebecca Armitage 2025

Rebecca Armitage asserts the moral right to be identified as the author of this work.
A catalogue record for this book is available from the British Library.

HB ISBN: 9780008757687
TPB ISBN: 9780008757694

This novel is entirely a work of fiction. The names, characters and incidents
portrayed in it are the work of the author's imagination. Any resemblance to
actual persons, living or dead, events or localities is entirely coincidental.

All rights reserved. No part of this publication may be reproduced, stored
in a retrieval system, or transmitted, in any form or by any means,
electronic, mechanical, photocopying, recording or otherwise,
without the prior permission of the publishers.

Without limiting the exclusive rights of any author, contributor or the publisher of
this publication, any unauthorized use of this publication to train generative artificial
intelligence (AI) technologies is expressly prohibited. HarperCollins also exercise
their rights under Article 4(3) of the Digital Single Market Directive 2019/790 and
expressly reserve this publication from the text and data mining exception.

Printed and bound in the UK using 100% Renewable
Electricity at CPI Group (UK) Ltd

For more information visit: www.harpercollins.co.uk/green

AUTHOR'S NOTE

Lexi's ancestor, Barbara Villiers, was a real person – a royal mistress who scandalised the kingdom with her beauty, her sexuality and her endless scheming. Barbara was a favourite of King Charles II – that much is true – but in *The Heir Apparent*, British history takes a wild turn. The House of Villiers may never have ruled Britain, but oh, how Barbara would have loved it if they did.

PART ONE

CHAPTER ONE

1 January 2023

I was about to kiss my best friend when the helicopter came.

It was New Year's Day, and for the third year in a row, Jack and I woke before the sun. I'd rolled up the rainfly on my tent during the night so I could look at the eruption of stars overhead. Now I saw only the first bloom of dawn. When I crawled outside, Jack's own tent was already unzipped, and he was sitting by the embers, rumpled and sleepy and smiling at me.

'Coffee?' he whispered.

Finn was still asleep in his dew-beaded tent, so we left him there and walked the sandy path from the campsite. There's nothing like morning in the Australian bush – it's magical. Those great beautiful gums were silhouetted against a pale sky. The first birds started their call. Wombats ambled around us, unafraid, as we walked towards the water tank.

This tradition of ours was a bit of an accident. The first time, the three of us had been at a New Year's Eve party at a bar in Japan when we drunkenly agreed to a snowboard instructor's invitation for a dawn run down the mountain. The next morning, when the alarm went off in our room at the ryokan, Jack had flinched under his giant doona, and our hangovers walloped us over the back of our skulls.

It would have been so easy for the two of us to roll over and go back to sleep, but Finn was staying at a place down the road with his sisters. He'd be standing at the ski lift waiting for us, looking fresh and miraculously sober, and he'd have been beyond pissed if we didn't show. So we had silently pushed back our blankets and put on our damp ski gear and trudged out into the inky snowfields to find him. It wasn't until the three of us reached the summit and the sun burst above the mountains that Jack and I looked at each other and smiled, our hangovers gone, the new day like a fresh sheet of paper. We'd agreed to watch the sun rise together every New Year's Day for the rest of our lives. Probably a strange vow for two friends, if anyone had bothered to ask. We certainly hadn't.

Last year I had been on call, and we'd watched the sun ascend over Hobart while we sat together on the roof of the hospital. This time, we were camping, a curious anticipation humming between us.

'We could probably still catch the sunrise if we head down to the beach now,' Jack said.

I left the bottle by the tap and we walked through the long grass in silence. When my boot got caught under a log, I steadied myself on Jack's down-covered wrist, my hand sliding into his. I left it there. Such a curious feeling, holding your best friend's hand, like edging your toes over a great precipice, or draining a champagne flute quickly.

Jack and I had been circling each other for weeks. A month earlier, soon after I'd broken up with Ben, he'd tickled me in the kitchen until I was breathless and hysterical and trying to pretend I didn't enjoy feeling him pressed against me while I grabbed his strong forearms.

So I didn't object when he squeezed my hand as we stood on the rocks above the beach, the sky blushing pink before us. Sunlight travelled through particles in the air, refracting and scattering in the atmosphere. It was simple science at work, but as the sun torched the sky it was hard not to believe it was just for us.

Now would be the time for Jack to ruin the moment, to say, 'Pretty spectacular, ay?' or maybe, 'Okay, I need that coffee.' This time he was silent as he wrapped an arm around my waist and pulled me close. He smelled of campfire and down feathers.

I barely heard the distant drone of the chopper as he looked at me. He brushed a leaf from my hair, and I stared at his lovely full lips, his dark eyes. But the droning got louder, and the grass around us began to ripple, then whip against our legs.

We turned towards the roaring helicopter as it descended on a sloping field. I hardly recognised Stewart when he emerged, crouching beneath the blades as if he weren't five foot five. When I realised it was him, I knew that someone had died. His mouth was set, his shoulders were hunched and his fists were clenched, just as they had been twelve years before when he'd hopped off the Italian coastguard boat and said my mother was still out there somewhere.

This time, they'd sent Stewart all the way to Australia. And not just to Sydney. He'd taken a plane to Hobart and found Jack's mum, who must have told him we were camping out east on Maria Island. Then he'd chartered a chopper at dawn to track me down.

Stewart had been the last one to give up on me. Even when Louis's texts dwindled from once a month to once a quarter and then to nothing, Stewart would still dutifully check in on me. His suggestions would arrive by Signal – *Unfortunate, this story about you putting a coffee cup in the recycling. It's best to assume the tabloids are always watching.* But I hadn't heard from him in three years.

Now he was wheezing from the effort of crossing the field, though he remembered his protocol and managed a crisp bow.

'Is it the Queen?' I asked.

He was in a dark suit and tie. They all kept a black outfit for the day it finally happened. I wondered whose idea it had been, this journey to the ends of the Earth to find me. Probably Stewart suggested it and Papa outright rejected it. 'She can open up the bloody newspaper like everyone else,' he probably said.

And then Stewart would have tactfully remarked that the newspapers might be most sympathetic to a father who did everything in his power to find his wayward daughter and break this terrible news to her.

But there was a strange look on Stewart's face as he stood before Jack and me, his breath shaky and deep. I realised, with alarm, that he was scared.

'I'm sorry, Your Royal Highness,' he breathed. 'I'm so sorry, no. It's not the Queen at all.'

*

It had been at least a decade since I'd flown private.

The family tried to avoid it where possible. At first, it was because seeing us climb the little steps to a private jet reminded our subjects that we were like very expensive house cats: lazy, ungrateful and, perhaps, ultimately useless. Then it was because the younger members of the family kept preaching about climate change before hopping on a rich friend's Cessna to pump six thousand kilograms of carbon dioxide through the skies on the way to Mustique.

But my father had died in the snow.

My brother Louis was holding on for now, but it didn't look good.

No one had bothered to tell me what was going on with Kris, our oldest friend in the world, but I heard whispers of 'brain death'.

And so the Queen had accepted an offer from a telco billionaire to fly me back to England on his Dassault Falcon. There were six people on the plane I didn't recognise, but they were all young and dressed in black suits. Junior aides, I assumed, from Papa's office.

The moment I sat down, an aide slid into the seat beside me and took my hand. I thought perhaps she was trying to console me, but she produced a bottle of acetone and started rubbing off my dark nail polish. Even after all these years, it was still a thrill to pick out a shade with a ridiculous name like Barbaric Burgundy or Poison Ivy at the salon. Even more intoxicating was to watch it chip at the edges and do nothing about it for weeks on end. Now I was watching my month-old Courgette Coquette nails disappear.

'Thank you,' I said.

'Of course, Your Royal Highness,' she whispered. She looked around and then, when she was satisfied no one could hear us, she leaned forward. 'I know it's ridiculous, this rule about dark nail polish. It's not very modern. If it were up to me, you'd wear what you wanted.'

I had got on the jet in Patagonia fleece and hiking boots, but I knew I'd come down the steps looking like the last eleven years had never happened. I wondered if she'd start sewing in extensions next, to boost my curls to their pre-Australian levels. They couldn't get me back under fifty kilos in fourteen hours, though, I was pretty sure.

Stewart took the seat in front of me and began texting. It was odd to see him on an iPhone. The last time we were close, I was still trying to convince him to play Snake on his Nokia. He had been Granny's private secretary for thirty years, but he seemed to have had a hand in all of our lives.

'Is there any more news about Louis?' I asked him.

He looked up from his phone and back down at the screen. 'No, ma'am. I'm sorry. They'll radio up to the pilot if they hear anything.'

We both knew we wouldn't discuss what had happened back at the house. After the chopper landed in Hobart, Stewart had taken me to the vineyard to pack a bag. I sat under the grape-leaf arbour while he ransacked my room. But then came a strange feeling, one I'd had before, like a black wave cresting and breaking over my head. The edges of my vision began to dissolve and I remembered, in quick succession, the feeling of Mum's fingers braiding my hair; the time I fell off my horse and

Papa ran across the wide, green lawns of the Scottish estate with something like fear in his eyes; and how, if a window fogged up, Louis and I drew a star each with our fingertips, one for him and one for me. Even after we'd stopped speaking, I still found myself smudging two stars on frosted glass on winter nights, wondering, as they clouded over, if he ever thought about me anymore.

By the time Stewart had come out of the cottage to ask where I kept my passport, I was doubled over in my chair. It was like hot claws had taken hold of my lungs, and I flinched when he put a hand on my shoulder.

'Breathe, ma'am,' he murmured. 'Just breathe.'

Palace aides are forbidden from touching members of the family. But Stewart had always been around when I was growing up, always giving me sweets and helping me onto my horse, and I adored him. He had constantly implored me to stop hugging him, but we both knew I held all the power and if I wanted to wrap my little arms around his knees and squeeze, I would. It was nice to feel his touch again. It was almost enough to stop the walls of my mind caving in.

'Here, ma'am,' he said, his hand still on my shoulder. 'This will calm you.'

I looked up and he was holding the bottle of amber liquid. I hadn't seen it since the week Mum died, all those photographers in boats bobbing in the waves just beyond the villa's dock. Back then, Stewart had drawn the blinds as I sat trembling on the edge of the bed, and then he came towards me as he pulled liquid into the dropper. It was meant to taste like blackcurrants, but it had burned my throat, and I wanted to say I didn't like it. But then the cold rush was back. It was as if the floor opened below me and I was falling, falling through black nothingness.

I took the bottle from Stewart's hands and tossed it as hard as I could. It landed somewhere among the pinot vines, and I imagined Jack finding it days or weeks later, wondering how a bottle of diazepam elixir had ended up on his property.

'Don't touch me again, Stewart,' I gasped, my chest heaving.

I was almost myself again by the time the jet took off from Hobart Airport. Stewart put his phone down and settled his elbows on his knees, his trouser legs riding up so I could see his compression socks. He was getting old.

'You should prepare yourself, ma'am. They were under the snow for more than twenty minutes. Prince Louis had a small air pocket, which is how he was able to survive being buried, but it's not … it was probably not enough,' he said.

We need 3.3 millilitres of oxygen for every 100 grams of brain tissue. I remembered writing that equation down again and again before exam time: *3.3 ml per 100 g.* I'd made a rhyme of it: *three-point-three per one hundred g, three-point-three per one hundred g.* If that number drops, the body redirects blood flow to the brain to try to save it. After five minutes in an oxygen-deprived state, brain cells start to die. That's when the permanent damage sets in, and it accelerates until the brain just stops.

My brother's brain.

'He was in extreme cold, though,' I heard myself say. 'It happens sometimes – a child falls in an icy lake and the temperature sort of flash-freezes the brain cells, and they come back with all function intact.'

Stewart looked down, and the bespectacled girl with the nail polish remover held my hand tenderly.

'I've read about it,' I told them.

'Yes, ma'am,' Stewart said. 'We pray for Prince Louis. But I do not want you to get your hopes up.'

An unspoken 'this time' hung in the air between us. I felt tears simmer in my eyes. Louis was the only one who'd hugged me after Mum died, even though he was furious with me. I didn't know then it would be one of the last times a family member took me in their arms and held me.

Unbidden, another memory: The four of us on a ski trip to Courchevel. Louis and I wore matching red jackets. Mum looked resplendent in a white Fendi snowsuit, her chic mirrored goggles hiding her tear-stained eyes. I'd heard our parents arguing again in their suite that morning. The slamming of doors, Mum's quiet sobs. The photographers were assembled a respectful distance away on a snowbank as she helped us with our poles and jackets. When Papa kneeled in front of me and tightened my already fastened buckles, the whirr of the camera shutters sounded like crickets all around us. He looked up at me and grinned.

'There you are, mignonette,' he said with the stagy brightness of a man who'd been fighting with his wife all morning and was holding it together for both the kids and the world's press.

The photograph of that moment was often run alongside stories about our deteriorating relationship. That was when things were good, the tabloids claimed. Often they'd include a picture from the day Louis and I were born, Mum looking young and overwhelmed with a baby in each arm, Papa beaming and relieved to be discharged of his duty. The photo from Mum's funeral was always there too, showing me and Louis, aged seventeen and completely blown apart. I didn't really remember anything from that day – the picture was the only proof I had that I was even there.

When my nails were clean, I excused myself and walked to the bathroom, where I could check my phone. I'd been clear-headed enough while we packed my suitcase for London to stick the phone in the waistband of my leggings when Stewart wasn't looking. Fifty-seven text messages had arrived in the space of twenty minutes. Seven missed calls from those old-fashioned enough to try to phone someone who'd just endured a family tragedy that already had its own Wikipedia page. Most were from Uncle James. If I'd picked up, he would have begged me not to get on this plane.

I tapped on the little nesting dolls of news alerts on the screen so I could start from the beginning.

BREAKING: Prince Frederick injured in ski accident in Switzerland, palace says.

BREAKING: Prince Frederick, son Prince Louis and Duchess Amira's brother Krishiv Shankar injured skiing in Zermatt, Switzerland. Follow our live blog for updates.

BREAKING: Heir to the throne Prince Frederick dead at 63 after avalanche, confirms Queen. Prince Louis in 'critical condition'.

BREAKING: Prince Louis reportedly critical and brother-in-law Krishiv Shankar 'brain dead' after Prince Frederick's death in ski accident.

WATCH LIVE NOW: UK PM Jenny Walsh addresses nation after darkest day in British monarchy's history. Follow our updates.

BREAKING: No sign of Princess Alexandrina after ski tragedy kills her father and leaves brother critical.

I whisked the remaining news alerts away and took a shaky breath. My text messages were all condolences and exclamation points and question marks.

Text me when you land okay? Call if you're up to it, I don't care what time it is, Jack had written just before we took off from Hobart.

Stewart hadn't allowed him or Finn onto the chopper, insisting he only had space for me. As the chopper darted away, I watched the two of them standing there, growing smaller. I suppose they ended the trip then, packing up the tents and taking the ferry home. I imagined them sitting in our cosy living room with the news on the TV – sleeping bags and boots on every surface, where they'd stay for weeks on end without me to insist they be dealt with immediately.

The mess would still be there when I returned, perhaps in a month. Six weeks tops. Finn would smirk and say, 'Sorry, dolly,' as I slipped back into my old skin and pretended to worry about the proper care and storage of expensive camping gear. Jack would be leaning against the doorjamb, smiling at me. Papa would still be dead, but Louis would be awake by then, his snap-frozen brain cells thoroughly thawed. The rightful heir spared, his aides would shoo me back to Australia in no time, I was sure of it.

The jet punched through the clouds over the island and into the light above. I looked down the list of missed calls and texts. I spotted a message from Amira, the first she'd sent me in three years.

Lexi, please come home now. I need you.

*

Louis and I were the first twins born in the line for more than three hundred years.

In 1660, King Charles II fell in love with our ancestor, Barbara Villiers, who was tall and luscious, with a tumble of dark hair and insouciant hips. She was from a noble but impoverished family and already married. So the king made Barbara his royal mistress and instead made a politically advantageous match in Catherine, a Portuguese Infanta who spoke little English and couldn't seem to bear him a child.

Barbara might have remained a footnote in history, but three years later an outbreak of smallpox tore through Whitehall. First, Barbara's husband died. Then, Queen Catherine was overcome. The next day, Charles married his mistress, and Barbara was England's 'uncrowned queen' no more. Within months, she was pregnant with twins, and the woman once deemed a royal whore was transformed into a vessel for the heir and spare.

Only one twin survived childbirth. There was something wrong with the girl, who was born very small and grey. Her brother, William, must have been feeding off her strength, because he arrived teeming with health, all dimpled knees and bread dough cheeks.

In delivering a healthy male, Barbara had catapulted herself into that most vaunted of all positions: the mother of a future king. But fate wasn't done with her yet. A few years later, when smallpox returned to London, Charles succumbed to the disease, making three-year-old William the new king. Barbara, who had spent years consolidating her power in court, became

Queen Regent, ruling until her son was old enough to accede the throne.

The England we know was shaped by Barbara's small, pale hands. A Scottish rebellion against her rule was brutally put down, and she retired the title of Prince of Wales forever, instead making her son, and all future male heirs, the Prince of Scotland. Charles's House of Stuart never technically ended, but we Villiers crept inside it like ivy, twisting around support beams and window frames until we flourished over the roof. It is her name we keep as our own. And all of it was possible because of her twins – the girl who died, and the boy who didn't.

Three centuries later, Louis and I were both expected to survive the perils of birth, and we promised to take the monarchy into interesting new territory. The question of which twin would rule had already been settled: the first child delivered was the heir. Unless she was a girl followed by a living boy, in which case she slid down the line of succession at the first sighting of his tiny regal penis.

The TV anchors of 1993 breakfast television giddily speculated about the constitutional implications of my mother's pregnancy. What if Princess Isla required a caesarean, and an obstetrician found two boys in her belly? He alone held the fate of the British monarchy in his hands. From the gaping wound that contained two babies curled together like fish, he would reach inside and pluck out a future king. There were also those who argued that the last twin out was the first implanted, and therefore the kingdom's rightful monarch.

The palace sensed a looming constitutional crisis. And so, when my mother's labour entered its twentieth hour and the doctor said it was time to consider a caesarean, the Queen was consulted over the phone. She made her ruling. Isla would have to work these babies out of herself naturally. Intervention would only take place if our lives were under threat. The life of Isla, then twenty years old and one of the most famous women in the world, was never discussed.

At the time, she was still desperate to do everything perfectly, and thirty-seven minutes after her mother-in-law refused to end her misery, Isla gave birth to a healthy baby boy. I followed two minutes later – pallid, silent and female.

As Papa clutched his heir, I was whisked to another room where I was surrounded by a dozen doctors and nurses wielding nasal cannulas and nitric oxide. My mother moaned in pain and fear until finally, either an eternity or sixty seconds later, I unleashed an almighty wail. She had done it. She had birthed an heir and a spare in one afternoon. I imagine every royal woman experiences that moment of deliverance the same way, whether it is 1664 or 1993. That intake of breath as the doctor or the midwife peers over the child. Will the baby thrive? Is it a boy? Am I finally, finally safe?

By the nineties, princesses had earned a certain cultural cachet. The tabloids wanted designer gowns, shiny hair and bad boyfriends. Then they wanted an Abbey wedding to a nice man who was the harbinger of ruddy-faced babies and postpartum weight-loss stories.

Louis was the future of the family; I was a decorative accent.

Six hours after she delivered us, Mum was helped out of bed, her black curls brushed until they shone. A blousy seafoam maternity dress was pulled over her head – this was years before she started to rebel with the men's blazers, Calvin Klein minimalism and oversized sweatshirts that haunt trend cycles to this day. She's the reason every woman in the world wears sneakers with dresses. Sometimes I'll be walking through town and a girl will pass me in old Levi's, a man's shirt and a baseball cap pulled over her hair. The post-divorce Isla aesthetic, they called it.

But on this day in 1993, she stood on the steps of the hospital in what was effectively a big green tent, the fabric so thin and pale she must have been terrified that one sneeze would destroy this antiseptic vision of postpartum perfection. Papa was beside her in his ubiquitous Savile Row, thirty-three years old, but looking far more nervous than his young wife.

The palace aides had choreographed the photo op perfectly. Isla would emerge with both of us in her arms, the teen bride transformed into a regal mother. After a moment, Papa would take the boy from her, and they would pose with one baby each. But in the glare of the camera flashes, he forgot his cue and did nothing but stand there. Mum, wobbly and in pain, gritted her teeth and held on to five kilos of sleeping babies while the world watched. Eventually, an aide opened the door to the hospital and ushered them back inside, taking the babies from her pale, spindly arms before she sank back into the wheelchair awaiting her.

They say four thousand people flocked to the palace to wait for the announcement of our names. An easel was placed at the gates:

Prince Louis Arthur Albert Lawrence, born 28 December 1993 at 2.02 pm

Princess Alexandrina Anne Barbara Mary born 28 December 1993 at 2.04 pm

Twenty-nine years later, another easel was placed outside the gates:

Prince Louis died peacefully at Visp Medical Centre this afternoon. His wife, Amira, Duchess of Somerset, was by his side. She will return to London tonight, where she will stay with the Queen. Princess Alexandrina is expected to arrive in London tomorrow.

Amira, after receiving permission from Granny, had agreed to turn off Louis's life support while I was somewhere over the Timor Sea. She had done the same for her brother, Kris, ten minutes earlier.

Later, the *Daily Post* reported that a Swiss doctor had phoned me on the plane to run through their clinical evaluation of Louis's chances of recovery. We'd conversed in French, apparently, and I'd tearfully agreed that it was time to remove life support. It was my idea that his organs should be harvested first. I couldn't work out who had leaked this falsehood to the *Post* – probably Granny's people, to cast her in a warmer light. Or perhaps it was Stewart, trying to help me save face.

Because in reality, they didn't radio the pilot as they'd promised, but waited to tell me when we landed for a fuel stop in Singapore.

'Oh,' I said to Stewart when he broke the news. I was so unsteady that the young female aide who'd cleaned my nails was now gripping my arm for fear I might collapse onto the tarmac. 'Can I speak to Louis now?'

Stewart and the girl exchanged a look.

'No, ma'am,' Stewart said slowly, 'As I just told you, Prince Louis died two hours ago.'

I shook my head. When we were babies, Louis and I could only sleep if we were swaddled together in the same cot. As toddlers, we chattered in the secret language we'd invented. He brought me a glow-worm in a jar; he gave me a piggyback when I cut my foot on an oyster shell. Louis and I were two little stars drawn on the glass, and I couldn't believe he was disappearing into the fog without me.

'No,' I said again. 'I'm sure there's been a mistake. If you could just let me talk to him—'

Suddenly my knees buckled, and the girl holding me up almost toppled over as she tried to catch me. Orphaned and alone, there was nothing to do but allow Stewart to help me back onto the plane that would return me to my family. But even as I flew closer to London, advancing further up the line of succession, I was still a pariah in the House of Villiers.

CHAPTER TWO

2 January 2023

Granny was a 23-year-old newlywed on her first international tour when she became queen. At some point, while she was dancing with dignitaries at an embassy party in Barbados, her father died in his sleep and the crown slipped invisibly to her head. The following day, she landed at RAF Northolt and her ladies-in-waiting realised they hadn't packed mourning attire. The new queen sat on the plane for forty-five minutes while a black dress was procured from Watford Castle. It's one of the most famous photos of her: Eleanor's bow-shaped mouth set in a grimace, her delicate hand holding the railing as she descended the steps towards the neat row of men who would schedule every minute of the rest of her life.

Five decades later, Stewart was determined not to make the same mistake. The girl who did my nails flicked through a rack of black clothing, pulling out Erdem dresses and Reiss blazers, glancing at me appraisingly and popping them back.

'She can't look too styled,' she whispered to Stewart as I stared out the window, lush green farmland giving way to sprawling suburbs. 'It needs to look like it came from her own closet. But also … you know.'

My wardrobe no longer included British designers, A-line hems or headbands. The only thing I'd really kept from my old life was Mum's waxed Barbour jacket. I rarely wore it, fearing I would disturb her last remaining essence still lurking in the fabric. When I did wear it, the *Daily Post* would inevitably run a photo of me alongside an old picture of Mum from the eighties, looking gorgeous and windswept on the moors.

'Just keep it simple and appropriate,' Stewart whispered. 'And nothing too flashy.'

We landed hard on the empty runway and I gripped my seat. It was the first time I'd been in England in three years. That last disastrous trip, I'd left two days early, booking a flight back to Australia on the train to Heathrow. It took me twenty-eight hours, including a nine-hour layover in Seoul, to get home. I wore sunglasses and a hoodie and dozed on airport carpets and no one gave me a second look.

Out the window, I saw the row of men in suits walking across the tarmac to meet the plane. It took a moment to realise one of the men was, in fact, a woman, dressed in a black pantsuit.

Stewart cleared his throat. 'Ma'am, just to reiterate the plan: there are no photographers and we've strung tarps against the fence to safeguard your privacy. Once you're in the car, we'll take you to the palace so you can be with the Queen.'

In the end, they dressed me in an Alexander McQueen skirt suit.

'Black looks good on you. You're a true winter,' the young female aide said as she rolled up the blazer's sleeves.

She had the mousy look of most female palace aides. They were all white; they were all rich. With her featureless blonde face, she could have been pure aristocracy. Her family must have been somewhere further down the food chain, but high enough that a £21,000 palace salary covered her tab at the Twenty Two hotel while she lived off a generous trust.

'Thank you,' I responded uneasily. 'What's your name again?'

She might have told me already, or I might have waited sixteen hours to ask – I couldn't recall.

'Mary,' she said with a flush. 'Mary Williams.'

'Right, yes, sorry. That's my middle name.'

'Yes, ma'am,' she said warmly. Again, she glanced around us. 'I'm a big admirer of yours.'

I looked at her, confused. No one ever said that. I was the one who had walked away. But before I had a chance to respond, Mary was standing back to admire her handiwork. Someone outside the plane opened the door. A mechanical thump, a whoosh of cold air and it was time.

Outside, I nodded my thanks to the Royal Navy pilot as he stood to attention at the top of the stairs, even though Stewart had reminded me to ignore him. I looked out across the tarmac and realised that while tarps had been flung across the fences, a couple of photographers were standing on stepladders so they could stick their lenses over the top. The images would be on the *Daily Post*'s website in moments. Very smart of Stewart, I thought.

I gripped the railing, suddenly terrified of falling, and eased myself slowly down the steps towards the line of faceless suits waiting for me below. They rippled like a black tide as they descended into deep bows. The woman was the prime minister, I realised.

'Your Royal Highness,' she said and took my hand between hers. 'On behalf of the United Kingdom, may I express my deepest condolences for your loss.'

I didn't know much about Jenny Walsh, except that Papa seemed to leak a lot of details of their conversations to his favourite reporter, trying to make himself look smart and her look feckless.

'Thank you,' I said breathlessly.

It hadn't really occurred to me until this moment who I was to these people. The prime minister had driven all the way to Northolt to meet my plane. A photographer was balancing a long-range lens over a fence to get a blurry photo of me. My hair had been straightened, re-curled and rendered lustrous. I was meant to be back at the hospital on the third of January, but I didn't even know what day it was or whether anyone had called to let them know I wouldn't be coming in for a while. Louis was gone forever, and I'd never told him how sorry I was.

'I'd like to sit down if that's okay,' I whispered.

Jenny nodded and, displaying all the crisis-management prowess of a woman in politics who was also a single mother of two teenagers, took my elbow and guided me towards a waiting car. Once I was inside, she went around and hopped in the other back passenger door. Sweat was pricking the nape of my neck, and I had the distinct urge to vomit. I rested my head back, closed my eyes and tried to breathe.

'Now, ma'am, if you think you're going to be sick, they've got these little baggies back here waiting for you,' I heard her say.

I nodded but kept my eyes closed. We were rolling down the tarmac towards the gates. I was pretty sure the windows were tinted, but if the flash hit the glass at the right angle, they'd have a vague sense that I was swooning in the back of the car with the prime minister. I remembered something Mum used to do: three big breaths, in and out, holding the last intake of air until your lungs burned. The hit of oxygen didn't really help, but I felt like I was in control of myself again.

'Sorry,' I said. 'Flying always makes me feel a bit sick.'

'Quite alright, ma'am.'

Jenny Walsh was different from the other PMs who'd traipsed through my grandmother's study every few years. Usually they got there by first passing through Eton, then Oxford, then some Mayfair hedge fund, before finally running for the seat of a retiring family friend. Jenny Walsh, meanwhile, came from Essex. She had made a name for herself in the union movement. She wore navy kohl smeared on her waterline. England, as far as I could tell, marvelled at her rise while quietly plotting to destroy her for it.

'We'll drive over to the palace now, and you can finally see your granny – er, the Queen,' she said.

As we passed through the gates, she was going through the same schedule Stewart had run through five minutes earlier. But it gave me something to focus on as the camera flashes bounced off the windows.

The photos, uploaded to the *Daily Post* twenty minutes later, showed just a glimpse of my face through the underwater-like depths of the tinted glass. My eyes were on Jenny Walsh, and I looked composed but appropriately mournful. My black hair, usually free and wild, was a little too polished, and it would be obvious to anyone with a critical eye that I'd had a blow-dry. The only question was whether they'd see this as proof of my preening, Isla-like narcissism or yet another piece of evidence that the monarchy was evil indeed. Imagine forcing a young woman who'd just lost her brother, her father, and her friend, to endure a mid-flight glam squad. I'd read the comments on the blogs later and see which version of reality prevailed.

'Prime Minister,' I said.

'Yes, ma'am.'

We were on the road to London then, the blue strobes of our police escort pulsing in the dreary afternoon sky.

'Could you tell me what happened on the mountain? Stewart won't say. I haven't looked at the news sites, and I'm not really sure I should.'

Jenny Walsh hesitated for a long moment. 'I think the Queen might prefer to be the one.'

'I don't want to ask her to do that.'

She'd applied a fresh line of kohl before she collected me from the airport, and it was starting to smudge. She looked bone-tired and steely. But somehow her eyes were still kind.

'Alright.'

CHAPTER THREE

30 December 2022

This is how it happened.

Louis, Amira and Kris went to Zermatt on Boxing Day as they did almost every year. They were there for Louis's and my twenty-ninth birthday – the first one that passed without any communication between us – and intended to stay through to New Year's Day.

Papa was never meant to join them. But at the last minute, Annabelle had decided to go on a health retreat in India. It was becoming an annual – if unsuccessful – pilgrimage to give up smoking. But this year she wanted to begin the detoxification process before the first of January, and she dropped her name to get the reservation rebooked.

Papa would ordinarily relish such isolation. He adored his second wife, but I don't think he was ever happier than when he had his Norfolk estate, Elton Park, all to himself. He would tend to his orchids, read academic papers on organic farming and write memos that government officials would politely ignore.

But for some reason, he instead decided to join his 29-year-old son, his daughter-in-law and her brother on a ski trip to Switzerland. Papa was a decent skier, but he'd grown finicky in his later years. He rarely did anything so reckless as book a last-minute holiday at a resort he'd never visited, run by staff he had not yet terrorised over decades with his whims and demands.

This was a man who travelled with a portable leather toilet seat, even when spending the weekend at the White House. Two personal attendants helped him dress every morning. He expected the butter with his breakfast to be served in three – not two, not four, but three – perfectly scooped little balls. It's not so much that he was a diva. But every day since he was able to eat toast, it had arrived on a tray alongside a bowl of three creamy pearls of butter. He simply couldn't bear to have it any other way.

So the idea that he'd spontaneously tag along on Louis, Kris and Amira's ski holiday was weird. I knew why the palace would have approved it – they would have been positively panting over the potential photos of the heir and his son on the crisp white slopes together. The masculine action shots, the fatherly arm slung over Louis's shoulder. How nice for a man to remain so close to his adult son, even after everything they'd been through. Kris would be discreetly cropped out of every shot. Amira never skied, but her absence from the photos would be enough to leave the tabloids speculating that she was pregnant.

On 29 December, they had a long day on the slopes. Papa was getting his legs under him again. Everyone was getting on. By midafternoon, Kris was ready to head back to the chalet, but Louis suggested one final run. An instructor had promised to take him down backcountry that was closed to the public. Kris was tired but agreed to one last run. Papa, confoundingly, wanted to come too.

It wasn't the instructor's fault. The conditions seemed fine that day. The trail was available to those who could afford it. The royal protection officers broke protocol by allowing two senior members of the family to ski off-piste together. But most of Papa's regular security team was on leave for the holidays, and the men filling in weren't sure how to handle him – and Louis's extracurriculars verged on suicidal at the best of times.

Worn down by years of bungee jumping and ultramarathons, his protection officers thought this ski run would be as simple as a walk in Hyde Park. They didn't have an inkling of danger until the snowbank shattered like glass.

They were descending difficult terrain at 2730 feet. Kris and Louis, both light and nimble skiers, glided over the top of the bank without destabilising things too much. But the instructor, who was further down the trail, said Papa was lumbering along at a slower pace. He didn't notice the jagged faultline appearing behind him as he manoeuvred down the mountain.

All around him, the snow seemed to turn into liquid, and he lost his balance. Gravity no longer made sense. A white cloud was building up at the front of the sliding snowbank, but Louis and Kris coasted just ahead, oblivious to the force gaining momentum behind them.

The instructor said it was at this point he shouted out. For what purpose, he wasn't sure. The tumbling snowbank was at least ten metres wide, and even the best skier would have struggled to avoid it. He grabbed onto a tree trunk and held his breath.

The officers, who had been trailing Papa, slowed to a stop and watched the scene unfold below them. It didn't seem that serious in the first moments – Papa sliding through a powdery sea on his backside, his poles waving in the air. They were mostly worried that he'd be embarrassed once he slowed to a stop.

It was when Kris was engulfed by the snow that they realised how bad this was. The slushy mess that had tripped up the ageing prince had transformed into something powerful and terrifying.

Papa vanished, then Kris.

Louis must have heard a shout, because he looked over his shoulder and saw it coming for him next. The guards said he maintained his grace in the second before he disappeared too. That was the last image of my brother – strong and elegant as he flew, looking over his shoulder for Kris.

Then he too was swallowed by that pristine monster.

Any experienced off-piste skier knows you really have only ten minutes to rescue someone trapped by an avalanche. After that, their chances of survival drop precipitously, to twenty per cent. The instructor knew what he was doing and had attached a beacon to every skier before they set out in the chopper. But he had brought only one probe and one shovel. He didn't have the heart to make royalty carry their own gear. By the time the officers made it down the trail, the instructor was already digging in the snow.

'There's someone here at three metres,' he shouted.

'We need to find the princes first. Where did the princes end up?' the guards asked.

But the instructor shook his head and kept shovelling. 'I dig as soon as I find a burial victim.' He threw them the probe. 'Hover this over the snow. Quickly. Call me if the beeps intensify and then one of you will take over here.'

By then, six minutes had elapsed since Papa, Louis and Kris were entombed in ice. The mountain was silent except for the intermittent beeps of the probe and the harsh breaths of the officers. The instructor had already sent an SOS to the resort, and he ached for the distant buzz of the rescue chopper. He was twenty-four years old. He had thought he'd end the day with €400 and a story to tell his friends. For the first time in his life, he prayed.

Twelve minutes after the avalanche, another group of skiers happened on the scene. Experts in backcountry skiing, they brought with them shovels, probes and a surge of hope. The thing about a crisis is this: you don't really know who you're going to be until you're standing in the wreckage of your daily life. Royal protection officers are trained over years to look out for stalkers and cream pies being hurled at their assets. They can shoot pistols and pack a gunshot wound. But on that mountain, with two members of the House of Villiers buried somewhere underneath their feet, they were at a loss.

Most disasters in our lives are so sudden, so quick, it's as if we can stomp back to the Before and undo what was just done. That car accident, that aneurysm. Just for one strange moment, time feels like a rope that can be gathered back up in your hands. But it doesn't stop – not if your toes lose traction on a yacht's swim step, not if five hundred kilograms per cubic metre of snow is squeezing your body. Time ticks on, a ruthless metronome, on and on and on and on.

The instructor had been silently sinking into a deep panic as he dug and dug and found only more glinting piles of snow. Every minute was agony. But as the skiers began searching the area and shouting instructions in French, the bumbling guards gratefully submitted to their leadership. Before the skiers coasted into their obliterated world, they'd been quietly adjusting their expectations for the future. If they saved the princes, everything might be alright. If they saved one of them, they would probably still lose their jobs, but their lives wouldn't be over. If they just kept digging, maybe the world wouldn't hate them.

Fourteen minutes after the avalanche, the probe found Papa beneath the snow. Two minutes later, they had Louis's location as well. The rescuers split into teams and dug frenziedly. Those who didn't have shovels used their hands. People who have survived avalanches say it's like being trapped in cement. It's completely dark in your tomb. You cannot wiggle your fingers; you cannot expand your lungs. Suspended in ice, you have no way of knowing which way is up and which way is down. As the search entered its seventeenth and then eighteenth minute, everyone knew the air was getting thin down there.

At minute twenty, the instructor's shovel hit something hard. He began to dig with his bare hands and uncovered Kris's frozen face. The shovel had nicked his cheek, but his eyes were glazed and unseeing. His lips were a frightful purple. The instructor cleared the packed snow from his chest, but Kris took no breath.

'He's gone. Come and help us, we've got the future bloody kings of England down here,' one of the officers hissed.

The instructor looked down at Kris, suspended in his snowy grave as if only a prince's kiss would revive him. In a decision that would earn him the ire of the British tabloids and threats from the darkest corners of the internet, he stayed with Kris. He pumped his chest and breathed air into his lungs until the rescue chopper landed.

He did not give up on him when the rescuers found Papa with a fractured skull and a mouth full of snow. He did not stop when Louis was prised from the ice just one metre from Kris, the flutter of a pulse beneath his skin like water under a frozen pond. He stopped when a rescuer laid a hand on his shoulder and offered to take over.

Papa was taken off the mountain in a body bag. Louis and Kris never woke up again.

CHAPTER FOUR

2 January 2023

Night had fallen by the time we pulled onto The Mall, which had been adorned with two rows of Union Jacks, slapping and rolling in the January winds.

'Why are there so many people?' I asked. The streets were packed, and I wondered if there was a festival underway at the park.

'They're here for your brother and your father, ma'am,' the PM said. 'They've been outside the palace for days now.'

The crowds saw the pulsing blue lights of our motorcade and stopped in unison to watch us pass. A few people waved, a few took pictures, and a handful broke out in awkward applause that quickly evaporated. They were mostly silent as they watched me make my return.

The palace's old iron gates yawned open and then swallowed us whole with a metallic gulp. The last time I'd been in London was for Louis and Amira's wedding. I'd caught glimpses of Granny throughout the day, but they'd deliberately arranged things so we'd never be alone. After we all waved from the balcony, I had changed my clothes and slipped out of a side entrance, walking unrecognised through the dense crowds that lingered outside the palace. When I'd looked behind me, the old building half hidden behind the plane trees, I knew I might never see it again.

Three years later, I was home. When Jenny and I pulled into the quadrangle, Stewart was waiting with a few other aides at the doors. I had no idea how he'd managed to beat me to the palace when I had left the airport before him. But here he was, pressed and cool in his black suit, ready to deliver me the last hundred steps of his 34,000-kilometre journey.

'Are you coming in, Prime Minister?' I asked.

Jenny Walsh shook her head. 'This is where I'll leave you.'

'I feel weird that the prime minister picked me up from the airport and doesn't even get a cup of tea at the end of it,' I tried to joke.

She smiled. 'You should probably get used to things like that.'

She bent forward to rummage through a black handbag at her feet. 'Here's my card – it's got my private mobile on it and my email. No assistants gatekeeping those ones.'

I slipped it into my bra and thanked her.

'You call me any time now. None of this is going to be easy, but I'm happy to talk whenever you need, even if it's just for a bit of a chat,' she said.

She had a way of staring into my eyes, unblinking and still and totally comfortable with the silence that opened up between us. She'd be a great therapist, I thought.

I wasn't ready to get out of the car and go upstairs.

'How do I do this?' I asked.

She smiled again. 'You go in there and you spend some time with your family. You mourn your brother and your father. We'll worry about the rest later.'

I nodded. She squeezed my hand and indicated to Stewart that I was ready.

The palace never really changed, but it was looking more tired than I'd ever seen it. With its marble busts and baroque gold frames, it was still grand. But the carpets were worn. A lurid green FIRE EXIT sign in the hallway was pulsing and emitting a dull buzz. Some of the stairs squeaked and groaned as we climbed them. I knew it needed work. I'd read it was in desperate need of structural repairs. But with a price tag of £369 million, the family was afraid of pulling at a public thread that could see the whole thing unravel. And so the Queen had delayed bringing the matter before the prime minister again and again as the old palace sagged and aged.

Stewart took me the familiar route to the private apartment on the north side of the building. The halls were empty, though I knew staff were hiding in dark corners. Once we passed, they would emerge to resume their duties. We reached the narrow door to Granny's apartment.

'One moment, ma'am,' Stewart whispered and slipped inside, closing the door behind him.

I heard the murmuring of voices and tried to calm my galloping heart. Too soon, he was back, ushering me inside. The private apartment always smelled different from the musty halls of the palace. Granny's chambermaids cleaned with lemon and eucalyptus. The tortured floral arrangements that cascaded over tables in the halls gave way to vases of lily of the valley. As I breathed in their soapy scent, I looped the roll of memories I'd forgotten I had. Grandfather sitting forward and stabbing his cane at the ancient TV to change the channel. The gold fringe of a heavy curtain tickling the tops of my feet during a game of hide and seek. Louis's dark eyes after Mum's funeral. Granny, still in her black suit, putting down a bowl of sausage rolls we wouldn't eat.

I turned the corner into the drawing room and saw her there, so much older and smaller than I remembered. Her blonde curls were perfectly set, and she was dressed in a black cardigan and kilt. But one look at her face and I could tell she had been annihilated by the news. I curtsied, wobbly and out of practice.

'Your Majesty.'

She looked up as if just noticing me. 'You must be so tired, dear girl.'

I walked over to her armchair and kissed her papery cheeks, one by one. Her eyes were shining, and she seemed to be searching for something to say. It would have been nice if she were the type of grandmother who'd pull me into her lap and rock me while we both wept. I hadn't cried yet, but I was fairly certain that if she took me in her arms, I would start and never stop. Instead, I pretended she was one of my patients and gently took her hand in mine.

'I'm so sorry, Granny – I can't believe it.'

She nodded and took a deep breath. When she opened her mouth to speak, she seemed to change her mind, and suddenly, she was up off the couch and striding towards the kitchen.

'You must be hungry, dear girl – what a long journey you've just had.'

My grandmother was never meant to be queen. When she was born, her uncle Albert was on the throne, but he died at the age of thirty-eight when he was bucked off his horse and trampled under its hooves. Albert's severed spinal cord and crushed chest saw his brother's life of planned obsolescence upended, along with his niece's destiny to be a pub trivia question no one ever got right.

When I went into the kitchen, she was looking into the open fridge, its buttery light casting a glow in the dark room.

'I'm not hungry, Granny – they fed me on the plane. But I can make us tea if you'd like?'

She turned around and nodded. 'Yes, alright, I suppose.'

She sat at the kitchen table and watched as I briskly moved around the room, turning on lights, filling the kettle and laying out tea the way I had been taught by one of Granny's ladies-in-waiting.

'I don't take sugar anymore,' she said. I stopped, the gold-trimmed Sèvres sugar bowl in my hands. She managed a small smile. 'Doctor's orders.'

I put the sugar bowl back and sat in the chair opposite her.

'Why don't we talk about everything tomorrow?' I said. 'Tonight we just drink our tea and then go to bed.'

She gazed at me, and I couldn't read her eyes. But then, I'd never been able to read her. I imagine the moment she saw the horse's hooves on her uncle's neck, everything inside her had been sealed off forever.

'Yes, alright, tomorrow.'

We were silent while we waited for the pot to steep. It was strange to be in her presence again. No matter how far I moved away, I still saw her face everywhere I went. Her profile on coins, her slightly dispassionate wave on television, her smile on the cover of a magazine by a patient's bedside. But that woman was mostly a different person to my grandmother. Granny complained about people leaving the heater on if they weren't using it and insisted no Christmas present cost more than £20 – and while the daily stack of papers on her desk received careful scrutiny, it was the health and breeding of her dogs and horses that consumed her.

The only time her two halves intersected was in her command of every room she entered, whether it was parliament or the dining room for family brunch. I didn't know how older women were really treated in this world until I went out and joined it. I was aghast to see my friends' grandmothers edged out, sat in the corner with a glass of wine and ignored. Out of habit, I was always deferential to older women, the way deep reverence for a white man in a suit is ingrained in everyone else. Needless to say, I was a hit when I did my geriatric medicine rotation.

I was never sure whether the crown turned her into a leader the moment it touched her head, or whether it just gave her the necessary armour to overcome her gender. She sat with her perfect posture, sipping her tea, unperturbed by the silence.

Finally I broke.

'Did no one come to stay with you, Granny?' I asked, for something to say.

'Amira is here. I think she might be asleep already.'

I started a little. 'Oh, I didn't know she was here. I thought she'd be with her parents.'

'The Shankars are in India. They're coming in the next day or so, I believe.'

She finished her tea and got up to set the cup in the sink for her chambermaid to deal with in the morning. I drained mine as well and propped it on top of hers. She had never stacked a dishwasher in her life, but she required her family to put their crockery in tidy piles for her staff if they ate in her apartment. A water glass on a sidetable would not be tolerated.

She smoothed the front of her kilt as she looked at me. 'I'm glad you've come.'

'Of course, Granny.'

'I know you did not part on good terms with your father and your brother, but they cared for you, and I know you cared for them.'

I nodded and tried to keep the hot tears pricking my eyes from spilling over. I didn't want to think about the last time I saw them.

'We have much to discuss, but now you should rest,' she said. 'They've set up your old room for you.'

I kissed her cheek again. She smelled like L'Heure Bleue and Earl Grey, as she always had.

'Goodnight, Granny,' I whispered and gave her the smallest of curtsies.

She smiled sadly and shook her head. 'The men in this family die too young. They always have.'

She drifted down the hallway towards the bedroom where she'd slept alone for twenty years. A jetlag-induced headache was firing up in my temple and I suddenly felt like I could lie down and sleep for days. Usually, I dreaded sleep. I feared it. I couldn't fathom how people simply lay down and succumbed to the darkness. The best part of being a doctor was that I worked endlessly, trudging up and down the wards, past the black windows and sleeping patients. I could go longer and harder than anyone else. But now my old bed was waiting for me with clean sheets, ironed with lavender water and warmed with an electric blanket. There would be a pitcher of water by the bed. Heavy drapes. Newspapers by the door in the morning.

It occurred to me with a jolt that I didn't have my passport. The customs officer had boarded the jet when we landed and processed us all then and there. Stewart had taken my passport from him and slipped it into his jacket pocket. I had been so careful to hold on to everything else, but I'd been distracted by the armfuls of black fit-and-flare dresses being unfurled in front of me.

I was too tired to deal with it then. It would have to wait until morning. I walked down the hallway, turned left at Granny's door and headed towards the old room that used to be mine.

Granny and Grandfather had converted two offices into bedrooms for us when we were children. Louis's was on the other side of the hall from mine, decorated in a gloomy Tweedside tartan. My room had a canopy bed with frilly white curtains. In the corner stood a huge dollhouse hand-built by Grandfather, an odd but sweet man who had spent his days constructing replicas of palaces and estates that belonged to the family. His wedding gift to Mum was a dollhouse that looked exactly like the Scottish estate where she had grown up. In one of the turrets, he had placed a porcelain Isla doll. After Louis and I were born, Grandfather added to the dollhouse two porcelain babies, both with black hair and storm-coloured eyes. Louis's doll was lost years ago, but mine was still there, forever in Isla's porcelain arms.

I could see the light under Louis's door. Amira was awake. Perhaps it was the jetlag, perhaps it was because I was a resident who spent fourteen hours a day having difficult conversations, but I knocked. Shave and a haircut. When we'd boarded together at Astley, she'd stomp or rap her knuckles on her desk to let me know it was safe to come in: two bits.

Nothing happened, so I opened the door a crack. She was standing by the bed in a Team GB Olympics t-shirt and a pair of men's boxers. I couldn't tell if she'd been coming to let me in or planning to hide in the bathroom. But she seemed surprised that I'd just opened the door as if we still had that kind of relationship.

Her hair looked expensive. Last time I'd seen her, at the wedding, it had been rolled into thick, gleaming sausage curls. But in the ensuing years, she'd backed off from the toppers and curling irons. Now she was sleek, her hair spilling over her shoulders. Only her eyes gave her away. She looked like she hadn't slept in days.

'Hi,' I said.

'Hello.'

Like Granny, she would not cross the room for me. But in her baggy boy's pyjamas, she looked fifteen again, and I felt a flare of protectiveness. It was like I'd opened the door and wandered back into our suite at Astley in 2008. I walked over and hugged her.

'I'm so sorry,' I said.

She was thinner than I'd ever seen her, her ribs like corrugated iron. She would not yield to my embrace, but she rested her chin on my shoulder and allowed me to hold her for a moment. I wondered if anyone had dared to touch her since she told the doctors to switch off the ventilators. Finally, she extracted herself from my arms and mopped up a few stray tears by hooking a finger under her lower lashes like all women who wear a lot of makeup do. She'd stopped wearing a stack of Cartier Love bracelets and was restricting herself to one. The remaining bracelet was diamond-paved, so it was probably worth all its predecessors combined. I couldn't imagine anything more claustrophobic than a piece of jewellery you couldn't remove without a screwdriver.

'Did they really charter a helicopter and come find you on some island?' she asked.

'Yes.'

If we weren't so uncomfortable at the sight of each other, I'd have turned the whole thing into a joke: Stewart, dressed in a suit, stuffing my things into a backpack as he flitted around a dirty campsite. But Amira had been the one to identify my father's body. Now was not the time for me to try to cajole a smile out of her like it was the old days.

'Was it awful?' I whispered.

By then, holding back her tears with her fingers was a lost cause.

'Kris was covered in bruises. I couldn't work out what caused them. I suppose it was the pressure of the snow? Or when he fell down? I couldn't work out how his body could bruise the way it did if he was dying. It doesn't make any sense.'

'Bruising can occur as long as there's blood flow,' I said.

She gave me a queer look. 'Right.'

She walked over to the bed and started removing the mountain of pillows there. Granny must have dismissed the staff for the day if we were turning down the beds ourselves. She pulled back the blankets and sprayed lavender mist on her pillow.

'I think we're talking about funeral preparations tomorrow,' she said. 'I don't know what time.'

'Okay,' I said.

I moved to leave the room, aware that I'd overstayed my welcome or crossed some line somewhere. My family was riddled with invisible tripwires and it often felt as if everyone but me had the map.

'Here,' she said and threw me something from a chest of drawers.

It was a pair of boxers and Louis's Astley rugby shirt.

'Just stay here tonight,' she muttered, still annoyed with me.

I hesitated. Another wave of jetlag crested just above my head. I ached at the thought of slipping into the white linen sheets waiting for me next door. But Amira wasn't in the habit of asking me for favours anymore, and Louis wouldn't want me to leave her in his childhood bedroom to stare at the ceiling until the bagpipes played.

'I just need to wash all this slap off my face.'

'There's oil cleanser in there,' she said, gesturing to the bathroom and arranging herself in the bed.

I clocked the prescription pill boxes stacked behind the tap. The sink was brimming with La Mer and Augustinus Bader and other heavy gold bottles that looked like goose eggs. The no-makeup makeup look they'd given me on the plane was a thick layer of clay settling on my face. I scrubbed it off with Amira's cleanser, which smelled like frankincense and rosehips.

Determined to ignore the pill boxes, I searched for a spare toothbrush under the sink. I stared at my reflection as I did my teeth and then braided my hair. They'd soon be at me with the extraction facials and lasers and eyebrow dye. I had my mother's face, but Barbara Villiers was fighting for a glimpse of herself in me too, and the result was slightly awkward. My jaw was a little too wide, my eyes hooded, my nose just the tiniest bit too heavy. In unison, it all worked. I knew that. But unlike my mother's beauty, which was otherworldly and indisputable, mine was something I had to chase after and suffer for.

I finally gave in and looked at the pill boxes. Prozac, 40 mg a day. The script had been written six months earlier. Clomid for ovulation. Temazepam prescribed on an extremely tight leash: one 12-tablet pack, no repeats. A generous box of Valium prescribed yesterday – probably by the Swiss doctor who'd turned off the machines keeping Amira's brother and husband alive. I told myself this violation of her privacy was necessary so I knew how to help her. Being a doctor gives you an almighty shield with which to justify some pretty abysmal behaviour.

In the bedroom, Amira had a silk eye mask over her face and an air purifier sending up a little smoke signal by the bed. I slipped in beside her. My jetlag was like an anchor dragging me to the bottom of an oceanic trench. I spiralled gratefully down towards its dark depths. I would worry about everything later. Granny, Amira, Jack, the line of succession, the location of my passport, the fact that I was meant to be on shift at the hospital in a matter of hours. But who knew what would become of my residency now? All of it could wait.

'Lexi.' Amira's quiet whisper brought me swimming back to the surface. 'What will she do with me now?'

I held my breath. How many women in the long history of this family have lain awake asking themselves this very question? The palace was silent for the night, and deep within its labyrinthine halls, a woman was fearful of her fate. I reached across the no-man's land between us and found her hand. I wanted to lie and tell her it was all going to be okay.

'I don't know,' I admitted. 'But I'm here now. And I won't let anything happen to you.'

'You won't leave again, will you?'

I was silent for a long time, and it felt like the palace itself had stopped to hear my answer.

'It's all going to be okay,' I said.

CHAPTER FIVE

1991

The thing about being an aristocrat is that you meet very few people.

With our garden parties and investitures, the royal family is unique in brushing up against the masses. But the ranks of nobility below us are cloistered in a suffocating circle of exclusivity.

From nursery schools to pony clubs, through to Eton and the Bullingdon, a small batch of people enriched by the transatlantic slave trade, generous inheritance taxes and colonial robbery rise up together. They play together, they study together, they marry each other, and then they have children together, braiding the gilded threads of this community even tighter.

Grown men wear their Eton cufflinks to their Berkeley Square offices – if they have a job at all. They order £30 Johnnie Walker Blue cocktails at Louie and complain that the influx of foreign oligarchs is driving up house prices in Chelsea. They mercilessly mock the Saudis and Russians arriving in London – as if their money isn't dripping in blood as well. They vacation in Mustique. Their wives wear neutral cashmere jumpers from JOSEPH, go to Pilates at Lanserhof, and get bi-weekly blowouts at Jo Hansford.

From the cradle to the grave, they associate only with each other. Hardly anyone is granted admittance. Occasionally a nobleman will marry a model to inject some height and cheekbones into his gene pool. But she is never truly one of them. Even fewer leave by choice. Mum and I are the only self-imposed exiles that I can name.

For many, it's cosy in this pond. You could spend your whole life swimming in its warm waters. As long as you don't roil its delicate ecosystem, the creatures that lurk in the mud would never open their snapping jaws on your feet.

Victoria Shankar wanted in.

She was born Vikki Yarborough, the daughter of a plumber and a doctor's receptionist, in Newcastle upon Tyne. She had long legs and a pleasing face, and she parlayed these assets into a job as a flight attendant for British Airways. Vikki wasn't just pretty; she was clever. She used her meagre salary to pay for elocution lessons, smoothing out the swooping vowels of her Geordie accent, emerging with a good approximation of Received Pronunciation.

Her counterfeit refinement and 25-inch waist propelled her straight to the front of the plane, where she walked the aisles with a tray of champagne flutes. Madhav Shankar, the son of a tech millionaire, was sitting in seat 4A when Vikki caught his eye. An hour before the plane landed in Milan, he slipped her his business card and said: 'I'm staying at the Grand Hotel.'

She smiled demurely and tucked the card under his dinner tray.

'That's very kind, sir, but I'm not allowed to see you outside of this plane. It's forbidden.'

She'd settled on the word months ago for this very scenario: handsome businessman, first-class seat, an invitation for a tryst. There was something about the word 'forbidden' that felt salty sweet on the tongue. Madhav's eyebrow quirked and she knew it had the desired effect.

'I would never wish to imperil your employment,' he said.

Again, she gave that smile, a slow blink and she moved along with her bottle of Bollinger.

It was a high-stakes gamble, but Vikki somehow knew that the right man with the right resources did not need a little thing like her phone number to find her. And she was right. When she emerged that evening from the hotel where the BA staff were staying in a velvet cocktail dress and the Alaïa heels she couldn't afford, Madhav was waiting for her. She blew off her colleagues for drinks that night.

From Frankfurt to Brussels, Madhav appeared outside Vikki's hotels. Usually he was leaning against a rented sports car, ready to take her to the most boring, most exclusive restaurant in town. At all times, she displayed a careful ambivalence to their relationship. She was too young for anything serious, she intimated. Her career was too much of an adventure to give up. She liked the pretty things he bought her, but she did not value them. When she went back to her grimy Bexley flat at the end of her flight rotation, she lay on her bed and plotted.

Four months in, she lowered the boom.

'I'm never going to marry you,' she breathed over a guttering candle and porto tonicos in Lisbon. Vikki kept it light and teasing, just how she'd practised.

'Is that right?' he asked.

They were married eight months later. A working-class Geordie was not the girl Madhav's wealthy Hindu parents had in mind for him, their first-born son and heir to the family company. Vikki had anticipated this and never pushed for an introduction during their courtship. She had rightly sensed he felt stifled by his family and yearned for someone to hand him the match to set fire to his life. When he told her he'd been disinherited, she held him in her arms.

'I've never cared about money, we can strike out on our own,' she said, again just as she'd practised.

The Chelsea apartment, the South African hunting lodge in the Kruger National Park, and a £5 million trust were beyond his parents' reach. It was a good start for the newly minted Victoria Shankar. When Krishiv was born in 1992, Mayfair IT (an extremely white name chosen by Vikki to obscure its foreign founder) was becoming increasingly popular in London's financial services sector for its systems integration. Madhav, set adrift from his family, had no qualms exploiting the connections they had forged in London when he worked for them. He also found that he could steal his father's clients by suggesting perhaps they'd prefer the services of a British-based company over an Indian one.

When Amira came along fifteen months later, the company was offering consulting services in the UK, Bangalore, Berlin and Munich.

By the time Kris and Amira were teenagers, Mayfair IT was as large as the Indian company from which Madhav had been cast out. They traded in the old flat for a £14 million five-storey townhouse, complete with a lift and the walk-in closet of Vikki's dreams. She shopped at Browns and drove a big black Range Rover. A diamond-encrusted Rolex slid up and down her slender wrist as she enacted a perfect plié at barre. Her metamorphosis was almost complete.

She had been pleasantly surprised to discover that Madhav was just as socially ambitious as she was. He wanted to conquer London. And what was the point of conquering a city if you couldn't breach its highest gates? He took lessons in deer stalking, as well as a whisky, cognac and armagnac appreciation course. He took up polo and carriage driving. Together, they planned Kris's and Amira's schooling like they were drawing the battlelines of a continental war.

From the moment Louis and I were born, London's upper class speculated feverishly about which schools we might attend. It became a favourite cocktail party conversation across the city: where will the royal twins be enrolled? Mum had received a rather lackadaisical education from Swiss boarding schools. Papa had been subjected to a Scottish institution, apparently chosen to toughen him up, which instead left him with PTSD and a determination that his children would go to a school that allowed you to close the windows in winter.

Many assumed Louis would head to Eton, a school that had educated kings and prime ministers for hundreds of years. That would surely be a tolerable compromise for the Queen, and for Papa, who was really rather insistent that his young son not be subjected to punishment runs and cold showers.

The institution chosen for me was of far less interest, given I was a girl and the fallback, but London's best families wanted their daughters to go where I went.

While almost every woman on the planet had a parasocial relationship with Isla, there were none more fixated than those who had their babies around the same time as her. They watched with fascination as her belly swelled and her limbs stayed ballerina thin. Somehow she made the billowy maternity fashion of the day both chic and child-like. Two weeks after she pushed not one but two babies out of her tiny body, she was back in her old Levi's.

Vikki desperately wanted to be her friend, but unlike everyone else, she was willing to do whatever it took to make it happen. For Vikki, the opportunity was obvious. Her ascent would always be limited by their circumstances. Madhav would never be white, and she would never not be the daughter of Barry Yarborough. Kris and Amira might have been rich and beautiful, but they were still relatively new money. Who better to help them transcend the traits deemed unforgivable by the upper classes than the royal twins?

The trick would be placing Kris and Amira in our path. In the end, all Vikki needed to make the introduction was what had always propelled her life: a high threshold for risk, guile, and a tiny bit of good luck.

When Louis and I were twelve, the decision about boarding school had still not been announced. Kris, a year older than us, was already at Whitmer Hall, an institution famed for accepting all the boys who failed to make it into Eton. Vikki could still be brought to tears by Eton's rejection of Kris, something she insisted was due to race. In reality, he'd deliberately flubbed the interview because he couldn't stand the idea of wearing tails to school every day.

One conversation changed everything.

At the time, Vikki's project was Genevieve Lambert, the Marchioness of Northampton. The Northamptons were the only true aristocratic family at Amira's junior school. Genevieve rarely did the drop-off herself, but on the rare occasion she breezed into the courtyard in a perfect Stella McCartney poncho, Vikki made a point of trying to talk to her. To Vikki's great delight, Amira had struck up a friendship with little Lady Sophie Northampton that year. Enrolling her in the same ballet class had paid off splendidly. Vikki used these rare opportunities to offer to buy two candy-pink leotards necessary for an upcoming recital – the girls so loved to be dressed the same. Or there'd be an exhibition at the British Museum, to which Vikki would be more than happy to chaperone the children.

Genevieve never removed her oversized sunglasses for these conversations, not once. Vikki couldn't quite tell if she was even looking at her behind those inscrutable shades. But she would take Vikki up on her grovelling offers about forty per cent of the time. It didn't seem as if the frequency was increasing, but Vikki was prepared to put in the work.

One day in 2006, the conversation turned to boarding school, as it always did for the mothers of twelve-year-olds.

'Kris is happy at Whitmer Hall,' Vikki said. 'Madhav wanted him to go to that awful Scottish school that Prince Frederick went to, but I said absolutely not.'

Genevieve smiled and said nothing.

'I suppose the royals will send Prince Louis there, poor lamb,' Vikki added.

She knew full well that Frederick and Isla would do no such thing. She read the tabloids as often as anyone else did. But feigning ignorance in front of a person who believed herself to be a natural authority on all things was one of Vikki's old tricks. The only way a friendship would blossom with Genevieve was if the marchioness saw Vikki as desperately in need of her guidance. They could never be equals, but Vikki might be a fun fixer-upper – if only Genevieve chose to take her on.

Genevieve sighed a laugh. Her mother had been a bridesmaid at the Queen's wedding. Her husband was the Lord Great Chamberlain, a hereditary role that required him to walk backwards in front of Queen Eleanor at the State Opening of parliament each year. Vikki had seen the Northamptons in paparazzi shots of Frederick and Isla's summer trip to Capri a few months back.

'She would never let them go,' Genevieve said smugly.

'You mean Isla?'

'Of course. I'm not sure how she'll cope with the children at boarding school at all. She's got no life beyond them.'

Vikki swallowed the dozens of questions brimming in her throat and made a sound she hoped would register as bored sympathy.

'She does seem a bit ... vulnerable,' she said.

'Miserable, more like it. She'll want them close to London. He'll acquiesce so she doesn't completely lose it,' Genevieve said.

She looked down at her watch, a Tank Louis Cartier on a crocodile band that made Vikki's beloved Rolex suddenly seem mortifyingly tacky.

'I've got to run, lovely to chat,' Genevieve breathed and walked away.

That night, Vikki went online and found a map of all the best boarding schools near London. There weren't many. The whole point was to get children into the countryside where they had space to play and run free.

Eton, just forty minutes from the palace, still seemed like a good bet. But something told Vikki that if Isla were as precious and demanding as Genevieve implied, she would want the twins together. That way she could drop them off and fetch them in one trip. Needy women, like Vikki's own mother, romanticised everything. She wondered if Isla was the type to believe that being separated from their mother was traumatic. She would insist the twins not be torn apart as well.

If her hunch was correct, it left only one option: Astley College. It was co-ed, breathtakingly expensive and just forty-five minutes from the palace. With its emphasis on tiny class sizes, 'academic experimentation' and scholarship pathways for the underprivileged, it was not a place Vikki had even considered before. It was a place where filmmakers and artists sent their children. It even let the girls wear trousers as part of their uniform if they wished.

But something told her this was the place Isla would enrol the twins. Everyone knew she had spurned hired help and did all the child rearing herself. She refused to go on international tours longer than a fortnight.

This was the place. Vikki knew it.

By the next week, Amira and Kris were enrolled in Astley to begin in the Michaelmas term of 2007. Kris, who had already spent a year at Whitmer, was incensed. His mother would not listen to his entreaties, his bargains or his tantrums. He was going to Astley with his sister. Madhav was concerned, but after thirteen years of marriage, he respected his wife's slightly witchy sense of the future. She would have made a great day trader, he often thought.

Six months before the term was due to start, the school asked the Shankars if they'd be willing to submit to a background check. They offered no more detail than this, but Vikki knew her gamble had paid off. She bought herself a Tank Louis on a gold and diamond bezel band to celebrate.

In September 2007, Louis and I stood at Astley's school gates in our stiff new uniforms, smiling for the cameras. My skirt was long and itchy, but Mum had assured me I could change into the trousers she'd bought once the photographers were gone. Louis stood between Mum and Papa, aware they'd spent most of the morning locked in one of the bitter arguments that never seemed to cease these days.

The headmistress suggested we divide into two groups – one parent and one twin – so we could go see our new boarding houses, which were on opposite ends of a grand quadrangle. Papa took my suitcase, engaging in a little vaudeville display for the cameras by pretending it was so heavy he simply couldn't budge it. I slapped his arm playfully.

I didn't meet Amira that day in Old Court. She was in the suite opposite mine, sharing with three other 'Shells', as we first years were known. We would meet three days later during a treasure hunt that was designed to acquaint Shells with the 200-acre campus.

Across the quad in Bishop's Quarters, Princess Isla and Prince Louis walked into the two-bed suite where the heir was to spend the next five years. Inside was the boy handpicked to be his suitemate. The palace had been intimately involved in the choice, finally settling on a slightly older boy of Indian descent. It was thought by several aides that a bit of diversity would play well with the British public, who were paying £82,000 a year for the two of us to attend this school. It was also considered a bonus that he was from Mayfair, and therefore was perhaps more inclined to honour the code of silence that governed the upper classes.

'Louis, please meet your suitemate for the year,' said the headmistress. 'This is Kris Shankar.'

The boys shook hands. They made eye contact as their fathers had taught them. They were both tall for their age, made confident by money and privilege and their adoring mothers.

'And ma'am, this is Kris's mother, Victoria Shankar.'

From the ancient stone bay window, Vikki stepped forward and curtsied. She was in a black Chanel skirt suit for the occasion, her hair twisted into a low chignon. It had taken her fifteen years to reach this place. She had no idea that beyond the casual meeting she had orchestrated, there were still miles and miles left for us all to travel together. She had no clue how much she would be willing to sacrifice to reach the summit of her ambitions.

'Your Royal Highness,' she said smoothly, just as she'd practised. 'I'm so glad our boys will be here to look after each other.'

CHAPTER SIX

3 January 2023

I'd been drifting on the edge of sleep, remembering the days when sleeping in these rooms was a regular occurrence. Mum, if she was staying over too, would often creep in at dawn and tuck herself in beside me.

'Let's make a raft,' she'd whisper as she wrapped me in her warm arms.

'Where are we going?' I'd murmur.

'How about Fiji?'

'That's so far. How are we going to get all the way there in a raft?'

'The trade winds will blow in our favour. I'll make a sail out of my coat and we'll glide all the way to the South Pacific.'

I blinked awake. Amira's side of the bed was empty. The velvet drapes kept the room almost completely dark, but the silver clock on the bedside table read 11 am. In Hobart, it would be dark by now. I'd be doing rounds in my squeaky Crocs, only the beeps and flashing lights of ICU machines to set the pulse of the night.

I fished out my phone from under the mattress where I'd stashed it before I went to sleep. I now had close to 120 messages. There were a few from Jack and I almost dialled his number, but he was probably asleep. He loved nothing more than going to bed at 9.30 pm. I called Finn instead.

'Doll!' he shouted above a cacophony of voices. 'Hang on babe, I'm at Sonny – I'll go outside.'

'No, you'll have to line up again!' I laughed. 'I'll call you later.'

'Nope, absolutely not. I'm walking away from an extremely handsome stranger as we speak.' He seemed to drop the phone from his cheek, and I could just make out his muffled voice as he spoke to someone next to him. 'Don't go anywhere, I just need to talk to my friend real quick. She's having a bit of a hard time.'

I waited as the bar noise faded to nothing. I imagined him standing on Elizabeth Street under the streetlights. 'Alright, I'm outside. How are you, doll?'

'I'm okay. It's weird being back here again.'

'When did you get in? We were worried about you. Jack's been trying to get through for ages.'

I remembered Jack's breath on my lips before the annoying distant buzz became a rapidly approaching helicopter.

'I got in last night, but they confiscated my phone. I only just got it back,' I lied, not really knowing why.

'Oh, wow, they're not messing around, are they.'

'Have you been to work?' I asked. 'I didn't even call them to ask for time off.'

'Babe, everyone on Earth knows you need a bit of time off, don't worry,' Finn said gently. 'I was on shift this morning and Ben said just to call in when you're ready and you can figure out a plan.'

I had a year left of my residency. Any longer than a few weeks off and I'd fall behind.

'Okay, I'll try to call him next,' I said, though I knew I absolutely would not. I'd procrastinate for days before I endured the inevitably frosty conversation with my boss. By now, we were doing a pretty good impression of a professional relationship. But the talk Ben and I needed to have was bound to stir things up that had been tightly packed down.

'You should call Jack first,' Finn said. 'He's been really worried about you.'

There was a light knock at the door, and a chambermaid stepped inside and curtsied. She was carrying a silver tray with tea, toast and a stack of newspapers. The pages were shiny, and I knew they were freshly ironed to ensure the ink didn't stain royal fingertips. I waved her in and smiled.

'I'll call him at the end of my day when he's awake,' I murmured, suddenly aware that everything I said would ripple through the palace whisper network.

The maid slid the tray onto the table beside me and cleared her throat. 'Her Majesty says the meeting for funeral preparations will begin at noon, Your Royal Highness.'

I nodded and she bobbed on her ankles again and left the room.

'Check you out, *Your Highness*,' Finn said. 'Are they waiting on you, hand and foot?'

I glanced at the tray: three slices of fruit toast in the rack, three gems of butter on a dish and a pot of strawberry jam. It was the same breakfast I'd been served every morning since I was a girl. The newspapers were fanned out beside the tray, and I saw my face on the front page of every single one. *The Prodigal Princess Returns*, one headline read.

'How's Ragu?' I asked suddenly.

'Oh my god, he's an absolute monster,' Finn said. 'He chased the chickens yesterday and nearly got one. And then he found a hole in the fence and ran down the creek.'

I yearned to be home then. I'd made up my bed with fresh sheets, imagining the luxury of slipping in there the night we were supposed to return from camping. The sweet peas in the jar by my bed would be shrivelled by now, the water slimy and cloudy. What I would give now to see that little room again. I loved its sloping ceilings and the spiders that took up residence in every corner. It was always dusty, and every time it rained, water seeped under the door. When Louis saw it during his one and only visit, he was bemused. Everything we had, in such embarrassing abundance, and I chose to give it all up to live in an old barn.

'Is there anything I can do, Lexi?' Finn asked, suddenly serious again.

I had the odd, panicky impulse to make things right with Louis. I never knew that there was a finite number of days left, each one ticking down towards zero. But too late now, too late for it all.

'Just send me lots of photos of Ragu. And tell everyone I'm fine. The funeral is next week, I think.'

Finn was quiet for a moment, which was unlike him. 'Have they talked to you about what happens next?'

'What do you mean?' I said, though I knew exactly what he meant. I had barely allowed myself to think of it from the moment Stewart told me they were all dead. The truth of it had been wrapping its cold fingers around my throat for days now, its grip tightening every moment.

'Well … you know, you're like, *it* now, aren't you,' Finn said, more a statement than a question.

It was never meant to be me, I thought. I cleared my throat and shook my head. 'I've got a meeting with them now actually, so I better go before they come looking for me.'

'Alright, dolly, call me anytime. Love you so much.'

'Love you too,' I said and hung up.

Finn vocalised his love for everyone, from his mother to the girl at Pigeon Whole Bakers who sold him the last croissant. The words had never sat easily in my mouth, but with Finn, they were as sweet and nutritionally complex as spun sugar. Sometimes I wondered if I'd latched onto him in medical school so I had someone to whom I could say the words.

I looked at the clock again. I had thirty minutes before they expected me in the drawing room, and Queen Eleanor did not tolerate lateness, even for the jet-lagged and recently bereaved.

I slipped out of Amira's bed and took my tray across the hall to my own room. An outfit was laid out for me on the bed – presumably for me to wear to this meeting. Even after a night tangled in a down pillow, my hair was silkier than it had been in years, so after a quick shower, I brushed it out and pinned it up. When I was done, I still had ten minutes left, so I sat on the edge of the bed and told myself I would emerge at five minutes to the hour.

The only sounds in the room were the ticking of the clock above the mantel and my quiet breaths. I had done this so many times as a child. I would sit and wait until the last possible moment to leave my room before another frosty dinner, another reception during which my parents could barely tolerate standing next to each other. My father's sulking was like an energy source for Mum. The more he glowered and pouted, the more she shone. By the end of the evening, the whole gathering encircled her, laughing and gasping at the twists in her story.

I looked at the old dollhouse. From the turret, the Isla doll peeked out, baby Lexi in her arms. Mum was dressed in a tiny replica of her wedding dress, the big folds of taffeta like spoonfuls of clotted cream. Even for the early nineties, it was objectively the ugliest dress that had ever existed, an affront to the menswear-inspired minimalism that would come to define Isla. I had always thought it looked like a dress designed by a little girl. It took me too long to realise that it had been – a nineteen-year-old eaten alive by her ridiculous gown. I took the dolls from their turret and stared into their faces. When I was small, Mum and I would plot their escape from the Scottish castle.

'They rip off her dress and tie it to the window sill, then they shimmy down and run for the moors,' Mum would say.

'But no one could survive a night on the moors in just their pants,' I insisted.

I wrapped the dolls up in the veil like a burial shroud and placed them back in the turret where they belonged. I was out of time. I needed to go to the drawing room or I'd be late.

Outside my door, the girl from the plane was standing with her fist poised to knock. We both startled at the sight of each other.

'I'm sorry, Your Royal Highness,' she said. 'I was sent to fetch you for the meeting.'

'I'm running a bit behind. It's Mary, right?'

She smiled, seeming heartened. 'Yes ma'am.'

We walked down the narrow hallway, and I could see that she expected us to make the journey in silence. She led me out of the private apartment with her mousy ponytail bouncing behind her.

'Whose office do you work in, Mary?'

'I'm at Wolseley House, ma'am. I run Prince Frederick and Duchess Annabelle's social media presence. Or *ran* it, I suppose.'

'Oh, I'm sorry. Did you know my father well?'

She shook her head. 'No, ma'am, not well. But he was very nice on the few occasions we did meet.'

He probably never bothered to learn her name, but likely erupted in her general direction when he didn't approve of the exact temperature on the office thermostat. I looked sideways at her. 'Was he really?'

She glanced at me over her glasses and gave me an impish grin. I decided I liked her.

'I couldn't possibly comment, except to say he was nicer than your stepmother.'

I refused to follow Annabelle's Instagram account, though I would sometimes look at it when I was feeling particularly self-destructive. I had noticed a drastic improvement in her grid in recent months. I wondered if that was Mary's influence.

'Annabelle hates you? Welcome to the club. We should get jackets or something.'

She laughed, then covered her mouth, remembering that we were supposed to be in mourning. She glanced over her shoulder to make sure no one was behind us and leaned in.

'All I can say is everyone at Wolseley is looking forward to working for you instead of her.'

Before I had a chance to respond, we'd arrived at the door of the drawing room. She knocked, waited a moment and then let us in.

'Her Royal Highness Princess Alexandrina, Your Majesty,' she said as she commenced a slow descent. Her curtsy had impressive depth.

Granny sat on a great gold brocade couch with Amira perched at the other end. The sheer size of it dwarfed them both. I had forgotten what it was like to be in rooms like this, cavernous and gilded and stuffed with mirrors and chandeliers. Everywhere you looked, faces lurked. There were lions carved into the mouldings, cherubs in the chair legs, disapproving ancestors in the paintings. As a child, I had felt as though a thousand eyes watched me constantly in these rooms. A cluster of aides including Stewart and Mary stood by a marble column and waited while we dispensed with family pleasantries.

I dropped into a curtsy and smiled. 'So sorry I'm late, just a bit jet-lagged.'

'Quite alright, dear girl,' Granny said.

'Lexi's always loved a sleep-in, hasn't she?' a booming voice said behind me.

I turned to see my father's brother standing there, picking at a lavish spread of pastries and fruit laid out on the table. Richard was in a flawlessly cut Savile Row suit, though there was nothing a skilled tailor could do about the cascade of neck skin over the collar of his £500 Tom Ford shirt. The 'Villiers droop' was an affliction no man in the family could avoid, no matter how handsome they had once been.

When he and Papa were young, Richard was the beautiful one. He was blond and dashing, where Papa was dark and shy. He got the magazine covers and the polo cup trophies and all the girls. In his twenties, Richard briefly worked as a search and rescue pilot in the Royal Air Force, once finding a little girl who had been missing on the North York Moors for over a week. The photos of him walking with the child gathered up in his biceps to return her to her weeping parents had earned him a lifetime of good will from a grateful kingdom.

But there was a public Richard and a private Richard. His pale eyes were as cold as ever, and I recalled that once, on a hunt, he had pushed my face into damp heather and hissed at me to be bloody quiet when I accidentally sneezed and disturbed the grouse.

'Uncle Richard,' I said.

He came towards me with his laden plate held aloft and kissed me on both cheeks. 'My poor little niece, what a tragedy. Gosh, you look more like Isla every day, don't you? Though better fed than your poor old mum, I suppose.'

He breezed past me to the chair next to Granny's elbow. Amira, clutching a teacup on her knee, barely contained her disdain. In the old days Richard and Papa would fight over this prime position by their mother's side, as if they were still boys and not middle-aged men.

'Perhaps, ma'am, we should get started?' said Stewart.

'Is Annabelle not here?' I asked.

The others exchanged glances. The aides busied themselves with papers or stared at their shoes. No one had said a word about my stepmother since I'd landed in London.

'The Dowager Duchess has elected to stay at Elton Park until the funeral. Her children are with her,' Stewart said.

'May as well enjoy it while she can,' Richard muttered.

In excruciating detail, Stewart began outlining the plans for the funeral. My father's and brother's coffins were to be placed side by side in Westminster Hall for four days so the public could say goodbye. After lying in state, they would be taken to the Abbey on two royal gun carriages, each drawn by a contingent of 140 sailors. In the interest of keeping calm and carrying on, it was decided that one funeral instead of two was more appropriate.

'As is tradition, we would expect His Royal Highness Prince Richard and Her Royal Highness Princess Alexandrina to lead the procession from the hall to the Abbey,' Stewart said.

'I'd like my girls with me,' Richard interjected, his mouth half-full of one of the muffins he'd piled onto his plate.

The room was silent for a moment. I glanced at Granny, but she was staring blankly out the window and barely seemed to be listening.

'Birdie and Demi have just lost their beloved uncle and cousin,' Richard continued. 'They're the Princesses of Clarence – and blood princesses at that.'

Amira, the target of this little shot across the bows, shrank in her seat. Stewart looked to Granny and then me for some kind of direction.

'Sir, traditionally only male members of the family join the procession,' he began.

'Lexi's walking, though.'

'Yes, sir. We thought given the circumstances—'

'She's not a working royal anymore. So if we're dispensing with old traditions – sexist traditions at that – then it's only fair that my girls walk too.'

A sunrise pink rose in Stewart's cheeks, and he glanced again towards the Queen for guidance. The tea in her hands had long gone cold and she put the cup on the table before her.

'Well, I have my view,' she said and suddenly looked at me with her brown eyes, so much like Papa's. 'But I'd like to hear what Lexi thinks first.'

Everyone turned and I felt my face grow hot. No one in this family had ever asked me for my opinion before.

'Richard is right,' I said. 'Demelza and Birdie should walk. If they want.'

Amira stared at me. She was wearing a full face of makeup, and her hair was pulled into a sleek bun at the nape of her neck. And yet she still looked like a woman close to her edge.

Richard wanted Demelza and Birdie in the procession for his own schemes, no doubt. But I had watched this family spiral into blood feuds over nonsensical, mediaeval traditions far too many times. After Mum died, Papa and Uncle James ended up in a screaming match over a spray of lilies placed atop her coffin. To the palace, it was the traditional symbol of mourning. For Isla's grief-struck twin brother, it was one too many insults to bury her under a mound of flowers she once declared 'smelled like cat piss'.

Stewart snapped his folder shut, relieved the worst was over.

'I think we've made great progress, and I thank you all for your patience,' he said, stacking papers and hustling aides from the room.

Granny eased herself from the couch. 'I think I'll go to my room for a rest.'

'Oh, yes, Mummy, you should. Amira, will you go with her?' Richard said.

The room emptied of everyone but the two of us and Richard fixed me with a smile that verged on a sneer. He was of the generation of British royals who never received braces or cared much for dental aesthetics. In recent years, he had his top teeth whittled down to fine points and then enveloped in blinding white veneers. But he left the bottom row untouched. His mouth reminded me of a freshly painted McMansion rimmed by a rickety picket fence.

'It was so good of you to come all this way,' he said. 'Your father was truly agonised by your estrangement. It was difficult to watch at times.'

My heart sank. Most of the time, I believed Papa barely noticed that I was no longer around.

'But Lexi, I have a favour to ask you,' he said. 'Mummy is not faring well, as I'm sure you've noticed, and I think it's best if I move in here for a while.'

What a sacrifice for a man who already lived in a thirty-room mansion for free, staffed with aides and maids for whom Granny paid.

'That makes sense,' I said.

'But here's the issue,' he said, leaning forward in his fussy gold chair and crossing his legs. He was wearing the same silk argyle socks Papa had favoured. 'I think Mummy would be more comfortable if Amira weren't here.'

I crossed my own legs and leaned forward, placing my chin in my hands. 'Is that right?'

'She doesn't really know her well, and I think it can be rather overwhelming when you're grieving your son and grandson to be somewhat … subsumed in someone else's grief. I just think it's best if she's surrounded by the people she's actually close to.'

It was a clever ruse – I had to give it to him. He could jettison both of us out of here, install himself as the Queen's favourite, and then tell the tabloids he was her pillar of strength. If I refused, he'd tell them we were two layabout princesses overstaying our welcome with a grieving sovereign.

'Fine,' I said. 'We'll go to Amira and Louis's apartment.'

He clasped his hands together, the way men always do when they've won the conversation, and grinned. 'Superb. Gosh, it's nice to have you back here, Lexi. The girls are going to be thrilled to see you. I don't think they even got to speak to you before you slipped out of Louis and Amira's wedding.'

I gave him an insincere smile. Demelza and Birdie had arrived at the wedding in dresses so ridiculous they instantly became internet memes. Demelza's dress had been composed entirely of hyperrealistic silk butterflies. Meanwhile, Twitter had branded Birdie's frilly ombré pink frock 'labia chic'.

'Oh, I can't wait to see them either,' I said.

I left him to his plate of pastries. Striding down the hall with my heart thudding, I understood why Mum and Papa had left every engagement that involved Richard with their jaws set and their knuckles white. It took me a moment to realise that Mary was trailing behind me, her leather binder pressed to her chest.

'Were you waiting for me, Mary?' I asked.

She broke into a trot until she reached my side. 'Yes, ma'am. I just wanted to see if I could be of any assistance.'

I realised I was deploying my hospital rounds stride. But it felt too good to stop. Maids, looking slightly alarmed, ceased their dusting and polishing and bobbed their heads as we stalked past. The palace's old floors buckled and sagged under our feet.

'The Dowager Duchess of Somerset and I need to move to her apartment at Cumberland Palace, probably tonight,' I said.

'Yes, ma'am, I was informed early this morning. Your things are being moved as we speak.'

Abruptly, I stopped, the anger sliding out of me and something heavier taking its place. Richard had never been going to give me the option to stay. His staff must have been making calls, arranging for me to be kicked out while I was still asleep in my childhood bed. I had the impulse to call Louis, who always knew how to handle the family. Then I remembered I would never speak to Louis again. With Mum, the cruelty of this one-two punch of absence still wounded me. It had been twelve years, and every time I heard a juicy piece of gossip or helped set a particularly grisly fracture, my first inclination was to tell her about it.

It occurred to me then that they were all gone. Father, mother, brother. We had once stood together in our snowsuits and goggles and posed as the ideal family. But they lived short lives. The last things they felt were fear and pain. And now I was all alone.

I went to the nearest window, but all I could see were trees.

'Are you alright, ma'am?' Mary asked.

'I don't know how to do this,' I said. She was silent and I turned from the window to look at her. 'Before … you said you were looking forward to working for me. I'm sorry, but I'm not planning to stay. I've got a life to get back to in Australia, so I'm only here for a few weeks at most.'

She looked crestfallen. 'I see.'

'I'm sorry. But I'm telling you this because I like you and hopefully this gives you time to find another job. I'm not sure what they'll do with the Wolseley staff.'

She nodded and pushed her glasses up her nose.

'I understand,' she said. 'I'd be happy to assist you as long as you're here, though. You'll need help with the funeral preparations. You haven't been here for such a long time – it might be useful having someone who knows the ropes.'

I smiled. Palace aides I'd known my entire life had stopped speaking to me the moment I moved to Australia. When I was still returning home every Christmas, they would turn on their heels and flee if they saw me walking down the halls.

'Mary, this is a complicated place, and I know I'm not exactly … popular here. If you want to stay working at the palace, your chances are better if you're not seen hanging around me.'

A row of stern-faced servants passed us, curtsying as they went. We were silent until they were safely down the hall. Mary looked up to meet my eyes. That smile of hers was back.

'I'm not very popular here either. Everyone thinks I have funny ideas. So perhaps it's fitting that we go out together.'

*

In Louis's room, I found Amira smoking by an open window.

'Have you heard the news?' I asked, flopping on the bed. 'We've both been evicted. Can I crash at your place at Cumberland? Or do you think you'll go stay with your parents?'

She said nothing but sighed smoke into the frosty London air. She had unpinned the bun from her head and her hair cascaded around her shoulders.

'I wouldn't worry. It doesn't mean anything,' I added. 'It's just Richard being a twat as usual.'

She took another drag of her cigarette. We used to smoke in our suite at Astley, sitting side by side in the alcove where we wouldn't be spotted from the grounds below. I don't know if we took much pleasure in the act itself, but it was forbidden and therefore appealing. A photo of me with a fag between my teenaged lips would have been worth £10,000 at least, which had only added to the allure.

'I was meant to have my egg retrieval next week,' she said quietly.

I lay on the bed propped on my elbows and stared at her. As the plane was cruising somewhere over Turkmenistan, I'd had a vivid fantasy that as soon as I arrived in London, Amira would tell me she and Louis had a few embryos on ice. We would have to act fast: the procedure would need to happen in a matter of days. But a nice big donation from Vikki's chequebook in exchange for the surgeon's silence would seal the deal. Vikki would do it – I was certain of it.

An ancestor of mine was nicknamed The Old Pretender because his rivals were utterly convinced the true heir to the throne had been stillborn, and a living infant procured and smuggled into the Queen's chambers inside a bed warmer. Was thawing out a speck of Villiers tissue and inserting it into the line of succession worse than what The Old Pretender's parents did? They would have done the same if the science were available to them. The line was a thousand years old, and it had rarely been straight and true.

I joined Amira by the window. We could see the red asphalt courtyard below. The cigarette switched hands between us.

'I'm sorry,' I said and inhaled. 'I didn't know you were trying.'

'I haven't drunk alcohol or coffee or smoked for three months in preparation for this week. Instead I'm going to his funeral.'

We stayed by the window for a long time. I hadn't smoked since secondary school and my head was swimming. I handed her the cigarette.

'Would you like to go get drunk at your apartment?'

*

Cumberland is a royal residence at the opposite end of Hyde Park from the sovereign's palace. Once a lavish gift to an old queen's favourite, it has since been converted into apartments for the monarch's relatives. Now it's sort of like an exhibit for endangered animals at the zoo: a safe place for these useless but fascinating creatures to loll about. Beyond its gilded wrought-iron gates, they had no chance of survival.

All the apartments looked inward to a central courtyard so that the inhabitants spent their days peering through their curtains to spy on each other. Mum caused an uproar in 1997 when she had wooden shutters fitted to finally grant herself some privacy.

'A middle-class monstrosity,' Granny's mean sister Beatrix had declared. But she'd always been resentful that Mum and Papa got Cumberland 1, the largest apartment, while she languished in the slightly smaller Cumberland 2.

I begged Stewart to let Amira and me walk across Hyde Park with hats and sunglasses to disguise ourselves.

'She needs the fresh air, Stewart,' I whispered at the entrance to the palace.

'Absolutely not,' he said and walked me to the waiting Range Rover. 'Now, ma'am, you understand that after the funeral there will be much to discuss. Prince Frederick's will … among other things.'

'Fine,' I said, relieved to hear I had four whole days during which no one would corner me and force me to decide everything at once.

When we got to the apartment, Amira disappeared to change her clothes and left me standing in the drawing room where I had grown up. I hadn't been inside Cumberland 1 since Granny gave it to Louis as an engagement gift. They'd had the place gutted and remodelled, the echoes of my childhood now almost imperceptible. The shutters were gone, replaced with chic linen curtains. A Hermès blanket was artfully draped across a white boucle couch. On top of a terrazzo coffee table were ruthlessly neat stacks of Tom Ford books and Diptyque candles the size of buckets.

I lit the enormous candles, deciphered the sleek and powerful bluetooth speakers to put on a Spotify playlist of 2010s throwback hits, and went into the kitchen in search of provisions. The abrupt end to their Zermatt ski trip and our decampment from the main palace meant no staff had yet had the chance to stock the fridge. But there was butter, half an onion, parmesan cheese and a shrivelling lemon. I went into the pantry and dug through packets of konjac noodles, bags of buckwheat flour, sugar-free chocolate, monk fruit sweeteners, powders and protein bars until I found an old box of orzo. Then I went looking for the gin.

By the time Amira emerged from her room dressed in an Olivia von Halle tracksuit, I had orzo al limone bubbling on the stovetop. She sat down at the kitchen island and eyed me suspiciously.

'Ready for your martini?' I asked and she shrugged. I took the shaker from the freezer and poured her an ice-cold dirty martini with three olives. As teenagers we'd split a VK mixed pack. But after lurking at the periphery of a few frosty family Christmases in the last decade, I knew that this was her drink.

'Cheers,' she muttered, took a gulp and closed her eyes. 'Goddamn it, that's good.'

I laughed.

'We shouldn't get too drunk though,' she added. 'I think they want us to inspect the flowers tomorrow.'

I took a sip. 'We don't have to do that, you know. It's a lot to ask of you. It's been, what? Four days?'

She gave me that strange look again. 'Your pot sounds like it's boiling.'

I gave the orzo a stir and sipped my drink. Jack's mum, Paula, horrified by my inability to do anything for myself, had taught me to cook a few years earlier. Until I was eighteen and out on my own, I had been unable to walk into a kitchen without a maid asking me how they could be of assistance. At boarding school, dinner was slopped onto a plate from a row of bains-marie. Through uni, I avoided the issue altogether with microwave meals and Thai takeaway.

Paula, who seemed to notice everything, had quietly taken me on as her project when I first moved onto the vineyard.

She and Jack's father, the first Jack Jennings, were a big deal in Tasmania. In the eighties, they were arrested for blockading the Franklin River to prevent it being dammed. In the nineties, Paula led the state's Yes Campaign to make Australia a republic and was devastated when they lost. She probably would have ended up in parliament, but Jack's father had died, and she took over his family's vineyard instead. She had still kept her hand in, though, risking arrest to stand in the path of a dozen bulldozers that were supposed to be razing an old-growth forest, and door-knocking for marriage equality in 2017.

I was not exactly the housemate she had in mind for her son. But, she'd concluded, if I was going to have a stab at life in the real world, the least I could do was learn how to handle a kitchen knife. First Paula had asked me to read out steps from the recipe while she cooked. I'd watched as she calmly moved about her space. Somehow she knew that Japanese noodles needed to be plunged in cold water after boiling so they didn't stick. She removed basil stems to keep the pesto from going brown and bitter. She knew that too much kale caused a stomach ache, but you could massage the leaves with oil to soften them. Eventually, she had placed a cutting board, a pile of vegetables and a knife before me. I was later mortified to find out it was a child's safety knife purchased specifically for me.

Now I could make a proper dinner from odds and ends in the fridge. More than my medical degree, more than my bank account in my own name containing my own salary, it was my capacity to take care of myself that made me proud. I could suture a laceration and barely leave a scar, but it was my ability to make soup that felt like alchemy.

I spooned the orzo into bowls and pushed one towards Amira. She looked at it warily. 'I can't remember the last time I had dairy or pasta.'

I ate a mouthful. In our school years, she had watched in bewilderment as I dieted and deprived myself down to the bone. I did two hours of ballet a day for no other reason than to arrest the development of my teenage body. I threw up every Christmas dinner until I was eighteen. I wondered, when she finally succumbed and joined this family, if she had vowed to herself that she would do it differently. But it could never be different. Mum was taller and slimmer than both of us, and she had denied herself so long her hair began to fall out. When Papa gave Isla the ring that now sat on Amira's finger, she had a 27-inch waist. By their wedding day, she had shrunk down to 23 inches. I knew this fact not because my mother told me but because every woman in England somehow knows about Isla's 'handspan waist'.

'I bet you've been so stressed, you probably haven't had a proper meal in days,' I said carefully.

It was an argument that might have worked on me once. Life was a relentless calculation of calories consumed. A few days of intense restriction might permit one indulgence like a full meal. She nodded slowly.

'I don't need extra cheese on top, it'll just hurt my stomach,' she said, pushing the plate of grated parmesan towards me.

'Would you like another martini?' I asked.

'Yes please,' she said, taking little pecks of individual orzo from the tines of her fork. 'This is nice, thank you.'

We ate in silence. I poured another round of drinks, and we listened to the relentlessly upbeat music of our childhood. When Adele came on again, Amira grabbed my phone and started skipping through songs in search of something she liked.

'Is this your dog?' she asked of my phone background.

This was the first time in the decade since I'd left that a family member had asked me a single question about my life. Once Papa had realised I wasn't coming back, he'd settled into an icy silence that lasted the rest of his life. The others followed his lead.

'That's Ragu, Jack's dog.'

'Is Jack your boyfriend?'

'He's my friend,' I said, flushing. 'I live in a cottage on his mum's vineyard with another friend.'

She nodded and looked again at my phone. 'Is Ragu a German short-haired pointer?'

'Yes, but they don't use him for hunting. I mean, he kills a lot of things – rabbits, blackbirds. But that's of his own accord,' I said, irrationally nervous.

'If his prey drive is that high, they need to train him to hunt,' she said absently. 'Do you have any more photos?'

I opened my photo app and handed the phone back to her. 'There's nothing saucy in there, except a few gnarly wounds from the hospital. Just flick around.'

I drained my martini as she swiped. Ed Sheeran crooned over the speakers, something a teenaged Amira would never have allowed. I wondered what she made of it all, the life I had chosen at the end of the world over the one to which I had been born, the life Vikki had been desperate to give her. The monotonous tap of her finger suddenly stopped. She stared for a long time at whatever she'd found on my phone, her eyes narrowing.

'Who's that?' she asked, turning the phone around for me to see.

I hesitated a moment. 'That's the other guy I live with, Finn. Would you like something else to drink?'

She stared at the screen. My phone displayed our 'family photo' taken on Christmas Day: the three of us with our arms looped around each other, Ragu bored and unimpressed at our feet. We'd posed for it at the end of a long day drinking Jennings sparkling wine. It had been taken ten days earlier, but it might as well have been a hundred years ago.

'Yes please,' she said, pushing forward her glass. 'What does Finn do for a living?'

'We're in the same residency program,' I said, trying to keep my voice light. I was never sure how many details of Louis's disastrous trip to the vineyard made it back to London. But clearly enough for her to still be furious at Finn and me.

She continued glaring, but seemed to decide to let it go when I proffered a fresh martini. She took the glass from my hands and sipped it.

'Okay, so that's three drinks,' I said, desperate to change the subject. Even after I abandoned Louis, even after I lost him, I was still in the habit of protecting him. 'If we stop now, we'll be fine to inspect the flowers tomorrow and not look totally minging.'

Drake came on the speaker, and Amira pushed the volume all the way up to its limit. For the first time since I'd come careening back into her life twenty-four hours earlier, she smiled at me.

'Fuck the flowers,' she said.

*

At 3 am, I staggered into a guest room and flopped onto the bed. Four and a half martinis, it turned out, was too much. We had listened to the 2010s throwbacks before dancing through the early 2000s. By the time I was queuing up Beyoncé's entire discography, Amira bent over the farmhouse sink in the kitchen and unleashed her dinner and drinks.

'Alright, bedtime,' I declared.

I helped her wash her face, knowing that wearing a full face of makeup to bed was a greater sin than eating pasta with cheese.

'Do you want me to sleep in here with you?' I asked as I tucked her into the enormous bed obscured under a seemingly endless topsoil of neutral linen cushions. 'Or I can just put a bucket by the bed.'

'I don't need you,' she moaned. 'You always think I need you.'

I couldn't find a bucket anywhere in the apartment, so I left a crystal punchbowl on the bedside table.

Upstairs, in the dark guestroom, the bed rolled under me like a ship. This room had once been Mum's office, but her desk had been replaced with one of those expensive stationary bikes.

Louis's dress watch sat on the bedside table next to a carafe of water. His clothes hung in the closet and his gym bag lay on the floor.

I pulled my phone out of my hoodie and called Jack. He picked up on the second ring.

'Lex,' he said.

'Hello.'

Even with a belly of gin, I was unaccountably shy, as if thousands of miles didn't separate us. I imagined the undersea cable running along the seafloor to connect our voices, passing through the Malacca Strait, the warm waters of the Arabian Sea, the Suez Canal, which laid bare my family's waning influence.

'What time is it there?'

'I dunno, 3 am? I'm a bit jet-lagged,' I said.

'How are you?'

I took a deep breath and closed my eyes, but found that just made the spins even worse.

'I'm alright,' I lied. 'I forgot what it's like here. My uncle's had me and Amira kicked out of the palace.'

'Where are you staying?'

'The apartment I grew up in.'

I could hear voices around him and I realised I'd caught him in the middle of his work day. He would be between the vines. His t-shirt would be dampened with sweat in the January sun and he would take off his hat so he could run his forearm across his brow.

'Is it really an apartment?' he asked.

'They call it an apartment but it's four storeys high.'

A comfortable silence settled between us, like it used to in the old days. The 'old days' were only days ago, but I suspected they were already lost to me. Sometimes we used to talk on the phone with just the wall separating our rooms. I would get into bed and dial his number. He wouldn't even say a word, just open the line and place the phone on the pillow beside him.

'What are you doing?' I would eventually ask.

'Just lying here. What are you doing?' he'd respond, his voice more vibration than sound, striking a chord inside me that I didn't care to examine.

Finn and I had moved in with Jack seven years earlier, when he needed housemates and we needed a safer place to live. His place was on the family property, a sandstone cottage, partially buried in a tumble of jasmine. The best part of the cottage was the converted, slope-roofed barn attached to its side. Jack insisted I have it, while he and Finn took the bedrooms in the main part of the cottage.

When we first moved in, I found Jack alarmingly attractive. I was relieved that he had a girlfriend, Georgia, who bought and restored antiques before selling them at a breathtaking mark-up on Instagram. She wore paint-splattered Blundstones and overalls. She came from a nice Tasmanian family, which, unlike mine, had never inflicted colonial trauma on the entire planet. With her sweet face and her useful hands, she was basically perfect for him. I swiftly turned her into my friend to annihilate my tiny crush on Jack and ensure he remained out of reach. But when Georgia received an offer to work with a famous furniture restorer in New York three years ago, Jack declined to go with her. On the night she left, I dialled his phone across the wall to make sure he was okay. It was a habit we had never attempted to break.

'I'm really sorry about your dad and Louis. I don't know if I had a chance to say that before.'

I said nothing for a long moment. 'How long did it take you to get over your dad's death?'

'Well, I was eight, so it's probably a bit different,' he said. His father had fallen off a ladder trying to fix a shingle on the roof of the main house. It was only a few metres, and he'd seemed fine. By the time anyone realised the knock to his head had triggered a catastrophic bleed, it was too late to save him. Jack had watched as his dad staggered, then swayed like a felled tree, dead before he hit the ground. 'How long did it take you to get over your mum?'

'I'm still waiting.'

He was quiet for a while. 'Yeah. Same, I guess.'

'Hey,' I asked suddenly, 'before the helicopter came, do you think we were about to kiss?'

I knew every iteration of his laugh, but this particular version was new to me. He hesitated. 'Are you drunk?'

'Maybe, why?'

I could hear him sifting through his thoughts, deciding which one he would share with me. 'I was going to kiss you, yeah.'

'Have you ever thought about doing that before?' I asked, my face flushing at my own recklessness. Our friendship was a delicate thing that depended on certain doors never being opened, even though we loved nothing more than to rattle the handles to see what would happen.

Again, he was silent. 'Well, yeah ... but maybe this is something we should talk about when you've sobered up.'

'Why?'

'Because you'll wake up in the morning and regret this conversation, and then you'll avoid me for a while.'

He was right. The helicopter coming in to break up our potentially life-altering kiss had been both maddening and a reprieve.

'You know,' I said, barely following my own thoughts as they flowed out of me, 'I've always suspected that if I didn't have my title, I wouldn't be half as interesting. Isn't that pathetic?'

I couldn't see him, but I knew he was smiling that smile of his, the annoying one he gave me when I was crabby in the morning or worried about an exam, the one that made me want to sink my teeth into his neck.

'You're the most interesting person I know, and I couldn't care less about your title,' he said.

He could name all 160 grape varieties that grow in Australia. He could easily have spent his life trading on his rebellious family's fame but never did. He still borrowed library books. He danced with old ladies at weddings. When we first met, I was oddly determined to scare him by telling him stories about my parents, the worst ones that never made it into the tabloids: The time Papa shoved her and she fell back into a mirror. The time Mum found Annabelle's nightgown in his bed and ran up to the roof with it. But Jack only listened intently and squeezed my shoulder. *Oh, shit,* I had thought. *Who is this?* He was undoubtedly the most interesting person I knew.

'Lex,' he said, 'you've got a lot going on right now. I don't want to pressure you.'

His voice in my ear and the gin in my blood was edging me to sleep.

'I wish you could come to the funeral,' I murmured. 'I have to go alone.'

'I would come. But it doesn't sound like the kind of funeral where anyone can just rock up and pay their respects.'

I thought of the impossible day that lay ahead, the second time I would have to trail a coffin as everyone watched.

'No, they're checking every manhole and lamppost in central London for explosives,' I said. 'Half the world's heads of state will be there.'

'I'll just grab a seat next to the Emperor of Japan then.'

'He can't come – he's having gallbladder surgery. He's sending his son instead.'

We both laughed softly. It was that hour of night when nothing really counted.

'Will you pat Ragu for me?' I asked.

'He keeps looking for you. Every time I go to find him, he's standing at the barn doors peering inside.'

My eyes were closing. 'I'm falling asleep.'

'That's okay. Go to sleep. Call me later.'

'Good night.'

'Night, Lex.'

CHAPTER SEVEN

2012

The thought that I must leave had first come to me when they found Mum's body. I'd never wanted to flee before. I was a good princess. Obedient. Eager to please. But when the police pulled her from the Ligurian Sea, a desire to escape surfaced in me as well.

During the fraught negotiations over her funeral, the Kilchurns confirmed that Isla's mysterious twin, James, would be the one to speak on her family's behalf. He lived in Australia, and I'd never seen him before he walked up the aisle of Westminster Abbey in his black suit. Once he stood at the pulpit, he abandoned the eulogy approved by Stewart and instead calmly disembowelled my father, my grandmother and the palace.

'If I had been a better brother, you would still be alive today,' he said before the stunned congregation. He had dark, wild hair and his eyes glowed with rage. 'You were seeking something your blood family failed to give you. Our neglect sent you down this path. I pledge to do all I can to make sure your fine children keep the open hearts you gave them.'

At the wake, he pulled me into an awkward embrace and slipped a piece of paper into my hand. I tucked it away before anyone saw. I always wondered if he did the same for Louis when

I wasn't looking. If he had, neither of them ever mentioned it to me. Later that night, I sat on my bed and fished the folded-up paper out from my pocket. It contained James's phone number and email address.

If you need someone to talk to – or if you need a rescue, it read.

Sometimes I think I might want out of this, I wrote to him that night.

We emailed for my remaining twelve months at Astley. Sometimes we chatted aimlessly, sometimes we edged closer to what might best be described as a plot. Both Louis and I were permitted a gap year after school if we used it to do volunteer work. At James's recommendation, I developed a very public fascination with Australia. He had been running a small merino wool farm in the midlands of Tasmania for fifteen years, and he was happy to facilitate my escape.

I didn't know much of his childhood except that he and Mum grew up in the family seat at the head of Loch Fyne on a 60,000-acre estate. Their father, the duke and local clan chief, was nothing more than a strong set of shoulders striding through the castle gates, and in a scandal that rippled all the way to London, their mother, the Duchess of Kilchurn, abandoned the family when her twins were two. Eventually, the duchess begged for the children to join her down south, but her ex-husband denied her.

Instead the twins were consigned to governesses and otherwise left to drift along draughty halls like ghosts. While James roamed the moors, Isla wandered into the kitchen and made friends with the servants. One afternoon when she was twelve, she took her small sailing dinghy and went out on the loch alone. Once she was on the water, she heard a rip and looked up to see a gash opening up in her mainsail. It would be nine hours before anyone noticed she was gone, and another four before a search party found her, shivering and terrified, on her drifting raft.

Without a parent to guide them, James and Isla never really knew their neighbours. They didn't attend the Highland Games, and they didn't dance reels with kids their age. They were sent to separate boarding schools at the age of thirteen – Isla to Switzerland and James to the Highlands – and neither of them returned to the castle on the loch. She moved to London after school, living briefly and disastrously with her mother, before she found herself being courted by the heir to the throne. When they became engaged, the Scottish press found issue with her plummy accent and her European education, branding her the 'Gall princess' – a Gaelic insult for stranger.

Their father died in 2005. But even though he was the new Duke of Kilchurn, James refused to spend another night in the castle where he grew up. To cover its considerable maintenance costs, he opened it to the public for guided tours – an enterprise that became especially lucrative after Mum's death.

I had the impression that he and his sister were never particularly close. By the time Isla went into the water, she and James were barely speaking. But there was no one more incensed by her death than her twin brother. Days after they found her, James turned on the television and saw Louis and me. They'd sent us out to inspect the flowers and work the teary crowds who would not leave the palace gates. We were seventeen. Somehow he knew I was drowning in the depths of my family, and he threw me a rope.

After finishing school, I was meant to be in Australia for six months. The palace had arranged for me to spend half the trip jillarooing at a cattle station in Far North Queensland before I was permitted to travel around the country on my own. I was then expected to head to the Shankar lodge in South Africa, where I would reunite with Louis, Kris and Amira and spend six months volunteering at a game reserve. By Michaelmas 2013, all four of us would walk into the University of St Andrews, where I planned to study chemistry.

As a blood princess, I had no expectations that I would ever have a job beyond being a 'working royal'. But I had noticed that science came remarkably easily to me, and with little effort.

In chemistry class, I could successfully make the mercury oscillate like a beating heart and turn flames blue or green with the correctly chosen chemical. And come exam time, the answers to the questions on the page seemed to surface in my mind like bubbles from the bottom of a dark lake. Papa thought it would be a suitable degree for me to acquire and never use.

But I never made it to Queensland, or to South Africa or to the gates of St Andrews. As soon as I landed in Australia, I'd abandoned my itinerary and headed straight for James's property in Tasmania. I never really thought I'd go through with it, but after a week spent immobile and unshowered on his couch, I decided to put the second phase of my plan into action. I applied for a student visa and enrolled in a chemistry degree. But rather than Sydney, as I had originally intended, I applied for a course in Tasmania.

To this day I cannot explain why I chose Hobart over the mainland. Somehow, I stepped off the plane and I knew. Below me was Antarctica. To the west was nothing but the vast expanse of the Indian Ocean all the way to Argentina. Everything was rugged and windswept. Hobart still has the air of a swashbuckling whaling town. Nestled into the slopes of kunanyi/Mount Wellington, the city uses the mountain as its thermometer, its playground, its spiritual touchstone. You don't bother with the weather forecast in Hobart. You simply look for a dusting of snow on the peak and dress accordingly. There is nothing more stirring than the sight of mist caught in its organ-pipe cliffs. In the afternoon, the sinking sun casts a chiffon shroud over the mountain's broad shoulders. The locals are the butt of national jokes and the victims of the poorest health outcomes in the country. They're consistently left off the map, both literally and figuratively. And yet no one wants to leave. They log off at 4 pm for a pottery class and they shut their tourism-dependent businesses to go bushwalking for the summer. They strip off naked and swim in nine-degree waters to celebrate the winter solstice. There are red wine and oysters and firepits. Somehow, everyone knows everyone. No one ever asks you what you do for a job because no one cares. Who could care about work when you're living on a magical island where everything glows, from the bioluminescent mushrooms to the seas edged with electric-blue algae to the aurora-filled skies? I had reached the southernmost edge of the world, and I decided to stay.

My email sent with shaking hands to inform Papa of my new plans received no response. A week later, Stewart appeared at the door of James's farmhouse.

'You've made a commitment to the station in Queensland,' he said, sitting awkwardly at the kitchen table across from me while James stood sentry in the doorway.

'She can do the same sort of volunteer work here,' James said.

When he first arrived in Tasmania, James had purchased his property as a hobby farm. Now, from a flock of five thousand sheep, he produced ultra-fine wool that was made into luxury Italian suits. I had not been much help in the fortnight since I arrived. Every morning, we ate breakfast together, and then I'd watch him walk down the hill, off to muster, or shear, or fence, or whatever it was sheep farmers did. I sat around reading in his living room until he texted me at exactly noon to remind me to eat the sandwich he'd left for me in the fridge. Then I moved to the porch to silently fret. Regretting and reaffirming my decision. Deciding to pack my bags and return to London. Realising the group chat with Kris, Louis and Amira had fallen silent. Knowing they'd started a spinoff without me.

But when the sun finally melted over the horizon, James would return, and I'd sit at the kitchen table while he chopped things for our dinner. For the first time in a long time, I ate. And I swallowed. And with each meal that James prepared, I thought less and less about the food inside me. It took me years to realise that he must have recognised this problem of mine, approaching it like a skittish lamb in one of his fields, quietly shooing it away before it imprinted on me and followed me around for the rest of my days.

I wasn't sure how he knew this about me, but I suppose he watched his own sister stalked by the very same shadow. Once she became a royal, the full face of her youth receded until her cheekbones pushed up like colliding tectonic plates. All her softness was replaced with right angles and a fine down that grew over her pale limbs, fluffing up against the cold so she looked like a little nestling. Everyone agreed she looked sick, but also sensational. Everyone wanted to be her.

But James and I had both read the autopsy report, and we knew she died with the skeleton of an eighty-year-old, with wrecked teeth and a listless heart. Worse, she died with a near-empty stomach, having almost forgotten what it was like to sit down and eat a full meal, to enjoy it and let it remain inside her.

'Ma'am, it has been a very trying few years, and you are entitled to a break,' Stewart had said, clearly delivering the lines he and Papa had agreed upon. 'But you have a duty to your family, and privilege entails responsibility.'

It was smart of Papa to send him. The speech James and I had agreed upon suddenly left me.

'I'm sorry, Stewart,' I said.

He had looked down at his hands for a long moment and then returned his gaze to my face. He had the soft golden eyes of a Saxon merino. I wondered if this might be the last time we ever saw each other.

'Ma'am,' he began. 'Prince Frederick cannot support this; he refuses to pay for this.'

The kettle on the stove took its breath and emitted a low whistle that escalated into an almighty wail. James shuffled across the kitchen and took it off the hob. Taking his time, he had prepared the tea, following the steps just as Mum had. A scoop for each person and one for the pot.

'It never seemed right to me that I got everything when our father died, and Isla got nothing,' James said with his back turned to us. 'It's the way things have always been done, I know. But it seems wrong to send a girl out into the world with nothing –

especially a girl who's never been taught how to take care of herself.'

He placed the pot on the table between us and laid out the cups and saucers. He sat down and made himself comfortable.

'I would like to pay for Lexi's education,' he said.

Stewart kept his gaze downward.

'I should have done more for Isla, and I didn't. Our father rarely spoke to us, but when he did, he would say to Isla, "Be careful, your face is your future." She always wanted to get away from him, but in the end, she married a man just like him,' James said, slowly preparing his own tea.

Our cups steamed untouched in front of Stewart and me.

'Your Grace, your dedication to your niece is admirable,' Stewart said. 'But I fear significant decisions are being made in the fog of grief.'

'Lexi is free to choose,' James said. 'I am simply facilitating her choice to have a different kind of life than the one to which she was born.'

Stewart turned to me. 'Once you head down this path, it will be enormously difficult to turn back.'

I began to cry, not because I was particularly scared, but because James had warned me they would try to coerce me back with an ultimatum. Stewart looked pained, but forged ahead.

'Prince Frederick wishes me to inform you that as executor of your trust, he has enacted a variance so that you will only be able to access your inheritance at age thirty, rather than twenty-five,' he said.

I nodded, hot tears and snot streaming down my chin. Stewart handed me a handkerchief, which I blindly accepted. Louis and I had been surprised to find that Mum had a will prepared before she died, though we couldn't understand why she made Papa the executor of the trust. I suppose she had no one else to ask.

She was almost broke by the last few months of her life – not that I particularly cared about the money. But I was also set to inherit her jewellery, including her engagement ring, which I yearned to hold in my fist until it dug into my flesh. I wanted that ring the same way I would have treasured her discarded apple cores, her pencils delicately marked by her teeth, a water glass with the ghost of her lipstick on the rim.

'Probably best you go now, don't you think?' James said calmly and Stewart nodded.

Six months later, I was living in a two-bedroom flat in Sandy Bay and ready to begin my new life as a science student. I was surprised to find that apartment living was not dissimilar from boarding school life. There were popular tenants and outcasts, villains and shut-ins. The block was filled with wealthy retirees who had downsized from the sagging mansions along the beachfront. Most seemed to fear the moment their adult children would find out about a fall or an accidental attempt to microwave a metal saucepan and move them into nursing homes. All disapproved of my presence since I came with a horde of photographers and 24/7 security guards who sat outside the block in their cars with the engines running.

James paid for my rent and school fees and gave me a credit card with a monthly limit for expenses. For the first three months, I was terrified by the concept of finite resources and lived on nothing but pasta and balsamic vinegar. Once James encouraged me to live normally, I blew it all in ten days. Over time, I slowly worked out what things cost, mostly by imitating my fellow students on their purchases. I learned that I could live on packets of Indomie Nasi Goreng noodles on the last days of the month, and that the most dreaded expense of all was university textbooks. I floated the idea of getting a job, but my security detail deemed it too dangerous. I got better over time, but I still had the stink of a rich girl pretending to be normal, scouring the Chemist Warehouse catalogue for bargains, and then dropping $350 on Miu Miu sunglasses because I forgot to ask the saleswoman the price before having her wrap them up.

The palace told the tabloids that Granny and Papa were thrilled by my choice and had counselled me by phone as I considered changing my long-held plans.

'*She's always had such a love of Australia. Prince Frederick was not at all surprised she wanted to stay there after finally having the chance to visit. She's truly a daddy's girl and he was there every step of the way as she rethought her plans to study at St Andrews with her brother,*' a 'friend' told the *Daily Post*.

'*Alexandrina still intends to be a working royal, but her dream is to focus her future philanthropic efforts on health and medical research. She'll simply be the most educated princess in British history.*'

I met Finn in my first week of classes. At first, no one dared approach me. It was a phenomenon I had seen only occur around Granny: when she walked into a room, she was like a shark swimming into a school of fish. Hordes of guests stepped back in unison, eyes averted, the path before her magically cleared. For lower-ranked royals it was quite the opposite. The socially ambitious swam alongside us like suckerfish. I had expected to be accosted at university, but instead I found myself friendless.

Finn was the most popular boy in Hobart. His family dated back to the first penal colony – the ultimate status symbol in the state and the Vanderville name was on street signs and buildings across the city. No one knew he was smart until he graduated at the top of his class and decided to study chemistry. Everywhere he went on campus, he was trailed by a swarm of recent grads from Hobart's private schools. With his blond curls and flushed cheeks, he had been a cherubic child who drew gasps everywhere he went, and he still had the confidence of a little boy who believed himself truly beautiful. On our first day of organic chemistry, our lecturer paired everyone off as lab partners by going down the class list alphabetically. Vanderville and Villiers were assigned to Bench 5.

When I approached him, he quirked a brow and grinned at me. 'I've been waiting for us to meet.'

And that was it. I had made my first friend outside the gates of palaces and boarding schools. I was aware that Finn initially saw me as a novelty prize from a circus sideshow. He displayed me at nightclubs and gay bars and family gatherings. He casually captured me in the background of his Instagram stories, which were so abundant that they looked more like tiny grains of rice than dashes at the top of his page. I was useful to him and I allowed myself to be used because he was fun and I was lonely.

In our second year of uni, he moved into the guest bedroom of my flat. Neither of us had any practical skills and it was a relief to find someone with whom I could sit on the floor and watch YouTube tutorials so we could figure out how to reboot the modem or remove red wine from the carpet. Being my hanger-on came with very few perks, except for being described as my 'unidentified male companion' by the *Daily Post*. The photographers who stalked me in packs eventually thinned out to just a few stragglers as the novelty of my desertion wore off. But still, Finn stayed by my side.

Through the relentless grind of university and then medical school and hospital night shifts, our relationship of convenience deepened into something else. We raised each other. Not once had he betrayed my confidence. He knew all my secrets and he held them close. In the end we succumbed to a real friendship.

I was shadowed by my security detail for the duration of my bachelor's studies in Australia. The *Daily Post* repeatedly reminded its readers that it was costing the British taxpayer £250,000 a year to guard an absconding princess. Leo, a thirty-year-old with a cheeky grin, was my protection officer for more than a year, and we carried on a frenzied affair that was fuelled almost entirely by the thrill of secret sex. But then Martin, his gruff older colleague, caught us kissing in the underground garage of my apartment block. The next day Leo was gone, put on a plane back to London, and replaced with a stern female protection officer called Susan.

I had been smart enough to keep my texts to Leo in code and avoid the sharing of nudes altogether. But when he tried to sell the details of our trysts to the tabloids, I was forced to issue an SOS to Stewart. A mysterious arrangement was made that likely involved a lump payment for Leo and a requirement that I return home for Christmas for the traditional family walk to church.

'This is why royals fuck other royals, doll,' Finn sighed. 'It's mutually assured destruction.'

My taxpayer-funded security was finally withdrawn when word reached Papa that I had sat the Graduate Medical School Admissions Test, the dreaded exam that determines whether undergrads will be admitted into the Doctor of Medicine master's program. Finn and I passed, and he posted the news, coupled with a boomerang of us clinking champagne flutes, on his Instagram stories.

A month later, I walked out of my building and got halfway down the street before I realised something was different. There had been no white Holden Commodores idling by the kerb when I left the house. No middle-aged man with a crew cut had given me a brusque hello. No one was following me. I stood on Sandy Bay Road in Tasmania's strange autumn light. I looked out at the jumble of masts on the boats docked at the marina. I realised this was only the second time in my entire life that I had been completely alone.

I went to my classes, met friends for drinks and said nothing to anyone. Finn and I bought a barbecue chicken and a pasta salad from Coles and walked home. I was aware that if any of the Isla obsessives who sent me ranting 72-page handwritten letters were to jump out of a bush, they could easily kill us both.

'Have you noticed anything different?' I asked.

Finn checked to see if I'd changed my hair. 'No?'

It was probably a testament to my security detail that they had managed to fade so skilfully into the backdrop of my life that no one even noticed when they left. They dressed down in black puffer coats and sneakers, so they looked like everyone else in Hobart. They mostly walked a few paces behind me or sat in the back row of my lectures. New friends found them fascinating and would always offer them a schooner or a handful of chips while they leaned against the wall of the pub, waiting for me to be done. With the exception of Leo, they always declined.

'My security disappeared this morning.'

Finn's eyes went wide, and he looked up and down the street for the officers who were no longer tailing us.

'Do you think your dad took them away?' he asked. 'Or do you think they're tied up in the garage right now and your killer is waiting for you in the apartment?'

There was no killer in our apartment. When I texted Stewart to ask if he knew anything, I got the answer I expected.

Yes, ma'am, you may wish to talk to Prince Frederick, he wrote back. *There was a review conducted by RAVEC into the security costs for the family. Best, Stewart.*

The Royal and VIP Executive Committee, or RAVEC, decides who among Britain's high-profile figures gets state-sponsored security and who doesn't. Stewart sat on the committee, but he never would have withdrawn my protection unless Papa had ordered him to do it. I left it for a week. But one night after I had three cocktails at the Grand Poobah, I dialled my father's direct line on the walk home. The phone rang out and sent me to his voicemail.

'Hello, Papa!' I chirped. 'Just thought I'd let you know it's about ten o'clock at night here and I'm cutting through a city park on my own. Gosh, it's quite overgrown, isn't it? It's very dark actually, and I'm quite drunk and stumbling about in a very short skirt. Anyway, they always say that if you find yourself alone at night, you should call someone. I'm not sure why. I suppose rapists hesitate to attack you because the other person on the phone might hear everything and call the police? But you didn't pick up, so I'm on my own here. Hope everything is well with you! Let's chat soon if I survive this walk home! Night night, Daddy.'

He never called me back.

A week later, the *Daily Post* published details of the RAVEC review into the protection of the royal family. I'd been stripped of my security detail because I was deemed a 'low-risk target'. The *Post* rather cattily described Demelza and Birdie as 'minor royals', but their protection arrangements were left intact.

'*With Alexandrina off on her own course, the girls have had to pick up so many public engagements, even though they're busy students as well,*' a royal 'source' told the *Post*.

'*Hundreds of charities are entirely dependent on the favour of the Royal Family, and they were left high and dry when the princess took off for a new life in Australia. Demelza and Birdie stepped into the breach beautifully, and they've made their grandmother extremely proud.*'

'*Demelza and Birdie have a higher profile thanks to their cousin,*' Richard's aide told the *Post*. '*It was not a role they sought, but they are loyal to the crown, and they've put themselves at great risk to take on the burden of Alexandrina's duties. It's entirely right she was stripped of her protection, given she is in the middle of nowhere and her cousins are picking up her slack.*'

When word reached James that my security detail was gone, he called an emergency meeting at his farm. Finn and I got in his old RAV4 and made the drive north, fearful we were about to be kicked out of our Sandy Bay flat. Despite being my benefactor and my only relative in a 14,000-kilometre radius, James and I only saw each other a couple of times a year. If I wasn't going to Norfolk for Christmas, I went to Finn's family lunch. James would almost always decline to join us. He worked the parched plains of central Tasmania in solitude and ate almost every meal alone.

He didn't seem particularly surprised that Papa had withdrawn my protection. 'It's classic Frederick – he was always going to lash out when you finished your undergrad and didn't go back.'

'I probably am low-risk, though,' I said. 'It's been four years now.'

James grimaced and shook his head. 'You're still third in line to the throne.'

'Would it make any difference if you took yourself out of contention for the throne, Lexi?' Finn asked while nibbling on an Arrowroot biscuit.

Regular people – Australians in particular – imagined that my HRH style, my title and my place in the line were things I could just hand back, like ugly candlesticks inherited from a distant aunt. When Mum and Papa had divorced, she was allowed to keep her title, but they stripped her of her HRH.

'He wants me to have to curtsy to my own children,' she said with big wet eyes.

'Don't worry, Mum,' Louis said, wrapping his skinny arms around her. 'I'll be able to give it back to you one day.'

I knew I had no use for the letters and titles that hung on my name like silver charms. But the idea of losing them, of being just Alexandrina, felt like I was being asked to stand naked in the midst of a huge crowd. Perhaps one day I would do it, when I could swap them out and become Dr Alexandrina Villiers, MD. Those letters were adornments I would drape across my name with pride, I thought.

Of course I got my doctorate a few years later, and still never considered – not even for a moment – giving up my HRH. I knew once I did that, there was no going back. Even as I drifted further and further from my family, I found that I couldn't sever the last bond between us. Sometimes, in the early days, when I was particularly lonely, I wondered if perhaps I should just go home. They were my family, after all. But then Papa's office would leak a lie to the tabloids – I was hitting him up for money again, I had fallen under the spell of my anti-establishment uncle – and I would remember what my future in London looked like. At least in Australia, whatever happened next was entirely up to me.

'It's a whole thing to give up the titles,' I said to Finn. 'I don't just hand them in. It would take an Act of Parliament. Or I'd have to become a Catholic.'

James probably saw through my excuses, but he said nothing and dipped his biscuit into his tea. He was a Scottish duke masquerading as an Australian wool farmer. He could sell the family seat tomorrow for millions of pounds to a Qatari emir, and yet he couldn't let it go.

It was decided that the Sandy Bay flat was not secure enough for us to stay. Without officers guarding the entrance to the garage, it was frighteningly easy for someone to slip inside by lurking behind the recycling bins and waiting for a resident to drive in. A ladder could be leaned against our balcony, and if our glass doors weren't locked, someone could be in our apartment in less than a minute. With toxic levels of charm emitted over the years we had lived there, Finn and I had managed to win over our sceptical neighbours. But they would not be happy if we asked them to withhold the door code from relatives and delivery men.

'I can't ask you to pay for security guards,' I said to James.

'I'm not offering,' he said. 'Look, you're never going to be a normal girl, no matter what you do. But that doesn't mean you have to go home. We just need to get you into a more secure living situation – and no more stumbling through town steamin', alright?'

James had a livestock manager who'd proven to be a hard worker and a good guy.

'In a few weeks, he's going back to work on his family's vineyard in the Coal River Valley. It's fully fenced, and it's not open to the public. His mother lives in the main house, but he's looking for housemates to share his cottage on the property,' James said.

We hopped into James's old LandCruiser and drove up to the lucerne paddock, where the flock was grazing. There is something so stark and haunting about the Australian landscape. It is neither green nor pleasant. It isn't trying to kill you, but it doesn't particularly care if you live or die in its pitiless surroundings either. It was my ancestor who sent James Cook to this place to claim it and bend it to the crown's will, to unleash disease, misery and pain on the people who lived here.

Centuries later, I was here too, hoping to be granted the land's benedictions. I vowed to tread lighter than the ghouls who came before me.

The wind was picking up that day and the grass swirled around us like skirts. James pulled the truck over, and Finn and I walked gingerly through the field in our inappropriate footwear. Surrounded by yapping kelpies, a man in Blundstones and jeans emerged in the near distance. When James stuck his fingers in his mouth and emitted an ear-piercing whistle, the man turned to look at us. He was tall. His shirtsleeves were rolled up to expose strong forearms and tanned skin.

'Uh oh,' Finn whispered as he ambled towards us. 'Is he going to be trouble for you or for me? I can't tell.'

'Calm down, you two. He has a girlfriend,' James muttered. Louder, he said: 'Jack, this is my niece, Lexi, and her friend Finn.'

His hand enveloped mine and he gave me a warm smile. He had a flop of brown hair, dark eyes and the smallest scar on his lips that only enhanced his looks.

'Hey, Lexi – really nice to meet you.'

Finn beamed as he shook Jack's hand. Despite the whipping autumn winds, I felt hot and breathless.

'I hear you're both studying to be doctors – that's amazing,' he said. 'James says you're looking for a place to stay. I hope you like wine. And dogs. The place is crawling with them.'

It was then that I knew I was the one who was in trouble.

CHAPTER EIGHT

4 January 2023

I spent all night dreaming of Mum, floating together on the imaginary raft she built for us.

'We're going down a stream in the Pyrenees,' I would whisper.

'How about the Ganges? The air smells like spices and people are throwing flowers into the water.'

'You always want to go to the most humid places,' I would moan. 'And we have curly hair.'

I snapped awake when I realised someone was in the room opening the curtains. Morning light scattered halos across my vision, and I pulled the blanket over my head. My martinis had gone rancid in my bloodstream, like battery acid. The poison was moving to my right temple in preparation for a drilling ten-hour headache.

'I might skip tea, thank you,' I said from under the blankets to the maid, who was making an awful lot of noise. 'But I'll take some paracetamol, please.'

When I felt the unmistakable weight of a person sitting down on the bed beside me, I pulled the sheets down. It didn't matter if she was about to faint – a Cumberland maid did not sit on a royal's bed.

'Hello, Lexi,' Vikki said.

For a woman who had just lost her only son, she was still somehow glowing with Pilates-induced health. She had stopped drawing thick lines of liquid eyeliner in sharp wings and replaced them with brown kohl pencil. She was in a sumptuous burnt-orange duster coat over a cream turtleneck, leggings and riding boots. The intervening years (or a surgeon's incisions) gave her the snatched, angular face of a runway model.

I sat up in bed and wrapped my arms around her.

'I'm so sorry,' I whispered.

'Good lord, you stink like a distillery,' she said airily, but there were tears in her eyes.

Papa had never been particularly kind to Vikki. He had a natural suspicion of anyone from outside the home counties, and there was something about Vikki's raw ambition he found frightening. Being born lucky did not stop a person yearning for more, but it satiated the appetites enough to be wary of the truly hungry.

When news first broke that Amira and Louis were dating, the tabloids took vicious delight in Vikki's history as a 'trolley dolly'. Someone – either a palace aide or one of Louis's friends – leaked to the tabloids that when invited to Scotland for a shooting weekend, Vikki showed up in a cloud of Chanel No 5. They claimed the Shankars failed to tip the keeper or thank the grouse beaters. They also apparently slammed doors, took multiple calls on their mobile phones and drank far too much at elevenses. At the end of the shoot, Vikki inquired after 'the toilet' instead of calling it the lavatory.

But the Shankars would never have done any of these things. No one would have been better researched on the etiquette of a dreary shooting party than Vikki and Madhav. I had no doubt Madhav procured a fat wad of £10 notes so that he could correctly pay the traditional thirty quid for the first hundred birds and a tenner for every hundred that followed. Vikki would have raided every Purdey store in West London for tweed caps and blazers and wellies. When food and drink was served out the back of a Range Rover at 11 am, they would have politely sipped one Bullshot each. The leaking of falsehoods to the tabloids was a threat and a reminder: you may learn our ways, you may be richer than us, you may even infuse your genetic code into the line by becoming grandparents to the future monarch. But you will never, ever be one of us.

'Granny said you'd been in India?' I asked.

'We were, but we went to Switzerland for Kris,' she said.

I was silent for a moment. 'They didn't transport him with Papa and Louis?'

Vikki coolly held my gaze. They would not make space for her son's body on our plane. They would have her book a commercial flight and go collect him herself.

'It was important to Madhav that we honour Hindu death rites, so we had him cremated in Bern,' she said in a strange voice. She took in an unsteady breath. 'There's a lovely waterhole at the Kruger lodge. I was thinking perhaps we spread his ashes there, but I don't know. Maybe he'd prefer to be here in England with us. Amira asked her lady-in-waiting to buy some pendants that can hold some of his ashes. But would he like that? Bits of him all over the place?'

I put my hand over hers. For a moment I was running across the main lawn of Astley at dusk, the sky bruising mauve and indigo above us. Amira screeching with laughter as she struggled to keep up. Kris shooting past me on his runner's legs. Me, wheezing as he doubled back, scooped me up effortlessly and took off again. Louis, as always, was ahead of us all, bounding like a gazelle towards a grove of mulberry trees. We were big, reckless kids grasping onto those final days of childhood.

'I think he'd like that, Vikki,' I said. 'Part of him gets to stay with the people he loves and part of him gets to watch every sunset at Kruger.'

She crumpled suddenly, bending forward, her face in her hands. I put my hands on her shoulders, but she pulled herself together more quickly than she needed to and brushed at the tears threatening to ruin her eye makeup.

'I came up to talk to you about something, actually,' she said, and dug in her pocket for her phone. She turned it to show me the *Daily Post*'s front page.

'*Partying princesses Amira and Lexi rock Cumberland Palace ALL NIGHT by playing wild music until dawn, leaving their royal neighbours wondering: Aren't they supposed to be in MOURNING??*' the front-page headline shouted.

It was one of the *Post*'s classic Photoshop jobs: our smiling faces were superimposed on an image of Cumberland with a disco ball cut-and-pasted where the flag post usually stood. The picture of Amira looked like it was taken recently. With her beaming smile, I assumed it was a visit to a children's hospital or a nursery. My picture was less flattering. My head was thrown back in abandon as I laughed at something. I couldn't quite place the photo, but it was probably taken by the pap who stalked through the crowds at last year's wine festival to get a few shots of me working the Jennings booth with Jack.

I looked at Vikki sheepishly.

'Read it,' she said.

The Royal Family members who call Cumberland Palace home were left stunned by the thumping sounds of a wild party being held by one of their neighbours until dawn this morning.

And who was holding this all-night rager?

It was Duchess Amira, who is supposed to be in mourning for her husband, Prince Louis, and her brother, Krishiv Shankar.

And the one guest at this party was none other than Princess Alexandrina.

The Daily Post *understands that Duchess Amira had been staying with Queen Eleanor for several days after returning from Switzerland, while Princess Alexandrina arrived on Monday from Australia.*

But the ageing monarch, who was devastated by the loss of her son and grandson, was unable to cope with the noise, mess and chaos made by the posh pair.

Yesterday it was finally suggested they return to Duchess Amira's Cumberland apartment, so that the 85-year-old could mourn in peace.

But the Queen did ask her youngest son, Prince Richard, to stay with her at the palace for the foreseeable future, with aides describing the Duke of Clarence as 'her golden child'.

'It was simply too much for the Queen, trying to grapple with this loss, while being expected to take care of these overgrown children,' a source tells the Post.

'Alexandrina hasn't stepped foot in this country for years, and she came here yesterday making wild demands, throwing tantrums and showing up extremely late to meetings.'

Prince Richard smoothed things over so that both women knew it was time to leave.

'Richard has always been a source of strength for his mother. Now is a time when she needs those closest to her to hold her up and support her,' the source said.

'Alexandrina has been MIA for years, barely staying in touch with anyone. Meanwhile, with her lavish spending, Amira has been burning through the allowance given to her by her father-in-law. The Queen doesn't need people asking her for favours right now.'

But once evicted, Amira and Lexi took their reign of terror to Cumberland Palace, blasting their dance music at window-shaking volume and keeping up their relatives until the early hours of the morning.

'It was extremely inconsiderate,' one Cumberland resident complained to a friend this morning.

It's understood the royal chums were taking a trip down memory lane, blaring many hits from their childhood and high school years.

*'C'est La Vie' by B*witched is understood to have been given a remarkably good run, with many repeat plays.*

While it is admirable for Duchess Amira to make amends with her old school pal, her boisterous behaviour just five days after her husband's death has raised many eyebrows within the Royal Family.

The couple had recently been dogged by rumours that one or both were no longer happy in the union.

Prince Louis had been spending much of his time in the couple's countryside bolthole in Norfolk, while Duchess Amira was often in London, either staying at their Cumberland apartment or her parents' opulent Mayfair townhouse.

For Amira to be partying just days after her husband's tragic death in a ski accident, along with her father-in-law, Prince Frederick, and her brother, Krishiv Shankar, is being seen as tacit confirmation that all was not well with the royal couple.

'If nothing else, it's poor form,' said royal commentator Harold Himmelhoch.

'I don't care what was happening in the marriage, she should be sombre, reflective and humble in the midst of this great tragedy to help Britain through its grief. But of course, Princess Alexandrina has always been a bad influence, so it's no surprise the duchess's behaviour took an unfortunate turn the moment the princess touched down in London.'

It's understood from royal courtiers that many palace insiders were bracing themselves for the return of Princess Alexandrina, who defected from the family and moved to Australia when she was 18.

The death of her mother, Princess Isla, is understood to have been the catalyst for Alexandrina's decision to step back from royal duties.

Princess Isla was vacationing on the Italian Riviera in 2011 with her children Louis and Alexandrina when she fell off a yacht and drowned.

The royal twins were asleep in their villa in Rapallo, unaware that their mother had taken the boat out late at night.

Princess Isla was an experienced yachtswoman, but a coroner concluded that she slipped from the boat while under the influence of prescription medication and alcohol.

When her children awoke the next morning and found their mother missing, they called local authorities.

After an extensive three-day search, Princess Isla's body was found floating at sea, 100 miles from her last known location.

Palace insiders say the tragedy had a profound impact on Alexandrina. She and Prince Louis were just 17 at the time.

But there have long been rumours of a spectacular row between

Alexandrina, Louis and Amira when the princess found out her brother was secretly in love with her best friend.

'Alexandrina reportedly disapproved of the match,' said Mr Himmelhoch.

'But I always suspected she simply couldn't stand having to share the attention with another pretty young woman. Instead she threw a great big tantrum and moved to Australia, hoping her father would beg her to come back.'

After the tragic deaths of Prince Frederick and Prince Louis, Alexandrina has now rocketed up the line of succession to be the Queen's heir.

It's understood that the Queen is yet to discuss with the young princess if she intends to claim her place on the throne or finally rescind the status that she has spurned for so long.

Princess Alexandrina is a second-year resident at Hobart General Hospital, and the Post hears that she hopes to pursue specialty training in obstetrics in a year's time.

'An admirable goal, to be sure,' Mr Himmelhoch said.

'But one cannot deliver babies on the throne. If she is to be queen one day, she can no longer have it both ways. She will have to make her choice.'

Alexandrina may be the first heir in British history to rescind her claim to the throne, in which case her uncle Prince Richard, the Duke of Clarence, will become first in line.

But Mr Himmelhoch is sceptical it will come to that.

'Like her mother before her, Alexandrina adores the spotlight. Like her mother, she cannot stand when eyes are not on her, and just like her mother she is prone to throwing a fit when she doesn't get her way,' he explained.

'I cannot say if she will make a good queen, but she will certainly be an eager one.'

I handed Vikki back her phone.

'I'm sorry, I was just trying to make her feel a bit better and I shouldn't have put the music on,' I said. 'This is all just Richard's usual shit – but his target is me, not her.'

She said nothing for a long while and I tried to look neutral while my gin-soaked bloodstream hummed inside me. The idea of a McDonald's breakfast – a bacon and egg McMuffin, two hash browns and a large chocolate thickshake – was simultaneously revolting and alluring.

'Lexi,' she finally said, 'have you decided what you're going to do?'

I hesitated, then decided she could always handle the truth. 'I think I should probably just go home. I'm not good at this.'

She rolled her eyes. 'It's not a question of talents or capabilities, Lexi. You're the heir now. It's yours.'

I stared at my hands clasped on top of my white linen duvet.

'A few days ago, my life was heading in one direction, and now I'm somewhere I never thought I would be,' I said.

'Yes, that's true for all of us.'

Vikki was once the only adult in my life who refused to cut me any slack. She admonished me when she caught Amira and me drinking, and she made clear it was my job to always take care of Amira. But she was also kind. By the time we were getting ready for our school leavers' ball, I was motherless. Vikki booked the private suite at Selfridges so Amira and I could choose our dresses. After two hours, she put both of our gowns on her credit card and took us to Home House in Marylebone for lunch.

'I haven't really had a chance to think about it all yet,' I said.

'I understand. But I also don't think you realise the danger you're in.' She reached across the bed and took my hands in hers. 'If you decide you want this, you're going to have to fight for it. The table's been upturned and everyone's down on the floor, wrestling each other for scraps. This article is just the beginning. If you don't want it, leave now. Otherwise they're going to destroy you – and you'll bring Amira down on the way.'

When Amira and Louis had decided to get married, Granny's lady-in-waiting offered the bride a tiara from the royal collection. The gifting of a tiara is an elaborate affair, steeped in tradition, and entirely dependent on the monarch's favour and mood swings.

Sometimes a woman marrying into the family is offered a range of choices. Sometimes one is selected for her, and it's up to the bride to make it work with her gown and hair. A wedding tiara is the bride's to keep for the remainder of her life. Not even the Villiers know exactly how many tiaras we own, but I've heard it's in the range of forty to fifty. From dozens of choices, the lady-in-waiting selected for Amira the Heart of India.

The dramatic headpiece is set with hundreds of diamonds and tipped with sapphires and pearls. But it got its name from the tiara's fifty-carat centrepiece, a diamond that was stolen from an eight-year-old maharajah at the behest of our ancestors. British history books still claim that the jewel was handed over as part of a contractual agreement reached after the maharajah's men could no longer hold off the advancing British troops. In reality, we held bayonets to the throat of a child and stole his gemstone. Now the reigning monarch expected the first British Indian woman to enter the royal family to pop it on her head and walk down the aisle.

The tiara put the Shankars in an impossible position: accept it, wear it in public and risk upsetting one billion people, or politely ask the Queen if there was another option and likely cause her great offence. In the end, Louis quietly intervened on the Shankars' behalf and another tiara was procured for the day. But the awkward exchange was like an arrow placed in the family quiver for future use.

A year after the wedding, Papa was criticised for taking a twenty-minute helicopter ride to a Cambridge speaking engagement, at a cost of £4000 to the British taxpayer. A train or even a chauffeured limousine would have had him on university grounds in an hour at a fraction of the price. As the disapproving news cycle stretched into a third day, Papa decided there was only one way to protect himself. He placed the arrow in the tabloid's bow and allowed them to take their shot at his own daughter-in-law. I often wondered if it was his idea or someone at Wolseley House. Did he have to be talked into it? Did he call the reporter himself? Did he feel any remorse at all? The story in the *Daily Post* was written by Posey Habsburg-Mollard, Papa's favourite reporter for planting stories. Posey cast Amira as a foot-stomping bridezilla whose fealty to her ancestral homeland was greater than it was to the British crown. The lady-in-waiting's choice of tiara was not insensitive, but a loving nod to the bride's ethnic origins. Papa's chopper joyride was immediately forgotten. Amira's pre-wedding 'tantrum' never was.

The practice of selling each other out to the tabloids to distract from our own scandals was a family addiction we all vowed to give up. But we never did. It was our version of getting drunk and arguing at Christmas, our phones at the dinner table, our days and days of the silent treatment. But for Amira, the trading of secrets and the distortion of family squabbles always became a question of loyalty. Like the disastrous shooting weekend, the whispers about Amira rose to a steady drumbeat of one claim: she is not one of us, she will never be one of us.

I knew Vikki was right. As the widow of an heir, Amira's future place in the family was always going to be uncertain. But as the House of Clarence sought to excise me from the line, they would relish the opportunity to snip out Amira as well.

'Okay,' I said to Vikki.

She nodded at me sceptically. 'Okay.'

She went back into her coat pocket and produced a strip of paracetamol tablets.

'For your head,' she said. 'I'll go check on Amira. She's been throwing up all morning.'

'Thank you – and sorry again.'

Once she was gone, I found my own phone under a pile of pillows and went to one of the American celebrity gossip sites that had pivoted hard to royal coverage since Louis and Amira's wedding.

'*Amira and Lexi played a couple of Beyoncé tracks last night and the old aristocratic crows who live at Cumberland Palace can't cope,*' the headline read.

I scanned the article and quickly made my way down to the comments. Americans, with their reality TV stars and Instagram influencers, were remarkably savvy when it came to parsing tabloid stories for the true intentions of the informant.

'*Does Mommy's precious little golden boy think this is how he'll get on the throne? Ragging on a couple of young women who dared put some music on IN THEIR OWN HOME??*' one commenter wrote.

'*So sick of these racist ghouls. They can do whatever they want, but they're pissed when Amira spends her allowance or plays music????*' wrote another.

A long, 75-comment thread was dedicated to what went wrong between us.

'*I'm so glad they're friends again. Maybe Amira can be her lady-in-waiting when Lexi's queen?*'

'*Girl, do your research. These two were lovers all the way through high school and Amira dumped Lexi and seduced Louis so she could be the queen. She's not waiting on her ex lololol.*'

'*Can you IMAGINE when England has a Queen and her Queen? LEXMIRA FOREVER.*'

'*Wow you all have it SO WRONG. The royal twins are both so gay it's RIDICULOUS. Kris and Amira were meant to be their beards, but Lexi got cold feet and bailed …*'

I shut my phone off, pulled the blankets over my head and sought refuge from my hangover in a dreamless, death-like sleep.

CHAPTER NINE

9 January 2023

There are royal families all over Europe, but none fell into the celebrity trap quite like the House of Villiers. The Second World War came as a turning point for monarchies. Europeans no longer had to wonder what they were capable of, whether it was great heroism or utter barbarism. Royals who had enjoyed centuries of unquestioned power felt the winds shifting and made their choices.

Some, like the House of Emanuele in Italy, were deposed and fled to the United States, where their descendants worked as graphic designers and bankers and TikTok creators. Most of the Scandinavian houses were clever enough to retreat into a largely symbolic presence. Only the monarch and the heir are visible. Everyone else lives in relative luxury, but they're expected to have jobs and bank accounts. We, the British, sneeringly call them bicycle monarchies, because it's not unusual to see a blood princess cycling around the Low Countries on her way to her job as an architect.

Whether it was a clever scheme or a catastrophic mistake, my grandparents transformed our family into tabloid stars. In exchange for millions of taxpayer pounds and a promise to remain at the centre of British life, we invited our subjects' scrutiny. Hours after we were born, Louis and I were presented to a pack of photographers, their camera flashes like a supernova. As toddlers, we learned to wave to crowds of strangers. Throughout our childhood, we were shadowed by security officers who intercepted frenzied, handwritten violent fantasies mailed to our homes. These days, we receive a world-class education and then spend the rest of our days cutting ribbons and planning our eighth vacation for the year. The curse of being a minor royal means slowly becoming addicted to attention and luxury, and then watching both evaporate with our youth and our beauty. My elders formed transactional friendships with shadowy billionaires who made them the guest of honour at every lavish dinner party and every yacht trip around Corsica. The great shame of minor royalty is that you become accustomed to a lifestyle that your taxpayer-funded allowance doesn't actually allow, and you have neither the work ethic nor the family's permission to get yourself a job.

The dark heart of our Faustian bargain was the hope that we could distract the British people with drama and intrigue so no one noticed they were paying for one family to cloak themselves with jewels and live in gilded palaces for free. Our lives became storylines, and there are no greater plot points than weddings, babies and funerals.

Amira and I were groomed and detoxed and lasered in preparation for our starring roles at Papa and Louis's funeral. Four days left the palace with no time to foist injectables or starvation diets upon us. But the changes to our appearances needed to be subtle anyway. Every morning, the doorbell rang at Cumberland 1 and an army of beauty professionals traipsed into the apartment. Mary Williams arrived at 7 am sharp to oversee their work and to shove a tumbler of hot lemon water in my hand. She declined my request for a croissant and double-shot flat white ('Ma'am, I'm sorry but your cleanse prohibits you from dairy, salt, caffeine *and* gluten'). For my part, I begrudgingly took part in the 'cleanse' while complaining to anyone who would listen that detoxing was a myth ('It's literally what the liver and kidneys are for'). I submitted to the LED light facials and microcurrent treatments, but politely declined the offer of colonic irrigation.

After years of silence, Amira and I slipped back into the familiar routine we developed once we became suitemates at boarding school. We picked at our so-called veggie glow bowls on the couch while watching so many episodes of *Love Island* that the TV occasionally asked if we were still there. We talked very little, but when we did, we stuck to old stories from our Astley days. Our reminiscences always stayed within the safe confines of the early years, before everything went wrong.

'Do you remember when Kris brought a screwdriver onto campus and then went around for months secretly unscrewing things?'

'Yeah, no one noticed for six months until locker doors started falling off and chairs were collapsing under people.'

'Do you remember when Louis changed Papa's voicemail message?'

'Everyone thought they'd accidentally called Pizza Express in Primrose Hill.'

The morning of the funeral arrived. It was a typical January day in London with a heavy pewter sky slung low overhead. On my phone that morning was a text from Jack, wishing me luck (*I'll be watching x*). In a show of austerity, Amira's style team dressed her in a repeat outfit: a black, calf-length Catherine Walker coat dress with a bow neckline that she had worn to a Remembrance Day service two years earlier. Her lacquered hair was pulled into a low bun with a little black hat attached to the crown. Her eyes were obscured by a mesh net veil. Around her wrist looped the three-strand pearl bracelet that once belonged to my mother. Louis had given it to Amira as a wedding gift. Mum's garish emerald engagement ring, also handed down to Amira, had soaked in a thimble of gin overnight so the moody stone glinted on her hand.

For my mourning clothes, Mary had chosen a Stella McCartney fitted dress with a matching cape coat. A seamstress stitched a thin fleece lining to the inside of the ensemble to keep me warm during the walk from Westminster Hall to the Abbey. Stockings lined with a flesh-coloured fleece to give the illusion of sheer black pantyhose were shipped express from Japan. It had been many years since I had worn anything but Blundstones or Crocs, so the ten-centimetre spires that Amira could balance on were deemed 'high risk' for me. They found a pair of black velvet Emmy London pumps with a block heel instead. A cobbler attached thick rubber pads to the soles to prevent slipping. Once I was dressed, Mary presented me with long leather gloves and a black wide-brimmed hat, free of netting, bows and other flourishes she knew I'd hate.

'The brim's wide enough so you can look down and have a bit of privacy if you need, ma'am,' she said, as if I'd been able to shed a single tear since this nightmare began.

The peach fuzz on my cheeks had been shaved away with a tiny razor. My brows were dyed. False individual lashes were trimmed and nestled among my own inferior lash line. Four separate lipsticks were blended on my mouth. My nipples were taped down in case they budded in the cold. Only about a third of the hair on my head was my own. From my neck to my knees, I was caught in the vice grip of shapewear. I looked in the mirror and saw the woman my family had always wanted me to be.

Five minutes before we were supposed to leave, there was another knock at the door. Mary went to answer it and came back with a velvet box.

'From the Queen, ma'am,' Mary said, holding the box with reverence. 'She thought you might like to wear something from the family collection today.'

Inside was a platinum brooch set with dozens of tiny diamonds. At first glance, it resembled a sword. But when you studied it, you realised it was shaped like a thistle. Papa and Mum had commissioned a Scottish jeweller to make the brooch for Granny's seventieth birthday. I had wanted the jeweller to use purple stones for its spiky petals but was overruled.

'We want it to be tasteful, mignonette,' Papa had laughed.

There were Instagram accounts and websites dedicated to cataloguing every piece of jewellery we owned. This brooch, which Granny had always worn to represent her love for Scotland and for her heir's family, would be immediately recognised.

Vikki was sitting in a genuine Pierre Jeanneret rattan armchair dressed in a replica Jackie Kennedy pillbox hat. She stood up and came over to admire the brooch that Mary had attached to the breast of my cape.

'This is a good sign,' she said quietly and squeezed my shoulder. 'She's claiming you as hers.'

The family assembled in the courtyard, waiting to be shepherded by aides to the correct vehicle. The lower ranked royals were to be taken directly to the Abbey where they would have to make ninety minutes of small talk with Commonwealth politicians in the pews. Amira would be one of the last mourners to enter, so that all eyes would be on her as she made the slow march up the same aisle that three years ago had delivered her to her husband.

Mary and I climbed into a Range Rover headed for Westminster Hall. The roads around the palace had been closed for the day and we glided through central London's empty streets. Mary looked out her window and sighed.

'Are you okay?' I asked.

Surprised, she looked at me. 'Yes, ma'am, thank you.'

'How old are you, Mary?'

'I'm twenty-four.'

'Have you ever worked for anyone but this family?' I asked, not quite sure why I had chosen this moment to quiz her about her life.

'This was the first job I got after I graduated.'

'What school did you go to?'

She hesitated. 'I went to Astley.'

I looked into her face and tried to peel back the years to when I would have been in the Upper Sixth and she would have been a Shell. I had trudged through the aftermath of Mum's death, conversations and classes swirling around me like a fine dust. I went to rowing practice and sat my exams and studied my textbooks. In between, I hurried around corners and into bathroom stalls for uncontrollable, silent crying jags.

'Did we ever meet?' I asked.

'No, ma'am,' she huffed, as if she found the notion absurd. 'I was thirteen and you were an upperclassman.'

'Sorry about all the random questions,' I said. 'I think I'm just nervous.'

'Of course, ma'am.'

At the back entrance to the hall, a huge contingent of Queen's guardsmen and sailors stood waiting for the procession to begin. Despite the size of the crowd, it was utterly silent. I knew they had released a falcon to soar above the Abbey to scare off the pigeons for the day, one of the ridiculous flourishes only my family could think was perfectly reasonable. I could hear my heels crunch in the gravel as I walked with Mary past rows of sailors in perfect white hats and square collars.

Stewart was waiting for us in the archway, and he bowed deeply. 'Your Highness, before the news crews arrive, we thought you might like a moment alone in the hall.'

I was surprised to find that I was moved by the gesture. 'Okay.'

'Just five minutes, and then we'll have you in position with your family to follow the procession to the Abbey.'

They shut the doors, and I was alone in that vast stone hall with its timber beam roof stretched high above me. A heady incense filled the air. The grey morning cast the room in gloomy shadows; at its centre, two coffins were surrounded by flickering candles. My footsteps echoed as I approached. Both were draped in the royal standard, but I could tell who was who by the flowers arranged on top of each coffin. The day before, I had watched from my window as Amira moved around the high-walled garden she had shared with Louis, cutting handfuls of winter heather and English lavender and piling them in a basket. Now they were arranged in a wild bundle and tied with a purple ribbon. It was right for my brother. For Papa, someone had procured mountains of jasmine, English roses, hothouse orchids, tall stems of delphiniums. He had spent his life expecting that upon his death the Sovereign's Orb and Sceptre would be placed on top of his casket. Instead he got a floral arrangement teased to perfection.

Standing inside Westminster Hall always made the arc of history feel very short to me. This was the room where Charles I was found guilty of treason and sentenced to death, where Charles II held his coronation feast a decade later after restoring the monarchy to its former glory. Guy Fawkes was tried here. Barbara Villiers watched from a secret balcony as her enemies were condemned to lose their heads. It was the place she lay in state when she finally died.

No matter how they came to be in St Edward's Chair, whether they were born to it, or they fought, killed and scrambled to heave themselves into the seat, all monarchs knew their destiny ended here. Their bodies would always be carried up onto the catafalque in Westminster Hall so their subjects could say goodbye.

And, I supposed, there was always someone like me standing at the end of the coffin, either shocked or thrilled to find that they might follow the same path. Were they frightened like I was? Did they swear, if they held their breath and stood very still, that they could hear the murmur in the walls of all the people who came before them? Did it feel like the DNA of their ancestors was coming awake until every cell in their body snapped and shimmered inside them?

On the stone steps in the farthest corner of the room, a shadow shifted, and for one insane moment it was Barbara herself, there to remind me that fate didn't care if you believed in it or not. Destiny knocked, and you either cowered behind the door or you flung it open to see what life held for you next. I took a few steps forward, desperate to ask her what to do. But the shadow moved again, and I saw that a family of birds roosting in the stained-glass windows had flown away.

I was alone again in the hall.

The last time I had stood here, I was flanked by Papa and Louis. After days of arguments over whether the mother of a future king was entitled to a traditional funeral, Mum's coffin was covered with the royal standard and obscured under the mound of offending white lilies. We stood at the edge of the red velvet catafalque and stared at her coffin. Louis told me they had placed Mum on a cooling plate to keep her body at three degrees so she wouldn't further decay until after the burial. The horror of it consumed me for days, finally hardening into a pebble that rolled to the back of my mind, bothersome and always there.

Papa had put a hand on each of our shoulders. 'We move forward after this. We don't talk of it again, do you hear me?'

Now he and Louis too were lying on cold plates in their twin coffins.

Finally, a hot tear rolled down my face.

I wasn't sure for whom it was shed.

The rest of the day passed in snatches of colour and sound. The brilliant red of a Queen's Guard tunic. A woman sobbing in the crowd of mourners who lined the streets. Richard's cold stare. The feel of Demelza's and Birdie's curious eyes as I stood ahead of them in the procession.

When we entered the Abbey, we walked across the worn floor, the two coffins bobbing on the shoulders of the Grenadier Guard pallbearers ahead of us. I looked up at the nave's familiar ceiling. When I was a child, its great stone spine and tapered ribs had made me feel like we'd climbed inside the belly of a dragon. Then we had squeezed through my favourite place, the quire screen with its arched roof painted like the night sky. Louis and I loved to linger in there so we could look up at the stars. 'Stop dillydallying,' Papa would whisper, grasping our hands.

Granny sat in her usual spot in the front row of the south lantern, staring rapt at the coffins that held her two heirs. Papa's widow, Annabelle, took her place beside me and I noticed distantly that her hands trembled in her lap. I made no effort to comfort her. Drifting through the prayers and eulogies, I snapped to attention as the piper began the funeral lament, 'Sleep, Dearie, Sleep'. It was over. We were shepherded back into our Range Rovers and driven to Watford Castle for the burial. The streets were lined with mourners and Amira put her head in my lap and fell into a deep sleep for the half-hour journey.

Whether their lives were long, glorious, ignoble or tragic, every monarch of the last two centuries had been interred beneath the smooth stone floors of St Edward's Chapel. Compared to the grand abbeys and palaces to which these sovereigns and their families grew accustomed, the chapel is beautiful in its simplicity.

Under the floor of a light-filled corner of the chapel lay sixteen members of the House of Villiers. Great Aunt Beatrix had been interred with her parents years ago, followed by my grandfather. We had all expected Granny to be next. Instead she stood staring at the gaping hole in the floor that led to the family's underground crypt. It was not ready for her yet.

Granny, Amira, Annabelle and I were the only ones invited to the burial service. Richard had no objection to being excluded, perhaps because there were no photographers to capture the moment. At the archbishop's quiet instruction, Annabelle and Amira stepped forward and scattered red earth from a silver bowl on the coffins of their husbands. After one final prayer, it was done. We would not be required to watch as the caskets were lowered underground.

Annabelle, who had yet to acknowledge anyone except Granny with a shallow curtsy, excused herself to find her children. She was the arch villain in my mother's story, my father's obsession, and the unspoken bogeyman of my and Louis's childhood. Even as I buried what remained of my family, I couldn't help but steal glances at her. There was a hard, haunted look in her eyes I'd never seen before. Now, Amira, Granny and I watched as she stalked from the chapel, followed by the archbishop.

'What a terrible waste,' Granny mused, tears gleaming in her eyes, as we lingered under the stone arches.

'Did you want to skip the reception, Granny?' I asked. 'You could just head upstairs if you'd prefer.'

She looked at me for a moment and then came forward to kiss me on both cheeks. She had given Papa his dark eyes and Louis his sharp jaw. She had given me the ability to take my feelings and bury them under hard stone.

'My dear girl, I'm so glad you're home,' she said. 'Yes, you stand in for me at the reception. You're the one they're all curious to see anyway.'

She picked up the order of service pamphlet she had carried all the way from the Abbey, and Amira and I curtsied as she slowly walked from the chapel. A boom echoed through us as the doors closed behind the Queen.

Amira began unpinning her hat from her hair.

'Do *you* need to go upstairs?' I asked.

'What?' she said around a mouthful of bobby pins. 'And leave you to face the hyenas alone?'

We walked around the middle ward at the heart of the castle grounds, heading for the state apartments where the reception for family and friends was underway. It was late afternoon, the drab day giving way to dusk. Our breath turned to twirling vapour in the winter air.

'What's going on with Annabelle?' I asked while I had the chance. 'Why isn't she talking to anyone?'

Amira walked on, gathering her thoughts before she answered. 'To be honest, I'm not really sure. But something happened around Christmas. That ashram trip was pretty hastily organised, and your father was acting strangely when he showed up in Zermatt.'

'Were they not happy anymore?' I asked.

She took a long time to respond. 'They were upset about something before he died, but I've no idea of the details. Louis knew more, but we didn't have a chance to talk about it.'

We were walking in the great shadow of the castle keep and I had the irrational thought that I must call Mum and tell her: Papa and Annabelle weren't *happy* anymore. She had been my father's first and only love. All buxom curves and bleached blonde curls, the divorced Catholic daughter of his horse breeder had enraptured him from their first meeting in 1980. They were forbidden to marry, but both assumed that like most kings, Papa would be able to keep a mistress on the sidelines of his life. He had been stupid to think that tabloid editors would be able to resist such a saucy storyline – or that my young romantic mother would be able to bear it. There was nothing quite like knowing my father's heart was somewhere outside his family, that my very existence was not what he yearned for or imagined for himself.

Granny finally gave in and allowed Papa to marry Annabelle seven years after Mum died. A war council, including the archbishop and the prime minister, was assembled to make the wedding palatable to the British people, who were still resolutely Team Isla. The bride was required to convert to the Church of England. She could never be the Princess of Scotland, a title that was now inextricably linked to my mother. Instead, she was bumped down to one of Papa's lesser titles and called the Duchess of Exeter. The mother of the groom could not attend a union of divorcées. Instead, she threw the newlyweds a lavish reception. Louis's and my involvement in the wedding was considered a crucial endorsement. Louis probably agreed to go because it was the mature thing to do, while my presence was secured through bribery. I'd been in Australia for six years by the time Papa remarried and was drifting ever further from his grasp. In exchange for showing up in a nice dress and hat, I was given early access to some investment bonds that I had received from my grandfather as a christening gift. I used the money to buy myself a second-hand Corolla.

Papa and Annabelle's civil ceremony was the first time she and I had ever really spoken. From the dark shadows she had cast over my childhood, I half-expected a bad fairy from a German folk tale. Instead I found Annabelle to be a busty countrywoman who liked a stiff drink and had trouble meeting my eyes. She was attractive for sure – what Granny would call a handsome woman. But Annabelle had the great misfortune to be publicly pitted against my mother, a five-foot-eleven stunner with a pre-Raphaelite complexion, bright-green eyes and the kind of lips many women paid for. No one – not the tabloids, not Granny, not even me – could fathom why Papa would spurn this perfect creature for a woman who was not a virgin, not young, and not in possession of the kind of beauty that could sell lipsticks and luxury cars.

The hushed conversations evaporated the moment Amira and I walked into the Crimson Drawing Room. Mouldering men in morning suits and women in 1960s vintage Chanel looked me up and down with unabashed curiosity. Richard was still stuffed into his ceremonial military uniform, draped in a gold braided aiguillette and his bright-blue Order of the Garter sash. How he'd earned the medals pinned to his breast after completing half of his basic training and then dropping out, I had no idea. He curled back his lips to expose his teeth, as natural as a row of china saucers, and raised his glass of scotch to us.

A waiter quietly approached and took our drink orders: a dirty martini for Amira, gin and tonic for me. Richard's wife, Lady Florence, a tiny sparrow of a woman, waved both hands at me and then wrapped them around my waist. She was so small her head was practically buried in my breasts.

'Lovely Lexi,' she said, rocking me back and forth. 'I am so sorry for your loss.'

'Thank you,' I said, relieved to see the waiter return with my drink so I could escape her embrace.

'Did Granny go up to bed?' she asked with an exaggerated, child-like frown.

Richard and Florence married the same year as my parents. She had been born into the kind of nobility that was all name and no money. The family's great hope was an offer of marriage from the Duke of Clarence. When Richard lost interest in the union, Florence had no choice but to hold on. Unlike my mother, who waged all-out war against my father, Florence made herself smaller and meeker. She did not make demands, and she did not ask questions. In the crater left by my parents' divorce, Richard saw an opportunity: He could be the brother who held on to his wife. And so, with Florence's permission to do as he pleased, he remained married in name only. I could never understand why she would endure such indignity, but in more ways than one, a royal family is like the Mafia; you never truly leave it behind.

'Come and see the girls!' she squeaked, digging her nails into my wrist and pulling me across the room.

Amira reluctantly followed as we approached Demelza and Birdie, who were standing by themselves, smirking and whispering to each other as their eyes roamed the room.

My cousins looked at me warily. In such a meeting of royal women, there were rules to follow. They were meant to curtsy before me, and Amira was meant to defer to them. But we dispensed with such formalities when Granny wasn't around. The dynamics were supposed to shift as we got older. If things had worked out and Amira had gone on to be queen, they would have been forced to bend at the knees for a woman they'd continually snubbed. Despite my howling objection to Louis and Amira's marriage, this image was one of the few future perks I had relished.

They clutched their glasses of sauvignon blanc and made no move to acknowledge us, so I deployed one of Isla's classic moves. In the face of scepticism, the only option was to beguile. I smiled warmly and kissed them on their cheeks.

'Hello, cousins,' I oozed. 'How are you holding up?'

'You're looking so … well, Lexi,' Demelza said, her gaze raking me up and down.

Demelza was four years younger than Louis and me. The tabloids, who loved to compare us, often declared her to be the prettier one. But she was not so much beautiful as devoid of flaws. I could not tell you a thing about her face except that it was neat and forgettable. Her hair was an expensive creamy blonde. She was naturally a size six, with tiny breasts and the sort of narrow hips that would have killed her in childbirth a century ago. Our parents' distaste for each other meant we had spent very little time together growing up. She had always struck me as the kind of girl who spent her life sulking in the passenger seat of a boy's car.

My leaving London was the best thing that had ever happened to Demelza. She sauntered out of her brunches at Scott's with a copy of the *Sunday Times* held up to shield her face from photographers. She dated interchangeable Greek polo players and Kate Kennedy club members. She spent four nights a week at the Connaught, where she suspiciously drank nothing but managed to stay awake until 2 am. She had a job assisting the window dresser at Harrods, but still spent a third of the year on vacation. Now and then, she'd put on one of her padded headbands to accompany Granny to a flower show, and the *Daily Post* would declare her a modern fashion icon.

But there was a bitterness in Demelza's eyes that gave her away. Being born fifth in the line was the worst thing that could happen to a person like her. The crown was right there, just beyond her grasp. She saw what life could have been if it had landed on her head, but she would never, ever feel its weight. Now fate had finally gifted her a small chance, and the only thing standing in her way was me.

'Shall we take a picture?' Flo brightly suggested, pulling her phone out of her purse. 'All the girls together at last.'

'Jesus Christ, Mum,' Demelza said, but she was already fluffing her hair up. 'Don't be naff, just take one while we're chatting.'

Amira and I made eye contact as everyone stiffened into what they imagined was a natural pose. We both knew it would be considered to be in poor taste to take a photo after the funeral. But one surreptitiously taken by messy old Lady Florence and posted to her Instagram account would be her misstep, not ours. All four of us approximated soft, closed-mouth smiles while Flo tapped her phone screen again and again. After an interminably long time, she saw someone across the room and wandered off to trap them in conversation.

'How are your studies going, Lexi?' Birdie asked.

'Uh yeah, okay. I've got a year left of residency.'

'Gosh,' she said. 'What kind of doctor do you plan to be?'

'She's not sure,' Amira said before I could respond. She hit me with a stern look.

Birdie's real name was Bernice. But from the moment two-year-old Demelza struggled to pronounce it and called her Birdie instead, the name on her birth certificate would be ignored for the rest of her life. She was the youngest cousin, sixth in line, homely and a bit dotty, and therefore ignored by pretty much everyone, including her own parents. All I really knew about her was that she was given, and promptly quit, an abundance of jobs that thousands of young people would kill for. She worked at a record label for a while, then did social media for an auction house, then went to New York to intern for *Saturday Night Live*, then was hired to be an accessories buyer for ASOS. Nothing seemed to stick for more than a few months.

While Demelza lived in a three-bedroom cottage on the grounds of Cumberland, Birdie still stayed with her parents at the Clarence family manor. There had been a minor scandal the year before that gave Birdie her first and only front page of the *Daily Post*. She had thrown a dinner party, and as the wine flowed, Birdie took a sword off the wall and pretended to knight one of her friends. The sword was far heavier and far sharper than she realised. She sliced off the tip of his ear, spattering blood on a £50,000 Persian rug on loan from the Royal Collection Trust. '*Blitzed Birdie brandishes blade and butchers buddy*', the *Daily Post* snickered.

'And what about you, Amira?' Demelza asked. 'What are your plans? I'm so sad we're not going to be neighbours anymore.'

I felt, rather than saw, Amira's posture become rigid under Demelza's gaze. A waiter carrying crab meat vol-au-vents gingerly approached the group. Birdie plucked one from the silver tray and inserted it into her mouth.

'What does that mean?' I asked.

Demelza's eyes slid over to me.

'Oh,' she said with faux innocence. 'I just presumed, you know. Cumberland 1 always goes to the heir, doesn't it?'

'Nothing's been decided,' I said and her eyes sparkled with obvious interest.

I felt an arm snake around my back.

'Look at all these beautiful girls,' Richard said, his grip tightening around my waist. 'How are we all feeling?'

'Fine,' Amira said in a small voice.

I was repelled by his scotch breath and quirking brows, but the feel of his scratchy tunic reminded me so viscerally of Papa that I didn't move away. The reception after Grandfather's funeral had been a night just like this one: silver trays of elaborate canapés, the quiet hum of dreary adult conversation. I had fallen asleep on a crimson silk couch, and at some point Papa scooped me into his arms to take me upstairs. He never did that. It was always Mum or a nanny putting us to bed. But on the night he buried his father, he had gathered me to him, and I got to rest my cheek against the rough wool at his chest. I spent the next year flopped over couches and under dining tables with my eyes squeezed shut, desperate for him to cradle me in his arms again. It must have been the only time he did it, and now I knew for sure it could never happen again. The riptide of memory took hold of me as Richard gripped my hip tightly. I felt desperately alone.

'I might turn in,' Amira said.

'Good idea,' said Richard. 'And don't be naughty and blast your music this time, eh?'

She bowed her head and hurried towards the door that led to the quadrangle. I freed myself from Richard's grasp.

'I might head out, too,' I said and stalked off before they had a chance to respond.

Outside, the moon, as round and smooth as a coin, showed Amira cutting across the lawn. Close family had been invited to spend the night in the private apartments before the fleet of Range Rovers returned them to their lives. The mourning period officially ended the next day. Flags would return to full mast, newscasters would take off their black suits, and I would have to make my decision.

'Hey,' I said.

Amira stopped walking but she did not turn around. I could tell by the sharp rise of her shoulders that she was upset.

'What are you doing here?' she asked.

'I don't want to talk to the bloody Clarences any more than you do,' I said. 'I'd rather just go to bed.'

She spun around and I saw pure fury in her face. 'No, what are you *doing* here? Are you staying? Are you going to take all this on?'

'I don't *know*,' I said. 'Everything's happening so fast. I don't know what I'm doing. Is that so hard to understand?'

'Yes, it is actually, because it's not meant to be a choice. The worst has happened. You're up. It's your turn.'

We stared at each other for a moment in the cold wash of moonlight, aware that our raised voices would echo against the stone bailey.

'I don't want Cumberland 1,' I said, softer now. 'You should stay there as long as you like.'

She rolled her eyes and huffed out a foggy breath. 'I don't care about the stupid bloody apartment.'

'Well, what *do* you care about then?' I asked. 'Because it seems like you've got a chance to get your life back now. You're not even thirty. You've got time to have a career, if that's what you want. You've got a business degree you've never used. You can have kids. Why are you so determined to stay in this thing?'

She stared at me, aghast. Her eyes were ringed black from exhaustion and smudged mascara. Wisps of hair were starting to curl out of her chignon. 'You are so conceited, you know that? You have *always* thought you were better than everyone else. You had to move to Australia to prove how much smarter and how much more special you are than the rest of us.'

'Amira—'

'You haven't spoken to me in three years, you haven't been properly in my life for more than a decade, and now you're back here telling me how I should live?'

She strode towards me and pointed a shaking finger in my direction.

'You were a shitty friend to me,' she said, tears cracking her voice. 'And an even worse sister to Louis. When you left, you trapped him here. All of this is your fault. And now you have the gall to stand before me and say you're still not sure what you're going to do? Your brother sacrificed so much for his duty to the crown, and you don't even care about it. Even after you bury him, you're still failing him.'

Somewhere in the stone battlements above us, a robin whistled an incongruously happy tune. Amira turned and walked away from me, disappearing into the dark castle.

I sat in the quadrangle for a long time, even as my hands and face began to ache in the cold, even as the robin's song fell silent.

CHAPTER TEN

2009

It was March Equinox and everyone at Astley was getting ready for the end of Lent Term. We always celebrated the arrival of spring holiday with a school dance. The next day, our parents came to watch the cadets parade through campus, and then we all went home for Easter break.

But first, I had to get through ballet class. I was up at dawn, trudging through grass that crackled underfoot as I made my way to the dance studio. My ears hurt in the cold. My nose streamed. The sun seemed as sleepy as I was, only deigning to rise at seven-thirty. I was fifteen, no longer a 'Shell' in boarding school parlance, but a 'Remove'. Breasts and hips had bloomed seemingly out of nowhere. My period had arrived a year earlier, bringing with it an onslaught of furious, fiery acne. To my great shame, a crisis meeting had been held at the palace to discuss my face. A doctor I'd never met prescribed me a contraceptive pill that is now banned in France for causing an inordinate number of strokes in young women. The little tablets, as sugary and delicate as silver cachous on a Christmas biscuit, were decanted into a vitamin bottle and sent to Astley in bulk to conceal the fact that I was a child on birth control.

But there was no cure for my unwieldy figure. I had always

been a tiny, beautiful child, with black curls cascading down my narrow shoulders. It was assumed that I would grow to be like my mother who, by then, was divorced from Papa and clambering out of Rolls-Royces with her collar bones protruding and her thigh gap on display. No one ever mentioned that her elegant body was achieved with a bony finger thrust to the back of her gullet. The courtiers who ran our lives never had much command of hereditary genetics. The classic Villiers hips and arse that suddenly sprouted from my teenage body were met with grave disappointment.

Dancing was my idea. I had seen an interview on television with a famous actress who seemed to be celebrated mostly for her childlike body. She looked like a twelve-year-old boy with B-cup breasts, a prominent sternum and veins that roped around her spindly arms. When the journalist asked how she maintained such an enviable figure, she tittered and claimed she ate nothing but burgers and ice cream.

'But I used to dance and that kind of changed my physicality,' she said. 'I started ballet as a child and I danced every day for four hours until I was nineteen when I became an actress.'

It was 2009, and this seemed like a pretty good deal to me. I signed up for ballet classes through Astley's dance program, and convinced Mum I should be allowed to do additional training in town on the weekends. The burgers and ice cream would have to wait until dancing successfully scrambled my genetic code. There were many days when I consumed nothing but watermelon.

On the morning of the end-of-term dance, I was walking past The Mound, a strange little hill on school grounds that may have been a neolithic structure for ancient rituals. Now it served as a convenient location for Astley kids to smoke and pash, away from the prying eyes of housemasters. I had put myself on a 'Diet Coke cleanse' that week and my heart was racing from the combination of caffeine and roaring hunger. When I felt myself lift off the ground, I wasn't sure if I'd finally pushed it too far and this was what fainting felt like.

'Creeping back to your suite after a wild night on the town?' Kris crooned in my ear.

Slung over his shoulder, I looked upside down to see Louis wandering up the path in his camo fatigues with two rifle bags under his arm.

'Put her down, mate,' my brother said.

Louis was already six feet tall and well muscled for a fifteen-year-old. His skin was clear and his braces had recently been unhooked from his teeth. As he ascended towards manhood, I wondered if the conditions on his side of the womb were fairer than mine. Was the amniotic fluid warmer? Did his cord deliver him an extra flush of oestrogen to create those big eyes that made him look like a Disney forest creature?

'I've got ballet,' I said. 'What are you two doing?'

'We've got cadets,' Kris said as he placed me back on the ground. 'We're learning to be men.'

Cadets was introduced to a handful of schools in the nineteenth century to give boys basic military training in case France ever invaded. In the intervening decades, it was decoupled from the British military and touted to parents as a program that taught teenagers discipline and wilderness skills.

'You joining us for a drink on The Mound before the dance?' Kris asked. 'It's Removes only – no Shells allowed.'

'Yep, we'll be there,' I said.

Louis nudged me with his rifle bag. 'Don't forget they'll be here tomorrow. Both of them.'

Since the divorce, Mum and Papa had studiously avoided each other, letting their aides manage the drudgery of parenting (permission slips, broken eyeglasses, poor exam results) on their behalf. But Louis was leading the Removes class cadets in tomorrow's parade. In increasingly passive-aggressive messages sent via their courtiers, neither Mum nor Papa would back down. In the end, there was no other option but for both to attend. For regular divorced couples, this wouldn't be an issue. Astley's immense quadrangle provided plenty of space to avoid contact while still being able to glower at one another over a pair of Ray-Ban Wayfarers. But a royal rota photographer was also being sent to capture Louis's display of masculinity and natural leadership in his military dress uniform. The Prince and Princess of Scotland simply had to stand together, or the tabloids would have their front-page story sorted for the next week. A compromise was struck: I would stand between them as a visual and emotional buffer.

'How could I forget?' I said, smirking.

Louis gave me his perfect smile. 'We'll see you at breakfast.'

I, of course, would not be at breakfast. I had a knack for disappearing at mealtimes, insisting to my boarding master that I simply had to spend all of lunch searching for a missing library book in my suite. Dinner, however, was inescapable, so I crowded out my plate with vegetables and hoped no one noticed. Half the residents in my boarding house were edging towards the same precipice as me. The hardcore girls ate nothing but carrot sticks and then had to hide their telltale tawny hands in their pockets. But I knew Louis saw everything, and I could sense he had been weighing up the consequences of reporting me to Mum or a school counsellor. So far, he hadn't said a word to anyone and was trying to coax me back from the brink by pressing a muffin or a latte into my hands.

The impending dance was causing me alarm because almost every other girl would be wearing a Hervé Léger bandage dress and I would not. Greater than my fear of being photographed in a tight dress on the front page of the *Daily Post* was looking bad in a tight dress on the front page of the *Daily Post*. I scrolled through the expensive sausage casings online and knew that if I attempted to wear one, I would only resemble one of those pythons that eats a whole deer and lolls on the side of the road, immobile and trapped in digestive hell. So I used the credit card given to me for emergencies to order a one-shouldered Jason Wu flowy mini dress in an ice-blue chiffon instead. I would look like the rich virgin I was, but I supposed there was power in that.

As we got ready that evening, Amira regarded the dress. 'You look so gorgeous,' she insisted.

We kept our suite door open, the custom before all dances and balls. Rihanna songs wafted down the halls on a cloud of Miss Dior. Amira was wearing a red bandage dress with a keyhole front that put curves on her where none existed. I was intensely jealous.

'No, *you* look amazing,' I said.

We zipped up our coats and hid our black cherry VKs in our pockets. Then we set off for The Mound, teetering on the matching black Christian Louboutin peeptoe platforms that Vikki had bought for us.

'I'm going to kiss Rafe tonight,' Amira declared.

Rafe Fernsby was Amira's current obsession, a boy whose father was caught up in Ireland's financial crash and currently dodging creditors in Turks and Caicos. The fact that Rafe continued to show up each term suggested the family's accounts had not yet been frozen – or that a wealthy grandparent had stepped in to keep him enrolled.

'Isn't Rafe's father going to jail?' I asked.

'His father is a *baron*,' she said. 'They'll never do it.'

I rolled my eyes, but said nothing. When I first met Amira, I avoided her. I had no time for those who were obsessed with rank, a stance that was easy for me to hold given that when it came to rankings, I was mere inches from the top. Amira's mother had been telling her since she was a toddler that she must see marriage as a ladder into the aristocracy. Consequently, she was like a walking copy of *Burke's Peerage*. The book, which lists in excruciating detail every duke, marquess and earl in Britain, is better known as the 'snob's Bible', and Amira was its greatest devotee.

We might never have been friends, but a few months into our Shell year, she spotted a photographer hiding in the elderflower shrubs that grew along Astley's hockey fields. She stopped our game, lined up a row of balls and then smacked each one in his direction. When he finally ran, she chased after him with her hockey stick in hand, unleashing a barrage of insults and threats.

She returned a few minutes later, sweaty and triumphant. 'Don't worry, Lexi, I made him delete the photos and I swore I'd murder him if he ever came back.'

We were friends after that.

She looked at me now and smiled. 'Rafe might have a friend for you, you know.'

'No thank you,' I said.

Most of the boys at school gave me a wide berth out of respect for Louis. They also probably feared the fuss and drama of dating someone like me. But this suited me fine since I was terrified of them. As a girl, I'd been repeatedly warned of the danger of boys who would coax me into sending nudes or who would hide a video camera in their room and record us having sex. These images would inevitably find their way onto the internet and into the tabloids, destroying my life and, with it, the thousand-year-old British monarchy.

'Things are different for your generation,' Papa said to me when I was eleven. 'You must assume that there is a camera watching you every moment of the day.'

My only option, I concluded, was to convince a boy to fall hopelessly in love with me so that he would never betray me. Such an arrangement had eluded me thus far.

I always felt strange on The Mound, the top of which was only accessible by a scrubby spiral path. It was rumoured to be a site for ancient Pagan rituals before becoming the motte of a Norman castle. Sometimes when I ascended The Mound, I thought of all the wars my family had fought, the invasions, the empire-building, the noblemen and women who had schemed and murdered and seduced their way to power. This hill had stood here for centuries as my ancestors came to rule these lands. Now it served as a hangout for rich teenagers. Including me, the unexceptional descendant of a great family.

Amira and I scrambled up the path in our ridiculous shoes to find half the Remove class, including Louis and Kris, already there. Despite the cold, Amira removed her coat, opened her VK and sauntered over to Rafe, who was sprawled on the bough of a tree with a few other boys. I planted myself on a bench between Kris and Louis but didn't dare to remove the bottle from my coat. Unless we were in our small circle of trusted friends, who always offered to pile their iPhones and Motorola RAZRs into a shoebox for good measure, Louis and I did not drink or smoke in public ever.

'Who's Amira talking to?' Kris asked.

'Rafe,' I said. 'She's got a thing for him.'

'He's a bit of a tosser, though,' Kris muttered.

'Yes, but he's a future *baron*.'

He laughed. 'Wow, her standards are really dropping if she's ready to step down from prince to baron.'

Like millions of other girls, Amira had grown up with a poster of Louis on her wall. She'd blown out every birthday candle with the sole wish that she would one day be his bride. She still hadn't forgiven Kris for telling us all this.

'I only wanted to marry you until I *met* you,' she said to Louis constantly.

The three of us sat on our bench as classmates drifted in and out of our orbit. We all looked over as Amira giggled and flicked that shining mane of perfectly curled hair over a shoulder. Rafe erupted into laughter at something she said, and Amira sipped delicately from her purple bottle, looking pleased with herself. The dance had started an hour earlier, but only Shells and nerds showed up on time. Most of the older kids partied in suites or hidden thickets before rolling in for the last hour, their mouths sticky from sugary vodka. Mum, who had grown up learning to make conversation with her father's house staff, had been utterly determined that Louis and I would have none of Papa's preciousness. While Astley was comprised of impenetrable cliques, Louis was already kingly in his benevolence. He was as comfortable in the presence of the rugby boys as he was the scholarship students, gifting everyone with his slow smile, his genuine interest in their lives. He was the star around which every other celestial object revolved, including me, his dwarf planet.

'Lexi, are you going to come with us to New Zealand this summer?' Kris asked.

'New Zealand?'

'Yeah, it'll be winter down there so we're going snowboarding over summer break for a week,' he said. 'Then a week in the Cook Islands to thaw out on the way back. It'll be mad.'

'We'll be in Scotland, won't we?' I asked Louis.

Every year, Granny went north to her estate in the Scottish Highlands for what could loosely be described as summer. We shivered through chilly mornings stalking deer and fishing for salmon. The stone house was a fake gothic structure, with decorative turrets designed by our great-great-grandmother. It was impossible to heat, so we spent our summer crouched over radiant heaters and turning our electric blankets up as high as they could go. We struggled out of damp wellies and moist woollen jumpers that seemed to latch onto our skin with scratching, sucking mouths.

So a week in the Cook Islands did, in fact, sound pretty great. But it was unlikely Papa would ever allow it when the custody arrangement dictated that this was his summer with us. Never mind that he'd spent much of his time up the road at the estate he inherited from his own grandmother. No one ever mentioned her by name, but I knew that he went there to see Annabelle.

'It would just be two weeks,' Louis said optimistically. 'I'm going to ask him tomorrow after the parade.'

'Just say you're going to check in on a few members of the Commonwealth, mate,' Kris said.

Finally, Louis decided that the moment had arrived; it was time for us to descend The Mound and head to the dance. We whooped and hollered in the dark as we crossed the great lawn.

Kris gave me a piggyback so I didn't have to struggle through the wet grass in my shoes. Amira and Rafe dawdled far behind the crowd, ignoring the titters and whispers of their peers who looked back to watch the new romance bloom. In many ways, it was the last night of my childhood, when my biggest problems were the size of my thighs and the pile of assignments on my desk that would ruin spring holidays.

Like most Astley events, the dance was overdone, with a DJ brought in from London, a professional photographer in a fedora roaming the dance floor, and a slushy-machine station that was under heavy guard by three teachers to prevent vodka being added to the mixes. Boys were required to wear shirts and ties, though most rebelled against the dress code by zipping a hoodie over the top. Many of the girls had squeezed themselves into bandage dresses, but there were enough Preen power dresses – with their unflattering bubble hem and bra back straps – that I did not feel the odd one out. I danced with the girls from my boarding house, throwing my hands in the air in a perfect approximation of youthful joy, always keeping an eye on the photographer as he wandered from group to group, blinding them with the white haze of his camera flash. I knew that if I appeared sweaty or tired, I would look drunk, so I kept my movements light and surreptitiously dabbed my forehead with a paper napkin.

When the photographer approached us, I saw a glimmer of recognition in his face. His contract would stipulate that he could not sell his images to third parties, but he would anyway, claiming the photos that wound up in the *Daily Post* must have been leaked by an Astley kid. The man nudged his fedora higher on his head and asked the girls to crowd around me, which they did eagerly, lining up with their hands on their hips like a row of teapots. I popped a knee slightly to give my body a flattering line and smiled as sweetly and soberly as I could.

'Alright, girls, lovely, thank you,' he said, revealing a gap-toothed grin.

'Hang on, mate, one more!' Kris shouted and loped over to sling his arm across my shoulder.

Amira, who had been grinding herself on Rafe's thigh, hopped off and teetered over on her heels to tuck herself in beside me. Louis, who had been chatting to a group of Shells, ran over and threw an arm around her.

'Okay, mate, now you've got the shot of the century,' Kris boomed, and we all laughed as the photographer pressed down on the shutter and bathed our retinas in a dazzling flare.

It's a photo that has been used by the *Post* again and again, the four of us so young and beautiful and happy, the pale blue of my dress setting off nicely against the fiery red of Amira's. Our teeth gleamed, our eyes twinkled. It would be the front page of the *Post* that weekend, with shots of Mum and Papa at the parade bumped to page three. The headline would read *Inside the luxe lives of the royal twins*, and the story would describe Amira and Kris as the *fabulously wealthy and exotic siblings who befriended the prince and princess*. Vikki would purchase copies of the photo and have them set in sterling silver Tiffany frames, one for each of us. After school, I never had the heart to display it, but it was always boxed up and taken with me when I moved from place to place. It was only in recent years that I finally noticed the thing everyone missed: Louis was at one end of the group, while Kris was at the other. Just behind my left shoulder, their fingers were gently clasped together.

The dance felt interminably long. Amira and Rafe sneaked outside, Kris and Louis were nowhere to be seen, and I finally succumbed to my hunger and ordered a hotdog from the stand, loading the bun with American mustard and relish and onions. I wolfed it down in three bites, knowing I'd hate myself as soon as all that dough and processed meat was inside me. But for a few moments, I finally felt anchored back to Earth. Hunger was like floating just above the surface of everything, the entire world hazy and bothersome below.

When the lights came on, the DJ told everyone they had fifteen minutes to return to their suites. I pulled on my coat and walked through the dark school grounds with a group of kids, who peeled off as they reached their boarding houses. As I passed the rifle range, I found Amira wandering across the grass with her shoes dangling from one hand and her hair wild.

'Where have *you* been?' I asked.

She grinned. 'Nowhere. But I'm bloody freezing. I can't find my coat.'

She was shivering in her dress, its right side damp and grassy.

'Did you leave it in the hall?'

She shook her head and rubbed her upper arms, trying to stay warm.

'I think it's up on The Mound. Will you come with me, Lexi, please? I can't lose another one. Mum will kill me.'

We walked quickly, trying to generate heat in our weary bodies. My shoes pinched my feet and my much-regretted hot dog burned my guts. In exchange for joining her up The Mound, Amira regaled me with the details of her hookup with Rafe – almost exclusively over the clothes, thanks in large part to the bandage dress that was impossible to push up or shove down.

'We're going to hang out over spring holidays,' she said.

'You'll have to "hang" at your place, since his house is about to be repossessed.'

The Mound was more haunted than ever at midnight. The tree branches looked like knobby fingers reaching towards us and we gripped hands as a barn owl wailed overhead. As we reached its peak, we heard music playing, soft and tinny, like it was coming from one of those plastic travel speakers that never work well.

'Is someone else up here?' I whispered to Amira.

'Must be a hookup. I just want to get my coat and go to bed,' she whined.

We crept through the tangling, shifting branches of a willow tree, still bare and yellow from winter. I stumbled on my heel and nearly crashed through the underbrush, but Amira grasped my elbow to steady me. When I looked back at her, she was staring straight ahead, her mouth agape.

'What?' I whispered, but she kept her gaze ahead of us.

When I finally looked through the willow's tendrils, I was struck by how beautiful they were. I had always been slightly repulsed by the pawing and open want of teenage couples. But as they swayed to the music in each other's arms, Kris and Louis were only tender. Louis's cheek rested on Kris's shoulder, his eyes closed, his face more peaceful than I had ever seen it. Kris, who was usually brash and bold, stroked his back gently as they turned. I knew our lives were all about to change, but in that moment, as he cradled this boy to him, I could only feel happy for my brother.

'We should go,' I whispered, and Amira nodded.

We tiptoed down the path, Amira's coat forgotten. We were silent as we walked back to our boarding house and scaled an ivy-covered trellis to get through the open window of our suite. We sloughed off the dresses we thought made us look like women. We said nothing as we pulled on the brightly coloured pyjamas that transformed us back into the girls we truly were. We went our separate ways into sleep, wondering what tomorrow would bring.

When our brothers died fourteen years later, most of Kris's ashes would be spread at the family's hunting lodge in South Africa. The tiniest scoop of him was saved for a trio of gold pendants that Vikki, Amira and Madhav would wear for the rest of their lives. But if you were to unscrew the top of the gold heart that hung from Amira's neck, you would find it empty. Before the funeral, she had been allowed one final private moment with her husband. When no one was looking, she slipped the real necklace containing Kris's ashes into the breast pocket of Louis's suit so the two men she loved could finally be together.

CHAPTER ELEVEN

10 January 2023

I woke up to the familiar wail of Granny's piper, who stood below her bedroom window and played for her every day at 7 am. I was fairly certain Granny was up hours before the bagpipes sounded, but it signified the official start of the morning in whichever home she was staying. Maids began bustling in the halls, phones rang, breakfast trays for the late sleepers were delivered. I looked out the window and found it was the first glorious day since I had arrived in London. Mists were rolling across the vast green lawns as the sun's rays burned off the slick.

We all preferred Watford Castle over the main palace, which was far too grand and required we be grand inside it. At Watford, we kept a kitchen garden and said things like 'I'm off to potter in the potager.' There were rosebuds in tiny glass vases on every available surface. We drank wine on mediaeval stone steps and watched the sun disappear behind the horizon.

I still had a few hours before the reading of Papa's will, so I got out of bed and crept downstairs. I found an old waxed coat and some wellies in my size and walked to the East Terrace, which led to a vast lawn, carved hedges and slumbering rose bushes that would explode in colour by spring. The garden was a mathematical marvel, all right angles and discipline. But beyond it were the wild, untamed oak groves where deer are allowed to roam. That's where I wanted to be.

Just as I was about to set off, a springer spaniel emerged from the hall and ran loops around my ankles, looking for love. It was Granny's dog Pudding, followed by the servant sent to walk off some of the dog's frantic energy. He started when he saw me, and then bowed.

'Morning,' I said. 'I can walk Pud if you like.'

'If it pleases you, Your Royal Highness.'

I trudged across the grass as Pud raced ahead of me. The sun and chilled air felt wonderful, even with the heaviness of the funeral still lingering. I had spent the few hours I was able to sleep dreaming of the crypt in which Papa and Louis were now sealed forever. Surely they would wander across the heath at any moment, back from an early-morning ride, Louis's cheeks blooming in the cold, Papa demanding his coffee tray.

When we reached the grove, Pud chased squirrels while I nestled myself in the giant smooth roots of an oak tree, as safe and strong as a parent's arms. I pulled my phone from my pocket and made the call I had been putting off in thirty-minute increments since the day I arrived.

Ben answered on the sixth ring when I was about to give up.

'Well, hello,' my boss at the hospital said. 'I was wondering when I'd hear from you.'

'Sorry.'

'Nah, don't be. Sorry about your dad and your brother. How you holding up?'

'Fine,' I lied. I imagined him in his oxford shirt and navy trousers, at odds with the shaggy blond hair he refused to cut. His stethoscope would be slung around his neck as he leaned against the nurses' station and read a few charts while we spoke. 'I have to ask you a couple of logistics questions.'

There was a long pause, and I heard the bustle of the hospital taper off to silence. He was moving to an empty room where the nurses wouldn't piece together the bits of our conversation and draw their conclusions.

'You're dropping out, aren't you,' he said.

'What? No.' I felt suddenly flushed. 'All I want to know at this stage is how much leave a resident can take.'

'Five weeks a year, and you're already down two,' he said, not giving me one inch, as usual.

'What happens if a resident loses their entire family and maybe needs time to sort things out?'

He was silent for a while. 'Lexi, you know we don't make exceptions. Even for you. You'd have to take the rest of the year off and then start your third year next January.'

'Has anyone ever done that before?'

'Sure they have. Usually it's because they get pregnant or have a mental breakdown, but yeah.'

Sometimes I marvelled at the younger version of me who had been so desirous of this man I would press him against the wall of the stairwell in the middle of a shift. I recalled those first frenzied interludes in his apartment, when I ripped the scrubs over his head and begged him to touch me. All I'd wanted was the full weight of his male body. I'd wanted him, even when he was bossy at the hospital, wrenching the endoscope from my hand and hissing, 'You're doing it wrong.'

'Lexi,' he said. 'What have I always said to you?'

'That the residency program is a huge expense to the Australian taxpayer, and I'm taking someone's spot for my own vanity exercise, and inevitably I'll drop out once I've proved whatever point I'm trying to make, and go back to where I came from?'

'I said that?'

'Yes, you twat.'

'Jesus, that's mean,' he said, laughing at the atrocious bedside manner he displayed in all the beds he lay in and stood over. 'Other than *that*, what I always say is that you'll be a doctor if you're meant to be one. If you need to take a year off to sort things out, you'll pick it back up next year and it won't be a problem.'

I watched Pud stick her head in a pile of rotting leaves and inhale deeply, trotting forward as she followed her nose.

'You looked hot at that funeral, by the way,' Ben added. 'Sorry, that's probably not appropriate to say, but you did.'

'You're a ghoul.'

'Yes.'

There was a long pause.

'Why do I feel like you're saying goodbye to me?' I asked him.

'Well ... you hardly said goodbye last time, did you.'

'You dumped *me*,' I reminded him, though what had happened in his flat five weeks before was more complicated than that and we both knew it.

'Look,' he said, 'if you want my two cents, I think you're better than what they're offering.'

'What, being Queen?' I asked, heat rising in my cheeks at the word finally spoken out loud.

'Yes. But it's up to you. Just decide soon, would you? Trying to do rosters when I'm one resident down is a pain in my arse.'

'I will.'

'Goodbye, Dr Villiers,' he said, but left us suspended in silence for a few moments before finally ending the call.

Ben had been a mistake that I enjoyed making. After Louis and Amira's wedding, when my family finally cut me off, sleep seemed to leave me entirely and I spent a lot of nights staring at the shadows on the ceiling. I was more numb than upset, but there was a deep-rooted thought inside me, one that was waiting to be plucked. If I took it by the stem and pulled, I knew the tears would come and they would never stop: *I just want my mum, I just want my mum, I just want my mum.*

My internship at the hospital had been all-consuming, but I was still restless for something I couldn't name. Ben, handsome, irritable and completely off-limits, seemed like a fine distraction.

The first time I felt his eyes on me, when Finn and I stood among the other hapless interns, his gaze lasted a moment longer than it should. A crackling little current, a swell of something. I couldn't tell if he liked me or disdained me. Two weeks after the wedding, I saw Ben at a bar in town and we ignored each other. But I lingered in my booth until everyone I knew was gone, and he did the same, finally sliding into the seat next to me right before last call. *What am I doing?* I thought later in the alleyway outside, running my fingers through his hair while I kissed him. *And who would care?*

I had told no one my secret, slipping into Ben's flat a few nights a week and going home to my own bed before anyone noticed. A month in, Jack told me he was taking Paula north so she and her friends could blockade loggers from razing an ancient forest.

'Want to come?' he'd asked. We were standing at the sink and his fingers brushed mine as he handed me a dripping dish. 'You don't have to actually stand in the path of the truck. I usually just watch in case things go awry. Mum's always pushing it a bit further than she probably should.'

'I would,' I said. 'But … you know I can't.'

He'd nodded, understanding as he always did. Paula was constantly asking me to come along to protests and blockades. She thought I was brave enough to wrap myself around a 200-year-old tree. When it was still just a sapling, my ancestors had taken possession of the land, razing forests, slaughtering humans, building industries, until this giant was destined to be cut down in its prime, and made into tissue paper and woodchips. But I would not embarrass my family by trying to defend it. Even after they had cast me out, I was still too afraid of their ire to take a stance on a single thing.

'You'll be okay on your own?' he asked quietly.

Jack seemed to be the only one who saw the blackness that had settled over me after the wedding. He also knew me well enough not to try to talk to me about it. Instead I felt his watchful eyes as I passed through the kitchen on the way back to the barn. He was constantly giving me things unsolicited: homemade lattes, a morning bun just because, his unyielding devotion.

'Of course.'

With Jack and Paula gone for the weekend and Finn at the hospital, I had the property to myself. I locked Ragu in his crate for the night and jogged down the dirt road so I could open the vineyard gates to let Ben in. Ordinarily I would never have let him stay the night, but our exertions left us exhausted, and he had fallen asleep in my bed. At dawn, I had hustled him out onto the sandstone verandah that ran from the cottage to my converted barn.

Jack was standing there with Ragu's dinner bowl in his hand. All three of us stood frozen, like actors on a stage who had forgotten the next line.

'I thought you were in the highlands,' I said.

Jack was silent for a moment, his eyes moving from the almost forty-year-old man in an unbuttoned shirt over to me. 'Uh, we all got arrested. So we had to leave early.'

I nodded, clearing my throat, absolutely dying to wrap this up before Ragu trotted around the corner and unleashed the almighty bark he reserved for men he didn't know.

Ben shuffled towards Jack with his hand outstretched. 'Hey, Ben. Lexi and I work together at the hospital.'

Jack nodded absently, taking his hand. 'Hi.'

I walked Ben to his car in silence along the dusty road. I wondered what Jack would make of it all. Would he think of me differently? Would he think less of me for sleeping with my boss? Jack's breakup with Georgia was still fresh, and as I plodded up the road in my pyjamas, I grew angry at him because he could go out with anyone he liked. Everything I did had to remain clandestine because all the details of my life had price tags dangling from them. I'd had to listen to him and Georgia through the wall between our bedrooms for four years, and I hadn't complained, not once.

'That wasn't your boyfriend, was it?' Ben asked when we got to the car, interrupting the silent nuclear fission of my thoughts.

'What?'

'That guy. You both were acting weird just now.'

'He's not my boyfriend,' I said irritably.

Back at the cottage, and for the three years that followed, Jack and I said nothing of that morning on the verandah. If I left the house, headed towards a destination I kept deliberately vague, I was sure Jack knew exactly where I was going. If he had any thoughts about that, he never voiced them. Occasionally, a pretty girl would emerge from Jack's room, her shoes dangling from her hand. I would nod politely at her until, finally, a few weeks later, she seemed to vanish. Through it all, Jack and I remained unlikely, determined friends. I might have slept in Ben's bed, but Jack was still the one who picked me up after I had my wisdom teeth out. He knew which brand of tea bags I liked. He called me late at night so we could share the silence. I kept things this way so I'd never have to lose him.

Thinking about it all now, I hugged myself closer to the roots of the old oak tree. I thought about Jack and the vineyard he loved. He should open it up to the public and do wine tastings. He should host weddings in the gloriously rundown shed that had stood on the property for a hundred years. But he couldn't do either because I lived there like an exotic, endangered bird that must be protected at all costs. I thought about my medical career. All those ninety-hour weeks, the orifices I'd stuck my fingers in, the first time I saved a life, the first time I watched someone die. I thought about Kris and Louis, who deserved an apology from me, and would never get it. I thought about Amira and her boxes of pills. I thought about the snow cloud swallowing Papa whole. I thought about Mum, the love of my life.

It all felt like a tangle I had no hope of ever undoing. I could only try pulling things straight and living with the knots that remained.

*

At the castle, I found Amira's room already empty. She must have returned to London early. I walked back to my own room, which Mary had filled with racks of clothing and a suitcase of heels.

'Good morning, Your Royal Highness,' she said, bobbing into a distracted curtsy. 'I'm just pulling together an outfit for the reading of the will. The funeral went very well, I think. Would you like to see the papers? Or perhaps I could provide a summation of your coverage?'

'I'll pass.'

'Well, suffice it to say you were very well received – even a few of your more strident critics praised you, and your ensemble in particular.'

'Mary,' I said, sharper than I intended. 'Please. Don't.'

Her little face tightened. 'I'm sorry, ma'am, forgive me.'

I looked at the garments strewn across the bed, the piles of impossible shoes. This is what it would be like. Garden parties. Investitures. The endless race to be declared the hardest working royal by stuffing my calendar with engagements towards the end of the year. Winning over tabloid reporters with off-the-record cocktail parties. Strategic leaks to keep them fed and watered. Louis had woken up every day and pushed this boulder up the hill without complaint. Now it had rolled to my feet.

'Mary ...' I sat down on the bed. 'Do you think there's a different way to do this? A better way?'

She eyed me cautiously. 'I'm not sure I follow.'

'If I were maybe to give this a go, do you think there's a way to do it so it's not just ... clothes and obsessing over the *Daily Post*?'

She went still. When I looked up, her eyes were blazing as she clutched a stiletto.

'I do, very much,' she breathed. 'Do you remember when your mum – Princess Isla, I mean – went to Darfur and she stood in that camp with her hair covered by the scarf? And she demanded the West go look into the faces of the children before they chose to ignore their pain? Everyone slammed her, but that was the moment everything should have changed.'

I did remember. When she got home from her unapproved trip to Sudan, Papa refused to speak to her for a month. The *Daily Post* called her the 'Darfur Ditz'. Even the American president implied that she was too much of a bimbo to understand the complexities of the situation.

'You could do it,' Mary said fiercely. 'You've been out in the world. You're a doctor. It should be you to finish what Princess Isla started. Who says the monarchy can't be a force for change? If it sits at the centre of British life, it should earn its place there. It should apologise for the past and be a moral leader of the future. Why not?'

I couldn't ignore the little swell of my heart, the heat rising in my face. Mum used to talk this way when we were alone. She had never dared say these things in front of Papa, especially when she was still trying to please him. But when it was just us, she would lean forwards and murmur in my ear: 'Can you imagine where we'd be if your father had one splinter of Barbara Villiers' backbone?'

Could I imagine a truly modern queen, who took all the nostalgia, all the love, all the unity that Britain felt for the crown and did something with it? Could I be the monarch my mother once longed for? Mary seemed to sense my thoughts, and she smiled at me.

'I could help you,' she said. 'If you decided to stay.'

I looked at the clock. Everything was happening too fast, and my excitement morphed into panic. Yesterday, I was fully prepared to walk into this meeting and ask them to draw up the paperwork so I could go home. Now I wasn't so sure.

'I should get dressed for this thing,' I said. 'I can't really keep the Queen waiting.'

She smiled again and nodded. With the mourning period officially over, it was time to emerge from our black garments.

Mary presented me with a boxy blazer and matching trousers in a deep hunter green. It was the colour of Mum's eyes, the colour she wore almost exclusively for her first few years as a royal woman.

'Now, I know we're staging a quiet revolution here,' Mary said, kneeling on the floor to dig through the suitcase of shoes. Her voice had transformed in the few moments we'd been speaking, so it was not quite so soft, no longer unsure. She was like the little mouse who roared. 'But fashion is power. If you dress the part, they'll accept you. Once we're on the inside, that's when we change everything.'

She held up a pair of tan suede heels and squinted at them. 'These are perfect.'

The meeting was held in Granny's private apartment, which overlooked the East Terrace Garden. I had expected Papa's lawyer, Antony Eastaughffe, to be there to read his last will and testament. Instead I found Granny seated at the head of the table, with Stewart on one side and the prime minister on the other. After tea was poured, Stewart spread his fingertips on the papers before him, as if divining their message by touch, and looked at me over the rims of his glasses.

'Now, ma'am,' he began. 'You'll understand that your father, the Prince of Scotland, was bound by the custom of male primogeniture in writing his will.'

I looked at Jenny, who managed to keep her face neutral. I knew she was pushing for a law to remove the last hereditary peers from the House of Lords. She had also called for the toppling of the monarchy when she was nineteen, in a video that resurfaced when she ran for office. What must she think of us, this family that played with expensive toys that didn't belong to us?

'Your stepmother, Annabelle, the Dowager Duchess of Exeter, will receive your father's possessions – his estate in Scotland, his jewellery and watches, the collection of lithographs, as well as the antique gramophones. Elton Park was bought with revenue from the Duchy of Exeter, so it therefore remains property of the duchy,' he said, his eyebrows rising and falling the way they did when he was working up to something.

'It's okay, Stewart, I know he didn't leave me anything.'

All three of them glanced up at me, surprised. A part of me hoped Papa might have thought of me when writing his will. He was far too traditional to leave me anything of value, but, against my better judgement, I had a fantasy that there was some souvenir from our past that would show he truly did love me, that he had forgiven me, that he was my father. I had no idea what this object would be. I could not think of a single thing that might hold deep significance to both of us. And that, perhaps, was the trouble with Papa and me. We were father and daughter, and we were also strangers to one another.

'That's right, ma'am,' Stewart said slowly. 'It is the way things are done, as you know. Prince Louis's portion of your mother's trust now goes to his wife, the Dowager Duchess of Somerset, when she turns thirty. We also thought it best if perhaps Cumberland 1 remains hers for as long as she wishes.'

Mum's divorce payout had been close to £18 million, though she had burned through almost all of it to cover her exorbitant security costs in her final years. No longer a working royal, she had been stripped of her taxpayer-funded protection, leaving her out in a world that hated her as much as it exalted her. I was fairly certain there had been only about £10,000 for Louis and me to share by the time she died, although it was a relief Amira would always have a place of her own.

'That's good,' I said. 'For Amira, I mean.'

'Yes, ma'am. Depending on your own intentions, Cumberland 3, which is just across the quadrangle, is undergoing renovations that will be completed by spring. It would make a fine home for you.'

He glanced at me, but when I said nothing, he returned to his papers.

'Now, on the matter of income. I am sure you're aware the Duchy of Exeter is reserved only for the monarch's eldest son and heir,' Stewart said, his eyebrows furrowing again. 'This is according to law. With your father and brother gone, you are the monarch's heir, but obviously not her male child, so the duchy – and its considerable profits – can never be yours.'

Granny met my gaze. I wondered if they had strategised beforehand, deciding who should deliver which strange bit of news. The Duchy of Exeter was set up nine hundred years ago to ensure that the king's son enjoyed a lucrative income while he waited to ascend the throne. Those who lived on the duchy's prime southern land – whether they were pensioners, the owners of sprawling farms, or big corporations – were expected to pay him rent. With more than 100,000 acres of land, as well as a few savvy investments, the duchy was today worth about £1 billion. The arrangement meant that Papa, with zero effort, had earned an annual income of £20 million to buy all the lithographs his heart desired.

'The duchy goes back to being administered by the crown estate?' I asked.

As children, Louis and I had been required to sit through weekly constitutional history lessons with a private tutor. I had only vaguely paid attention, knowing none of it would ever be my problem. But a £1 billion parcel of land that would never be mine, under any circumstances, purely because I was a girl, was a fact that had stuck.

'Her Majesty the Queen will support you financially – if you choose to stay,' Stewart said. 'But yes, the revenue from the duchy will flow back to the government.'

'Well,' I said, looking at Jenny, 'congrats to you, I guess?'

She laughed a little, then stopped when Stewart shot her a look. Her face sobered as she turned back to me.

'We're at the point where we must discuss your future, ma'am,' she said. 'You are now first in line to the throne. Do you intend to wear the crown when it comes to you?'

I looked at their weary faces, these three people who made momentous decisions behind closed doors. I had spent the last eleven years believing the crown should be quietly tossed into a city dumpster like a murder weapon. It had turned siblings against each other, triggered wars, broken up marriages, enslaved millions, destroyed civilisations. What did it say about me that I would now consider bearing its weight?

'She doesn't know,' Granny said. Everyone turned to look at her. It was the first time she had spoken since I'd come into the room. 'She simply doesn't know.'

She rose from her chair, so we all stood too. We watched as she wandered over to look at the garden through the window.

'I wasn't sure either, to be honest,' she said. 'Though I was never given a choice. I was just a girl. Everyone believed it was God's plan, and who would question such a thing? But the world feels like it's on a precipice, doesn't it? The next monarch's reign is likely to be the hardest in our family's history.'

She left the window and walked back to the table to prepare herself another cup of tea, waving Stewart away when he tried to help.

'The greatest challenge for my successor will be guiding this family through whatever lies ahead. I'd like to believe this planet isn't doomed, but there will be sacrifices to make and people will be afraid. I've lived through wars. When people are scared, they can become ... irrational. The next monarch could be a symbol of hope, a great unifier, a stabiliser,' she said, sipping from her cup. 'But if they fail, they'll be tossed on the scrapheap.'

The woman who was my grandmother had vanished. Her radiant alter ego, Queen Eleanor, had emerged. She sat back down and wordlessly encouraged us to do the same.

'I still believe the crown lands on the head that God chooses. But perhaps He needs to guide his chosen one,' she said. 'If Alexandrina needs a little time, she may have it. I propose that a year from now, I proclaim my heir to be the next Princess –

or perhaps Prince – of Scotland. I didn't give Freddy the title until he was five, so a year won't hurt. I also think Scotland probably deserves time to get used to the idea, don't you? The independence movement is stronger than ever.'

Stewart and Jenny looked at each other and something invisible passed between them.

'Ma'am,' Stewart said, 'a female heir presumptive has never received the title of Princess of Scotland before.'

'Yes, thank you, Stewart,' Queen Eleanor said. 'I was educated by some of this nation's greatest constitutional and legal scholars, I am Great Britain's longest reigning monarch, and I read and sign every piece of legislation presented to me by parliament. I'm quite aware of the title's history.'

Stewart flushed, but the Queen cut him off before he could speak.

'Unlike the duchy, the Scottish title is the monarch's personal gift to their heir – traditionally their firstborn son. But this week, we find ourselves in exceptional circumstances. For the first time in a very long time, a woman is not the heir presumptive, but the heir apparent.'

I looked at her, stunned. Women who are first in line to the throne are almost always relegated to the title of heir presumptive – a placeholder just in case the monarch manages to replace her with a son. To be heir apparent is to be untouchable. In the long history of our family, no woman had enjoyed this inviolable position. No woman except, now, potentially, me.

'Freddy is gone. Louis is gone. There is no possibility that a son will be born with a better claim to the throne than Alexandrina,' Granny said, folding her hands before her. 'So it is hers. Unless, of course, she doesn't want it.'

She rose from the table and scooped up the black patent handbag that had been resting on a stool by her chair. We all stood as well.

'Prime Minister, if Alexandrina decides to give up her place in the line, you can draw up the bill for parliament, and we'll proceed with Prince Richard,' the Queen said. 'I'm going for a ride. I'd like to reflect on the week's events in peace.'

She left the room with Stewart trailing behind her, and I wondered if he would attempt to change her mind. Jenny and I watched them leave. As soon as they were out of sight, I collapsed back into my chair, my head swimming.

One year. I had one year to choose. I had expected to be forced to come to a decision, but instead I'd been granted a reprieve.

'Well,' Jenny said, raising her eyebrows, 'that was unexpected. But I suppose we have a plan now.'

'You must find all these archaic rules insane,' I breathed.

She shrugged. 'I have two kids. I can't imagine ranking them like that, or giving everything to my son simply because he's a boy, and leaving my daughter with absolutely nothing.'

'Do you think she's right?' I asked. 'The next monarch's reign will be the hardest?'

'I think all institutions are being re-examined, and they'll have to justify their place,' she said. 'Those that don't evolve will be cast out before they even know it's happening.'

I looked at her. 'My mother always thought the crown could do more, but everyone told her we have to stay out of politics.'

She thought for a moment as she tried to force her binder into an already overstuffed bag.

'What are the three rights of the modern sovereign? To consult, to encourage and to warn? I imagine a queen who's been a physician would have every right to encourage her government to invest more in the NHS, to advocate for more funding for cancer research and improve maternal health.'

'Surely that queen would be very controversial.'

She gave me an enigmatic smile. 'I don't know. I think she could effect a lot of change. She would be a role model for many people. I know I'd certainly like to have a weekly audience with that queen.'

I leaned back in my chair, feeling like I'd woken up in the driver's seat of a car I had no idea how to operate. Maybe all I had to do was take the wheel. Or maybe I should open the door and roll myself onto the ground before I crashed.

'If it's not me, it'll be Richard, and everything will probably be fine.'

Jenny hesitated and then looked around the room to make sure it was empty. She leaned towards me.

'All I can tell you is that if it's King bloody Richard, it'll end with a guillotine,' she whispered. 'And I know plenty of people who'd be happy to be the executioner.'

She started gathering her things to leave. I wondered what she knew that I didn't.

'Prime Minister,' I called as she walked to the door, 'say I don't want it. What happens to the Duchy of Exeter?'

She turned to look at me. 'Well, I suppose in that case, Prince Richard becomes both the monarch's eldest son and her heir apparent, which means, legally, possession of the duchy goes to him.'

'So for Richard, the only thing standing between the crown and £1 billion ... is me,' I said.

She narrowed her eyes and looked at me for a long time.

'Your grandmother loves her son and seems to have a certain blind spot when it comes to him. But I do not,' she said. 'And I hope you don't either.'

*

A Range Rover waited in the quadrangle to take me to London. The sky was an optimistic blue, and a house sparrow took a dust bath on the drive, burrowing in the sandy gravel to distribute it all through his tortoiseshell plumage. From the shadow of an archway, I moved into the blinding sunlight and stepped into a cloud of cigarette smoke.

'I hear congratulations are in order,' Annabelle said.

She was leaning against the wall in a tartan coat and black sunglasses.

'I think congrats are reserved for the winner of the antique gramophones, don't you?'

She smirked at me. 'Freddy always said you were funny.'

I smarted at the mention of his name. His heart was never with us, perhaps not even for one moment, but I still felt a claim to this man who had always been hers. When I was four, Mum went to Jamaica on an official trip with Louis. I was struck down with conjunctivitis and stayed at Elton Park with Papa. One morning, I padded along the hallway, my eyes streaming and burning, and found Annabelle in his dressing gown, curled up on his bed. She looked stunned to see me, but then smiled and pressed a finger to her lips as we heard the squeak of taps turning in the bathroom. Fearing trouble if Papa emerged to find me there, I retreated on my sock feet, nearly stumbling down the staircase as I ran.

That was the year my nightmares began, when I woke up the estate with my screams, claiming that I was being terrorised by 'The Scary Lady'.

'Well, my car's waiting,' I said.

'You probably shouldn't have let her delay everything by a year,' she said. 'That gives Richard his window.'

'Okay. Goodbye, Annabelle.'

'I'm quite interested in how you intend to navigate all this. People out there look at this castle and wish they could live here.' She took a long puff of her cigarette. 'Little do they know it's the world's nicest prison.'

'Well, your time is served and now you're free,' I said. 'You made my mother's life hell, you broke up a family, you leaked against me and Louis. Goodbye.'

Briefly, she looked chastened, the same way she had when I'd discovered her in Papa's bed, then she set her face back into its familiar smirk. My father's widow dropped her cigarette and crushed it, sizzling, under her toe.

'You know,' she began, 'I'm not proud of it all, far from it. But I think you'll soon find yourself bound by the same constraints that your father and I did. The truth is, Frederick never really thought himself worthy of the crown. That's why he was always so fussy and spoilt. He thought if his surroundings were regal, he could be kingly as well. And yes, he would occasionally leak against you, and I suspect that was his way of trying to bring you back to him. But he never gave up your biggest secret, did he?'

My heart fell through the elevator shaft of my chest all the way to my stomach. I stepped forward, unsure of what I wanted to do, only knowing that my fists were clenched tighter than my jaw. I thought of this woman lying against my father's chest, learning all the confidences we had made because we were supposed to be family.

'Fuck you,' I said, and turned and walked to my Range Rover.

'Alexandrina,' she called, but I did not stop. 'One last piece of advice: watch out for that little twit Mary. She's not what you think.'

I slid into the back of the car and slammed the door so hard it shuddered. With a shaking hand, I pressed the button to roll down the window.

'The fact that you don't like her is the only reference I need,' I said. 'She's hired.'

*

When I reached the door of Cumberland 1, I knocked and waited. If Amira refused to let me in, I didn't really have anywhere else to go. My apartment-to-be was still a construction site. I'd have to crash with Stewart in the staff quarters over the garage. Barely a week back in London and I'd already made a mess of things.

A servant answered the door, bowed and let me in. From the drawing room came the thundering of feet and a bark like a sonic boom. A German shorthaired pointer slid across the hardwood floors on his nails, running in place to correct himself and then bounded towards me. For one moment, I thought it was Ragu. But this dog had white spots speckled through his coat, where Ragu was dark and sleek. He jumped and placed his big paws on my shoulders, looked deeply into my eyes and unleashed another barrage of ear-piercing woofs.

Amira came running down the stairs, already dressed in pyjamas, even though it was 5 pm.

'Chino, down,' she scolded.

The dog, all long limbs he could barely control, galloped back to the drawing room. Amira and I smiled tentatively at each other.

'That's Louis's dog, Chino,' she said. 'It's funny you both had pointers at the same time. We had him up at Norfolk, but I asked that they bring him down. I figured you might be missing your dog.'

Chino returned with a tennis ball in his mouth, which he dropped at my feet. I threw the ball up the stairs, and he barrelled after it, rattling priceless artworks on the wall as he went. I smiled at Amira.

'Thank you,' I said. 'And, about last night, I'm so sorry.'

She held up her hand. 'No, I'm sorry,' she said. Chino tumbled back down the stairs, and triumphantly dropped the ball on my foot, ready for round two. 'Everything's upside down and I'm not coping. I didn't really mean what I said.'

'It's true, though. I failed you and Louis. And Kris. I just ran out of here and left you all.'

Chino howled with frustration as Amira and I looked at each other, leaving the ball untouched at our feet. I remembered our last year at Astley, when I had been sick with grief, moving through the dark tunnel of each day, only to succumb to my hot tears when we finally turned the lights off in our suite. Amira would reach across the void between our twin beds and take my hand.

'Well, you're here now,' she said. 'At least for a little while?'

'Yes, I've decided to stay,' I said. 'For now.'

We sank onto the couch, the lush Hermès blanket finally put to use as we unfurled it over our knees. Chino settled himself between us and put his heavy head in my lap. I tried not to think of the little life I had created for myself in Tasmania, the one that was waiting for me as I slipped into the existence my brother left behind. I was sitting on his couch, stroking his dog, sleeping in his bed, contemplating the possibility that I might take his place in the line. At the worst moment of our lives, Louis had lied for me.

I had a year to decide if this was how I could finally make it up to him.

PART TWO

CHAPTER TWELVE

2 December 2022

A month before the helicopter landed, I was on shift at the hospital when I got a text from Ben.

Ur flatmate is in emergency, it read.

I looked at the screen with an almost reptilian detachment. The worst had happened. Again. As it always would. Distantly, I thought of the horrors that usually awaited me in the emergency department. Car accidents that annihilated the soft human body. Cardiac arrest in the young. Feet losing purchase on the highest rung of the ladder. A drowned woman, dripping and waterlogged on a gurney. I didn't realise I was running down the hall until I was already in motion. At the nurses' station, I checked the patient list with shaking hands and found him there: *J. Jennings*.

When I ripped back the curtain of his cubicle, he was sitting on the bed with his hand balanced on the steel tray beside him. Ben looked over his glasses at me and scowled.

'That was quick, Dr Villiers,' he said.

I ignored him and went to Jack's side, trying to pretend I wasn't breathing quite so hard.

'What happened?' I rasped. My heart was cantering in my chest, even as I saw him whole and alive on the bed before me. There was a rose petal of blood on his t-shirt.

'Hey, I'm fine,' he said, smiling at me. Briefly, he put his good hand on the small of my back. 'We were splitting trellises with the table saw and the wood kicked up and I got a splinter.'

I bent over the wound. The splinter was a monster. He'd clenched his hand the moment the wood pierced his skin, shattering it into fragments that would need to be plucked out individually. When I looked up, he was giving me his best Don't Be Mad at Me smile.

'I told you to wear gloves when you use that thing,' I said.

'I know.'

'Do you know how dangerous table saws are? Johnny Cash's brother was killed by one and that's why his music is so sad.' He tried not to laugh at that, which only incensed me further. 'You absolutely shouldn't be standing at the end of it. I don't know how many times I've told you that.'

'Dr Villiers,' Ben said in a low voice, 'can you please not berate my patient?'

The overhead paging system crackled, and a voice called for Ben to check in at the nurses' station immediately. We eyed each other while Jack, sensing the mood, pretended to inspect his hand.

'You go,' I said to Ben. 'I can handle this.'

He narrowed his eyes. 'You've got three patients already. I'll take care of Mr Jennings.'

'All discharged. I'll do this.'

Ben looked between us. The nurses' station called his name again. 'Can I talk to you for a moment in the hallway, Dr Villiers?'

After he closed the curtain, he took his time scribbling notes on his chart before finally passing it over. I stood there, glowering at him.

'You know I don't let doctors treat their friends – it's unprofessional,' he said in the imperious voice that used to thrill me. 'How do I know you're going to make the best possible decisions when you're this attached to the patient?'

'We're understaffed. It's a shallow puncture wound. We can't let patients sit around all day while you enforce arbitrary rules.'

He clicked his pen the way he did when he was annoyed. A man in a hospital gown staggered past us, clutching a bucket. At work, I was Ben's student. At night, I was in his bed. Life's other joys and complications – birthday dinners that needed planning, airport runs, grocery bills, camping trips – all of it happened in another world that had nothing to do with him. For three years, this arrangement suited Ben fine. But I was newly aware of a certain impatience in him that was spiralling towards exasperation. Suddenly, he wanted my weekends and my early mornings. Jack and Finn, who held dominion over those parts of my life, were becoming the subject of many furtive arguments. Any mention of Jack in particular could lead to days of silence.

'Also,' I said, now on a roll with my grievances, 'you didn't want to add any more details to that text? Or were you trying to make me think the worst had happened?'

He smirked, looked up and down the hallway to make sure no one was around and then leaned towards me. 'That's the whole point of a text. It's light on details. Enjoy your patient.'

I went back behind the curtain. Jack eyed me warily as I snapped on gloves and took his pierced hand in mine. The hospital murmured and beeped around us.

'I'll need to do an ultrasound,' I said, keeping my eyes on the wound, 'so I can locate the shards. Then I'll make an incision to remove them. We won't need to put you under – local anaesthetic will do it. Then we'll clean the wound, and you'll probably need a stitch or two in these parts where it's deepest. When was the last time you had a tetanus shot?'

When I looked up, I found that he had been watching my face while I worked. He smiled. 'I'm sorry about the saw. You're right. We were rushing and I was stupid.'

I peeled off my gloves, softening. 'Sorry I scolded you.'

He looked meaningfully in the direction of the curtain. 'Everything okay there?'

I rolled my eyes and shrugged. The Ben situation was not something we discussed. 'Need me to call anyone? I can get Paula down here. You'll probably be here for hours.'

He shook his head. 'You're here.'

In reality, I wasn't around much. I booked him in for an ultrasound and left him there while I attended to two new admissions in the ED. I came back with a chocolate bar, and he ate it while I examined his ultrasound results. No wooden shards had reached the bone. It was another hour before I could inject his hand with local anaesthetic and send his nerve endings into a deep slumber. When he was numb, I carefully made my cut into the heel of his palm while Rachel, my favourite nurse, watched on. Jack had taken a photo of me looking stony-faced with a scalpel in my hand and put it in the vineyard group chat. Now both our phones were buzzing with responses.

'How's your pain level there?' I asked, bent over his hand in scrubs and a mask. 'It's probably better if you don't look.'

'I'm fine,' he said.

I started picking the pieces with my forceps. It was strange to cut into flesh that I knew. I removed the slivers of wood from his curled hand as gently as I could.

'Is Lexi the best doctor at the hospital?' Jack asked Rachel and she snorted. She was holding his good hand while I worked. She was the toughest nurse on the ward, terrifying to everyone as she marched down the halls with her cropped pink hair and fierce eyes. She'd been at the hospital for thirty years and refused to retire, even as her shoes wore down and her back gave out. She always took a patient's fingers in hers when there might be pain.

'Lexi cares too much, if you ask me,' Rachel said. 'Most of the doctors forget a patient as soon as they walk out of here. Lexi's still worried about them days later.'

I glanced at Jack's face over my magnifying lenses. He was smiling. 'That sounds about right.'

'Is Lexi a terrible flatmate?' Rachel asked and barked her wheezing laugh.

'No, she's the best,' he said. 'She lines up all the workers at the vineyard and gives them flu shots every year. And every time someone's got a sick relative, she's on the phone to them asking about their symptoms. Last year, my grandma needed a hip replacement, and she went with her to meet the surgeon.'

I was grateful for the mask that obscured my pink cheeks. The last wood fragment slipped from his skin and blood beaded in its place.

'Too soft for this world.' Rachel smiled.

By the time Jack was sutured, bandaged, shot up with tetanus, and lectured about the importance of staying off work for a few days, my shift was over. I drove him back to the vineyard. Ignoring a text from Ben asking if I was coming over, I made us dinner and we collapsed on the couch. Finn was out with a new guy and we had the house to ourselves. It was a warm night, so we left the door open to hear the humming of insects. Ragu lay across the threshold to get the evening breeze on his belly.

'It's kind of incredible what you can do,' he murmured. We were both sleepy as we stared into the TV. A respectable distance remained between us on the couch. 'I mean, I know what you can do, but it's something else to see you doing it.'

I shrugged, even as I felt myself folding up his words and tucking them into my tender heart. 'It's not brain surgery or anything.'

'I mean it,' he said and looked at me. 'I know it's complicated with your family, and they didn't really ... give you credit for it. But I think you're amazing.'

I turned to look at his face in the television's aquarium glow. He was smiling at me, a drowsy pile on the couch, his bandaged hand on his chest. The sound of the TV seemed to drown to nothing as our eyes met, and I wondered, as I often did in those last days, what was going to happen next. My phone rang. We both started as Ben's name lit up the screen. We watched passively as it ground along the coffee table. When it finally went black, we turned our eyes back to the television in silence, only the cicadas filling the space.

*

Two nights later, I was lying on Ben's bed, reading one of the medical journals he kept on the bedside table. He came out of the bathroom brushing his teeth, a towel slung low on his waist. He prowled around his gleaming apartment, shutting off lights.

'What are you reading?' he asked around the toothbrush in his mouth.

'Hmm?'

'What are you reading?'

'Nothing much.'

He wrapped a hand around my ankle, pulling me down until I was flat on the bed. He was still damp from the shower as he crawled on top of me. Absently, I dragged my nails down his back. I kept reading.

'I love when you wear my shirt,' he said into my neck.

'You're all foamy.'

He climbed out of my arms and went to spit in the sink. I rarely spent the whole night at his place, though I had not allowed him in the barn since the morning Jack saw us. Even after all these years, I was still paranoid that a photographer would snap me going into Ben's building and lie in wait until I came out again at dawn.

'Hey,' he said from the bathroom, 'I've got that conference in Launceston this weekend. Why don't you come?'

I put the medical journal down on my chest. The collar of my shirt was wet with droplets that had fallen from his hair. I imagined hiding in a Launceston hotel room so none of my senior colleagues would see me there, eating room service because it was too small a town to go anywhere without being spotted.

'This weekend? I can't.'

'You're not rostered on.'

It was riddling day at the vineyard that weekend. The Jennings still did it manually, even though most growers used machines now. They insisted you could taste the difference, so every season, we all filed into the shed to rotate row upon row of sparkling wine, each bottle requiring a quarter of a turn to coax the sediment up the neck.

I hesitated. 'I promised to help on the vineyard this weekend.'

There was silence in the bathroom, and I waited for him to come out. Choosing manual labour with Jack over a weekend in a hotel with him was bound to cause a fight. Finally, I heard the light switch and Ben walked in, his trousers back on as if we weren't about to go to sleep. There was a challenge in his eye.

'Just blow it off. I've got a nice room and everything.'

I sat up on the bed. 'I can't, I promised.'

He stared at me for a while and then he walked to the glass doors that led to the balcony. It was too dark to see anything but our own reflection. I usually insisted he draw the blinds at night, convinced a photographer would somehow get into the building across the street, *Rear Window*-style. When the blinds were up, I could feel the shiny black lens of the camera trailing over my skin.

'I think we should stop doing this,' he said to his own reflection in the glass. 'You're too young.'

I was very still. He lived on a busy block in town, and we could hear people laughing and staggering out of the pub below.

'Okay,' I said. 'Didn't seem like I was too young for you three years ago, though.'

He turned to look at me, his hands in his pockets. He was wearing the same expression he did when he pronounced a patient dead.

'I know. But you're not really getting any older. I think maybe you're always going to be like this.'

I stared at him. Then I got off the bed. With my back turned, I took off his shirt and put my own clothes back on. Even as I had chased him, I always believed I'd be the one to walk away first. He was sleeping with his student, after all. I'd pursued him and then judged him for giving in to me.

'You shouldn't leave this late,' he said quietly. 'Just stay here.'

'My car's downstairs, it's fine.'

I knew his eyes were on me as I gathered my things: my favourite hospital shoes, Mum's watch on the table, the toothbrush I left under his sink. I cleaned up like I was fleeing a crime scene, pushing everything into my bag.

'Are we really not going to talk about this?'

I hoisted the bag onto my shoulder and avoided his eyes. The beat of my heart was methodical but peculiar. 'It's fine. You're my boss. It always had to end.'

He put a finger under my chin so that I would look at him. 'Have you ever had a real conversation in your life?'

I squirmed away from his touch, hotly embarrassed. There was something about the silence that made me think of home. Mum and Papa's unspoken rage over the dining table. Louis's eyes glancing at the clock on the mantel again. My queasy heart.

'I'll see you at work,' I said.

He shook his head, marvelling at me like I was a patient who'd rolled into the hospital with Living Statue Syndrome or Blue Skin Disorder or some other exotic condition we'd never see.

'I think you were with me because we had to keep it a secret,' he said. 'That's how you like it. You'd be incapable of living a real life, out in the open.'

My face was aflame as I left the apartment, but I didn't cry. Whenever I saw people weeping at the hospital, I eyed them curiously, wondering what it was like to do that in public where anyone could see. Even Mum, with her enormous, unwieldy emotions, only shed her tears once the door was shut.

Outside, the pub's patrons crowded the pavement, and I walked among them gingerly, keeping my face down so no one would recognise me. It felt good to be outside, even in the smoke and beer stench, and I breathed deeply as I walked to my Corolla parked under a single streetlight.

In the hushed safety of my car, I put the key in the ignition, but nothing happened. I tried again and again, the lights on the dash flickering and the car giving the smallest pant before falling silent again. I sighed, remembering Jack's warning that the battery was getting on and would need to be replaced soon. I rested my face against the steering wheel and ran through my options. I was never good at these things. I had forgotten to renew my roadside assistance. I didn't carry jumper cables because I didn't know how to use them. Late in a small city, a cab or an Uber would be hard to find. And even if I flagged one down, the driver might tell the press he'd picked me up looking rumpled and frazzled in the middle of the night. I was out in a world I barely knew how to live in, and now I was on a dark street near a footpath full of strange, drunk men.

I could go back upstairs. But if I did that, we would end up on the bed, my teeth scraping his shoulder, my hair wrapped around his fist. In the morning, we would pretend the previous evening had never happened and limp along for a few more months until he found another defect in me that he could no longer ignore.

I pulled my phone from my bag.

U awake? I texted Jack, sure he wasn't. It wasn't a proper night's sleep if he hadn't already completed his first REM cycle by 10 pm.

I could walk to the hospital and crash for the night in the on-call room, I decided.

My phone buzzed in my hand. *Yep what's up?*

Fifteen minutes later, the silver headlights of his ute swept into the street. His hair was mussed from his pillow and Ragu was with him, curled up asleep on the back seat. Our cars parked nose to nose, he strung the cables between them. It was like jumpstarting a heart, though mine refused to stir. He killed his engine, came over and leaned his forearms against my open window. The dressing on his hand needed changing, I thought to myself.

'I think it's dead,' he said. 'We'll buy a new battery in the morning, and we'll come back and I can change it.'

I nodded, gazing out the windshield. Something dripped from my jaw, landing wetly on my collarbone.

'Lex,' Jack said softly. He reached through the window and brushed the tear off my cheek. By the time he had the door open, my forehead was pressed against the steering wheel again. I felt a warm hand on my back. 'Come on. Let's go home.'

I was silent in the passenger seat as he drove back to the vineyard, the roads black under a canopy of bush. The gums were lit up by headlights in the dark, frightening and beautiful. Ragu snored in the back.

'You sure you're okay?' Jack asked again.

'Yeah. Thanks for coming to get me.'

'Of course,' he said, stealing a glance at me. I'd lived with him for seven years and he'd never seen me cry before.

'Do you think I'm incapable of living a real life?' I asked.

He looked at me again. 'Did Ben say that to you?'

I stared ahead, unable to speak. The road's centre line passed beneath us like Morse code. I suddenly felt very far from home. The grey Atlantic skies. The trees in St James's Park that made me feel small when I walked beneath them. The enormous marble statue of Barbara that stood outside the palace to protect us. No one wanted me there, I remembered. I'd made sure of that.

We rumbled up the long drive and he parked his ute under the poplar trees. Out on the gravel, Ragu swooped into a deep stretch, yawned and trotted towards the cottage. We followed him in silence.

At the door, Jack paused. 'Do you want to come in? We can sit up for a while. I'll make you a drink.'

I shook my head and managed a smile. I could feel a bout of tears coming on and fought to hold them back. I knew if I started crying, some long-term debts I'd never settled would demand to be paid as well. 'I might try to sleep. But thank you. Again. For everything.'

Wearily, I walked down the porch, knowing that he was watching me go. Ragu plodded along the sandstone path beside me. I was the only one who let him up on the bed and, consequently, he spent his life trying to get into my barn. I waited for Jack to call him off.

'Lex,' he said, and I turned. A moth careened into the verandah light, casting fluttering shadows over his face. 'I don't know what happened tonight. But I meant what I said the other day. What you did – starting your life over, becoming a doctor – no one ever tells you how brave that was. You made yourself a real life. You're living it.'

I knew my eyes were wet and shining, and this time I didn't try to hide it. We stood under the dark stars, smiling at each other, believing there was still more time.

Somewhere in the Swiss Alps, flurries fell on a steep slope, snowpack quietly accumulating.

'He can sleep with you if you like,' Jack said, gesturing at Ragu, who leaned against my legs. 'For tonight.'

In my barn, I slipped gratefully into bed. Ragu nosed his way under the covers and pressed the length of his warm body against mine. I was smoothing his velvet ears when my phone rang. I opened the line, tethering us, even as the wall stood sentry between our beds. We said nothing for a while.

'Are you working over New Year's?' he mumbled.

'No, somehow I got the whole week off.'

I suspected Ben had arranged the roster that way, but there was no point wondering what he might have had planned.

'I was thinking we could go camping. Maria Island maybe? Can't beat the sunrise there.'

A new year, a new chance.

I smiled. 'Yes please.'

CHAPTER THIRTEEN

13 March 2023

It was one of those March days in London that brings with it just the slightest hint of spring, like a whispered promise on the breeze. There had been weeks of relentless rain. Then, on Commonwealth Day, we woke to find an impossibly clear sky.

The service to celebrate the Commonwealth was one of the most important events on the royal calendar, which every member of the family was expected to attend. The event dictated that we be publicly ranked in the pews according to our place in the line of succession. This year's service, our first family appearance since the funeral, was expected to be heavily scrutinised. After a childhood spent in the second row, I was now by Granny's side. Richard, Demelza and Birdie had also moved forward, taking the seats left vacant by Papa, Louis and Annabelle. In a move the *Daily Post* described as 'a touching but somewhat unorthodox gesture', Amira sat behind me.

Evicted from Elton Park, Annabelle had moved to Papa's estate in Scotland after the funeral. She wasn't in touch with anyone from the family, not even bothering to RSVP to the service.

The *Daily Post* ran a photo from the Abbey on its homepage: Granny, me, Richard and Demelza sitting solemn-faced in our pew. Poor Birdie must have been clipped out. The gap between

Richard and me would give body language experts enough content for a week's worth of interviews. The headline read: '*The New Royal Order*'.

Once we got home, I went straight to the bathroom to remove the bobby pins from my elaborate updo. Tucked into the mirror was a polaroid I'd found under the sink weeks earlier: Louis and Kris, their arms looped around each other. On the back, Louis had scrawled: *I wish everyone could know how happy we are*. In a different pen, Kris had added: *Maybe one day – after we're gone*. I kept meaning to move it. It was risky keeping it out in the open where a maid might pull it out and see the tender secret on the back. But I liked to imagine that Louis kept it above the sink where he could see it as he got ready for his day.

Just as I relieved the source of my tension headache, I heard the phone ring from the bedroom.

'Is that mine, Mary?' I called, plucking the tiny metal rod that was menacing my temporalis muscle. 'Could you answer it for me?'

'Princess Alexandrina's phone, this is Mary,' I heard her say in her phone voice, two full octaves lower than the way she spoke to me. 'Yes, one moment, sir.' To me, she called, 'It's Mr Jennings, ma'am.'

I looked at my reflection in the mirror and smiled. She would never call him Jack, no matter how much we both insisted. My hair free, I came out of the bathroom and took the phone.

'Hey,' he said, 'do you ever think the Commonwealth is just a way of keeping everyone in the empire under a new name?'

I smiled. He was never afraid to say things like this to me.

When dusk finally fell on the British empire, an ancestor transitioned this rapidly unravelling collection of colonies into a modern economic bloc. Fans of the Commonwealth say we are richer and stronger together. Critics call it Empire 2.0.

'Well, I don't know if it's that simple,' I said, one of the mealy-mouthed non-responses I had become very good at delivering after three months back home. 'I'm sure there's a way to acknowledge its colonial past but make it work better for everyone.'

'Ahh, so it just needs a better CEO then,' Jack said. 'You sure spend a lot of time in churches these days.'

'A weird place for a bastard love child to hang out,' I tried to joke.

For the past week, the tabloids had speculated about my and Louis's paternity, based on 'whispers travelling around the palace' that Mum had an affair with a doctor from Médecins Sans Frontières. Their evidence for this theory was a photo of an admittedly saucy-looking Mum seated next to a handsome young man at a charity gala in 1992. One 'royal watcher', who clearly had a sophisticated understanding of genetics, claimed that since this man and I were both doctors, we were obviously father and daughter. The doctor now lived in Angola and was refusing to speak at all – a strategy Mary thought prudent for everyone involved, though I knew for a fact that Mum didn't give up on the marriage and seek comfort elsewhere until I was thirteen. I could also point out that the shape and circumference of my hips marked me as a true Villiers woman.

'Tell me something that's happening at home,' I said, suddenly keen to change the subject. I lay on the bed in my dressing gown.

'Well,' Jack said, 'the harvest starts next week, so Ragu and I are up early. He caught a blackbird this morning, so he's happy.'

I could hear the gravel and leaves under his feet. The sun had just left me and was currently rising above his head. It was hard to believe he was 14,000 kilometres away when I could almost see him ambling between the vines, his full lips curving into a smile.

'What are you wearing?' I asked, realising too late the innuendo lurking in the question.

We laughed softly. Mary, who had been packing up my suit in the closet, made a swift exit and closed the door behind her.

'A very sexy outfit,' he said. 'I'm in Blunnies, which are getting a hole at the toe. And those jeans you keep trying to make me throw out. Ragu's wearing his collar and no pants.'

'Classic ensembles.'

'Your turn,' he said, his voice lowering to smokier notes that fanned the flames inside me.

'I was in this suit with a big hat,' I said.

'Was?'

'Well, the suit had to go back to the designer.'

'So you're just in the hat,' he said teasingly, always giving me an out, always sensing when we were drifting into territory I might find dangerous.

'Just the hat.'

In the days after the helicopter broke up our kiss, we barely spoke. Grieving and overwhelmed, I couldn't cope with the idea that my friendship with Jack might change too. So I'd panicked and avoided his calls for weeks. But once I had committed to spending some time in England, we eased back into regular conversation. He usually called when he woke just before dawn, which was dinner time in London. If I had an evening event, I would call him from bed, the phone on my pillow, just as it had been when I lay in the barn, his voice all around me as I tried to sleep. We talked about everything. Except what I planned to do at the end of the year.

'Do you remember when we went swimming at Wineglass Bay?' I asked, though I knew he remembered. He had still been with Georgia then, but she'd had a furniture show in Melbourne and couldn't come camping. After dinner, Jack and I went down to the beach alone, took off our clothes and strode through the waves so we could float where it was calm. Intoxicated by the moment, I forgot that I was scared of the night sea. I couldn't look at black water without imagining Mum slipping below. But suddenly I was up to my neck in it, looking at Jack, who was slick and glowing under the moonlight, and the fear returned.

Sensing it, he swam towards me. 'Want to go back in?'

I shook my head and breathed. 'Just give me a minute.'

Tentatively, he wrapped his hands around my waist to buoy me, ruffling the nerve endings under my skin. I eased closer, folding my arms around his shoulders, disturbing the droplets there, feeling the strong lines of his neck. We floated like that, quietly, until Jack's eyes darkened and he cleared his throat. 'We should go back in,' he'd said.

His voice brought me back to the present. 'I remember,' he said. 'Are you going to ask if I was thinking about kissing you then? Because, as I said, it's your turn.'

My stomach went warm, and I felt the old precipitous danger. 'You had a girlfriend. I didn't want to be that person.'

'No. Same,' he said, and then he laughed. 'I regret it now.'

'Don't ever regret being a good guy.' We were quiet for a minute, and I could just make out the fluty warble of the magpies on the vineyard. I felt a craving for home, even as I sat in the house I grew up in. 'What are you doing today?'

He paused. 'James is in town. I'm having a beer with him later.'

I nodded, even though he couldn't see me. James's disapproval of my decision to return to my family had been like a southerly buster, an icy wind blowing all the way to London from Tasmania. He did not return my calls and texts, only voicing his disappointment via Jack or Finn.

'Well, say hello for me, I guess.'

'I will,' he said.

There was a clatter of metal that I knew to be the bolt on the main shed.

'You're about to lose reception – I should let you go,' I said.

'I don't need to go in yet,' he said, and I imagined him settling on the old wooden bench outside. 'You're not worried about these tabloid rumours, are you?'

I thought for a moment. 'I don't think so. It's more that I don't know what Richard will do next. It's always waiting for the other shoe to drop.'

'Does he know … you know, about Louis?'

'No,' I said. 'Hardly anyone knows now.'

'Try not to worry, okay?'

I smiled.

'Are you really just wearing a hat and nothing else?' he suddenly asked, and I laughed.

'Just a hat,' I lied. 'Goodnight.'

'Good morning,' he said and severed the line between us.

I gave into my worst instincts and checked the news sites that were analysing my high-stakes performance of walking into a church, sitting through a service and walking out again. The outfit Mary had constructed for me seemed to have done the trick in shifting the conversation away from my paternity. Rather than the ubiquitous floral dresses favoured by royal women, she had pulled for me a menswear-inspired cream suit by Vivienne Westwood. We were a bit daring in using the waistcoat as a shirt, but, once paired with the oversized blazer and wide-leg trousers, no one could argue it was inappropriate for church. It was just weird enough to confuse the tabloids, while sending *Vogue* and the blogs into a spin.

I closed my phone. I was slightly embarrassed that, only months ago, I'd been diagnosing heart attacks and ordering MRIs, and now I seemed to spend all my time telegraphing secret messages through my outfits and staring at polling numbers that suggested Britons were still sceptical of me. Since January, my popularity had risen five points to forty per cent, but Mary seemed most preoccupied with winning over the swathe of people who described themselves as 'neutral' on my existence.

'The trouble is, no one really knows you,' she explained. 'You've been gone eleven years, and now we need to reintroduce you so we can build your support back up.'

Richard knew Granny had given me a year to make my decision and it wasn't long before the tabloids knew as well. There was an entire page on the *Daily Post* website called *Lexi's Choice*, filled with speculation about whether I would stay or go. There was even a timer in the corner, counting down the number of days I had left before my dithering must finally end. *Lexi's Choice* tracked my approval rating against Richard, who maintained a far more respectable figure of sixty-eight per cent.

It also kept a tally of our public appearances, sending us both on separate charity binges so we could top the leaderboard. Even as I dismissed the whole thing as ridiculous, I could feel myself longing to see my name edge above his in the rankings, the triumph that came when a lunch I hosted for International Women's Day briefly put me on top, the frustration when he packed his itinerary during a trip to Northern Ireland so that I slid back down again. We were gamifying charity and I was horrified to admit that I was becoming rapidly addicted.

Though we had successfully avoided seeing each other for weeks at a time, Richard's tabloid campaign against me was relentless. Last month, the *Daily Post* reported that I was self-prescribing semaglutide injections in a desperate attempt to be as slender as Demelza. There were rumours that the palace had quashed multiple malpractice suits against me in Australia, that I planned to evict Amira from Cumberland 1, that Granny's secret, ardent hope was that I would give up my place in the line.

But I didn't have the heart to retaliate. Louis and I had a pact to always keep each other's secrets, even as our own father leaked against us. Once I got down in the mud with Richard, I would never be able to get out again, something Mary couldn't seem to understand. We'd had an argument two weeks before when I refused to let her leak to the press that Richard had crashed the function I'd hosted for NHS care home staff.

'But he's doing it to *us*,' she had insisted.

'I don't give a shit,' I said. 'I don't do that. I never have, not once.'

She shook her head. 'I know you want to change things, but you can't do that until you have everyone playing by the same rules. The Duke of Clarence's office is briefing the media against you, and right now you're not giving them anything in return. You need to build relationships with reporters – you need to have a few of them in your corner. The media narrative is there to be shaped, and unless you grab onto it, you're letting Prince Richard chisel it into whatever he wants.'

She stopped and looked down both ends of the long hall to make sure no one was listening.

'This was your *biggest* mistake when you were in Australia,' she whispered. 'The Prince of Scotland painted you as some sort of deserter, and I was always astounded that you never fought back against us. You could have easily won over the public, if only you'd tried to bring a few sympathetic journalists onto your side.'

She had finally taken a breath and seen my face. I thought of all those stories that had flooded the front pages after I left. The jokes they had made as my body healed itself after years of deprivation. The way they had whispered about my state of mind, speculating about involuntary psychiatric holds and conservatorships. The unnamed Wolseley House aides who gave quotes to the tabloids about how selfish and spoilt I was, how much I had broken Papa's heart.

'Mary,' I said, 'when you worked for my father, did you brief the press against me?'

'No, of course not. I was a junior aide, I was there for social media only.'

'But you were there for those conversations.'

She hesitated. 'No.'

'It's okay if you were. That was the job. I'm just curious.'

In the three months Mary had worked for me, she seemed to have grown taller. She stood straighter, adding length to her spine, taking up more space in rooms where she was now the boss. But she shrank back down as I watched her.

'No,' she said meekly. 'I swear to you.'

I wasn't sure I believed her, and I thought briefly of what Annabelle had said to me at Watford Castle. *Watch out for Mary. She's not what you think.* But if I had to choose between the word of my stepmother, who had briefed the press against me whenever she needed to divert attention from herself, and the word of the junior aide who had sat in the room while these instructions were given, I would choose Mary every time.

So I had decided to leave it in the past, that strange territory that would probably always lie between us. I had given Mary permission to issue on-the-record denials whenever a reporter called to inquire whether I was an alcoholic, or a bully, or secretly married. But she was not to leak, and, if she did, she would be terminated as my private secretary.

'In a couple of years, when you have a proper power base, and the Queen starts giving you more duties, we can ban the family from leaking altogether,' Mary had promised.

At first, when she said these things, I would remind her that I was committed to one year only. But the more Mary talked of the future, the less I reminded her that mine was yet to be determined. As we planned out this new, modern monarchy that would require members of the family to be loyal and true, the more real it became in my mind.

*

When I came downstairs after the phone call with Jack, Amira was cooking in the kitchen with Vikki. Chino was getting underfoot, hoping someone would either throw him a scrap or kick the tennis ball he plopped down at strategic locations as they tried to move around him.

'Did Mary leave?' I asked.

'She said she'll be back at 7 am sharp tomorrow,' Amira said, cracking pepper over a bowl of foaming eggs. 'Meticulous Mary.'

'She's always been a strange girl, hasn't she,' Vikki said absently. 'But she does have a wonderful sense of style.'

She found me a spare glass and filled it up with a pinot from Alsace that was a little too sweet for my liking. I would need to ask Jack to send me a shipment of Jennings wine to get me through the year.

I looked at Vikki. 'I didn't know you knew Mary.'

'Mum,' Amira said sternly, gesturing at the eggs. 'Where's the salt? You're meant to be helping.'

Vikki put her wineglass down and went in search of the Maldon.

'Mary used to occasionally help with my styling,' Amira said to me. 'You know, if you're visiting a school or going to a concert, you need that Gen Z perspective.'

Vikki tossed a pinch of salt over the eggs and then picked up her wineglass again. 'You looked perfect today, Lexi darling, very chic, a little bit daring. This family mustn't know what's hit them.'

Clouds seemed to gather in Amira's face as she bent over her frittata mixture. I was conscious of two troublesome facts. One was that Amira would never, ever be able to break with tradition and wear trousers to church. Her missteps, even as mild as a skirt billowing in the wind, became week-long media catastrophes. She did not have the luxury to experiment like I did. If, like Birdie, she wore a hat shaped like a birdcage to church, it was not just meme fodder, but a symbol of her ill breeding. Worse still was the knowledge that I had taken her place in the family, consigning her to the seat behind me, the next page in the tabloid. She had once been part of the family's shining future but was now part of its tragic past. A widow with no children, there was no modern precedent for what to do with Amira. But Granny had always liked her, and she continued to invite her to family gatherings, which Amira dutifully attended. As long as she was sanctioned by the sovereign, her place in the inner circle was assured.

'What was Richard saying to you?' Amira asked.

'He was saying they're all coming to Scotland this summer.'

'Nightmare.'

Earlier that day at the Commonwealth service, when he sank down into the red chair between Demelza's and mine, his body oozing into my space, I'd stiffened, but smiled brightly as Mary had instructed.

'Uncle Richard,' I crooned.

'Lovely little Lexi, aren't you a knockout in that suit? Very KD Lang, I must say.'

'Oh, I'm sorry, I don't know who that is, but I'll assume it's a great compliment,' I said, laughing for the cameras. 'And where is Florence this morning?'

He grinned and unbuttoned his suit jacket. 'Migraine, unfortunately.'

'Oh, dear, she does have a delicate constitution, doesn't she?'

From the corner of my eye, I could see the BBC camera operator twist his lens towards us. As the final entrants to the church, we only had to make a minute or so of small talk before Granny arrived and the service would begin. But the seconds stretched out before me like an Olympic hurdling track.

'Hi, Lexi,' Demelza breathed, flicking her hair over her shoulder as she turned towards me. She was wearing a calf-skimming pastel coat dress. 'Are you bored of us all yet?'

'Impossible,' I said, leaning across Richard like he didn't exist. 'Every morning brings a new surprise, doesn't it?'

We spoke of the weather (finally turning), their plans for the summer (Mustique, followed by the Scottish estate), and the operas chosen for Glyndebourne's upcoming autumn season (honestly, fucking kill me), and then finally the organist's first notes rattled our rib cages and we could be quiet.

When the service was over, Richard, Demelza and Birdie glided past Amira without acknowledging her. Outside the Abbey, they walked by a Māori kapa haka performing, not even lingering to hear their song.

'That man is truly vile,' Vikki said as she rattled around in a utensil drawer. 'You know when we went to Scotland that time, he called me a cart tart?'

Amira covered her mouth to swallow her laugh.

'I don't think I can ever go back there again,' Vikki said mournfully. 'And it's such a shame, because I really loved it there.'

CHAPTER FOURTEEN

2009

Even those who hated going to Scotland for the summer couldn't help but be charmed by my grandmother's estate. She required all her prime ministers to visit for at least one weekend a year, something the public school boys loved and most Labour leaders and female PMs dreaded. But even for those who didn't relish the idea of spending summer shivering in long grass while trying to murder a beautiful stag, there was something about the Highlands. The scale of it humbles you. Its beauty is stark and honest. It's a wild place that demands you be wild in it.

When Louis and I were children, our annual Scottish pilgrimage was non-negotiable. But for our sixteenth summer, Papa relented to our incessant pleas to join the Shankars in New Zealand and the Cook Islands. In exchange, we had to spend the rest of our holidays with him in Scotland.

Mum planned to spend our first summer as a broken family drifting around the globe doing charity work and lounging on acquaintances' yachts. But she made sure to be in Edinburgh when we landed in the Highlands. Her plan was to drive three hours north to fetch us from Aberdeen Airport, make the sixty-minute journey to the estate to drop us off, and then return to the city alone.

'Mum, that's insane — we'll get someone from the estate to pick us up,' Louis had insisted.

But this was her tiny window in which to spend time with us before we were back at Astley for Michaelmas. Our Remove year was finally done and we were joining the ranks of the Hundred. The end of our school years felt aeons away, but I could tell that for Mum it was imminent. She was just thirty-six, had already survived a disastrous marriage and was nearly done raising two children. She was more beautiful than ever. But I sensed that the decades of life ahead of her were more frightening than inspiring. Papa was suddenly interested in enforcing the terms of the custody arrangement, and her time with us was strictly curtailed. For the first time since her childhood, she was alone. I felt a deep shame that I had negotiated with Papa to spend two weeks with my friends instead of Mum.

'Can I drive?' I asked, knowing that she loved to teach me things.

'Oh, dearest, I've had this bloody photographer up my arse since Edinburgh,' she said, peering over the top of her sunglasses and out the rear window of the car. 'Can you imagine what they'd say if they saw photos of me letting you drive without a licence?'

There were far too many indistinct cars lingering outside the airport for me to tell if anyone was trailing us, apart from our security detail. Louis thought she imagined it at least half the time, but after years of being hunted by men with long lenses, Mum had the reflexes of a Mafia don or an MI5 agent. Sometimes we'd be shopping or eating brunch and her sharp shoulders would rise. She would swivel her head around and say: 'Someone's watching us.' I never knew what to say because everyone was watching us, always.

'So,' she said, glancing in her rear-vision mirror as we swung out of the airport car park, tailed by our security officers, 'how was the holiday? Tell me everything.'

'Yeah, it was pretty good,' Louis said, his eyes hidden behind his Ray-Bans.

'What, that's all I get?'

'Kris and I went down a few double-black diamond runs on Mount Hutt,' Louis offered.

'That sounds a bit dangerous, dearest.'

'It's alright if you know what you're doing. Kris is the best skier I've ever met.'

From the back seat, I watched Louis's body language and listened to his intonation for clues. Trying to figure out what was happening between him and Kris had become a fixation of mine. Amira and I still avoided talking about it directly, only hinting at what we had seen up on The Mound. If it weren't for what we had glimpsed through the trees, I would have no idea they were anything but mates. During our time in New Zealand and the Cook Islands, Kris and Louis stayed in hotel suites next to ours. But their rooms were rank-smelling, chaotic messes, and they were always roughhousing and calling each other filthy names, and I started to wonder if perhaps boys just like to tenderly hold each other now and then and it didn't mean anything.

Mum grew quiet as we approached the castle gates. Our security officers had radioed ahead, so they swung open and Mum barely had to brake as we passed a clutch of curious tourists. After a week in the glorious sun of the South Pacific, I could feel the cold settling back into me. I didn't want to imagine Mum driving all the way back to Edinburgh alone. I didn't understand how this was preferable to our previous arrangement, in which Mum and Papa stayed apart at all costs, but no one had to spend summer alone.

At the main entrance, she kept her sunglasses on while she watched a house porter unload our bags from the trunk.

'Hi, Barney,' she said sweetly to the man, who blushed and bowed, even though she was no longer an HRH. She had a magical ability to hear a name once and retain it for the rest of her days. I was struck by the urge to ask Mum to come inside, at least for a little while. But I knew neither she nor Papa wanted that. The wound left by their separation was no longer fresh, but it festered and refused to properly heal. Granny had a coolly practical view of the whole thing and would see it as neither appropriate nor necessary for our mother to come inside.

'Well, my dear ones,' she said, opening her arms. 'I'll miss you.'

The three of us embraced for a long time. She was still bony in my arms, but she had lost the frailty of the previous summer. Deprivation had never been her style. She preferred to lose control entirely, black out for minutes at a time, gorge herself to the point of pain and then undo it all in the privacy of the bathroom. But when the divorce papers were finally signed, she seemed to stop eating altogether. Control had always been my preferred method, though I always seemed to yield to my titanic hunger by dinner time. Like everything else, Mum turned out to be far better at self-harm than me.

'Are you going to be okay?' I asked.

'Of course, dearest,' she said, sniffing a little and trying to cover it with her famous smile. 'I'll be in Edinburgh for the rest of the week, and then I'll be in Europe for a month. I'm so busy, it's ridiculous.'

'We'll be with you the week before school starts,' Louis reminded her.

She kissed both of us on the cheeks and climbed in the car. 'Be good for Granny!'

We were silent as we watched her drive down the long road, our lonely mother with none of the guard rails that kept her life moving forwards. Inside the castle, we learned that Papa had been 'detained by business' at his own estate and wouldn't be arriving for another few days, at least. I saw the hard edge of Louis's jaw set in a grimace, but he said nothing.

Richard and his girls had already been there for weeks. I barely knew Demelza and Birdie, who were twelve and ten at the time, but they grabbed the chairs on either side of me at the table and spent the whole evening whispering in my ear and fighting for my attention. I tried to keep my mind hazy on the long summer ahead. These holidays seemed to exist solely to wear Louis out with vigorous bloodsports. Meanwhile, I would be left to wander around, my little cousins trailing behind while I pretended not to watch the castle gates for Papa's car. Granny and Richard ordered us all to bed at 8 pm so we'd be fresh for stalking in the morning.

'Be ready to leave at 4 am, my boy,' Richard boomed at Louis, twirling his brandy glass. Our uncle had an almost masochistic drive to make a man of my brother. As the heir, Louis was more important than all of us. So Richard delighted in doing things like pushing him face first into cold water while we fished. When we were five, Richard had forced Louis to break a grouse's neck when the birdshot had failed to kill it. I'd always made a point of avoiding my uncle, though he didn't seem to notice. I was no one to him.

The week passed this way, Louis's participation in stalking and fishing mandatory, mine optional. I walked the moors and read fashion magazines in the library with the girls. Demelza, who wore denim cutoffs that showed off the crease of her prepubescent arse, did everything she could to give Birdie the slip so she could have me to herself.

'I told her we'd meet her on the terrace, so she won't know where to find us,' she snickered.

Demelza seemed to have been born sophisticated and mean. Fully grown adults found themselves vying for her approval. Our great-aunt Beatrix had a quick and devastating tongue, but even she steered clear of little Demi when her eyes narrowed and her mouth quirked into a grin.

I sighed. 'Let's go get her. We can't let her spend the whole day alone.'

Demelza groaned. 'God, you're lame.' She rolled her eyes but did as I said.

Louis, who was up before dawn every morning, sank into sofas in the afternoon and promptly fell asleep. Papa's unavoidable business up the road spilled into a second week. After ten identical days, a red stag with fourteen points was spotted a few miles from the castle. Eager to lose my little shadows, I trudged to the car in the blue morning light to join Richard and Louis for the hunt.

I did not enjoy killing animals, no matter how much Richard, the stalkers and the ghillies insisted that it was not only tradition, but conservation. They said we needed to keep the deer population under control, but there was something about an animal's wild eyes when the bullet pierced its flesh, the way its herd abandoned it to the humans who planned to bleed and strip it. When I was eight, Granny had told me about a wounded stag that had once stumbled over the moors for three days, travelling eleven miles, before it finally collapsed into a stream and drowned. I put my face in my hands and wept. But I did like being in the bracing northern air. If I joined the hunt, I mostly lay down in the heather and looked up at the sky while the others whispered and crawled around like boys pretending to be soldiers.

The stag was being hunted by everyone in the Highlands, but so far he was proving elusive. I imagined him hiding in the tall grass, standing perfectly still as men swung their rifle scopes right past him. Richard and the ghillies went further up the hill, while Louis and I were ordered to huddle between two smooth rocks on the slope. I picked at my cuticles while Louis kept a lookout, watching the horizon through his binoculars, just as Richard ordered. The relentless early mornings were catching up with him, dark circles under his eyes.

'When do you think Papa will get here?' I asked.

'I don't know,' he whispered.

My jacket was becoming wet in the sodden grass, but I still felt quite cheery to be with my brother on the blustery moors. A sunrise was blooming violet over the mountains.

'Do you think he's with Annabelle?'

Louis frowned at me and then returned his gaze to the binoculars. We rarely mentioned Annabelle by name. She was known only as 'her', delivered with a certain breathless intonation that left the other in no doubt who you were talking about.

'Probably,' he said quietly. 'But they're single now. They're going to see other people.'

'It's always been her, though, hasn't it? He's not going to see anyone else, because he never stopped seeing her.'

We fell silent. Louis obscured his face with his binoculars, but I knew he was gathering his thoughts.

'I think …' he said slowly, 'he loves her and probably always has. I don't know how he felt about Mum. It's probably easy to say now that it's over that he never loved her, but I don't think it's that simple.'

'Why didn't they just let him marry Annabelle?'

'You know why,' he said. 'The Catholic thing and the whole divorce thing. She was kind of old. I don't know, maybe he didn't fight hard enough.'

I thought of Louis's cheek resting on Kris's shoulder, his eyes closed, his face soft. I didn't want him to give that up.

'Do you think you'll fight?' I whispered.

He looked at me quizzically. 'For, like, a girlfriend or whatever? Yeah, I guess.'

'Will you fight for Kris?' I whispered into the heather, my heart lolloping in my chest. I had no idea what I was even doing, but I was suddenly terrified for him.

Louis stiffened so that the lines of his face were as fine as cut glass. He said nothing. Only the quivering muscles in his jaw gave away that he had heard me. After a minute of silence, he crawled over the rocks, slowly ascending the hill to join Richard on the peak. I lay there for a long time, buffeted by the stinging winds. Finally, a gunshot cracked overheard and echoed through the valley.

Louis avoided my eyes for the rest of the day, riding up front with Richard in the Range Rover, accepting the back slaps and praise of the ghillies for his exceptional shot – he had brought the stag down with a single shot through his heart.

After dinner, which was dedicated entirely to re-enacting every moment of the stag's demise, Louis disappeared to his room and kept his door closed. The next morning, I woke at dawn and looked out the window and there he was, marching wearily towards Richard, who insisted they pivot to fly-fishing for the rest of the week. Bereft, I went back to spending my days wandering the castle with Demelza and Birdie in tow. Granny's springer spaniel Pearl was pregnant, so we helped Granny prepare a whelping box for the birth, sitting on the floor shredding newspapers and taking stock of old towels. We discussed names for the litter, too, even though Granny had found homes for all the puppies but one, kept to ensure her spaniel's line continued alongside her.

Silence was the weapon of choice for our family, but it was one Louis and I rarely used against each other. Three days later, I was in bed, listening to the crackle of the fire, when I heard a knock on my door. He came in, looking wearier than ever. He was dressed in his Astley hoodie, and he sat on the edge of my bed, leaning against the Scottish oak bedpost. We looked at each other for a long time. I wondered if perhaps we would say nothing, but I should take his presence at the foot of my bed as forgiveness.

'Did you see us in New Zealand?' he finally asked.

'No,' I said. 'At school.'

He looked surprised. 'Where?'

'The Mound, after the spring dance.'

I watched the shadows and warm light from the fire dance across his face. He didn't look angry or frightened, only exhausted.

'Have you told anyone?' he asked quietly.

'No, but Amira was with me. She'd lost her coat and we went up to find it and we saw you dancing. But we haven't told anyone.'

He nodded and then leaned his head back against the post and closed his eyes.

'Louis,' I said, 'it's not a big deal.'

His eyes snapped open. 'Not a big deal?'

'I just mean … it's not a big deal to me, you know, if you like boys. That's cool – I don't care.'

He crossed his arms over his broad chest. 'Don't be naive, Lexi. It is a big deal, and you know it.'

I was quiet for a moment. 'Do you love him?'

He snorted, as if out of habit, and then his face became soft. How long had they been obscuring their soft hearts behind roughhousing and machismo? Our ancestor, one of the Edwards, felt the kind of all-consuming adoration for his favourite that saw him lavish the young man with silver and land. His obsession was so offensive to the court that Edward's father ripped great fistfuls of hair from his son's head. The favourite was exiled multiple times, but he and Edward could not be apart. On his fourth and final attempt to return to court, the barons kidnapped the man, put him on trial and beheaded him.

'You know, things are different now,' I said. 'At some point there's going to be a gay king, and they'll just have to deal with it.'

He blanched at the word. 'I don't know if I'm that.'

'Okay,' I said, feeling childish and out of my depth. 'That's okay too. Whatever you are, or whatever you want to be, it's fine.'

He snorted again, but his eyes were wet. 'Thanks. But you know it's more complicated than that.'

'If you told Mum, she wouldn't mind at all. You know that, right?'

It was suddenly important to me that he know that. I had no clue how Papa would react, and the prospect that he would ever find out filled me with terror. But Mum's devotion to us was like gravity. It was as dependable as the rising sun, the tick of the clock, the slow, relentless expansion of the universe. There was nothing we could do or say that would make her let go.

'I know,' Louis sighed. 'But don't tell her. She's got too much going on. We need to take care of her right now, not the other way around.'

The two minutes in age between us always felt like an era to me. I assumed that whatever he had gleaned about life in that sliver of time before my arrival had made him as sage and worn as an old man. When Mum was sobbing in the bathroom, it was Louis who put the music on loud in my bedroom and went to comfort her. When Papa and Mum were fighting again, he would take me for a long walk around Elton Park so I couldn't hear the insults they threw at each other. Now I wished he could be the boy he was supposed to be without the crown winking at him in the distance.

'How about we just … don't do anything for now? It's just you, me, Kris and Amira. Like it's always been,' I said.

He nodded, gazing at nothing. After a while he surfaced from the depths of himself and smiled at me. 'Yeah, okay.'

There was a rap at the door and Granny came in, wearing her burgundy dressing gown and slippers.

'Oh, you're here too,' she said to Louis brightly.

She was breathing a little hard, as if she had been running. Her face was glowing with excitement and adventure.

'Pearl has gone into labour,' she said to me. 'The first of the litter should be here within the hour. Would you like to join me while I help her?'

'Sure,' I said.

'Louis, you can come too, but you'll have to watch from the back. This is women's business,' Granny said as she left the room.

I pulled a jumper over my head and shuffled into my ugg boots. Louis was still on my bed, his arms wrapped around himself. He had a fragile look, like he had been crying a long time, and now he was sated and spent.

'Come on,' I said, placing a hand on his shoulder. 'It'll be fun.'

We hurried through the dark halls of the castle together, ready to stay up all night, just so we could watch new life burst into the world.

CHAPTER FIFTEEN

2 May 2023

An explosion of light filled the car as we drove past the pack of photographers and through the palace gates. Amira and I glanced at each other, remembering Mary's instruction: 'Engage in conversation and smile slightly when they get the car shot. You want something in between a big grin and a neutral expression. There's no photo more unflattering or more open to misinterpretation than a nighttime shot taken of you in a car.'

She wasn't wrong. In the early days of Louis and Amira, the overexposed photos of them in the back of black cabs, sweaty and exhausted after a night at a club, were positively seamy. When the tabloids were trying to cast my escape to Australia as a Britney-style breakdown, I learned that the photo taken of me at the end of the night was far more important than the one taken at the beginning. Finn and Jack would dawdle at the pub's entrance before we left, making small talk with the bouncer, while I powdered my face and brushed out my hair in the ladies' room for the drive home.

'Are you smiling slightly, my friend?' I asked.

'Just a smidge more than a neutral expression.'

A real smile broke out on my face as another flashbulb dazzled us. That, of course, was the photo they would use in the tabloids the next day, much to Mary's chagrin.

The state banquet for the Bahamian prime minister had been a year in the making. Every time I had visited Granny, I would see a bustle of activity: staff carefully laying out six crystal glasses for each place setting, using a ruler to ensure each seat was precisely forty-five centimetres apart, folding towers of napkins into Dutch bonnets. Granny had been tempted to call it off when Papa and Louis died, but she ultimately decided to persevere. The idea of their half-tailored tuxedos hanging limply somewhere on Savile Row was rankling me in the lead-up to the dinner.

Mary had started sourcing a gown for me the day I'd landed in London. She had spent the subsequent five months locked in quiet negotiations with Stewart and Granny over the medals I would need for the evening. As an absconder, I hadn't been given a single honour. Demelza and Birdie would wear the deep-blue sash that signified their status as Dames Grand Cross. Granny had bestowed the honour upon them on their twenty-third birthdays. I had spent the night of my own twenty-third vomiting off the roof of the Jennings shed, so my sash was still pending.

Ultimately, Stewart and Mary had agreed it would be far too conspicuous for me to become a Grand Dame Cross after a few months and the tabloids would rightly call it out. That was fine with me. Mum had been a royal woman for fourteen years, birthed an heir, endured the humiliations of Papa's indifference, and Granny still hadn't bothered to admit her. It would feel like a betrayal to wear the sash she was denied. But Mary had been able to secure for me a brooch that signified I was part of the Royal Family Order. Reserved for women and awarded entirely at the pleasure of the monarch, the brooch featured a tiny portrait of Granny affixed to a yellow silk ribbon.

The question of tiaras was a more vexed one. Stewart had thought it appropriate that Amira wear her wedding tiara and I borrow Mum's. According to tradition, royal women did not wear their first tiara until their wedding. But I was a dubious heir, pushing thirty and desperately in need of royal legitimacy, so Stewart bent the rules. However, once Richard got wind of the plan, he launched a sustained campaign to ensure the Clarence sisters were also given access to the collection. With the dispute threatening to spill into the tabloids, Stewart had quietly recommended to Granny that she dispense with tradition and give us each a sparkly plaything for the evening.

On the morning of the banquet, Mum's wedding tiara and my Royal Family Order were delivered to Cumberland 1 by a footman and two security guards. I sat with the tiara in my lap, remembering how, as a child, I had perched on the bed and watched Mum's stylist sew it into her hair for important events. I brought it to my face and inhaled, as if its glistening edges might hold her scent.

Now it was stitched to my own hair as we passed through the palace entrance. Our Rolls-Royce slowed to a stop and two footmen came forth to open our car doors. Amira and I were shown into the grand hall, where all the eyes in the room surreptitiously turned to look at us as we walked in. Five months back in London, and I was still an object of fascination to the people I'd once left behind.

Jenny Walsh was, as always, the first to approach us. She kissed our cheeks and smiled. Her business card was still hidden under my mattress, though I was yet to call her. She had less to do with the family than most prime ministers, but on the occasions I saw her, we seemed to fall easily into our own conversation.

'How's it going?' I asked quietly, trying to ignore the openly curious gazes of the people around us.

'Well, this is definitely not my scene. But it's all part of the job, isn't it?' She looked at us. 'You both look great. These things always make me feel rather frumpy.'

'Nonsense, Prime Minister,' Amira said. 'If you saw the armies of people who dress us, you'd think us ridiculous.'

Amira's gown for the banquet had been ordered and tailored months before she had toppled down the ranks of the family:

a simple white Emilia Wickstead column dress with a draping train that would fan out behind her when she walked. The gown was positively bridal and, as a new widow, she had considered wearing something else. But she didn't want to let down the designer, and Mary reminded her that almost every royal woman chooses white for formal occasions because it doesn't compete with the sashes and military stars that garnish their outfits.

Since I would only have the yellow-ribbon brooch to hide behind, Mary was determined that my dress should stand out. She'd found a young Bahamian designer who had delivered to Cumberland 1 a flowing aquamarine dress the same colour as the nation's flag.

As guests poured into the hall, Jenny was pulled away from us, and people began to drift towards me, curious and eager to chat. Working in hospitals had only enhanced my command of the art of small talk. Encountering people on the worst day of their lives, distracting them while I popped their shoulder back in its socket, sitting with an older patient who had no visitors – this was where I shone.

After Amira and I chatted to an emerging cookbook author, a nightmare Tory MP and several members of the Bahamian delegation, I suddenly felt a presence at my side. It was a very tall man, about my age, with a swirl of red hair. He bowed solicitously.

'Your Royal Highness,' he said, 'I have been instructed by the Queen to personally escort you to the ballroom for dinner.'

'Is that right?' I asked.

I could tell by the way he wore his tailcoat as easily as if it were a fuzzy dressing gown that he was an Eton boy. The Patek Philippe on his wrist shimmered in the candlelight. He had blue eyes and a friendly smattering of freckles across his nose.

'Knock it off, Colin, would you?' Amira muttered.

His solemn expression dissolved into a grin, and he leaned forward and kissed Amira on both cheeks. 'How are you, darling? Her Maj really did send me over here, you know.'

'Lexi, this is Colin.' Amira sighed. 'He's one of Louis's vile friends.'

He waited until I offered him my hand and then he shook it.

'We've actually met before, you know,' he said. 'You whacked me across the head with a croquet mallet when we were children.'

I could finally place him: Colin Bellingham, the Earl Amherst. His father was the Duke of Hereford, and therefore one of the richest men in Britain. Colin's family owned tens of thousands of acres of land, including the prime London suburbs of Mayfair and Belgravia. When his father died, Colin was set to inherit the whole £10 billion fortune over his four older sisters. At the age of seven, I had lost my mind when he pulled my skirt up during a game of croquet.

'Well, that's what you get for showing everyone my knickers,' I said.

'I never did apologise for that, did I?' He held out his elbow as the pipers began to play, signifying it was time for dinner. 'Allow me to escort you to your seat, ma'am.'

I took his arm. It was a state banquet tradition for a man to escort a woman down the long hallway to the ballroom. Amira was making the walk with the Bahamian finance minister, while I could just glimpse a bored-looking Demelza in a one-shouldered silver gown on the arm of the Lord Chamberlain. The official palace photographer held the shutter down as the couples streamed by.

'So,' Colin said, 'how is it being back in town?'

'I don't get to see much of it, I'm afraid. I feel like I spend all of my time behind the walls of the palace.'

'Well, that's not entirely true. I see you on the front page of the *Daily Post* every other day. Weren't you dancing with schoolkids in Hackney last week?'

'That's some highbrow reading you're doing,' I laughed.

Mary had been particularly happy with the Hackney school visit, which culminated in a dance session in the assembly hall.

I had thought nothing of joining in – what else are you supposed to do when little kids ask you to dance with them? But I could see in Mary's face on the drive home that she was nervous about how my antics would be received. That afternoon, the *Daily Post* had published a photo of me doing the twist with an adorable boy in glasses, my hair swishing around my shoulders. The next day, the photo was picked up by most of the UK broadsheets, and by the week's end it was the cover of an American gossip magazine.

It was a surprise to discover that I might be good at these things. I'd once believed that such abilities had passed through me like a recessive gene, flowing instead to Louis, so that all the warmth, all the charm, all the magic of our mother was possessed by him. Even more surprising was the possibility that I might like doing it.

Colin and I reached the doorway to the ballroom, my arm still through his as the photographer trained his lens on us.

He leaned in close to my ear. 'I swear, I usually stick to the broadsheets, but I take a peek at the tabloids now and then to see what you're up to.'

I felt heat rise in my cheeks. We were among the final couples to enter the room, just ahead of Granny and the Bahamian prime minister, Edward Knowles. A hundred and seventy guests standing behind their chairs stared openly as we walked by them. When we reached the head of the table, I stopped and Colin bowed again. After a battle between Mary and Richard's officer over who would be seated next to Granny, the head of the table had been arranged by rank, with the result that I – Granny's heir – was placed in Papa's old seat to her left. Richard had ended up two seats down on her right, sandwiched between the British and Bahamian prime ministers.

Colin grinned and leaned forwards. 'My seat's quite a bit further up the horseshoe than this,' he whispered. 'But we're all going to Demelza's cottage after dinner. I hope to see you there.'

He turned and walked away before I could respond, finding his seat next to Amira and smiling back at me over the candelabras. Granny glided past her guests with Prime Minister Knowles, and the room was totally silent as she took her seat and got herself settled. Then there was a collective exhalation, the orchestra began to play and everyone sank into their chairs.

After the toasts, a line of pages in red coats entered the ballroom carrying plates, which they placed before each guest in perfect unison. Once the entrée was served, guests relaxed a little and began to engage in polite conversation. The Bahamian prime minister's wife, Sonia Knowles, was to my left. As it turned out, she had been a virologist in Miami before her husband entered politics. We discussed India's newly achieved status as a polio-free country and breakthroughs in mRNA vaccine development.

'And if you stay in England, will you return to being a doctor, Your Highness?' she asked me.

I picked at the steamed halibut before me. 'I'm taking a year off, but there is always a possibility I could finish the final year of my residency here.'

'A junior doctor in the NHS who is also heir to the British throne,' she said, smiling like she had a secret.

'We're not sure exactly how or where I could practise,' I admitted. 'But I would like to try. Right now, I'm just taking a break.'

'Yes, I remember that first year off – how nice it was to rest. It was only meant to be a year for me as well.' She smiled enigmatically again and sipped from her water glass. 'Now it's been fifteen.'

I chewed carefully and swallowed. 'Whatever happens, I would like to dedicate my life to public health. Either as a doctor … or a monarch.'

She shrugged. 'The republican movement is very strong in the Bahamas these days, so who's to say whether you'll ever be our head of state.'

'I understand.'

'But either way, I would watch your reign with interest.'

A fleet of lamb rumps was placed before us with military precision. At the sight of the main course, Granny turned towards me with a sigh. She always spent the first half of a meal conversing with the guest of honour on her right before switching to the person on her left. Papa had once told me the nicest gift he could give Granny in these moments was a little chat about dogs and horses. Five months after the death of her son and grandson, the luminosity of her face was returning. But she continued to wear black, and I suspected she would remain in mourning for the rest of her life.

'How is Chino's training coming along?' she asked.

'I've got to be honest – he's still sleeping in my bed.'

'Oh, dear girl, no.'

'And he still pulls terribly on the lead. I let him off at Richmond Park the other day and he chased a herd of deer around for fifteen minutes.'

Granny tittered behind her hand. The official photographer, who was standing in the centre of the horseshoe, surreptitiously snapped a shot.

After coffee and dessert, the pipers glided into the room; their deafening song signalled that the meal was over. Granny rose, prompting all the guests to get to their feet as well. I always marvelled at her serenity in moments like this. She was unhurried as she gathered her purse and signalled for the Knowleses and me to follow her from the room. An undulation of bows and curtsies moved through the crowd as she passed.

In the grand hall, Granny shook hands with the Knowleses, said goodnight and left me to see them out of the palace. Sonia took my hands between hers.

'I will pray for you as you make your decision.'

'Thank you,' I said, and watched as she followed her husband to their waiting car.

I wondered if she had kept up with her virology literature after fifteen years outside the lab. I was still quietly studying.

With no more hospital rounds to occupy my sleepless nights, I had been reading medical journals by lamplight. But perhaps I'd eventually miss a few papers, and then it would become easier to let the discoveries accumulate on my bedside table. Eventually I would be a scientist in name only.

The hall swelled with people as the guests made their way out of the ballroom. I had arranged with Amira to meet behind the main staircase so we could make a quick getaway. Moments later, she appeared on Colin's arm.

'He wants us to go to Demelza's house,' she groaned.

'Yeah, come on, let's go,' Colin said.

I hesitated. 'I don't know.'

Demelza and I had spent the past five months pretending the other didn't exist. If I passed her in the Cumberland quadrangle, she would nod at me, her gaze landing somewhere left of my face. Sometimes I would arrive at the palace for an audience with Granny only to find Demelza and Richard by her side, teacups perched on their knees and smirks on their lips. Mary was convinced they somehow knew my schedule and were inserting themselves into Granny's calendar in the hope their social calls would roll into our official business. They were rarely invited to stay on for our meetings, but the tabloids were always told otherwise.

'Oh, come on,' Colin said. 'It'll be fun.'

'Yes, you should come,' Demelza said, suddenly turning the corner and appearing before us. She looked me up and down. 'Everyone's invited, especially my dear cousin.'

I gave in and nodded. My days were spent in the presence of greying courtiers, most of whom seemed to disapprove of me. I wore pantyhose and drank tea. I saw London from the window of a speeding town car. The idea of some mindless conversation and a few drinks with people my own age was appealing.

We had our driver meet us at the back entrance so we could avoid the photographers waiting at the gates. How ridiculous we must have looked – three girls in tiaras and a boy in tails squeezing into the back of a Rolls-Royce.

'Oh, shit, we forgot Birdie!' Demelza screeched as the car approached the gates of Cumberland.

'Shall I turn back, ma'am?' the driver asked, alarmed.

'No, she'll sort herself out. Onwards, driver.'

Demelza's cottage was among a cluster of buildings on the outer edge of Cumberland Palace. With three bedrooms, it was considered one of the humbler abodes available to family members, but it had the best view of the gardens and could be accessed without passing through the inner quadrangle, meaning that, unlike Amira and me, Demelza avoided the older relatives who watched our every move. The house had clearly been styled by an interior designer, with antiques borrowed from the Royal Collection Trust interspersed among the trendy pieces ubiquitous on every rich girl's Instagram. But the place was a mess, with piles of clothes everywhere, teabags mouldering on saucers and three mismatched stilettos on a stained marble coffee table. A baby-pink Ultrafragola mirror was badly in need of a spray and wipe.

'Jesus, Demi, get a cleaner in here, would you?' Colin said, pulling bottles of Bollinger from the fridge.

She stuck her tongue out at him as she tossed her heels and flopped onto her couch. The doorbell kept ringing as all the young people from the banquet arrived, still dressed in their gowns and tails. Had there been a group chat? Had Colin and Demelza whispered the plan in the ear of every guest who looked under thirty-five? Birdie was the last to arrive, dressed in her big blousy Erdem gown, which looked like an old lady's floral bedsheet on her.

'You *forgot* me,' she wailed. 'I had to get a lift with a staffer from Number 10. I was wearing a ballgown in a Ford Focus.'

Demelza, now half in the lap of a man on the couch, tried to hide her laughter. 'Sorry, darling, it was utter chaos, and I thought you'd want to go home with Daddy.'

As people came to say hello to me, I realised I had met most of them at one time or another. Whether it was from Pony Club or parties at Elton Park, nearly every name and face resurrected a long-forgotten memory.

Soon Colin came over with two glasses of champagne. 'How are you doing?' he asked. 'You're looking a little overwhelmed.'

'No, I'm fine. It's just I can't believe how many of these people I know.'

Amira was crouched by an open window with a cigarette between her lips, chatting to two women I recognised from Astley.

'Ours is a tight circle,' he said and sipped his drink. 'All our parents know each other. We all went to school together, and we've all shagged each other – or assaulted each other during an innocent game of croquet.'

'I'm still waiting for my apology. The kids called me Frilly Knickers for about a year after that.'

He laughed. 'No, look, I am sorry. I think I was just trying to get your attention. If it's any consolation, Lou stole my clothes during swimming practice a few days after that, and I had to wander around school in my Speedos trying to find them.'

A wave of loss rushed up around me. In spite of myself, my eyes became wet. Colin looked into my face and placed a gentle hand on my shoulder.

'Sorry, it must still be raw.'

'I actually love hearing things like that – stories about him I've never heard before. We weren't really in touch for the last couple of years. I don't even really know if he was happy at the end.'

He nodded. 'He seemed good. Though it was difficult to tell with him, you know? He always made me think of a mosquito flying over water, just kind of brushing the surface.'

I thought of my brother's unfathomable depths, the secrets he had been drowning in.

'Growing up as the heir ... I think that was hard for him,' I said.

'Yes,' he said. 'And now it's you.'

I shook my head and looked at the crowd, feeling like I was sinking into something I couldn't name. 'It was meant to be him.'

I drained my champagne flute, immediately regretting my words. I was confiding in a man I hardly knew, who was close to the one person who wanted nothing more than for me to board the first Qantas flight out of here: Demelza. The *Daily Post* had an entire team of reporters dedicated to covering my every move, and here I was, at a party where people were spending a suspiciously long time in the bathroom.

'Sorry. Don't tell anyone I said that.'

He smiled. 'Don't worry about that. You know we used to call Lou "Brian" so if anyone overheard us, they'd think we were just talking about someone else? You're safe here.'

I glanced at Demelza, who was watching us from her seat on the couch. Somehow she'd been able to get her tiara off her head, even though it had been stitched in like mine. Now she had it looped over her shoulder. Colin followed my gaze and then turned back to me with another smile.

'You don't have anything to worry about there,' he said.

'Didn't you say you read the *Daily Post*? Where do you think those leaks are coming from?'

He paused, as if gathering his thoughts, or perhaps choosing how much to share. 'Sometimes it's the courtiers behind all the drama, not so much the people they serve. They're the ones climbing the greasy pole.'

I thought of Mum, who had spoken endlessly of the 'grey men in grey suits' with paranoid fervour. At the end, she had insisted they were tapping her phone and using location trackers on her car, though I was never sure whether to believe her.

Amira appeared by my side. 'I've got to get this bloody tiara off. I'm going home.'

'I'll come with you,' I said.

Colin put his champagne flute down on Demelza's dining table, between shoeboxes, shopping bags and a half-eaten pear.

196

'I can walk you home if you like,' he offered.

'Colin, we're a hundred steps up the path,' Amira said, massaging her fingers into the crown of her head. 'Ask for the girl's number and say goodnight.'

He and I smiled at each other as Amira went to say goodbye to Demelza and the rest of the crowd in the living room. He pulled his phone from his pocket, and I put my number into it.

'You can talk to me, if you like,' he said. 'I know that was hard for Louis – trusting people.'

'Thank you.'

I was quiet as Amira and I teetered home on our aching feet in the crisp spring air. Even though I had grown up beneath the London stars, they were now foreign to me. At night, I looked up expecting to see the flickers of Carina, Crux and Centaurus, and every night I found the sky scrambled and unfamiliar.

'Do you think you'll go out with Colin?' Amira asked suddenly.

'What? I don't know.'

'Because you talk to that farmer twice a day?'

'He's not a farmer, he's a winemaker.'

'I think Colin's a good match for you, really,' she said, ignoring me. 'It makes a lot of sense: a future queen and a future Duke of Hereford. He's got his own inheritance – perhaps even more than you're in for. He understands this life, he's comfortable in it. I see why she got him to escort you tonight. That's the kind of match she'll support. She'll never let you marry a farmer.'

My cheeks were growing hot. 'You sound like one of the insane old women in a Jane Austen novel.'

Amira shrugged as we walked past Cumberland 3; the remodelling had been completed two weeks prior. Neither of us had yet discussed the possibility that I would move in.

'Those women weren't wrong, especially for people like us – well, you. Not me anymore. But you've got to get married and stay married and produce an heir. That's your job.'

We were a few steps from the door and I was desperate to go inside and crawl beneath my duvet.

'What about …' I faltered and said nothing more.

'What about what? What about love?' Amira said, stopping to look at me.

There had come a point many years earlier when she had stopped being honest with me. We didn't talk like this anymore. There was something frightening about the look on her face, triumphant and ready to fight.

'Have you ever been in love?' she asked.

I thought suddenly of Jack, his big hands and his relentless cheer. When we first met, he'd confided in me that he had once spurned the vineyard. He looked at his father's vines and felt the cordon of his own life creeping forward, every tendril that might take it in a surprising direction pruned back. And so he left. He went overseas for a year and then he wound up on James's sheep station. But the longer he had been away from the grapes, the more he yearned for them. He loved that stretch of earth like it was a part of him.

'I don't know,' I huffed. 'Have *you*?'

'No,' she said immediately. 'Do you think love is what makes marriage work?'

'My parents—'

'Love wasn't the problem for your parents – it was compatibility.'

I looked up at the strange sky to stop the tears from rolling down my face. It was an accusation I had heard many times – that it had all been Mum's fault, that she'd been naive and wanted too much and should have known better. If she had tolerated Papa's obsession with Annabelle, if she had dimmed her own light so it glowed just enough to shine on him, if she hadn't been so sensitive, she would be alive today and she would be the future queen. I had heard it all. I'd just never thought Amira and Louis agreed.

I was really crying then – for the first time since I had returned to London. I walked past Amira and left her standing in the quadrangle. All the windows around us were dark, but we knew better than to assume no one was watching and listening.

'Lexi,' she whispered. 'I'm not trying to be cruel, I promise. I just want you to open your eyes.'

CHAPTER SIXTEEN

2 0 1 2

According to the tabloid version of our lives, the trouble between Louis and me began the night before I flew to Australia. There are two books about our severed bond: *Royal Twins* and *This Is Not What Isla Wanted*. In public accounts, the story follows a familiar script: Louis and Amira had fallen hopelessly in love during our Upper Sixth year, but when I'd discovered them kissing (according to *Royal Twins*) or chastely holding hands (*This Is Not What Isla Wanted*) or shagging (various tabloids), they had insisted it was just a fling. Right before we were all meant to go our separate ways for our gap year, I had learned their relationship was far more serious than I had been led to believe. Rather than waiting six months to reunite in South Africa, as we had planned, they intended to travel the world together as a proper couple. I had been so offended by their duplicity, or so jealous in unspecified ways, that I'd immediately decided to move halfway around the world. It was clearly a storyline fed to the writers by Somerset staff, and I did nothing to correct it, even though it made me look demented.

But here's what really happened.

The tabloids had largely obeyed the palace's order to leave us alone until we had finished secondary school. But once we turned eighteen, the media collectively decided they were free to break their promise. They began to speculate about our sex lives, basing their wild conjecture on our body language in blurry photographs taken through long lenses. I didn't give them much to work with: trapped under the crushing weight of Mum's death, all I knew how to do was study and starve.

That term, I joined the rowing club. I liked the idea of an all-consuming sport that required dawn starts, burning lungs and enough cardio to whittle my body down to nothing. One day our boat got bogged in river silt, and a photographer hidden behind a public toilet block snapped a picture of a crewmate's brother taking my hand to help me onto shore. The *Post* declared him my 'crush' and camped outside his family's house for a month. The poor guy is still described as my 'first love' in articles about my romantic history, even though we barely spoke.

Kris had finished at Astley the summer before us and spent our final year doing officer training down at Sandhurst. Once the rest of us completed our schooling, Kris and Louis would take their gap year together. But as we counted down the days and weeks until we were free, Louis and Amira started heading into London on weekends to sneak into clubs. Astley policy stated that all students, regardless of whether they were of drinking age or not, should stay out of licensed premises. But no one was going to punish the heir – especially since he had just lost his mother.

One night, which I spent staring up at the ceiling in my suite, the three of them went to Madame JoJo's in Soho, where a fellow clubber surreptitiously took a photo. It showed Louis, tall and sweating through his shirt with his arms around Amira's peplum-accented waist. His face was in the crook of her shoulder and, with his heavy-lidded eyes and parted lips, it gave the impression of unbridled teenage desire. In the background, I could just make out Kris's shoulders as he turned away from them. But for the public, the photo was confirmation: the future king had a girlfriend.

The next day, when it was on the front page of every news site in the English-speaking world, they had both laughed and said Louis was simply asking Amira what she'd like from the bar. I don't think it had occurred to him until he saw the photo that this was something he could do: occasionally give the tabloids a morsel of heterosexuality to feast upon so they would never make him the meal. He and Kris kept their love for each other a secret from everyone but Amira and me. They held hands in front of us; they were tender and true. We assumed our parents had no idea, although there was something in Vikki's sly eyes that gave me the sense she was starting to see what everyone else missed. The fact that she read the tabloid rumours about Amira and Louis, but never demanded the truth from either of them, was surely a sign.

As the end of our Astley days grew near, the tabloid fanfiction went into overdrive. Louis had always maintained a certain mystique at school, so none of our classmates could confirm if he was dating Amira. But given how much time they spent together, it made a certain sense. If Amira and I went to his rugby match, a photographer made sure to get a picture of her looking proud in the stands. They captured her enigmatic smile as we watched Louis march in the Astley Tattoo. They went to the school leavers' ball together: Louis resplendent in his tuxedo, Amira in a turquoise Marc Jacobs gown seen on Sienna Miller three months earlier. I took Kris as my date so he and Louis could be together, but he spent most of the evening glowering across the table at my brother.

We sat our final exams. We packed up our suites. We smeared shaving cream and confetti on every surface. We were finally done. Now it was time for our gap year – twelve months that were wholly our own.

We had broken our year into two halves. We planned to spend the first six months apart – I would go to Australia, Amira to Europe, and Louis and Kris to South America. We would then come back together for the second half in Africa. I never mentioned to any of them that Uncle James and I had spent the better part of a year working on a plan that meant I would never actually show up for this reunion.

Even as I emailed James daily, my secret plan to stay with him in Australia never felt quite real to me. It was a game I was playing with myself, a fantasy I enacted with the help of props.

At worst, I would bail on the volunteer work in Queensland and cause a minor rift with Papa by spending six months on James's farm instead. I fully expected that I would lose my nerve and show up at the Shankar lodge by January. I thought I knew myself well enough to be sure of that.

Three days before we were due to go our separate ways, we were in Amira's room, helping her sort through her mountain of clothes. The boys were being no help, lounging on Amira's bed and using her pile of clothes as a pillow, their heads nestled together among the mess as they looked at their phones. I was always the organised one, and I sat on the floor, rooting around in an overstuffed suitcase looking for her missing passport.

'I need chic outfits for France,' she said, pulling a top from underneath Kris's shoulder. 'But then I'll need practical outfits for Africa, which feels like an entirely different packing approach.'

'You're coming back here for Christmas,' Kris muttered. 'Just repack then.'

I finally found the passport lodged inside a sneaker and pulled it free.

'Here it is,' I said, holding it above my head.

'Lexi, you're a lifesaver,' she exclaimed.

She took the passport from me, but as it changed hands, a folded piece of paper tucked in the sleeve slipped free and fluttered into my lap. Absently, I picked it up, intending to pass it to her as well. A word in the top-right corner caught my eye: *Santiago*. I don't know why I looked. I had barely paid attention to Louis and Amira's antics all year, but one glimpse of the city's name and I understood everything. I unfolded the document, an itinerary, and read it top to bottom. Amira was due to fly from Charles de Gaulle to Chile in a month.

'What is this?' I asked, staring at the paper.

Louis and Kris looked up from their phones. Amira, who was by her desk, turned and saw what I was holding. There was a brief flash of panic on her face, but she quickly brightened and snatched the paper from me.

'Oh, nothing … That's an old itinerary from when the travel agent mixed up our bookings.'

I watched as she folded it back up and slipped it beneath a pile of travel books on her desk. She was feigning casual indifference, but the set of her shoulders gave her away. I looked over at Louis and Kris, who had both returned to staring at their phones. The room was heady with conspiratorial tension. I had been so consumed by grief in the last year that I'd barely been aware of what was happening around me. I felt like the glossy black bubble I'd been trapped in had just been pricked with a needle.

'Are you going to Patagonia?' I asked, but she didn't turn to face me, continuing to shuffle things around on her desk. 'Amira?'

Louis and Kris were supposed to fly south to walk Patagonia in a month. It was all they talked about. Lakes so pure they reflected the snow-capped mountains like a mirror. No one would know them there. They could be themselves within its unfathomable beauty.

'Amira,' I said again.

'Just tell her, you two,' Kris moaned.

Amira turned and looked at Louis. They had grown close that year, with Kris at Sandhurst and me present in body but utterly gone in every other way. I was aware that my brother had lost his mother as well, and that I was not being a good sister to him.

I looked at Louis. 'What are you doing?'

He hesitated, keeping his eyes on Amira, as he decided what to say. 'Amira's going to come for a bit when we go to Patagonia.'

'And why would Amira do that when she hates exercise and the outdoors?' I asked, turning to look at her.

Her head fell forward so her face was obscured by a curtain of hair. 'I'm just doing them a favour, Lexi. I go, they get a picture of me and Louis together, everyone thinks we're an item. It's just misdirection.'

'And how long do you plan to do this for?' I asked Louis, ignoring her. 'Are you going to pretend Amira's your girlfriend forever?'

'What do you want me to do, Lexi? Come out to the world?' He sat up but refused to look at me. 'You know I can't do that.'

The question of coming out was one we'd discussed often after that first conversation at the Scottish estate. Louis, who'd had far longer to ponder the issue, was set in his belief that it was impossible. But I was desperate for there to be a way. I had even surreptitiously pulled a few books on UK constitutional history from the Astley library, hoping to glean some wisdom from their pages. We had learned as children that our kingdom had no written constitution. If that were true, then how hard could it be to declare that the boy who would one day be king had no need for a queen? But no matter how many shiny crowns we wore and how many balconies we waved from, ours was an institution built on ruthless conservatism. If Louis came out as gay, it would trigger a crisis in the church and the state. I had no doubt it was a fight worth having, a fight we could win with a groundswell of public support. But it was Louis's choice, and he didn't want to be the one to do it.

'There's a thousand girls in London right now who'd grind up on you in a club,' I said. 'Why do you need to use Amira? You know what's going to happen, don't you? Have you read a tabloid recently? Have you thought about how all this looks for Amira if you get found out?'

'Hey,' Amira said sharply, 'I can look after myself.'

Amira now appeared on the *Daily Post* website every other day, whether she was walking into Maddox Club with Louis or shopping on Old Bond Street with Vikki. She was quickly becoming one of the most famous girls in Britain, described by the tabloids as 'exotic' and 'ethnically mixed'. A right-wing MP caused a mild furore after he claimed Amira could not be trusted because she wasn't 'British'. A breakfast television host wondered aloud if we should expect her to wear henna on her hands if the relationship with Louis went all the way to Westminster Abbey. His co-host responded that at least their children would 'keep a nice tan all year round'. With their relationship neither confirmed nor denied by the palace, the royal household remained silent on all the hateful things being said about the woman shielding the heir.

'Lexi,' Louis said, 'you said you'd support me no matter what.'

'I didn't mean something like *this*.' I looked at Kris, who was still lying in the chaos of Amira's bed. 'Are you really okay with this? Were you part of this? Or was he talking your little sister into this when we weren't looking?'

'Hey,' Louis said. 'That's enough.'

Kris considered me coolly, his phone now placed against his chest. His feelings on our predicament had always been a mystery to me.

'It's so easy for you, isn't it, Lexi. You have no idea what it's like for any of us. No matter what *you* do, you can just go running to Daddy and he'll clean up all your messes, won't he?'

An unbearable stillness filled the room. Hurt beyond words, I looked to Louis, but my brother still would not meet my eyes. We had made a pact of secrecy, and I thought that meant something. More than our twin connection or our tragic mother, I believed it was our secrets that bound us. I dared not look at Amira, because if he had told her my secret as well, I wouldn't be able to bear it. It had once been the four of us. But now he needed them more than he needed me.

Blindly, I rose, grabbing my backpack as I left. No one called after me. When the lift opened on the ground floor, I found Vikki walking through the front door, huge sunglasses on her face and a row of orange Hermès shopping bags on her arm.

'Oh, darling, are you off?' she asked. 'I thought you and Louis were staying for dinner.'

'I have to go,' I muttered.

She put her bags down on the floor and gently took me by the wrists. In the year since Mum's death, I had veered between craving and avoiding Vikki's touch.

'Do you know what's going on up there?' I asked, suddenly furious. 'Do you know what they're planning?'

'Lexi, what do you mean?'

I hesitated, still bound by my vow to Louis, even if he was not. Finally I spoke. 'Amira's going to fly to Chile to be with Louis in the summer.'

'Yes,' she said, unsurprised.

A maid was lurking on the steps behind us, wondering whether to come collect the shopping bags or make herself scarce. Vikki shooed her away.

'Yes,' she said again, pushing her sunglasses to the top of her head and staring into my eyes. 'It's a beautiful thing she's doing for her brother.'

I gaped at her. 'You know.'

'Yes. For a while now.'

'And you're okay with them using Amira like that?'

She dropped her head for a moment, thinking. She was so calm that I realised she must have known about Louis and Kris for far longer than I might have guessed. Had they gone to her seeking advice? Had she known before Amira and I did? She was the first person I would go to if I had an unsolvable problem. But then I realised that wasn't quite right. The first phone call I had made was to Papa.

'My son is a gay British Indian boy who's in love with the future king,' she said. 'If that becomes public knowledge, it'll be difficult for everyone. But do you know how awful it will be for Kris? What they'll say about him? What they'll do to him? Amira can protect him.'

'But what about *her* life?'

Vikki took me by the hands again. 'This is not forever – it's just for a little while. And I know that you're savvy enough to see how it would help her prospects to be linked to your brother.'

I wanted to shake her. Everyone wanted to join the swirling nebula of our family. No one seemed to realise there was a gaping, insatiable black hole at its centre. By the time they were trapped in our orbit, it was too late to free themselves.

'Vikki, this entire plan depends on Louis and Kris breaking up, and everyone going on with their lives. What happens if they stay together?'

She smiled mournfully. 'I don't know. I haven't thought that far ahead. My son is in love with someone under impossible circumstances. I'm doing my best to protect him.'

'You're doing that at Amira's expense,' I said. 'You said it was up to me to look out for her. I'm telling you. This is a mistake.'

Vikki brushed my cheek, and it was then I realised I was crying. 'Darling, I know you're thinking of your mum right now, but this is different. Amira has a family to protect her.'

I thought of Mum: a motherless girl whose father had often forgotten she existed. When they had found her body, she was floating in a huge nest of sargassum. That's why the search took so long – they didn't notice her at first, nestled among the seaweed. I couldn't stop thinking of her long, dark hair intermingled with the algae. Would things have ended differently if her parents had loved her enough?

'I can't be a part of this,' I said and opened the Shankars' front door.

'Lexi,' Vikki called as I hurried down the steps and onto the street, my security detail giving chase to keep up with me. 'What are you planning to do, Lexi?'

But I was already running. I didn't stop until I was in Tasmania.

CHAPTER SEVENTEEN

10 June 2023

'Don't wave so much, dear girl.' Granny sighed as our carriage glided down The Mall beneath two rows of plane trees, now lush and green as spring edged towards summer. The Band of the Grenadier Guards led the way, clashing their cymbals and beating their drums, but we could still hear the crowd lining the road as we passed. 'You were the same as a child, constantly flapping that hand around.'

I returned my fingers to my lap. 'Sorry. It's hard not to get carried away,' I said.

Granny gave her famously fluttery wave, which Louis always said looked like she was changing an invisible light bulb.

She smiled at the crowd. 'Yes, they are rather nice, aren't they?'

Trooping the Colour came every June, filling central London with a sea of red tunics, horses, Union Jacks, regiments and brass instruments. The parade is a birthday gift from the Household Division to the monarch and culminates with a flypast by the Red Arrows, who leave a smear of red, white and blue through the sky.

Much to Richard's consternation, Granny had invited me to ride in her carriage down The Mall. Instead, he had to lead the procession on horseback, swaddled in his army regalia with a black, woolly bearskin atop his head. Mary declared the day a draw, since we'd both walk away with a winning photo opportunity.

'Are you enjoying your time back home, dear girl?'

I was surprised by the question. No one had asked me that before. 'Yes, Granny, I am.'

'You must miss your life in Australia.'

I thought of the cottage, smoke rising from the chimney, making it look like the cosy storybook house it was. I missed its jasmine-covered walls, the firewood chopped and stacked under the eaves, all our boots jumbled together by the door. I missed working on the wards and then coming home, Jack greeting me with a smile and a glass of pinot. The simple little life that I'd believed to be hopelessly complicated was just a memory now.

'I miss my friends,' I admitted. 'And I miss the hospital.'

'You should invite your friends to visit. I like being in the company of young people,' she said. 'As for the hospital, well ...'

In the emergency department, chaos reigned, and it was up to me to restore order. I missed the stench of bleach, freshly opened packages of gauze and the iron scent of blood. I pestered Finn for photos of the injuries he was treating. I kept feeling the phantom shiver of my pager on my waist, even though it was no longer there.

'Before I became the heir, I dreamed of being a horsewoman,' Granny said. 'When I was twelve years old, I watched the first woman compete in equestrian events at the Olympics, and I turned to my parents and informed them I would be a rider in the next Games. Of course, four years later, we were living in the palace. It always struck me as ironic that a horse killed Uncle Albert and changed our fates.'

The horse drawing our carriage was a black-brown mare named Lady Macbeth. She had a velvet muzzle and two white stars between her eyes. Before we had set off from the palace, Granny had fed her a sugar lump to thank her for her service.

'Do you ever wish it had worked out differently?' I asked.

'One can ride, and one can reign,' Granny said. 'I was lucky in that regard. It's more difficult to treat the sick from a throne, I admit.'

We both fell silent and waved to the crowd for a while.

'When it comes to our great ancestor, Barbara Villiers,' Granny went on, 'most remember her beauty or her ambition. Many believe she wanted power for power's sake, but she really did enjoy being queen regent, you know.'

Granny was a scholar of the family history. She knew Barbara so well, at times it felt like she had conjured her to sit at the table with us.

'She demanded religious tolerance at a time of great division,' Granny said. 'And she was a lover of the arts. She reopened the theatres and the music halls that had been closed down by the puritans. Barbara left her mark.'

'Is it true her groom tried to assassinate her by spreading poison over the horn of her saddle?'

'Yes.' She laughed lightly. 'But she caught him, and from then on, she made every groom lick her saddle and her boots before a ride.'

Through the trees, we could just glimpse the great marble statue of Barbara that stood outside the palace. Before it was the monarch's official residence, the building was a grace-and-favour home bestowed on Barbara by her son. But the place was so grand, so beloved by the people, that when his mother died, King William moved in and made it the centre of British power. He commissioned the statue in her honour, surrounding her with carved cherubs, as well as the angels of truth, justice and motherhood.

'I think what made Barbara special for so many people was that no one ever doubted she wanted to be queen,' Granny said. 'I'm not sure what people look for in their king, but in a queen, everyone wants a mother. And do you know what children want from their mother? Complete sacrifice, total devotion. Every single one of us, at one point, expected to be the centre of our mother's world. People feel the same way about their queen.'

I focused on the twitch of Lady Macbeth's ears, the sleek power of her muscles as she pulled us behind her.

'Does that ever make you feel ... suffocated?' I asked quietly.

She looked at me and smiled. 'A mother never feels suffocated by the love of her children.'

We were quiet while I contemplated this. I wasn't sure whether I wanted my own children, let alone millions of them. It was hard to summon the bravery for parenthood when I knew how tragically it could end.

Granny gave another wave, and the crowd erupted. 'I've been meaning to discuss something with you. In November, the palace holds a reception for a charity that isn't one of our usual patronages. It's a chance to lift up a worthy cause that otherwise struggles for the spotlight. This year was meant to be Louis's turn, but I thought in his absence perhaps you would like to take it over.'

Since I'd been home, I had pledged to fulfil Papa's and Louis's calendars, honouring their commitments and making sure their patronages weren't left in the lurch. I'd never been able to choose my own cause before.

'I'd love to.'

'Very good.'

'Which charity did Louis pick?'

'We never got that far,' she said. 'But rather than doing what your brother would have wanted, I suggest you think about the things that matter to you. Have your office contact Stewart when you've decided.'

Once Lady Macbeth pulled us to a stop in the palace's inner courtyard, we went up to the Central Room, where the rest of the family was assembled for our appearance on the balcony. Richard was standing before a gilt mirror in his crimson tunic, frowning at himself as he tried to fluff up his hair, which had been flattened by his bearskin. I gave him a wide berth, heading for Amira at the other end of the room. She had already looped the length of The Mall in a carriage with Birdie and Demelza, and the three of them stood murmuring to each other, looking like hand-painted Easter eggs in their pastel suits and hats.

Amira smiled as I approached them. 'How was it?'

'Apparently I wave too much.'

Birdie started rooting around in her clutch. 'I have your phone. It didn't fit in Amira's bag, so I carried it for you.'

Granny forbade phones in her carriage, leaving me no choice but to toss mine to Amira before we set off. Birdie held it out to me and smiled.

'You get a lot of messages from boys,' she said admiringly. 'You must teach me your ways.'

'Colin texted you,' Demelza added with the quirk of a bladed brow. 'And some Jack character also texted to say he's out late tonight, so you should call him when you're free.'

I snatched my phone from Birdie. When I shot a dark look at Amira, she only shrugged.

'I can't exactly wrestle the phone out of their hands when we're hurtling down The Mall while the BBC watches our every move, can I?'

Amira and I had reconciled after the state banquet, but there was still a slight distance between us. It was clear that we were unable to discuss the past without one of us being gripped by rage and the other being deeply hurt. After our fight, I had offered to move into Cumberland 3 so we could have space from each other.

'But what about Chino?' Amira had asked in a small voice. 'He thinks we're a family now.'

I thought fleetingly of the little family I had made for myself at the bottom of the world. But family was the one thing I had in short supply, so I stayed. Every morning, Amira and I ate breakfast together and took Chino to the park to wear him out. After that, I went off to the meetings and engagements that used to be hers and Louis's responsibility, while she did Pilates or visited Vikki. I gently suggested that she perhaps reach out to her patronages or even start a foundation for young people dealing with loss. She gave me a polite, if enigmatic, smile.

'I will,' she said. 'Just not yet.'

I was trying to keep her busy, but her new favourite diversion seemed to be the mess I'd made of things with Jack and Colin.

Ever since the state banquet, speculation that Colin and I were a couple had been feverish. The images of us walking arm in arm towards the ballroom made us look like an inevitable bride and groom. But it was the picture taken as he escorted me to my seat that had become a tabloid favourite. He was beaming down at me while I gazed up at him with my mouth parted and pouty. I looked positively feral in my low-cut gown, ready to pump out a bunch of his aristo babies. The day after the banquet, I had woken to a dozen texts from Finn, most of them a cascade of fire emojis and question marks.

Who's the hot ginge????????? he wrote above a link to a *Daily Post* story with the headline, '*Sparks fly as Princess Lexi openly FLIRTS with UK's most eligible bachelor, Colin Bellingham, who will one day be a Duke worth BILLIONS.*'

There was also, I noted with alarm, no text from Jack that morning. It was the first day since I had returned to London that I didn't wake up to a photo of Ragu, or an update from Jack's day.

Omg lol, I had responded to Finn, mindful he would relay this message back to Jack. *That's just one of Louis's friends. I don't really know him. He was awful to me when we were kids. I bashed him over the head with a croquet mallet once.*

EVEN HOTTER, he wrote back immediately. *Enemies to lovers, my fave x.*

I had been tempted to keep going with my denials, but I knew Finn loved nothing more than revelling in the drama of someone else's life. Exhausted, I'd stuck the phone back under my pillow, pulled the duvet over my head and languished there for the rest of the morning. By nightfall, I was still hiding from Amira in my room. I finally relented and texted Jack: *What are you doing?* But I didn't receive a response and went to sleep feeling friendless, repulsive and alone. Jack was not a game-player. He had been raised in a house where people said what they meant and went to sleep with their disagreements sorted and their consciences clear. The Jennings farm was a weird place for me and Finn. We had grown up in homes where the only way to voice your displeasure was to go so quiet that your silence was like a scream.

The next day, I'd awoken to a notification from Jack: a photo sent without comment. It was Ragu lying on the gravel road. It took a few days until the tenor of our conversation returned to normal. By then, Colin was texting me too. It had started with a few photos of Louis from their junior school rugby days. *Found these the other day. Thought you might like them*, he wrote. I responded to thank him, and from there he began to text me every other day.

'Look at you, stringing along all the boys,' Amira had said a few weeks later when we were friends again and she watched my phone pulse with messages from Hobart and Belgravia.

'I'm not stringing anyone along,' I said, worried that I was, in fact, doing exactly that.

'String Colin along all you like, he's a nightmare,' she said, sipping her wine. 'But you might want to be more careful of the farmer's feelings, don't you think?'

'He's not a farmer,' I muttered. I had talked Amira into letting me make spaghetti bolognese for dinner – with proper pasta instead of zucchini noodles – and the sauce was giving me trouble. 'Also why do you hate Colin?'

Amira looked surprised. 'I don't hate him.'

'You just said he's a nightmare.'

'Oh, well he is. I mean, he's *fine*,' she'd said, her face twisting in contempt. 'He's just kind of a nightmare for women.'

She hesitated and then looked away.

'One time he was seeing a girl in our circle, but after a few months he met someone else. Rather than break up with her, he just brought the new girl to a dinner party at our house. So we had to sit through a whole meal with Colin and his new girlfriend on one side of the table and the poor woman he'd been sleeping with on the other side.'

'Jesus,' I said, though I hadn't been particularly surprised. It sounded like any other dinner party at a Norfolk estate – Elton Park included.

'Anyway, I wouldn't worry about that if you like him. You're the big prize – he's not going to screw that up.'

Surrounded by my family in the gold leaf and brocade opulence of the Central Room, I glanced at my phone and saw that Colin had invited Amira and me to his family seat for a weekend over the summer. Jack had texted as well, but I decided to save those messages for when I was alone. I was wedging my phone in the waistband of my skirt when Stewart appeared in his charcoal suit, a sedate pocket square folded like origami at the breast.

'Make sure that phone doesn't make an appearance on the balcony, ma'am,' he said gently. 'When you're out there, stand to Her Majesty's left. And try to smile.'

'I won't cry this time, Stewart, I promise.'

We smiled at each other. Louis and I had made our balcony debut at the age of three, but I was so overwhelmed by the carpet of people before me, followed by the scream of the planes overhead, that I had burst into tears, and Mum had to take me inside. The next year, Stewart had arranged for the balcony to be opened up the night before the parade so he could lead me onto the narrow stone ledge and describe all the things I would see the next day. Together, we watched the night traffic swirl around Queen Barbara's memorial, the workmen setting up barricades for the people who were coming to see us in the morning, and Stewart explained that there was nothing to fear. I'd never really got used to the feeling of all those eyes on me, but with his help, I always managed a smile and a wave.

Now it was time for my first balcony appearance in three years, and when a footman pushed the doors open, the wind tumbled through the sheer curtains, bringing with it the murmur of a thousand voices below. Granny led us into the light. As my eyes adjusted, I saw them all before us, a huge mass of people just beyond the gates, climbing up onto Barbara's marble lap for a better view, filling the parks and the roads, the horde accumulating so far down The Mall that I could hardly see where it ended. Everyone was always happy to see Granny. But the roar of this crowd rolled in like thunder, so loud I could feel their voices echo in my chest. Startled, I glanced at Richard who was standing on the other side of Granny. I wondered if perhaps everyone had become far more vocal in the years I'd been gone, but I saw surprise on his face as well. Demelza and Birdie beside him looked astonished.

There were Union Jacks fluttering in people's hands and tears in their eyes, and I understood that they were enveloping us in their love, as they would any family who had lost all we had lost. Amira was standing to my left. When she took my hand, our eyes met, and I saw that tears were tracing down her cheeks. The summer solstice was approaching, the Earth's relentless grind around the sun almost halfway done. We'd made it to the tipping point of the year without Louis and Papa, fumbling through it, fighting and reconciling, trying every day to be better. I squeezed her fingers hard and smiled through my own tears.

Later, the press said that while Granny was clearly moved by the outpouring of support from her subjects, unlike the rest of us, she refrained from crying. But I was standing by her side that day, and I saw the tear caught in her lashes, the bobbing of her throat as her subjects shouted her name. For the first time, perhaps in my entire life, I saw what she meant to these people, and what they meant to her. I understood why she could never possibly be suffocated by their love.

*

When the parade was finally done, a light lunch was served in the drawing room, but I slipped outside for a moment alone and headed straight across the lawn for the sunken garden. Hidden from view by hedges on all sides, I stepped within its whispering green walls and took off my heels, wandering along the terraces that descended to a stretch of chamomile lawn, satin soft under my bare feet.

It was midafternoon in London, which meant it was creeping past 1 am in Hobart. Jack had texted to say that he was out late with Finn, but I doubted he was still awake. The yearly vintage had just been completed, which always left him exhausted. He would now be spending all his time in the winery, crushing, pressing and fermenting grapes, somehow turning those enormous vats of fruit into something special.

I pulled my phone from my skirt and dialled his number.

'Hey,' he said in a sleep-roughened voice.

'I woke you up.'

'No, you didn't.'

'Sorry, I thought you might still be awake. Go back to sleep. I'll talk to you later.'

I heard the rustling of blankets. 'I was going to watch you do the balcony thing, but I must have fallen asleep. How did it go?'

I sat on the grass. 'Usually I hate doing it, but it was nice, actually. Emotional.'

'Let's switch to FaceTime, I want to see you.'

'No, I have hat hair.'

But he had already sent the video chat request, and I found that I wanted to see him too, so I tapped the accept button. He was lying shirtless in bed, with sleepy eyes and his messy tumble of hair, and I tried to ignore the flush that started in my stomach and seemed to drift downwards. We smiled at each other like idiots.

'I haven't seen you in so long,' I said.

'I see you everywhere. I go to buy groceries and your face is on every single magazine at the checkout. Go on, show me your dress.'

I stood up, leaned my phone against a pot of lavender and stepped back so he could see me in my white skirt suit, with my hair ironed so flat I barely recognised myself.

'I look silly.'

'You look good. Different, but good.'

I scooped up the phone so I could have him gathered in my hands again. 'I'm the same old person.'

We looked at each other for a while in the light pools of our screens, and it was almost like I was curled up in the bed beside him. I so rarely went into his room that I was unfailingly curious about it. Whenever I found myself in there, I quietly inhaled as many details as possible. I had an odd temptation to rifle through his drawers until I uncovered all of his secrets.

'Where did you and Finn go tonight?' I asked.

'Just to Poobah for a bit.'

'*You* at the Grand Poobah?'

He smiled, adjusting the bare arm folded behind his head, distracting me. 'Well, what else am I supposed to do when you're not around?'

It occurred to me that he might meet someone on these nights out with Finn, that he could be talking to other girls already. He had every right to do so, even if it caused a hot bubble of jealousy to rise up in my gut.

'Tell me what you've been doing,' he said. 'What's your approval rating at now?'

'I don't know, forty something,' I said, as if I didn't know it was precisely 48.8 per cent. How I ached for it to reach fifty, the moment the British people were officially split on my character.

'Well, get the people doing the survey to call me next time, and I'll give you full marks. That's sure to bump you up a percentage point.'

'Full marks?' I said doubtfully. 'What about how I'm always leaving my washing on the line, and you have to bring it in for me?'

'I'd still give you a ten out of ten.'

'What about how I let Ragu lick the plates?'

'Ugh, you're *right*, your fatal flaw. Okay, nine out of ten.'

The sun finally broke through the clouds and warmed my already pink face.

'I have to think of a worthy cause,' I said. 'In November, they want me to host a reception for a charity that doesn't get enough attention.'

He smiled, but it was a strained smile, and I realised that by November, I would have been in London for almost twelve months. Sometimes, the end of the year felt like the sheer drop off a dark cliff. Either I would crash-land or float to the ground.

'Who are you going to pick?'

'I don't know. It's the first time I get to choose something, and now I can't seem to think of anything.'

He thought for a while. 'What about that place you went when you were a kid? The hospital in Africa that helps women after childbirth. It's perfect. It's everything you care about, and the hospital probably needs the support.'

I stared into the phone, wondering how he could possibly remember that. When had I told him? Four years ago? Six? Probably it had happened on a long bushwalk when we were trudging across weatherbeaten plateaus, my feet aching, all civilised small talk exhausted a few kilometres back, so that the real conversation between us began to unfurl.

Whether we were walking through a dripping rainforest, or wading along the shores of Narcissus Bay, I had told him about the time I went to Kenya with Mum to visit a hospital that treated obstetric fistula, a horror pregnancy complication that ruined the lives of millions of women in sub-Saharan Africa. While we were there, a fifteen-year-old girl had burst through the doors of the hospital, and she wept when the staff said they could help her.

That was the moment I'd decided to be a doctor. It was why I'd always planned to choose obstetrics as my specialty when my residency was done.

'Can I ask you something?' I said to him.

'Of course.'

'And you have to be honest.'

'Okay.'

'Would it not be better that I finish my training and then go volunteer at that hospital? Wouldn't that have more impact than just throwing a party to raise awareness about it?'

Jack's parents were legendary protesters who had saved a pristine waterway from government greed. I couldn't imagine that he would ever think charity functions were a worthy use of my time.

But he shrugged. 'Both options make the world better. You're a great doctor. But when you speak, the world sits up and pays attention. So maybe you just need to decide which one would make you happier. Sometimes you just have to choose.'

I nodded.

'I'll come,' he added. 'In November, I'll come to the reception thing. If you invite me, that is. I mean, I can't make a huge donation or anything, but I'll be there if you want me to be, and maybe ...'

He trailed off, and I saw that he was nervous.

'Would you?' I asked.

'Yeah.'

'You'll come to London in November?'

'Yeah.'

We exchanged fluttery smiles. Until Granny had mentioned it, I'd never considered that I could just ask him to board a plane and come see me. In five months, he might be standing among all those men in ties and tails, out of place among the British establishment, but warm and solid by my side.

'Okay,' I said. 'That means I've picked a charitable cause, and I've put someone on the guest list.'

'Good.'

I was tempted to ask that he leave the line open while he slept, so that whenever I wanted to see him, I'd pull my phone out of my pocket and find him there, steeped in shadows, his eyelashes fanned against his cheek.

'I should let you go,' I said finally. 'It's late.'

'Okay.'

'I miss you,' I said softly, and then realised the truth had slipped out. 'And Finn. And Ragu. I miss you guys. Is the cottage a complete frat house without me?'

He smiled. 'We're doing okay, but it's not the same. We miss you too, Lex.'

Reluctantly, we said goodbye, and I was alone again in the sunken garden. I ran my fingers through the daisy-studded grass. The UK's maternal death rate was the highest it had been in twenty years. Pregnancy was four times deadlier for Black Britons than white. Up to 100,000 people worldwide suffered an obstetric fistula during childbirth every year. I might never help deliver a baby again, but there were other things I could do with my time.

Maybe.

I needed time to examine it from every angle, like a jewel placed on my palm.

CHAPTER EIGHTEEN

12 July 2023

I stood on the sun-warmed deck at the Hampstead Heath ladies' pond and yawned. It was still early, just after 7 am, and there were only a few women in the water. A family of ducks glided through the light shards scattered across the surface. You weren't really meant to take pictures but, when the lifeguard wasn't looking, I snapped a photo of the scene and texted it to Jack. Then I strode to the edge and tried to decide what was the order of the day – lowering myself slowly by the ladder or jumping straight in. I was feeling bold, so I leapt from the deck. The ponds were never particularly warm, even in July, and I had become addicted to the clean slap the water gave me, the tiny victory of plunging myself into unknowable depths.

Once I was in, my heart steadied and my blood seemed to cool, and I rolled onto my back and drifted towards the centre of the pond. My new protection officer, Rita, lingered on the deck with her thermos of tea. Scotland Yard had been slightly annoyed by my recent ritual because it meant they had to find a female officer to come with me. But they managed to rustle up Rita, who didn't seem to mind the assignment too much.

'Beautiful day,' I heard a voice say behind me.

I turned to see a woman paddling by, her white hair tied in a knot at the crown of her head. She had blue eyes and a marvellously lined face. She was radiant in the way only older women could be. Age enriched her beauty.

'It's perfect, isn't it,' I said.

Like all women-only spaces, the pond had a convivial atmosphere, and it wasn't unusual for people to chat to me. With wet hair and no makeup, I was barely recognisable anyway.

'I started coming here in 1978,' she said, treading water.

'That's amazing. Has it changed much?'

She shook her head. 'The trees are a bit taller, the swimming costumes are skimpier, the water's not quite so cold in the winter, but not really.'

'I imagine that consistency is nice.'

She smiled at me like she had a secret. 'You know, your mum used to come here now and then. I don't think anyone realised it was her. You look so much like her, I got quite the shock the first time you swam past me, I must say.'

I looked at her in surprise. My memories of Mum were like papery flowers pressed in the pages of a book, and suddenly here was a decadently scented, dew-dropped rose picked fresh from the garden. She must have come out here after the divorce, when she was occasionally forced by the custody arrangement to spend time without us. She was still the little girl who'd wandered into the scullery of Kilchurn Castle and charmed the kitchen staff into letting her sit by the warm oven and chat to them.

'Thank you,' I said, as I always did when someone told me something I had never heard about Mum before.

The woman winked at me. 'Don't worry. I never told anyone about your mum coming here, and I won't tell them about you.'

I smiled at her, and then she kicked her legs through the water with the grace of a frog and was gone. I floated for a bit longer, feeling the sun on my face. The pond was formed by the headwater springs of the River Fleet, a secret waterway that flows underneath the city. The water that had buoyed Mum was long gone, seeping into the River Thames and out to the raging North Sea. But I couldn't stop imagining that the same water she had swum in now cradled me too.

Then I remembered how she had died. Stinking, rotting sargassum had wound through her hair like a crown, while scavenging sea creatures nibbled on her hands and feet. The springwater surrounding me suddenly gave way to the stinging brine of the Ligurian Sea. My skin was no longer clean gooseflesh, but swollen and blood-flecked from a thousand sandfly bites. The friendly mallards weren't ducks at all, but gulls prepared to pluck out my vacant eyes.

I was overcome by the desperate urge to get out of the pond, and I made my way back to the deck with efficient strokes.

'Are you all right, ma'am?' asked Rita as I climbed the ladder.

'Yep, fine! I've just got a busy day.'

It was the Wimbledon women's semifinals and I was due in the Royal Box to watch the match at noon. If I was late for the makeup artist, who was likely arriving at the house within the hour, Mary would be annoyed at me. But Rita's father had been a cabbie for forty years, so she knew how to get us anywhere in London in thirty minutes. When I opened the door at Cumberland 1, I was greeted only by Chino's galloping paws and the whirr of Amira's hairdryer coming from her bedroom. Mary was leaning over the kitchen island, tapping on her phone, and hardly looked up.

'You're late, Your Highness,' she said mildly.

'I beat the makeup artist, didn't I?' I called from the floor where Chino had me pinned so he could nuzzle my face.

'You've got pond hair,' she said, typing away. 'Go shower and I'll have the makeup artist attend to the Dowager Duchess first.'

I managed to wrestle free from the dog's frenzied attention so I could make my way upstairs.

'Oh, and congratulations,' Mary added. 'We cracked fifty.'

I stopped and turned. She was still tapping at her screen, trying to keep a neutral expression on her face, although I could see that grin of hers tugging at the corners of her mouth while she tried not to gloat about my improving likeability score.

I walked over and gave her a high five. She smirked, holding up her hand reluctantly, though I could see her eyes were sparkling.

'Thank you, Mary,' I said. 'Only half the British population is suspicious of me, and that's entirely due to your efforts.'

She smiled and turned back to her phone. 'Actually, only twenty per cent are truly suspicious. The other thirty just aren't sure yet. But we'll get them in our column soon enough.'

Almost everyone wonders how much people like them, but very few have it quantified down to the decimal point. It was hard not to become fixated on the number and the many ways it could be shifted. I was not a politician who could simply enact good policies. I couldn't give charming interviews like a celebrity. My job was only to be. Winning back the favour of the British public was a lengthy process that might take the rest of my life. Focus groups suggested my critics could never forgive that I once shirked my duty to the family. 'Selfish' was a word that came up a lot. I pointed out to Mary that people had used the same word to describe my mother, along with 'vulnerable' and 'hysterical'. Now she was revered, even by people who were too young to remember her when she was alive.

'There's only one way to get numbers like Princess Isla, ma'am,' Mary said, unmoved.

It was true. In death, Papa finally got the one thing he had always wanted: the adoration of the British people. He was easy to admire once they didn't have to endure his lectures, his cantankerous nature or his devotion to the woman he loved instead of the woman they loved. Louis, who had been cherished from the moment he was born, was well on his way to sainthood. Our young king who never was.

The Wimbledon match was part of Mary's strategy to demonstrate that my family had welcomed me back. When

Amira and I were offered tickets, Mary had suggested that I invite Demelza and Birdie along as well. The tabloids adored a 'young royals' story, and we were guaranteed the *Daily Post*'s front page. My relationship with the Clarence girls had thawed over the last few months, but I would hardly describe them as my friends. And while Demelza now had enough information to cause some serious damage to my reputation, none ever emerged. I could never decide whether that meant she could be trusted, or that she was smart enough to know I would be able to trace it back to her.

Once I was showered, dressed and made up, I met Amira in the car. I was in a navy and white striped shirt, tucked into matching trousers that could almost pass for pyjamas. But with a pair of stilettos, the outfit was effortless and tailored. In every public appearance, Mary insisted that one element of my outfit read as slightly rebellious – a bending rather than breaking of convention. This time, it was a vivid red lipstick, which had never been expressly forbidden for royal women but was rarely worn.

'How was the pond?' Amira asked. She was in a white sundress and a black YSL logo belt, sure to make Demelza curl her lip in disdain. Most royals preferred to buy a belt that looked like it came from Marks and Spencer but actually cost £1000.

'Nice,' I said. 'You should come with me one day.'

She guffawed. 'Never.'

We set off down the gravel drive, beneath the old oak trees that formed a rustling canopy over the palace entrance in summer.

'You know who'll be there today, don't you?' Amira asked.

'No.'

She looked at me, something hard and gleaming in her gaze. 'Colin.'

'How do you know?'

'He texted me this morning to ask if you were coming.'

I leaned back against the headrest and swallowed. We hadn't seen each other since our disastrous visit to Colin's country estate that ended with me making a mistake in a library and Birdie slipping over in her own blood. And now we would be reunited while the world's media watched.

*

A few weeks earlier, Amira and I had driven up to Lincolnshire in her Range Rover to spend the weekend at Colin's family seat. I was used to lavish homes – I was Papa's daughter after all – but Lutton Hall was unlike anything I had ever seen before. It was twice the size of Elton Park, and the main home had been demolished and rebuilt several times since the fifteenth century to ensure its architectural lines remained fashionable. The estate had its own chapel with a 55-metre clock tower; there were turrets, arched windows and an enormous two-storey library. I had never been there before, but when I heard my footsteps echo through the cold stone cave they called a drawing room, I remembered that Papa had once described the Bellingham estate as 'a garish mongrel that makes Versailles look chic'.

'It's awful, isn't it,' Colin said as he welcomed us into the house. Like Louis, he wore £250 Ralph Lauren knits with ratty holes in the sleeves and at the elbows.

'No,' I said. 'It's—'

'It's terrible,' he insisted. 'My great-grandfather didn't have the best taste, but no one can justify the cost of undoing it again. It'd be tens of millions of pounds.'

'Well, if there's one thing you don't have, it's tens of millions.' Amira sighed. 'Am I staying in my usual room?'

For the weekend we were joined by a few of his friends – all Old Etonians – as well as Demelza and Birdie. We spent most of the day drinking champagne and shooting clay pigeons. I had never learned how to do it, so every target sailed through the air unscathed when I tried to bring it down with my shotgun. After a while, Colin appeared behind me and wrapped me in his arms as he murmured instructions in my ear.

'You're focusing too much on the target and not its destination,' he whispered. 'This is more about instinct than precision. Now take one deep breath and slowly exhale.'

The trap flung the clay into the air, and Colin guided the direction of my shotgun with his hands around my elbows.

'Now,' he breathed.

I squeezed the trigger, the force of the shot sending me back against his chest, and we watched as the clay pigeon burst into a cloud of orange dust. When I looked over my shoulder at him, he was smiling.

'You're a natural. You were *born* to do this.'

The combination of champagne in my bloodstream, the shot still reverberating through my body and his arms around me was a confusing one.

'Lexi!' Demelza called from the stone terrace where everyone was sitting and watching. She held up my phone. 'That Jack character is trying to reach you again. Gosh, he's persistent, isn't he?'

His name out of context in this grand place sobered me, and I immediately eased myself from Colin's embrace like I'd been caught. When I walked over to Demelza, she smiled at me sweetly and held out my phone. Jack had called twenty minutes ago, and then followed up with a text to say he was going to bed but would try me later. We hadn't spoken in more than a fortnight, my summer schedule packed with early meetings, garden parties, Royal Ascot, and so many evening engagements that we couldn't quite seem to make the time zones work.

Demelza cocked her head. 'Still stuck in the talking phase? It's such a bore when boys do that.'

When the sun set over the sprawling gardens, the Lutton staff laid out a lavish feast for us on the terrace. There was Oscietra caviar, whole cracked Devon cock crab and Dublin Bay prawns.

'Okay, okay, okay!' Demelza screeched across the table, which was lit by a scatter of tealight candles. 'Never have I ever had sex with someone at this dinner tonight.'

'Gross, Demi,' Birdie muttered.

Everyone sipped their drinks – except for Amira and me – setting off a shriek of drunken laughter and confirming my suspicions about Colin and Demelza. Colin's eyes darted towards me briefly, though I pretended not to notice. The champagne gave way to red wine, which was followed by negronis and then brandy. I was thoroughly drunk for the first time in six months, and every drop helped as the man beside me droned on and on about the carbon-fibre superyacht his father recently commissioned.

'And what do you do?' I asked, feeling restless. 'For work, I mean.'

I recognised him as one of Louis's friends, though I had already forgotten his name again. The only thing I could remember about him was that he once burned £50 notes in front of homeless people as part of an initiation ceremony for one of Oxford's secret societies. His father had to pay the *Daily Post* to catch and kill the video taken on a bystander's phone.

'Well, I'm a landowner. What about you?'

'I'm … a princess,' I said, and the table roared like I had told the most dazzling joke anyone had ever heard.

When the staff began clearing away the table, Colin asked that they turn off all the lights inside.

'Hide and seek time, gang,' he said, rising from his chair.

'What? In the house?' I asked.

'It's so fun,' Demelza slurred, her spaghetti strap slipping off her shoulder again. Dr Villiers, who felt like she was buried fathoms and fathoms inside me, wondered if Demelza was one drink away from alcohol poisoning. 'Anything can happen in a big dark house.'

'Okay, so for Lexi's benefit, I'll recount the rules,' Colin said. 'Two people hide. East Wing only. Everyone else splits up into two groups to hunt down their prey. First team to bring a captive back to the terrace wins. Now, who's going to run?'

'Oh, it has to be you and Lexi!' Demelza shouted, and the men beat their hands on the tabletop in agreement, knocking over candles and sloshing wine out of glasses.

My head felt foggy, but my heart was racing. I was distantly aware that Amira had gone still beside me. But then everyone was counting down from sixty, Colin was grabbing my hand, and we were running into the vast black belly of Lutton Hall. I could hear our bare feet on the stone floor as we tore through the East Wing.

'Aren't we meant to split up?' I panted.

But he said nothing as he dragged me along by his hot hand. I was too full of wine to protest. At a door towards the darkest end of the hall, he stopped and pulled me inside. It was the ridiculous library, bigger than the state-owned centre in Hobart, with lush mahogany shelves and Persian rugs on the floor. He held me close to him and placed a finger to his lips, but I heard nothing except our breaths. It would take the others ages to sweep every black room to find us here. In the dark, he led me to a spiral staircase that took us to the second storey of the library: a mezzanine that wrapped around the entire room.

I could smell leather and dust and brandy. I leaned against the shelves to try to steady myself against something solid. In the near darkness, Colin was just an outline of a man. My stomach felt heavy and my blood ran hot as his shadow loomed over me. It had been so long since I'd been touched. All I could think was what a good princess I had been for six long months, exactly what Papa had always wanted. Now, finally, finally, I was in the dark where no one could see me for what I really was. Colin's hands slid up my arms and I felt his breath on my face. It was me who kissed him. I leaned forward into the black void and my lips found his. Then he was pushing me into the bookshelf, his hips holding me there as his hands plunged into my hair. I pulled him closer, wanting him, wanting to be obliterated. He was kissing me thoroughly and I realised Demelza was right: anything could happen in a big dark house.

By the time she stumbled into the library, I had most of his shirt untucked and his belt unbuckled.

'Caught in the act!' Demelza squealed.

'Well, well, what's going on here?' the landowner boomed as he staggered in behind her. 'Come down here, prey. We are your captors. You'll have to finish that later.'

We returned to the terrace mussed and swollen-lipped. Amira lowered her eyes and said nothing. For the next round of hide and seek, Birdie and the landowner went shrieking into the house. Once the hunters followed, we heard a shattering of glass and a proper scream. Birdie had knocked over a vase and trodden in the broken shards. As she sat sobbing among her bloody footprints, everyone froze, but Dr Villiers kicked and thrashed back to the surface of me. The alcohol and dopamine in my bloodstream were subsumed by a rush of adrenaline, and I calmly asked Colin to find me a first-aid kit. *This is who I am*, I thought. Who needs desperate frottage in a library when there's blood and chaos to mop up? The others watched silently as I tended to Birdie's wounds, which had barely nicked the dermis. I hadn't practised in six months, and a few minor cuts were as thrilling as the time Ben had let me perform a needle cricothyroidotomy unassisted. Birdie hiccupped and squeaked as I flushed the last remaining cut and applied antibiotic ointment, wrapping it tightly with a dressing.

'You're alright, Birds,' I said, taking her hand. 'I don't think you need stitches, but we can check again in the morning. If it's not quite right, we'll run you over to A&E for a look.'

The sight of blood smeared on the slate floors brought the evening to a natural end. I sat with Birdie in her huge bed, stroking her hair like she was a child. I was too afraid to leave her since she kept reaching for the 'xannies' in her purse, insisting they would help her sleep. I gently reminded her that benzos in her state would likely make her sleep forever. Hiding out in Birdie's room also meant I could avoid any soft knocks at my door in the middle of the night.

That was so fucking hot watching you do doctor things, Colin texted the day after we all returned to London.

I didn't respond. Instead, I called Jack.

'Come visit me,' I said when he answered. 'In August, we'll be going to my family's house in Scotland. You and Finn should both come. I know we talked about November for the reception, but that's too far away. Come earlier. I miss you.'

'Okay,' he said immediately.

'You can check with Paula,' I said, suddenly shy. 'I know it's pruning season and—'

'Lex, I'm coming.'

'Okay, it's just I know you don't love spontaneity – and that's fine. I'm always forcing you into things, like that time I said I didn't feel like going to the garlic festival and then changed my mind because—'

'You really wanted a squidlipop.'

I'd wanted a barbecued squid on a stick that could only be purchased at a festival two hours away, and Jack had dragged himself off the couch to go with me.

'I had to have a squidlipop, and I know that was kind of annoying—'

'I wasn't annoyed.'

'Okay, but I'm just saying, it's a big ask – coming to Scotland in a month. I'm around people who can just drop everything and fly around the world on a whim, so maybe I've forgotten what it's like to have actual responsibilities and—'

'Lex,' he said, 'do you want me to come or not?'

And now Jack and Finn were booked to fly to London in exactly a month. I paid for the tickets myself using the substantial monthly allowance Granny provided, much to Finn's delight. He somehow convinced Jack that I used frequent flyer points on the verge of expiring to cover the trip. Amira raised an eyebrow when I tried to casually slip my plan into conversation.

'Well, I can't wait to meet the farmer,' she said. Then she frowned. 'And his little friend.'

Our reunion loomed, but I had to get through July first, which was always busy, with Holyrood Week taking me on a tour of Scotland, a string of investitures and summer garden parties, and, of course, the tennis.

*

At Wimbledon, Amira and I were greeted by the chairman of the club, a bald, spectacled man who shook my hand and bowed to me, then greeted Amira with a nod. I was keenly aware in these moments that just a year earlier, Amira and Louis had breezed into this place, hands intertwined, wearing matching Jacques Marie Mage sunglasses, all camera lenses and eyes trained on them. Now she was often treated like my lady-in-waiting.

Plenty of royal women found themselves without the protection of an anointed man, and most vanished before history even bothered to jot down where they had gone. But the institution wasn't any more ready to let go of Amira than she was to leave it. She was hugely popular in the Commonwealth, not to mention that cutting loose a grieving widow would make the family look too much like the ruthless business it was. But I knew that if I were to ever let Richard take my place, he would have us both turfed out of the palace on his very first day as heir.

After we chatted to the ball boys and girls, we met Demelza and Birdie on a footbridge leading to the Royal Box. We hadn't seen them since our weekend away at Colin's family seat. We exchanged air kisses and surreptitiously assessed each other's outfits.

'Cute belt,' Demelza crooned to Amira.

As the door pushed open and we walked down the steps to find our seats, we were met with a great roar of applause. The Wimbledon crowd was always unfailingly polite. With 14,000 pairs of eyes on us, our conversation became more animated, our smiles brighter. I asked Birdie questions about her new job working as a production assistant on an action movie, and nodded as she told me she was likely to quit a few weeks early so she could go to Croatia with friends. Our seats were at the very front of the box, where we would have the best view of the court and the cameras would have the best view of us.

'How are your feet, Birdie?' I asked when she sat between Amira and me, preventing us from talking only to each other for the rest of the afternoon.

'Oh my god, awful, I can barely walk.' She pouted.

'One cut looks absolutely rank – you'll have to check it for her, Lexi,' Demelza said. 'I keep telling her she's got gangrene.'

'I don't have gangrene.'

'Daddy was very impressed by what you did,' Demelza went on. 'We told him all about our little trip away.'

I kept my smile rigid, imagining all the things she'd told Richard about our weekend, and how they would be planted among the royal rota to bloom like hemlock and oleander.

'Where do you go every morning, Lexi?' she asked. 'I see you hopping in your car at dawn most days.'

'Oh, just off for some exercise,' I said.

I would not tell her about the pond for anything, even if it meant the next few weeks held for me a dozen stories about my desperate, but necessary, efforts to lose weight at a nameless gym. After six months back inside, I was still the same average-sized woman I had been the day I arrived. Even with Demelza's boyish thighs crossed beside me, I was resisting the lure of deprivation.

'Where do you go? I do Pilates at Exhale – you should come with me one day.'

A hand on Demi's shoulder saved me from further questioning. We turned to see Colin with a couple of men settling into the seats behind us. They were all dressed in pale, half-buttoned shirts, their eyes behind Persol sunglasses.

'Hi girls, how are we?' Colin asked. He looked at me and smiled. 'Your Royal Highness, long time no see.'

I was relieved he didn't try to kiss my burning cheeks. The photos of this exchange so far would already be enough to knock any 'fab four' headlines off the tabloid front pages. Despite the near-constant gossip in the tabloids, Colin and I hadn't been caught in the same frame since the night of the state banquet. After we left Lutton Hall, I'd gone directly to Pakistan and Sri Lanka for a tour that Papa had been supposed to take.

'Colin, we've just been reliving our weekend at Lutton Hall,' Demelza said.

'Oh, good, I haven't been able to stop reliving it either.'

There was a burst of applause as the players walked onto the court, and then the commentator came over the loudspeaker to remind everyone to be quiet. I kept my eyes forward for the entire match, though I couldn't tell you who won or by how many points. I clapped when the crowd did, I gasped at their cue, putting on the performance of my life until one of the players fell to her knees and sobbed, the spectators leapt to their feet, and it was over. Soon, the chairman of the club was by our side, ready to escort us downstairs to meet the players.

'Bye bye, Colin,' Demelza said, waving to the row of white-teethed men before she led us up the stairs.

Just as I passed, Colin reached out and grabbed my wrist. He pulled me towards him so he could whisper in my ear, guaranteeing the tabloids the tight shot they desired.

'Hey,' he whispered, 'I keep thinking about the library. Text me back, okay? I want to see you again.'

I thought about Colin's hands on my waist, his decisive mouth on mine. I managed a smile and some non-committal noises before I said, 'I better go do this – they're waiting for me.'

After we shook hands with the players and said goodbye to Birdie and Demelza, Amira and I finally climbed back into the car and headed home.

'So,' Amira said, as I'd known she would when we were alone, 'if you're trying to get him to leave you alone, ignoring him like this isn't going to work. He loves the chase. This is probably driving him wild.'

I stared out the window.

'Really, though,' she said. 'Do you like him? Are you just making him work for it? Because I totally support that.'

'I don't know. I'm not playing games,' I said irritably.

I felt Amira roll her eyes. I knew she found my indecision intolerable. I knew that inviting Jack to London was asking for trouble, but I'd done it anyway. We had made no promises to each other; we had never even kissed. And yet, what had happened with Colin in the library felt like a betrayal.

At home, I went to my room to take off my makeup. I told myself that I would not check the news sites, that I would wait for Mary's assessment in the morning. But once I lay on the bed with Chino beside me, I was pulling up the *Daily Post* on my phone. '*LOVE SET MATCH? Princess Lexi whispers sweet nothings to rumoured suitor Colin Bellingham during fab four Wimbledon outing*,' it read. It was a nice photo, really. We were both smiling as he looped his hand around my forearm and I leaned in conspiratorially. For someone to touch a member of the royal family in public was like releasing a written statement to confirm that, yes, you had dry humped them in a library. Mary would not be happy. Granny and Stewart, who wanted to keep the focus on the Pakistan tour, would not be happy. This was the kind of thing Mum would do after the divorce – smile at a man, walk in the vague proximity of a man – and I would hear Granny and Papa's disappointed whispers at the breakfast table as they discussed the fallout.

My phone rang, and I expected it to be Mary. But it wasn't – it was Jack.

'Hi,' I said in a small voice, wondering if he'd somehow seen the photos already, if he was calling to cancel the trip. 'You're up early.'

'Hey, yeah,' he said.

'Everything okay?'

It was the middle of the night in Hobart, just past winter solstice, when the air is still and cold. There would be snow on the mountain and frost on the grass. The previous winter, Jack and I had sat on the roof of the main shed one clear night to watch the Aurora Australis set fire to the sky. As a solar storm raged in front of my eyes, I felt like a speck, like a clump of cells, like stardust in a universe that neither loved nor hated me, as anonymous and unimportant as every other living creature on the planet.

'Yeah, everything's fine. I don't want to freak you out, but I just thought you should know that we've noticed a guy hanging around,' he said. 'He sits outside the gates in his car and follows us to town. And he was in the waiting room at the hospital when Finn was on shift a couple of times.'

My stomach churned as I ran through the possibilities: a reporter delving into my lost years, a stalker who had latched onto those closest to me.

'Does he have a camera?' I asked.

'I don't know, maybe,' Jack said. 'The thing is, Mum didn't realise, and he came onto the vineyard posing as a distributor. She showed him around, but he kept asking all these questions about you. I don't think she told him anything really, and when she realised he wasn't there about business, she asked him to leave.'

'Okay,' I said, closing my eyes. 'Tell Paula I'm sorry.'

I could hear Ragu's nails on the hardwood floors as he followed Jack through the halls of our cottage. My heart felt like a tight fist inside me. In all the years I had known Jack, I'd kept this kind of scrutiny and intrusion out of his home.

'Don't be sorry, I just thought you should know,' he said.

'Have you seen him since then?' I asked.

'No,' he said. 'I'd throw him against the wall if I did.'

'It's probably a reporter. I'll tell my security detail, and we'll figure it out.'

'Really, it's all good,' he said. 'It's not like we have anything to hide, do we?'

CHAPTER NINETEEN

2020

I cruised down the Tasman Highway in my old Corolla, the windows rolled down so I could feel the dry February heat. It was a rare forty-degree day in Hobart, the kind of weather that enveloped the city for a maximum of twelve hours, leaving its cold-blooded residents wilted and cranky. But inevitably, gloriously, winds from the Southern Ocean would blow in, and everyone would open their doors to let a cross-draught through the house. By bedtime, you could sleep comfortably with the blankets pulled up to your nose.

'Are you sure you want to pick me up?' Louis had asked when we were planning his visit.

'Of course,' I said. 'Hobartians pick everyone up from the airport. It's how we show our love.'

It was an easy fifteen-minute drive from town, over the bridge and through the bushy surrounds of Mount Rumney. When I had first moved to Hobart, I was surprised by how eager everyone was to shuttle you to and from the airport, even if they didn't know you particularly well. It was partly because there were no good public transport options, but it was mostly a point of honour for the city.

When I pulled into the pick-up lane, I immediately spotted Louis among the other travellers waiting for their loved ones. His cap was pulled low over his eyes, and he had sloughed off all his layers in the heat. He could pass for any other guy in his twenties, though the four-wheel drive loitering at the kerb just ahead was clearly his security detail. They would keep a respectful distance as we pretended to be any other brother and sister spending a few days together.

'Hey,' he said, jumping into the passenger seat, 'I thought you said it's chilly here.'

'The cool change is coming.'

I pulled back into the lane and watched the four-wheel drive follow us out of the airport car park. We hadn't seen each other for more than a year, but we were silent as I drove up the highway towards the vineyard. I realised I should have brought Finn with me so he could fill the car with his charm.

'How was the flight?'

'Yeah, fine. Long. He made me fly commercial.'

'Right,' I said. I'd skipped family Christmas the year before because my car had needed new brakes a few months earlier, and I couldn't afford the flights home. I texted Papa to apologise. He never responded, but a week later the *Post* reported that I had tried to shake him down for money.

'How is he?'

Louis sighed and looked out the window, his cap slung so low I couldn't see his eyes. 'He's the same old bastard.'

'I told James we'd try to see him, but you might run out of time.'

'Yeah, thanks,' he said. 'I don't think I should. I'm trying to keep Papa on side before the wedding.'

The lead-up to the wedding was always going to be a treacherous time for Louis. Papa's greatest fear was that his subjects saw him as the caretaker king, a throne warmer in between the illustrious rule of Queen Eleanor and the accession of his shining boy. I had been surprised that Louis wanted to risk Papa's ire by coming to visit me so close to the ceremony, but he'd done it anyway. If Louis met up with the man who had facilitated my escape as well, it would likely cost him too much.

At the vineyard, Louis and I put on our brightest smiles for Paula, Jack and Finn. Our posture was straighter, our voices clear and eager. We were the royal twins, after all. Louis put his hands on his hips and surveyed the hills adorned with pinot grapes. The vineyard was putting on a show of its own that day. The vines were fat with fruit, the grass was luscious from a wet start to summer, and the estuary sparkled in the distance.

'It's truly magical, Paula,' Louis said. 'Tell me about the house. That stone wall is extraordinary.'

Paula, who was suspicious of celebrities and openly hostile to anyone with inherited power, was beaming at my irresistible brother. She took him over to show off the high stone wall that surrounded the house, built by convicts in the nineteenth century.

'He's so gorgeous,' Finn whispered to me. 'I've seen his photo, but it's totally different up close, isn't it? He looks like the prince in *The Little Mermaid*.'

'Then who do I look like?' I asked.

He stepped back to study me, as if he hadn't seen my face every morning for the past seven years. 'I can't remember her name, but you know when the sea witch disguises herself as a hot girl? You look like her.'

For dinner, Paula had gone down the road for fresh oysters, crayfish and scallops. We opened a few bottles of the 2010 Jennings sparkling and ate in the arbour. A century-old vine had slowly woven its tendrils around the wooden shelter that joined the main house to our cottage. It no longer bore fruit, but its frilly green leaves shielded us from the sun as we ate and read and talked beneath it.

Jack raised his glass for a toast. 'To Louis. We're really happy to finally meet you. Congratulations on your wedding.'

Everyone sipped and Louis's eyes briefly met mine.

'Honestly, this is the best champagne I've ever had,' he said, turning to Paula.

'It's sparkling wine!' she corrected him, laughing. 'We don't want to be sued by the French.'

'Well, it's better than anything they've done.'

Finn put down his glass, his unspoken request for our attention. 'Tell us about the worst thing Lexi did when she was a kid. I bet she was a terror.'

There are public and private answers to this question.

There was the time Mum threw herself down a flight of stairs in front of me. Papa was in Wales at the time, but I immediately called up Granny and insisted that he was the one who pushed her. Or there was the time I hid Papa's passport in the treehouse, hoping to keep him from an eight-week tour of the Pacific. When Louis eventually discovered it, he burned it in the wood behind Elton Park so Papa would never find out what I had done. At twelve, I discovered a mobile phone wedged between the cushions in Papa's study and quickly established that it belonged to Annabelle. It was the era before pincode-locked smartphones, and I had a marvellous few days texting everyone in her contacts: *I'M A BIG OLD BITCH* and *LET'S HAVE SEX PLEASE* and *CAN I BORROW MONEY? I'M SUCH A POOR OLD BITCH*. After two days of fun, I confessed to Louis what I'd done. He took the phone off me, sent one text to Papa reading *LET'S BREAK UP* and then crept back into Papa's study to put it back where I'd found it.

But the story deemed fit for public consumption goes like this: as a toddler, I was fascinated by Papa's signet ring. Engraved with the official crest of the Prince of Scotland, he wore it every day on his left pinky. When I was three, I took it from the dish on his bedside table and played with it on the floor. I remember holding the gold ring in my palm, wondering if I could drop it into the wide gap between two floorboards below me, like a letter in a letterbox. I had never mailed a letter, even though people seemed to do it on television all the time. The ring, I quickly found, slipped straight through the black slit with a little thud. Papa appeared in the doorway moments later, and I famously rose from the floor, turned to him and said: 'Your Highness, I've been very naughty.'

When recounting this story at dinner parties and on television, Papa said his anger immediately dissolved in the face of such childish decorum, and he procured a toolbox so that we could remove the plank and fish out the ring together. In reality, a groundsman was called to complete the job, but Papa had told the story so often and so vividly that I could almost picture him crouched beside me on the floor with a chisel. I could almost believe he wasn't irritated, but instead had given me a gentle lecture on the importance of respecting other people's treasures.

When the groundsman pried up the floorboard and plucked out the ring, we noticed something strange about the underside of the plank in his hands. It was covered in crude carvings – crisscrosses and squiggles that made the hair on the back of my neck stand up.

'Those are witch marks,' the groundsman said and then smiled at me when he saw my alarm. 'They've been found under the floors of many old houses in which kings once slept. These etchings were thought to protect you from witches – back when people believed such things were real.'

The plank was carefully placed back where it belonged. For years after, I would sit on the floor and stroke my hand along the surface of the wood. I imagined that the witch marks ringed his bed, keeping him safe from demons as he slept. Whenever he went away, I would ask if the bed he'd be sleeping in was surrounded by carvings.

'Of course, mignonette,' he would always say. 'There are witch marks everywhere I go.'

But Louis didn't reach for this familiar tale.

'When we were five, our nanny took us to the shops and I stole a creme egg,' Louis said. 'We rarely went to public places, and I was so excited seeing them displayed in the box like that, so I just nicked one and put it in my pocket. Mum found it in the nursery an hour later, of course. But when she confronted us, Lexi said she did it. I was too scared to own up to it, so the next day, Mum marched her down to the shop to apologise and return it.'

'Oh, don't tell them this,' I groaned.

Louis went on, ignoring me. 'The shopkeeper told Mum she'd seen me steal the egg but didn't want to get me into trouble, because she knew who I was. So when Mum asked Lexi why she was covering for me, she said, "I didn't want people to be angry at the future king."'

There was an awkward silence. It was an odd story for Louis to choose, because it captured our family in all its weirdness and dysfunction. Nanny-reared children who thought the supermarket was exotic. A sad little kid who sensed she was worth less than her sibling. My texting spree on Annabelle's phone would have gone down much better. Louis was ordinarily so good with civilians. He had Mum's gift of bewitching them while bonding with them at the same time. Then I realised this story was for me.

Jack laughed, breaking the silence. 'That's not a bad story,' he said. He had an innate sense of the collective mood and a knack for shifting it back into cheery territory whenever it drifted. 'That's Lexi, being brave and selfless.'

Paula circled the table, topping up everyone's glasses. She placed a gentle hand on Louis's shoulder as she filled his flute. It was a mother's touch, warm and unheeding. Paula wore her hair down to her waist. She had tattoos and multiple piercings. But there was something about her that always reminded me of Mum. Louis's eyes met mine again.

'What a strange way you two grew up,' Paula mused. 'Now tell us all about the wedding. Are they letting your fiancée have any Hindu traditions during the ceremony?'

The next day, we drove down to the peninsula to camp for a few days. Paula held Ragu by the collar as he watched us pile into the car and drive away without him. Jack's aunt lived on an acreage that overlooked the sand flats of Bellettes Bay. She spent most of the year travelling abroad and encouraged us to use the beach whenever we liked. It was technically a coastal reserve, but since it could only be accessed by the sandy path from her property, the beach was as good as hers. We packed our things into her wheelbarrow and ambled down the tree-lined slopes so that we could set up our tents on the water's edge. Pine trees planted a couple of centuries ago had begun to yield to the shifting sands. Their great trunks swayed towards the water and their roots rose up like the tentacles of an enormous sea creature. When the tide was out, the vast beach was like an unfamiliar planet. Creatures skittered around our feet. Strange craters pockmarked the sand where stingrays once burrowed. Birds arrived for their evening feast. All around us were the haunting hills of the Tasman Peninsula. The pale trunks of the gums looked like skeletons in the distance. Whenever I was here, I thought of the men who dared to escape the penal colonies to try their luck in the southern wilds. How frightening it must have been to walk into the ancient forest with no food and no plan. What horrors awaited them if they chose to remain in the convict camps.

It was strange to see Louis and Jack together. They were the two halves of my life, and now they were building a fire, discussing the best options for kindling and fuel wood. I could tell that they liked each other, and I was inexplicably relieved by this. Finn and I made dinner while Louis and Jack tended the fire and talked. We had gone to the farmers market the day before so we could make fresh pasta with smoked mozzarella and tomatoes from Paula's garden. We ate by firelight and the fading summer sun that refused to set until 8 pm.

'This is good, Lexi,' Louis said, surprised. 'How did you learn to cook?'

'It turns out cooking is chemistry.'

I had been nervous about him seeing this life of mine, in which I worried about bank overdrafts and filed tax returns and tried to remember how long it had been since I'd been to the dentist. But he was here, and he was getting on with the two most important people I had.

'Once we were walking the Overland Track and possums broke into our stash and ate all the food Lexi had insisted on bringing,' Jack said.

'Oh, yeah, we had to have pasta with olive oil and salt,' I said, remembering the driving rain and clinging mud of our seven-day odyssey through the bush. 'Honestly, it's still the best meal I've ever had.'

'It was so good,' Jack agreed, his face a marvel in the campfire's flickering light.

'Pretty sure we were just starving, guys,' Finn said around a mouthful of linguine. He turned in his camp chair. 'Where are you going for your honeymoon, Louis?'

My brother looked up. 'Oh, uh, South Africa. Amira's family has a hunting lodge there. It's our favourite place. It's totally isolated, and there's a waterhole. You can watch animals gathering at dusk. It's pretty great.'

Amira cared little for the lodge. I would have thought she'd want a honeymoon in the Maldives or Bora Bora. But I had also assumed she wanted a husband who would have sex with her, and I was wrong about that too. I'd told no one of their arrangement, even as the carefully arranged paparazzo set-ups gave way to a formalised agreement that was taking them all the way to the altar at Westminster Abbey. The deliberately grainy photos from Patagonia had escalated into handholding on ski slopes and kissing on the dancefloor of Mahiki. Like almost everyone else in the world, Jack and Finn believed Louis had fallen in love with my best friend.

I had learned Louis and Amira were engaged along with everyone else when they posed for photographs at Wolseley House. Amira looked radiant on Louis's arm, dressed in a forest-green Victoria Beckham dress that perfectly offset Mum's hunk of emerald on her finger.

But the ring belonged to me. The terms of the will stated that it be kept in a safe deposit box until my own engagement or until I turned thirty – whichever came first. The palace had told the tabloids that I had been so overjoyed my twin was marrying my best friend that I immediately gifted him the ring. When it suited them, I was the selfish, preening princess who refused to speak to her poor family for reasons unknown; the next week I was a cherished sister who handed over one of the few reminders of her mother in support of her brother's marriage. I had never seen myself as the marrying kind, but in the weeks after the engagement announcement, I found myself googling photos of the ring on Amira's hand, pinching and zooming in so I could get a better look. I wondered whose idea it had been to undermine Mum's will yet again – Papa's or Louis's – so they could deny me one more piece of her.

At first, I'd refused to have anything to do with the wedding, ignoring Stewart's quiet inquiries about whether I might be willing to be Amira's bridesmaid. But a few weeks later, I found myself in need of his help. Finn and I had met Jack and Georgia at a pub in town for drinks, and when we came out a few hours later, a photographer was waiting for me on the kerb. Most of the men who followed me used long lenses and hid behind trees and postboxes, but this one rushed forward, blinding us with his incessant flashes.

'On the turps again, sweetheart?' he said. 'Making Daddy proud, are you? Nasty little tart.'

I was more ashamed than afraid, but the lights were making me dizzy, and I nearly stumbled over. Finn grabbed Georgia and me by the hands and pulled us away.

'Off you run, you stupid bitch!' The photographer laughed. 'I know where you live.'

Dazed by the cameras, it took us a moment to realise Jack wasn't with us. When we went back, he had the photographer pinned to the wall of the pub. Jack's eyes were blazing, and the man gasped and struggled in his grip.

'Stay away from her,' Jack seethed. 'If I see you again, I'll kill you.'

A week later, a police car had pulled up at the vineyard. The photographer wanted to press charges, and the investigation had got far enough that they were going to check the pub's CCTV cameras. When Jack started looking for a lawyer, I called Stewart, who had a knack for making problems disappear. In exchange for settling matters with the photographer, Stewart asked that I come to London in a few months' time and hold Amira's train while she walked down the aisle.

I never admitted to Jack that I had struck this bargain to keep him out of trouble. But Georgia was clearly suspicious when the charges were dropped on the same day the palace announced that I was to be Amira's bridesmaid. Georgia and I had been friends for years, but she suddenly became distant, and then cold, and finally outright hostile. She and Jack began to argue constantly, and when she asked him to move to New York with her, the atmosphere in the cottage went from uncomfortable to unbearable. I hated the idea that he might leave, though I pretended to be agnostic about the decision he had to make. Two weeks before Louis's visit, I'd been getting into my car as Georgia stalked across the gravel towards her own. She said nothing, but she looked at me with such barely contained hatred that I knew she and Jack had just broken up. She moved to New York alone, blocked my number and never spoke to me or Jack again.

I wasn't sure if Louis knew how my presence in the wedding party was secured, but I was hardly going to ask him about it when he'd come all this way to see me. After dinner, we listened to Louis's stories from his travels. He had taken up extreme sports – cave diving, heli-skiing and whitewater rafting.

'I really want to try volcano boarding next,' he said. 'They do it in Indonesia and Vanuatu – nice and close if you ever wanted to do it. It's supposed to be an incredible rush.'

'Wait, so you snowboard *into* a volcano?' Finn asked.

'Not into its mouth. The slopes are covered in ash and gravel after they erupt, and you coast down that.'

'Sounds wild,' Finn said.

'Sounds suicidal,' I muttered, embarrassed for him.

Finn and Jack made meaningful eye contact across the fire.

'Nature is there to be conquered,' Louis said.

It was the kind of boneheaded thing his friends might say, but never him.

'I don't know,' Jack said lightly. 'I feel like anyone who tries to conquer nature pays the price. The natural world has its own rules, and if we break them, we die.'

Louis shook his head, grinning in a way that made him look like a stranger to me. 'There are no rules out there, that's the thing.'

We were all quiet for a while. I glowered at Louis over the campfire while he pretended not to notice.

'Well, I'm knackered. I might turn in,' Jack said, getting up from his chair.

'Me too,' Finn said.

Pots were washed, teeth were brushed, and Jack and Finn were swiftly zipped up in their tents. Louis's security team, who had set themselves up at a respectful distance along the beach, hid among the melaleuca trees, though we knew they were keeping watch with their night-vision goggles.

When I came back from peeing in the bushes, I found Louis alone. He was staring into the fire and hardly seemed to notice when I sat down beside him. Without the others, the sizzling tension between us eased. We sat quietly by the fire for a while, listening to its hiss and sputter as it split a log in two.

'Can I tell you something?' he asked softly. His bravado was gone.

'Yeah.'

'Last Guy Fawkes Day, we went to a friend's place in Scotland for a bonfire. Some guy brought peyote, and I took it,' he said. 'And the next day I woke up locked in a room. They'd bound my wrists with a scarf. Kris and Amira said they'd had to sit with me all night to calm me down.'

'What happened?'

'They said I'd kept running towards the fire. I was fighting them off and screaming that I needed to get into the fire. It took four guys to get me locked up inside. I told everyone that I didn't remember what happened. But I remember.'

He was staring into the fire now, the flames lighting up his storm-coloured eyes.

'What do you remember?' I asked.

He looked at me. 'I could hear Mum screaming from inside the bonfire. She was begging me to come get her. She was calling both our names, screaming for our help. And no one would let me get to her. It was so real.'

We said nothing for a long time, but we both had tears in our eyes. We looked into the fire, and I tried not to imagine Mum trapped inside it. We had never talked about what had happened. After she was gone, we rarely spoke of her again.

'Do you think she was calling for us at the end? Out there on her own?' he asked.

I covered my face to hide my tears, because that was all I ever thought about. Louis put his arms around me, and I buried my face in his shoulder. We held each other for a long time as the fire began to dwindle. In the days after her death, there had been too much to do, too much to hide, and we'd never sought much comfort from each other.

'You're the only one I can talk to about it – the only one who understands,' I said. I felt him nod as his head rested against mine. 'I don't want this distance between us.'

We were motherless children who'd been stupid enough to lose each other as well as her. Finally we broke apart and looked at each other with shining eyes.

'I know you don't support what I'm doing,' he said. 'But I can't do the other thing, I can't. Amira and I are friends – we'll take care of each other. Granny's giving us Sherbourne

House after the wedding. Amira's happy for me and Kris. And she wants this life – she wants to be queen.'

I wiped my face and nodded, trying to understand. 'Does Papa know?'

'He knows and he doesn't know,' Louis said, looking towards the pearly moon on the horizon. 'We've never really spoken about it, but, yeah, he knows.'

We hadn't been this honest with each other since the night in the Highlands when we were still children.

'I want you to be happy,' I said. 'I want Amira to be happy. I want Kris to be happy. I just worry someone's going to get hurt in all this. I worry someone will use this against you. I'm just … worried, I guess.'

'So am I,' he admitted. 'But no one's figured it out yet. And the thing is, I think we can all be happy this way. No one ever gets everything they want. But this way, we get pretty close.'

We knew that life was a ledger and that happiness would always be offset by pain and sacrifice. Kris and Louis could be together under the guise of close brothers-in-law. Amira could have the life of Vikki's dreams and a marriage of convenience.

'This feels like an insane conversation to be having in this day and age,' I said.

'It is, but you know our family's about a hundred years behind everyone else,' Louis said. 'You don't have to support what we're doing. But I do need you.'

I grabbed his hand and squeezed, the way Mum used to. We would be at a dreary Easter service or a garden show or yet another polo game, and she would absently take our little fists in her hand and knead them.

'It's a good life you have here,' Louis said. 'I'm really happy to see you so healthy. I was worried about you at the end.'

'Yeah, same.' I sniffed. 'I'm sorry I left you like that. I just … it felt necessary.'

He nodded. 'Are you really going to be a doctor?'

'My hospital internship starts next week.'

'Jesus Christ.' He laughed. 'I think Papa's secretly impressed. He'd never, ever admit it, though.'

We drove back to Hobart two days later, salt-crusted, tanned and triumphant. Louis and I had waded out until, finally, the sand flats gave way to deep water. We swam in the frigid bay, watching a glossy seal pirouette past us. We drank red wine by the campfire and walked the great length of the sand when the tide receded. I dozed in my tent in the afternoon sun and listened to Jack tell Louis about his dreams for the vineyard. When we got back to the property, Ragu galloped towards us and leapt into Louis's arms. By his last night, I was almost looking forward to the wedding, when we would be together again.

Paula had approached me about the possibility of throwing a party in Louis's honour, just for a few friends and the Jennings vineyard staffers. To my surprise, Louis agreed. There was no way to stop people taking his photo and sharing his location, but by the time anything hit the tabloids, he'd already be back on the plane to London. And, I had to admit, the revelation that he'd come to visit me a few weeks before the wedding would play extremely well with the public.

We threw the party in the main shed, with fairy lights wound around the rafters and sheepskins draped across the chairs for warmth. Deep inside that vast space was a chamber once used by Jack's great-grandfather to store apples from his thriving orchard. Its thick walls were filled with coal, and it was always deliciously cool in there. Jack's friends, who played seventies cover songs in the pub on weekends, set up their gear so they could croon to the swaying crowd on the dance floor. Almost every guest who arrived at the shed worked at a vineyard or a distillery, bringing with them promising new blends or daring experiments in unmarked glass bottles. Out on the grass, Finn filled a few disused steel wine vats with wood and set them alight for the smokers and the kissing couples to keep themselves warm on the cool summer night.

Friends arrived in their best shirts and summer dresses, carrying wheels of local cheese and fruity homemade craft beers, a rather polite and timid crowd. It was always this way in the beginning, and it was always up to me and Louis to break the ice.

I was wearing a black cotton sundress with delicate straps, my hair scrunched and manipulated into wild curls. I escorted Louis from cluster to cluster, making introductions. Then he would take over, flashing the audience his Isla smile – the slightest dip of his chin, the curl of his lips – before asking them sweet and insightful questions. Within the hour, the crowd had loosened up in the presence of a future king. When a winemaker from the Coal River Valley turned out to be a free climber who had just ascended Cape Pillar, I left them to their extremely technical and fervent chat.

I walked into the shed's makeshift kitchen as Jack was pulling a tray of sausage rolls out of an ancient oven. He shook them into a big bamboo steamer on the bench, which was stacked with loaves of Turkish bread, tubs of hummus, chopped up vegetables and two boxes of frozen spring rolls.

'Ah, just in time,' he said. 'Make yourself useful and take these around, would you?'

'Sure,' I said, dunking one into tomato sauce and eating it. 'Louis's doing alright, don't you think?'

'Yeah, he's a good guy,' he said, emptying a box of spinach and ricotta triangles onto the tray. I could see that he was working through something in his mind. 'He seems a bit ... I don't know. Tortured? But then ...'

He went quiet and I looked at him.

'What?' I asked. 'So did I?'

He popped the tray in the oven and came back, resting his hands against the only available bench space, his rolled-up shirtsleeves showing off his shapely forearms. He was annoyingly handsome in the summer, when his skin went bronze and his dark mop of hair was kissed by the sun. A string of lightbulbs draped between the support beams above us lit up the blond tips of his eyelashes. He smiled, but looked unsure how to proceed.

'All I needed was some good Jennings hospitality to fix me,' I said, smiling back at him. The Finnish brandy I had consumed made me feel loose-limbed and slightly irresponsible.

Since Georgia left a few weeks ago, a curious energy had hummed between us.

'You didn't need fixing,' he said, leaning towards me across the bench. 'You were perfect just the way you were.'

I smiled, knowing he was lying, but also that he wasn't. I picked up the bamboo steamer, which was so ridiculously large I had to hoist it onto my hip. 'Save me a dance, will you?'

I went back into the crowded main shed, wondering if he was watching me leave. By the time I'd distributed the sausage rolls, the evening had reached its raucous peak and everyone was ready to dance. Finn and Louis were singing along to the band's rendition of 'Free Fallin''.

'I want to move here!' Louis shouted in my ear when I was nearby. 'I'll become a vintner and we can live here together!'

The band began playing 'Wouldn't It Be Nice' and the shed, packed with sweaty dancers, immediately paired off into couples. Louis and Finn were swaying to the music, arm in arm. Jack appeared, and he pulled me into the centre of the dance floor, his big hands on my waist. It was one of those moments when it feels like the movie credits are rolling on your life, when all the thoughts in your head go quiet, and you can only feel gratitude for the people around you. I slung my arms around Jack's neck, unbothered by the consequences of our proximity for once. The heat of his body was radiating through his shirt collar and the band's plodding bass reverberated through me. We stayed intertwined through four songs, ignoring Paula's curious eye and the smash of a dropped glass from somewhere in the shed. Unchecked, my fingers combed through his bristly nape.

When two sweaty hands landed on our shoulders, we broke apart, guilty and confused. It was Tom the wine wholesaler, who'd arrived at the party late, drunk and thrilled to see Jack. Jack's arms left my waist, and he reached forward to shake

Tom's hand, looking dazed. I left them to catch up, relieved and disappointed in equal measure. It wasn't until I went outside to cool off that I realised I didn't know where Louis had gone. I looked for him in the crowds hovering around the bonfires and in the grape arbour before heading back into the shed to search for him among the slow-dancing couples.

'He said he was off to bed,' Paula said, collecting the abandoned glasses that had accumulated on every surface. 'He's got an early start tomorrow.'

It had been a good night. Everyone was sweat-slick and drunk and stinking of woodsmoke. As the crowd dwindled, I wheeled the recycling bin inside and began picking up empty glass bottles and napkins. The band packed up their gear and chatted in low, hoarse voices. I could see Jack through the shed doors cleaning up the kitchen and farewelling the guests as they wandered past him and into the dark. I was weary, but my heart was full. As I started to sweep up, Paula came over and took the broom from my hands.

'You've done enough – go to bed. We'll finish everything off in the morning,' she said. She looked over my shoulder as Jack approached the shed doors. 'You too, love. Thanks, but go to bed.'

We left the shed in silence, heading back to the cottage on the hill. It was a clear night, laden with stars. I wrapped my bare arms around myself to stay warm, and Jack draped his jacket over my shoulders. How many times had we done this? On so many nights, we'd walked out of noisy bars and movie theatres and fallen into a companionable silence as we approached our shared cottage and the wall that separated us.

'Want to come in for one more drink?' Jack asked.

'Sure,' I said lightly, trying to pretend it was nothing. 'Did you have a good night?'

'Yeah. I think Louis had a good time – once he stopped worrying about everyone looking at him to make sure he was having a good time.' He glanced at me. 'You used to do the same thing.'

I felt my face go warm. We were cutting through the narrow path between the vines, the grape leaves brushing our arms as we walked.

'I did?'

'Not so much anymore,' he said.

I imagined him watching me in those first few years, when we were new to each other and I was still coming out of the fog of my old life. When Finn and I first met Jack, we were practically children – immature and half-formed, spoilt and largely incompetent, learning how to save lives rather than tending to our own.

'You've been comparing Louis and me,' I said. 'I'm the experiment, he's the control group.'

He stopped and looked at me in the dim glow of the stars.

'You're the wine stored in oak – he's the wine stored in steel,' he said, smiling. His jacket wrapped me in the scent of him, and I pretended not to enjoy it. We kept walking, the gravel crunching under our feet.

'It's not a comparison,' he added. 'I just feel like I understand you better, that's all.'

'We've been watched our whole lives.'

'I know.'

'It makes you … I don't know … unable to tell the difference between reality and what you're trying to make seem real.'

'It makes sense. Everyone's probably doing that. For you two, it's just on a whole different level.'

'I don't know what happened to him, actually,' I said, eager to change the subject before I said too much. 'He must have gone to bed an hour ago.'

As we turned the corner on our verandah, we saw them: Louis and Finn kissing among the vines. They were under a halo of starlight, and they were oblivious to us. They were laughing and necking, two young people drunk on wine and each other. I glanced at Jack, who seemed briefly stunned but rearranged his face when he caught my gaze. He must have sensed my discomfort, because he looked at me kindly and shrugged.

'Time to call it a night,' he whispered. I watched as he slipped through the cottage door. Before he closed himself in for the night, he gestured with his chin towards my barn, telling me without words that it was none of our business. I was to go to bed and leave my brother to his own reality.

Louis's flight was at dawn, but when I came to the cottage at the agreed-upon hour, the living room was dark and empty. My irrational anger rising, I found the guest bed empty. I went back to the living room again and stood there, wondering what to do, wondering what Jack would do. But there was no other option. I stalked over to Finn's door and knocked softly, though my fist was ready to punch it wide open.

'Louis,' I murmured, 'we've got to go. Your flight's in an hour.'

There was a deep silence, then a rustling of bedclothes, the padding of bare feet on the wooden floors. The door opened a crack and Louis peered through it, his hair a mess but his face still perfect in its hungover state.

'Come on,' I urged. 'Are you packed?'

'Yeah,' he croaked. 'Give me a second, would you?'

'I'll be in the car.'

Through the windshield, I watched the clouds turn gold to herald the rising sun. The clock counted down the minutes to Louis's flight. By the time he came out of the cottage with his bag over his shoulder, his security guards had twice knocked on my window to ask where he was. He barely had the door shut before I hit the pedal and kicked up a spurt of gravel as I accelerated down the path.

A van was idling outside the gate, and it flicked on its high beams once I turned onto the road. I had no doubt it was a photographer. Someone must have posted photos from the party on social media. They would have torn through the internet in a few hours, landing in the inbox of a tabloid editor with just enough time and plenty of hustle to hire a stringer in southern Tasmania.

Louis was silent in the passenger seat as we drove. His security team managed to put their four-wheel drive between us and the photographer's van.

'Louis,' I said.

'What?'

'What happened last night—'

'Is none of your business.'

'Okay, sure, yes. But I have to say this.' He sighed and looked out the window, but I went on. 'You said you're being careful. Do you really think going to a party with a bunch of strangers and then sleeping with a guy you barely know is being careful?'

He sighed again.

'Are you sure no one else saw you but me? What do you know about Finn except that he's my friend?'

'Are you saying you're friends with someone who's not trustworthy?' he snapped.

'I just ...' I faltered. 'What about Kris?'

'You don't know anything about us.'

'Look, do what you want,' I said, shaking my head. 'I'm just saying that you're taking a lot of risks. You're skiing down volcanoes and hooking up with guys you don't know that well. It just seems like you either have a death wish or you want to get caught.'

We were silent for the rest of the drive to the airport, which didn't take long since I was doing ninety in a sixty zone. He was making this flight and getting off this island if it killed me. I couldn't contemplate the possibility of him missing his plane and having to mope around the vineyard for another day. When I pulled into the drop-off zone, he got out of the car and retrieved his bag from the boot.

The four-wheel drive pulled up behind us, and Rory, a long-time officer on Louis's detail, got out and approached us.

'Sir, we should get you inside immediately,' he said. 'There's press arriving, but we've called ahead and the airport staff will let you wait for your flight in a private area.'

'Thanks, Rory,' I heard Louis say. 'Just give me a moment.'

The boot slammed and my brother came around to lean through the open passenger window.

'Look, you don't get to tell me what to do,' he said in a low voice. 'You left. You left me to carry this whole thing on my shoulders. You want me to come out and tell everyone the truth. But even if I wanted to do that, I couldn't. And you know why? Because you *left me.*'

I stared through the windshield as a flush of adrenaline made my heart race. 'You stole her ring.'

'Huh?'

'Mum's ring,' I said, louder. I looked over at him. 'She left that to me. You and Papa stole it.'

He rested his head on his forearms and sighed. When he looked back up, I could tell he was through with me. 'And what are you going to do with it, Lexi? Pawn it so you don't have to rely on James for money anymore? Grow up.'

All around us, travellers were getting out of cars. Their loved ones got out too, helping them with their bags, hugging them tight and wishing them a safe journey. Meanwhile, I stayed where I was.

'The photographer's back there,' I said quietly. He had pulled up to the kerb opposite us and cracked a window open just enough to reveal the glinting shark eye of a camera lens. 'You should go.'

Louis smiled at me, but the smile was for the camera.

'See you at the wedding,' he said.

That was the last time Louis and I were alone together. The next time I saw him, ten days later, I would be invited to as many prenuptial celebrations as a problematic distant cousin. I stood at the altar behind Amira in a gown made according to measurements I had sent to her designer's atelier via email. It was baggy around the waist, but there was no one to ask about a seamstress who could help me, so I'd pinned the inside with safety pins instead. Kris stood solemnly behind Louis, his best man and the love of his life. All three of them avoided my eyes for the thirty-six hours I was in London.

After the wedding pictures were taken, Stewart took me aside and slipped me a manila envelope. It was a non-disclosure agreement, demanding that I acknowledge the intimate relationship between Louis, Papa and myself and vow never to disclose confidential information to outsiders. If I spoke about my father or my brother, I would open myself to legal action. It was a unilateral contract: while I was silenced, they were free to talk about me.

We had always kept each other's secrets. But now theirs would be protected by law and mine could be wielded like a weapon.

'Have your lawyer look it over,' Stewart said.

'I can't afford a lawyer.'

He bowed his head and said nothing. I knew that he had delivered the same papers to Mum when the divorce became final. That was the moment she knew she'd been cast out of the family. When he handed me a fountain pen, I scrawled my signature on the lines marked with cartoonish yellow arrows and handed the papers back to him.

'Goodbye, Stewart,' I said and went back to the room in the palace where I was staying, removed my ill-fitting dress, packed my things and took a train to the airport. When I got home, I lay on the couch in the cottage for three days and stared at the television while Jack silently fretted and brought me buttered toast and tea.

But back then, as I idled at the kerb while Louis swung his bag over his shoulder and walked away from me, we didn't know that was it.

If I had known what was coming – a terse text exchange every year on our birthday, a wall of snow that would obliterate him – I would have climbed out of the car and thrown my arms around him.

CHAPTER TWENTY

5 August 2023

'Your Highness, Mr Jennings and Dr Vanderville have just passed the gates,' a house porter said from the doorway.

My heart lurched, but I put down my teacup and smiled. 'Thank you, Barney.'

Amira smirked at me from her tartan armchair and then looked back down to the book in her lap.

'I'll go meet them,' I said, rising from my spot in the bay window, then hesitated. 'Are you coming?' I asked Amira.

She snorted. 'No, off you go. Have your big reunion with your farmer.'

A week prior, the entire family had descended on the estate for the remainder of the summer. Granny, Amira and I had flown to Edinburgh and taken the train the rest of the way, while the Clarences arrived by private plane. Richard assured anyone who would listen that it was a free ride, provided by an unnamed wealthy friend who was passing through. The Highlands were Granny's favourite place in the world, the place where she could be herself, dressed in slacks, with dirt under her fingernails and a cluster of dogs at her heels. It was my first time there as an adult, and I was learning that it was not as simple as my childhood summers spent lying in the tall grass.

There were multiple outfit changes, an unending schedule of outdoor activities and cocktails so strong they made your eyes sting. Some nights Granny decided we should all eat in front of the television. The next night she'd ask that we sit down for a seven-course meal dressed in evening wear. By my second day at the estate, with its etiquette traps and gin-loosened tongues, I had wondered if I'd made a mistake inviting Jack and Finn there. But it was too late to undo things. And besides, Jenny was up north for the weekend at Granny's request. She would at least tip the scales in favour of sanity.

I left the drawing room and walked through the labyrinth of hallways towards the main entrance. The walls were lined with the heads of glass-eyed stags that had met the wrong end of a rifle, dusty old tapestries and the portraits of my ancestors. Usually a guest who arrived at the estate was greeted by porters, taken to their quarters and handed an itinerary that would tell them exactly when they were allowed to appear in the castle's main rooms for cocktail hour. But I had deliberately dropped out of the stag hunt at the last moment so that I could be there to meet Finn and Jack. It was eight months since I'd been strapped into the belly of the chopper and pulled away from them. It felt like no time had passed. It felt like years had passed.

When I approached the sloping stone archway, my heart was a wild thing. I could see them, backlit in the August sun. Jack turned when he heard my footsteps on the slate floor and I was struck anew by him, his broad shoulders and his brown eyes. He was in a t-shirt I'd never seen, and his hair was an inch longer than I was used to, but it was him. We both stopped and smiled, and I found myself embarrassed by the swell of emotion inside me.

'Lexi!' Finn shouted. His familiar sunglasses were hooked through his shirt collar. He had the vampiric look we both used to get when we were enduring the endless grind of night shifts in Hobart winter. He lifted me off the floor when I reached them and I laughed against his shoulder, realising how much I had missed him. For more than a decade, we had barely spent a day apart and now I'd muddled through nearly a year alone without him. At last he put me down and stepped back. 'You look so *fancy.*'

Mary had me on a strict schedule of hydrafacials, hair treatments, peels, lasers, skin needling, manicures, lymphatic drainage massages and juices. I was shiny-haired, clear-skinned and perfectly groomed. I had deliberately dressed down that morning, pulling on old Levi's and a grey sweatshirt, hoping I would look like myself, even as I stood barefoot and soignée in a castle.

Finn stepped aside and Jack and I exchanged tremulous smiles. I was rooted to the spot, overcome by the sight of him, and he stepped forward and gathered me in his arms. He smelled like the Jennings cottage, like home, and I imagined a PET scan of my brain positively glowing as the scent of him lit up everything inside me. He was warm and real and in my arms, no longer the distant voice on the phone.

'Hey,' he said softly. I could feel the fluttering pulse in his neck.

'Hi,' I whispered.

'Er, ma'am,' Barney said as he appeared next to the pile of bags in the doorway. 'We'll get Mr Jennings and Dr Vanderville's luggage into their rooms now.'

'Thank you, Barney,' I said, distractedly. Jack and I had pulled apart but could not take our eyes off each other. 'I'll come as well.'

This, of course, was a great breach of etiquette, though I did not care, and Barney, who'd always adored Mum, allowed me to do whatever I wanted without raising an eyebrow. He led us through the halls to the guest lodgings in the east wing of the building. My fingertips brushed against Jack's as we walked, our eyes forward, smiles on our faces as Finn regaled me with every detail of their journey.

'We flew via Perth, which is kind of an unending nightmare, but you do get to London quicker that way,' he said, stopping momentarily to glance at a wall adorned with antique pistols and rows of trophy antlers. 'Anyway, business class rules, I loved it. Thanks, doll.'

'Yeah, about that—' Jack started.

'It was all paid for with points,' Finn and I responded in unison.

'I don't know if I believe you two,' Jack said. 'But I'm never going to get a straight answer, am I?'

'Nope,' we said. Jack reached out and caught my fingers in his.

Barney led us to the narrow halls of the guest apartments, where the gloom of the castle gave way to pastel paint shades and soft-pile carpeting. This extension had been added centuries after the main estate, and it was the only part of the house with any warmth. Members of the family insisted on remaining in the draughty sleeping quarters of the west wing because that was what we had always done.

At the end of a long hall, we came to a large guest room painted duck-egg blue. Barney stopped and extended a hand. 'Your quarters, Mr Jennings. I can have a valet unpack for you.'

I had asked for this room to be reserved for Jack because it overlooked the gardens of the south lawn, where the Scottish bluebells and primrose had been allowed to flourish. It was my favourite room, the place my mother had stayed the first time she visited the estate at age eighteen, charming Papa's parents and leaving him no choice but to marry her. I liked to imagine her staying in this jewel box, barely out of girlhood, brimming with optimism that this was the place where she would be loved, where she could be part of a family.

'I, uh, thanks, no, I can do that,' Jack said, wandering into the room, which was the size of our living room in Hobart.

'Very good, sir,' Barney said in his lilting brogue and turned to Finn. 'Dr Vanderville, you're across the hall, if you'll follow me.'

When they left, Jack and I were alone for the first time since New Year's Day. We stood in silence and again traded shy smiles that seemed to dissolve from our faces in a moment. His eyes told me everything I needed to know, and before I had even decided what to do, he was walking across the room and taking me into his arms. He held my face as he kissed me, his hands cupping my cheeks, running down my shoulders and to my waist. I'd felt his hands before, of course: our fingers had brushed when he passed me the Vegemite jar, or when he picked a thistledown out of my hair, or when I'd carefully extracted the splinter from his palm. But when he used those hands to pull me flat against him, holding me closer than I thought was possible, it was like I'd never felt them before. All the years that had passed between us, all the pain I'd inflicted on him, Georgia and Ben, the monumental decision I was yet to make – none of it mattered as I tasted his mouth for the first time.

Distantly, I heard Barney leaving Finn's room in search of a valet to unpack his luggage. I pulled out of Jack's embrace while I still had the willpower.

'Guys, this place is crazy,' Finn said, walking back into the room. 'There's a whole wardrobe full of clothes in my size in that room. Are they for me?'

'They are,' I said, clearing my throat. 'Just a few spares of things you might need.'

My voice was as raw as my nerve endings, but Finn was too overwhelmed by his surroundings to notice that Jack and I were standing together looking stunned and glossy-lipped.

He opened Jack's closet and briefly rifled through the contents. 'Your suit's nice,' he said.

I had asked Mary to stock Finn and Jack's wardrobes with everything they would need, including tuxedos and kilts. The castle was a rather treacherous place for guests. It seemed lovely and old-fashioned and relaxed by royal standards, but every outsider was silently judged for failing the thousands of little tests the family set for them. Not only were you expected to bring your own outdoor shoes – despite the piles and piles of wellies in every corner – your choice of brand could sink you. Hunters were always sneered at, especially the polished black ones. Only mud-splattered Le Chameaus were acceptable. You should have the right clothes for fishing, hiking, church, a rainstorm, an unseasonable thirty-degree day, a black-tie dinner and a highland fling. There was no way of telling which of these events might unfold during your stay at the estate, so it was best to overpack. But if you brought too much luggage, the staff might also gossip about you. If you brought no gift for Granny, you were low-bred. If you arrived with something extravagant, you were gauche. You absolutely had to tip your valet. You had to participate in parlour games. You had to drink the cocktail put down in front of you. It was no wonder Mum had started coming down with unspecified ailments every summer in the days before we were meant to head north for Scotland.

'Anyway, what should we do now?' Finn asked. 'When do we get to meet the big cheese?'

We did what country estate owners always do when they have a guest to entertain and no plan: we went for a long walk. Jack and Finn pulled on their box-fresh wellies so we could walk along the river that wove its way through the estate. The kitchen staff, used to the whims of my family, swiftly put together a picnic that we could take with us.

'Did you notice how everyone just *stopped* and went totally quiet when you walked in?' Finn whispered as we left the kitchen with our basket.

I hadn't noticed. After a few months here, I'd stopped being startled by the hush that fell over every room I entered. I wondered now if perhaps I had begun to enjoy it.

Out on the terrace, we found Amira and Chino lounging in the sunshine. Amira grinned at Jack over the top of her movie-star sunglasses, shaking his hand daintily and looking at me as if she knew exactly what we'd been up to in his room. In Finn, she feigned icy disinterest, though he pretended not to notice. I still wasn't sure exactly how much she knew, but we were all privately determined not to bring up what had happened between Louis and Finn at the vineyard.

'Would you like to come for a walk?' I asked her as Chino sniffed Finn's and Jack's shoes.

'Oh, I suppose so,' she sighed. 'I haven't done a single thing since we arrived.'

We walked along the river's rocky shore, watching Chino plod through the shallows. Finn set about eroding Amira's defences with a cascade of compliments and questions about herself. They drifted slightly ahead, and Jack and I went silent.

'How's it been for you, being back here?'

'Strange,' I said, feeling the slightest graze of his elbow against mine as we walked. 'But good. I think I needed to come back and make things right.'

He nodded, and I knew he understood. 'We've missed you ...' he said. 'I've missed you.'

'Same.'

'Though this looks like quite a life,' he said, gesturing at the verdant hills and the castle on the horizon. 'I remember when you first moved in, I didn't really know anything about you. I spent those first few weeks googling the royal family.'

I smiled. 'Did you read my Wikipedia page?'

'Yeah, I read your Wikipedia page.' He laughed. 'I remember seeing this one photo of you when you were a kid. I think it must have been taken here. You were on a pony, and you were in the fanciest, frilliest dress, and I thought, *What is this girl doing renting my shitty barn?*'

I had never heard any of this before. He'd always seemed completely indifferent to my past, only bemused that I didn't know how to send a package by express post, or change a vacuum cleaner bag or put wiper fluid in my car.

'I googled a lot about wine in the beginning,' I admitted. 'So that I could impress you with my knowledge.'

He raised his eyebrows. 'But you know a lot about wine.'

'I do now.'

He laughed again and put an arm around my shoulder, and it was like the last eight months had never happened and we were back where we should have been, before the avalanche and the helicopter and the crown came between us.

Up ahead, Amira and Finn were locked in conversation. Suddenly she turned around.

'Lexi! You never told me you delivered a baby for one of those girls who goes into labour but had no idea she was pregnant. I *love* those stories.'

'Oh, yeah,' I said, allowing Jack to keep the warm length of his arm around my back, even as Amira and Finn looked at us and pretended not to notice. 'She thought her appendix had burst.'

We sat by the stream and opened the basket that the kitchen staff had packed for us: crumbly cheddar, apples, shortbread and a thermos of tea. Amira seemed to be thawing to Finn, albeit reluctantly. He was impossible to resist, even if he had slept with your husband just weeks before your wedding.

'Are you ready for tonight, you two?' she asked.

'What do we need to be ready for?' Finn asked, intrigued.

Amira sipped her tea and threw a piece of cheese to Chino, lolling in the grass beside us. 'You're fresh meat, and this family is absolutely starving. There's nothing they love more than having common folk like us at the table.'

'Amira, you're hardly common folk,' I said.

'I don't decide who's common – they do. It doesn't matter if you're the prime minister or a millionaire's daughter,' she said, and then looked at Finn and Jack. 'But don't be scared. It took me years to understand all the insults that had flown right over my head. You'll be long gone by the time you figure out the slights that seemed like jokes.'

'Amira,' I said, glancing at Jack, who was rubbing Chino's belly but listening intently, 'you're scaring them.'

Finn laughed. 'I'm actually excited – this sounds nuts.'

Amira sighed and leaned back on her elbows in the long grass. 'You're not the one they're waiting to meet.'

I hid my flaming cheeks behind my enamel teacup. I could hardly scold her when she was speaking the truth.

'I think I can handle whatever they've got, Amira,' Jack said.

She smiled enigmatically behind her sunglasses, her hair tangling across her face in the breeze. There was something dangerous about her in this mood. Most of the time I felt like she was just beyond my reach, the truth of her hidden behind her duchess sheen.

'I'm glad to hear it,' she said.

Back at the house, we dressed for drinks, which the staff had communicated via handwritten note would be followed by a sit-down dinner in the dining room. I'd hoped for something more casual, then realised that Granny would be unwilling to balance a TV dinner on her knees in front of strangers.

I ordered a brandy to my room to try to calm my nerves as cocktail hour approached. Why hadn't I taken Jack and Finn to Croatia for a week instead of this? I put on a halterneck gown in a heavy navy silk that tied at the nape of my neck and then piled my hair on top of my head. I applied, then removed, red lipstick. I put on dangly earrings, then took them off. I took a sip of my brandy and stared at my reflection. The Algarve, I thought. That's where we should have gone. Clams and nightclubs and beaches packed with burnt British tourists.

My phone buzzed.

You were right, Finn's text said. *We need help with the bow ties.*

I made the long march through the hallway, my heart jangling as I approached the guest wing. They were in Finn's room, standing before the mirror and murmuring in low voices, and they turned when I knocked on the open door.

'I hear you need help in here,' I said, affecting a nonchalant air that was unlikely to convince anyone.

Jack's eyes met mine. I'd never seen him out of jeans and Blundstones before and I felt a girlish thrill at the sight of him in his suit, the black tie draped loosely around his collar.

'Oh, you look hot, babe,' Finn said, turning back to the mirror. 'These things are impossible. Even an eight-minute YouTube tutorial didn't help.'

I stood before Jack, remembering the lessons Papa used to give Louis while I sat on the bed and watched. 'A gentleman must always know how to tie his own tie,' Papa would say, Louis frowning in the mirror beside him.

Jack looked down at me as I reached to take hold of the scrap of silk around his neck. It had the effect of drawing us closer.

'You look ...' he whispered, his eyes wandering.

'Thank you. You too.' I cleared my throat, pushing up the collar of his shirt and allowing one finger to brush against his jaw. 'Okay so ...' My hands skimmed his collarbones as I talked him through the steps. 'You pull one side down and hold it taut, fold the front ... loop the loop and tighten it while holding all four points.'

I spent more time adjusting the knot than was strictly necessary, then smoothed down his collar and picked an imaginary piece of lint from his chest. His eyes never left my face as I worked.

'Not bad,' I breathed.

'Are you kidding?' Finn laughed. 'We look amazing. I want to wear this every night for the rest of my life.'

When they were both dressed, I noticed the etiquette guide lying on the bed. I'd hesitated before sending it, imagining how it would land for two Australians, who had grown up in a place where the greatest show of respect for an authority figure was to treat them as casually as a friend. Now they were being told never to show the monarch their back. Shaking hands is acceptable, but only if she reaches first. 'Ma'am' should always sound like 'jam', never 'palm'. When dining with the Queen, one must stop eating as soon as she is done.

I looked at them, embarrassed. 'Any questions about meeting her? You know how to bow?'

'How's this?' Finn swooped his arms like a dancer and performed a full court curtsy that ended with him on the floor.

'Okay, that's perfect for a Texas debutante, but keeping your hands by your side and nodding once from the neck will do it.'

Jack's hand hovered at the small of my back, his fingertips grazing the bare skin there. 'Seriously, we're good – I made him practise.'

As we entered the main drawing room, murmuring voices hushed to nothing and the huddled groups turned in unison to look at us. Richard and Demelza were by the bar waiting for their martinis. They inspected us briefly, then turned away. Amira was on the couch with Birdie. Granny and Jenny were chatting in the corner, the set of their brows suggesting they were discussing business, not pleasure. While I still had the courage, I pulled Jack and Finn with me across the room.

'Granny, these are my friends,' I said. 'This is Jack and Finn, from Tasmania.'

She looked at them kindly while they bowed. 'Yes, of course, how nice of you to come all this way. And thank you for the wine. My grandson talked endlessly of your sparkling after he visited your vineyard.'

For her entire life, Granny had been the woman on the banknote and the portrait in the government building, but there was no one more adept at making herself a flesh-and-blood human when she encountered her subjects. My nerves evaporated like snowmelt on the first day of spring as she asked Jack about the vineyard and its history. A tray of martinis arrived. The candles burned. The Clarences sat down and offered Jack and Finn limp handshakes and superior smiles.

The others were talking in intricate detail about the stag they'd been hunting for two days, so I retreated to another sofa with Jenny. 'He's doing well,' she whispered to me. 'Is he … the reason for your hesitation?'

'My hesitation?' I asked.

'Well, the end of the year is five months away, and you haven't told us if you've decided you'll be staying on.'

'Oh.' I took a gulp of my drink.

The question of what I planned to do was rarely broached by anyone in the family, although it was the only thing I thought about. There were occasions when I was determined to stay and do this – small, stirring moments I had so far kept a secret. The way the crowd had roared for Granny when we came out on the balcony during Trooping the Colour. The little girls waiting behind the rope line to give me their hand-picked posies and their drawings. The day the obstetric fistula hospital in Nairobi had accepted the offer of my patronage and said they hoped this was the beginning of a long and beautiful relationship. But whenever I thought about going to Granny, or Stewart, or Jenny, to inform them that I was ready to commit to this life, I couldn't do it. I'd put it off, and put it off, until the end of the year was in sight.

'Have you ever heard the saying that the most important decision a woman makes in her career is her choice of partner?' Jenny asked. 'I think that's true of women like you as well. If you intend to do this, you'll need the right man by your side.'

I looked at Jack, sleek in his tux, talking easily with Granny. She laughed a little at something he said. I turned back to Jenny, who was watching me. She was more serious than I'd ever seen her.

'I debated telling you this, but I think we have the kind of relationship where we can be honest with each other.'

I nodded, suddenly nervous. 'Of course.'

'When you invited your friends up here, Scotland Yard ran a background check – standard stuff when someone new meets the family.'

My throat felt very tight. 'Did they send someone to the house in Hobart? Jack said a man's been hanging around asking questions. I thought maybe he was a reporter, but nothing ever came of it.'

She looked at me, confused. 'No, they wouldn't need to do that. They just source documents from their Australian partners – police reports and such.'

We fell silent as a servant arrived carrying a silver tray of fresh martinis. I took one. When he left, Jenny turned to me and spoke quietly. 'What I want to tell you is that the palace seemed very concerned by Jack's background. His mother is rather ... radical? A republican? And Jack himself was arrested a few years ago at a protest.'

I imagined Jack and Paula becoming grist for the tabloids, all the things they had done to keep Tasmania pristine made to look rotten and sinister, and all of it happening because I had come smashing into their lives. When Jenny saw the look on my face, she gave me her kindest smile.

'Look, none of this is a problem for me. I rather like it myself.' She grew serious again and hesitated. 'I should tell you, though, that if there were a scenario where he were to move here on a more permanent basis, it would be ... difficult. I can help, of course, and if it's what you want, it will be worth it. But I imagine that both the Queen and the public will take some convincing. You would have to prepare yourself – and him. The press can be very cruel, as you know.'

I was quiet for a long time, and she let me dwell in the silence. Finally, I spoke. 'People keep telling me love isn't enough to hold a relationship together.'

She thought for a moment and then looked at the aristocrats lounging around us. In the shadows, servants waited to attend to our every whim. 'I wouldn't know the answer to that. All I can tell you is that the right person will know who you really are, and they'll love you anyway.'

A footman announced that dinner was served, and we moved to the dining room. I was surprised to find that Jack was seated to Granny's right – the place usually reserved for the guest of honour. Finn and I were way down the other side with the Clarences. For Richard, life was a constant, slippery struggle to be as close as possible to power. Stuck at the kids' end of the table, he would probably spend most of the night craning his neck, trying to listen to the conversation between the monarch and the prime minister.

'And what kind of doctor do you plan to be, Finn?' Demelza asked primly.

'Oh, well, I've actually just applied for the surgical program,' he said, his eyes cautiously on me as I turned to look at him between two candelabras. 'So if that works out, I'll be a surgical resident next year.'

I smiled thinly at him. 'That's great.'

The last I'd heard, he'd been planning to be a paediatrician. I would go into obstetrics and deliver the babies, and he would take over from there. It had been our joke for years. But, a quiet voice in my head reminded me, I had been the one to chuck it all in first.

'So what kind of ... I mean, what part of the body would you operate on?' Birdie asked.

'I don't want to get ahead of myself – I haven't been accepted yet. But I like orthopaedics – bones and stuff.'

'My friend's father is an orthopaedic surgeon,' Demelza said. 'He does 250 knee replacements a year, and it's all about to be done by robots anyway.'

'Yeah, robotic systems have revolutionised joint replacements, but there's still a surgeon guiding the machine,' Finn said.

Richard, who had barely acknowledged us the entire meal, suddenly turned.

'Sounds like lucrative work, just pushing a few buttons,' he said to Finn, smiling. He swivelled towards the other end of the table. 'And what about you, young Jack?' Everyone turned to look at Richard, whose top row of teeth gleamed. 'Tell us about this vineyard of yours. Is it successful?'

'By our own standards, it is,' Jack said. I watched the play of candlelight and shadows across his face. 'We're a small-batch vineyard. We're not so concerned with volume, at least not yet. I want us to expand, but right now we hand-tend to the vines. For us, it's about the pinot grape. We're just trying to capture a bit of its magic in our bottles.'

This was not the spiel he gave at wine shows. This was how he really felt. I smiled at him across the table, and he smiled back.

'Well, that all sounds very credible, doesn't it, Mummy?' Richard said. 'Dare I say it, almost plausible.' Whether she heard him or not, Granny gave no sign. Richard grinned at Jack. 'We're all country folk at heart, you know. We are honoured to serve, of course, but if it were up to us, we'd all be up here with our animals and our land.'

'Not me,' said Amira.

'Yes, well …' Richard smirked. 'You've always been a wild creature from the urban jungle, haven't you?'

Amira gazed at him for a moment, then she tipped her head back and drained her wine. She rose from her chair and turned to Granny. 'I have a headache coming on, so, ma'am, if it's alright, I might turn in.'

'Of course, dear,' Granny said.

After the bagpiper marched around the table, emitting his ear-piercing whine, we returned to the drawing room for a mandatory round of parlour games. More martinis were mixed, the icy glasses placed into our hands. I texted Amira to ask if she was alright and she said she was going to bed.

'Am I dreaming or are we really playing charades with the Queen?' Finn whispered. The three of us were squeezed onto a velvet sofa as we watched Birdie flap her hands to act out the title of a literary masterpiece she'd never read. The warm, solid length of Jack was pressed against my side.

'Yes,' I said. 'Though she only really observes these days.'

'Okay, good – I think I'd pass out if she got up there,' Jack whispered, and we laughed quietly.

After three rounds of charades, which Jenny and Demelza dominated, Granny retired to bed. We all stood as she glided from the room.

'For god's sake, sit down, it's much too late for that.' She sighed. 'See you all in the morning. It'll be a good day for fishing.'

With Granny gone, the parlour games ceased by wordless agreement, and everyone sank into their chairs and sipped their drinks. Birdie was explaining to a blank-faced Jenny that after a few months in the movie business, she was now considering a career in the art world. It was quite by accident that my hand slipped into Jack's. Between us, our fingers wove together, though we didn't look at each other. I pretended to concentrate on Birdie's professional aspirations, while my stomach did a little flip.

'Well, I might head off to bed,' Finn said suddenly. 'The jetlag, you know, it *hits*. Goodnight, all.'

'Night, mate,' Jack said, and I felt the vibration of his voice course through me, even though there were just two of us remaining on the couch. From the doorway, Finn winked at me and then he was gone. The conversation continued, though I barely heard a word of it. My heart began to thud as Jack squeezed my hand. I ran my thumb along the thin ridge of the splinter scar I had stitched up last year. It was healing well. After a few minutes, I stood up, unthreading my fingers from his as I rose.

'I am ... also heading to bed. Goodnight, everyone.'

'Yeah, good idea,' I heard Jack say as I reached the door. 'I might turn in as well. Night, all.'

Ignoring the knowing smiles of my family, I left the room and began walking up the stairs towards the guest wing, past the portrait of Barbara who seemed to wink as I passed her. Soon I could hear Jack's footsteps behind me. We continued through the dark halls, me a few paces ahead, not daring to look over my shoulder. I wondered if I had chosen this dress for this moment, with its revealing back and the tie hanging loosely down my spine. I felt oddly serene, even on the edge of something I had fought against and denied myself for seven years. I didn't doubt he was following me.

I entered his room and by the time he came through the door, I was standing at the dark window with my back to him. I heard the latch, and then the slide of the lock as he closed us in for the evening. I felt as untamed as the garden outside, where the summer mists swirled under a heavy moon and the heather glowed red in its light. Then Jack's arms were sliding around my waist. His breath was in my hair and his warm lips against my neck. His hands were surer this time, and when he gripped my hips, I turned in the circumference of his arms, finally ready. That same glimmer of danger I'd felt on New Year's Day was back, but now I knew the dangerous thing was me. I looked at this man, with his hopeful eyes and his endless patience and all that love he offered with two open palms, and I knew that he was mine to treasure or mine to ruin. As our mouths came together, I did not allow myself to think that this was goodbye.

PART THREE

CHAPTER TWENTY-ONE

10 October 2023

I was drifting on Mum's raft under a moonless sky when I felt his hand skim down my back and settle on my waist.

'Time to wake up,' he whispered, and I moaned, the dull thrum of a hangover in my temples. He kissed my neck as his hands crept lower. 'Come on. You said 8 am no matter what, remember?'

I opened my eyes. The last red leaves were falling off the row of sycamores that lined the window. There were six more weeks of autumn, but an icy gloom had already descended on London. My crumpled skirt from the night before was pooled on the floor. Two paracetamol lay on his palm.

'You shouldn't have made me that last gimlet,' I said and popped the pills in my mouth. I took the water glass he offered next.

'But you're so *fun* when you're tipsy.' Colin nuzzled my neck. He was crisp, showered and dressed in a dry-clean fresh suit. 'Oh, that drab little lady-in-waiting of yours is blowing up your phone.'

I groaned.

He rose from the bed and took his cashmere coat off the hook in the corner. 'What are you doing tonight? Dinner?'

'I can't remember – I might have another reception,' I said, stalling for time. 'I'll check with Mary.'

He smiled, came back to the bed and kissed me. 'Don't go disappearing on me again, Your Highness.'

I lay in the bed for a few more minutes staring at the ceiling. My face was going to be puffy from the gin, and Mary would be annoyed at me. Finally, I got up, put on Colin's dressing gown and went to the kitchen to attempt to make coffee with his elaborate machine.

Out the window, Belgravia's gleaming white buildings looked like wedding cakes. Young men in suits who drove cars and opened doors for the surrounding embassies loitered and smoked on the kerb below, waiting for something to happen. I could no longer ignore the wasp-like buzzing of my phone and answered Mary's call.

'Hi.'

'Oh, Your Royal Highness,' Mary said, 'I've been trying to reach you. We're due at the hospital soon, but you're … not home. Did you go swimming this morning?'

I pinched the bridge of my nose. I'd forgotten all about it. 'No, I'll text you the address. Swing by and pick me up. I'll change in the car.'

There was a long pause. 'Will you be camera-ready?'

I looked at my reflection in Colin's glossy oven door. 'Maybe bring some makeup.'

Later, in the back of the car, I struggled into the candy-pink suit Mary had brought with her – clearly I was being punished for my bad behaviour – and tried to swipe neat swoops of liquid liner along my lids. I was due to open a refurbished obstetrics ward. It was my biggest engagement yet, an issue that was all mine, not a patronage I'd picked up on Papa or Louis's behalf.

'Your numbers are up again, ma'am,' Mary said, pecking at her phone.

'Okay.'

'Sixty-nine per cent approval. Very good. We're officially ahead of the Duke of Clarence now.'

I closed my eyes, wondering if a quick nap would deflate my puffy eyes or only make me look worse. The appearance at the hospital would last an hour and then I could go back to bed.

'Ma'am,' Mary said sternly, 'is something the matter?'

'I'm just tired, sorry. I'll perk up.'

'No, that's not it,' she said, and I turned to her, surprised. 'You've been off for two months now. Today is the day. This is the first day of your campaign, the start of everything we've been planning: you're going to show them a new monarchy that doesn't shy away from the issues. Maternal health is the one thing you wanted to focus on above all else. Then we'd do sexual violence. Then we'd start addressing the injustices of colonialism.'

I laughed. I could not believe I'd once had the gall to think I could fix those things. Mary looked astonished, and I sobered. 'Sorry, sorry. I'm not laughing at you,' I said. 'I'm just in a weird mood. You're right. It is a good day.'

She studied me for a minute and then turned to her window. 'You're dropping weight too. If you lose any more, the tabloids will notice.'

Chastened, I tried to remember the last thing I'd eaten. There had been no time for breakfast because I was running late. Had I eaten dinner? I'd been to the palace in the evening for a reception and headed to Colin's as soon as it was over. There had been talk of pizza. But then he'd made a pitcher of gimlets while I perched on his kitchen counter to watch, and then he was kissing me and undoing my blazer, and then he pinned me, gasping, against the cold marble benchtop. I closed my eyes again. Hunger pangs had woken me up in the middle of the night, but instead of getting up to search for food, I'd found my phone in the mess of clothes on the floor and googled the name again and again: *David Rossi, Who is David Rossi?, Rossi + David, LinkedIn David Rossi, Instagram David Rossi*. Now was the time to tell Mary about David Rossi, to ask her to use the palace's shadowy connections and her sheer bloody-mindedness to track this person down. But I hadn't told a soul since I'd heard the name ten weeks earlier.

When the car pulled up at the hospital, the royal rota photographer was waiting alongside a Wolseley House videographer who would capture my every move so he could splice it together in a meaningless montage, set to an upbeat pop song, and upload it to Instagram. The family wasn't on TikTok yet, but that was another silly little idea that Mary and I had thought up which would never be realised. I got out of the car, winched up my brightest smile and shook the hands of the doctors and hospital administrators lined up to greet me.

It was nice to be in a hospital again, even with the unfamiliar rat-a-tat of my stilettos on the floor. The chemical iodoform, used as a disinfectant, is what gives hospitals their ubiquitous, astringent odour. For most people, it hits the olfactory nerve and triggers a trauma response. For me, it's the scent of comfort, of the one place I am totally myself. Coffee, exhaustion, Finn, the chaos of the human life cycle. It all came back to me as Dr Jacqueline Rockcliffe, the newly minted head of obstetrics at Prince Frederick Memorial Hospital NHS Trust, showed me from room to room. A woman who had just given birth was pre-screened and served up for a seemingly natural conversation with me as the cameras rolled. My hand, guided by the muscle memory developed over a thousand night shifts, rested on the chart hanging from the edge of her bed. I intertwined my fingers to keep myself from picking it up and reading it. She handed me her scrunchy-faced baby and I held him in my arms as the camera shutters clicked.

'His stomach is a bit rounder today. Do you think that's normal?' the woman asked.

'Probably just a bit of gas,' I murmured, feeling his distended belly. Then I caught myself. Quickly, I smiled. 'Ask your doctor about it. Obviously we're not going to try to sort that out with the cameras rolling!'

The photographers and assembled doctors laughed, and the pinched expression cleared from Mary's face. This event was the closest we had come to acknowledging the fact that I had once been a member of the professional class. It was a potent, but perilous, part of my story. The thinking was that by the time I was a ninety-year-old monarch, everyone would remember fondly that I once was a doctor, that I'd once made use of my hands before my function became entirely symbolic. But while my future subjects were still getting to know me, my MD could be problematic. It suggested I didn't want to really play this role, that I thought I was better than everyone else. That's what the focus groups said, anyway.

After my visit with the new mother, the event was done, and the rota photographer was thrilled to move on with his day. I lingered for a moment to chat to Dr Rockcliffe at the nurses' station while Mary and the team waited, checking their watches and exchanging meaningful glances. Palace scheduling was practically set by an atomic clock, and we were now ten minutes behind.

Dr Rockcliffe looked over my shoulder and brightened. 'This here is the junior doctor assigned to the patient we just met.'

I turned to see a man my age, looking crumpled in his green scrubs. He dropped his charts on the bench and shook my hand, too exhausted to smile or bow. His eyes were ringed in black shadows, and his hair was flat from a recent nap against a hard surface.

'I'm Dr Lee. Nice to meet you,' he said.

'A real pleasure,' I trilled, suddenly aware of my lurid pink outfit and stage makeup, detesting myself. 'What year are you in, Dr Lee?'

'I'm an F2,' he said. 'Second year.'

I leaned in conspiratorially and whispered, 'Are you exhausted?'

After a moment, he laughed, his reflexes as slow as if he were moving underwater. 'A little. But it's okay.'

I nodded. 'Well, thank you for your service. The NHS is Britain's greatest achievement, and it's entirely made up by people like you.'

He smirked and plunged his hands into his pockets. 'Everyone loves it – no one wants to pay for it. Am I right? I did ninety hours last week, but I'll be paid for forty-eight.'

Everyone stiffened. Dr Rockcliffe shot a dark look at Dr Lee, the kind of warning shots I used to dread from my own superiors at Hobart General. It took him a moment to realise what he'd said, and then the tips of his ears went pink. Mary came forward and grasped my elbow.

'I'm terribly sorry to interrupt, ma'am, but we're already late. We probably should be going now.'

A couple of nurses in lab coats were wandering down the hall, but when they saw us, they stopped, turned around and went back the way they came. They must have been told we'd be gone by ten-fifteen.

'Yes, alright,' I said and extended my hand. 'It was lovely to meet you, Dr Lee.'

He shook it absently, his mind already back on the dozen tasks he had to complete in the next ten minutes, my insipid chat only slowing him down. 'Yes, uh, thank you, ma'am.'

I tapped down the hall in my ridiculous shoes, surrounded by my entourage of handlers and security guards.

'Oh, hey, Your, um, Highness,' Dr Lee called, and I stopped and turned back to look at him. A strip of fluorescent lights overhead blurred his edges and bathed him in a synthetic glow. 'You were right about Arlo – the baby. Just a bit of gas.'

When I got home, Cumberland 1 was empty, except for Chino. I closed the door behind me, and he put his heavy paws on my shoulders – a bad habit we were trying to break – but I pretended he was trying to embrace me and wrapped my arms around his solid trunk while he squirmed and sniffed. In the bedroom, I stripped off my pink outfit, pulled on Jack's t-shirt and crawled under the covers. Chino slipped in beside me.

I was getting very good at pushing all thoughts of Jack from my mind, even if I did sleep in his shirt every night. When the maid washed it, I'd been devastated and sent a lengthy text to Finn explaining why I needed him to go into Jack's laundry and pilfer me a new one, and that while this might *seem* like worrying behaviour, it was entirely reasonable.

Honey, he wrote back. *That wouldn't be a good idea. You get that, right?*

Finn was still texting me daily as if none of it had ever happened. He told me about the wounds he was treating at the hospital. He updated me on Hobart gossip and told me what Ragu was doing. But he refused to talk about Jack, insisting a no-contact rule was essential so that we could both move on.

He's okay, he wrote after I spent an hour trying to steer our text conversation towards Jack. *But that's all you get xxxxx*

If I could have ripped my heart out of my chest to cure me of this ache, I would have done it. I knew I needed to cry at some point, but no tears would come. The only relief I could find was in sleep. For the first time since I was seventeen, I couldn't seem to get enough of it. I'd been more alert when I worked hundred-hour weeks at the hospital. But now I trudged through each day under the impossible weight of exhaustion. As soon as I pressed my head into the pillow, I succumbed gratefully to the darkness that would erase me for a while.

The bedroom was cast in late-afternoon shadows by the time Amira put a cool hand on my forehead.

'Hey,' she whispered. She was dressed in her Pilates gear. 'You alright?'

'Yeah, just tired.'

She picked up a takeaway cup from the side table and handed it to me. 'I got you one of those smoothies you like from that place.'

'I don't know if I'm hungry,' I said. I was beginning to like the self-flagellation of emptiness again.

She pushed the cup into my hands and smiled. 'If I have to eat, you have to eat. Drink as much as you can, and I'll finish it.'

I took a sip while Amira crawled into the bed. Thrilled by this development, Chino curled himself between us and sighed deeply. The smoothie felt cloying on my tongue. Eventually I gave up and passed the cup to Amira. I could hear the familiar sounds of the house staff in the kitchen, the clicking of the gas hob, the fridge sucking closed.

'We'll be too full for dinner after that,' I said.

'No,' Amira said firmly. 'They're making roast chicken.'

She finished the smoothie with a slurp and put the cup on the side table.

'So do you want to, like, talk about it?' she asked.

'When do we ever want to talk about it?'

She put her face in Chino's neck while I stared at the ceiling. 'I know, it would be very middle class of us. But it's just ... I hate seeing you like this. Maybe you'd feel better if you told someone what happened.'

What *had* happened? I would tell someone if I knew. I thought of those first few days of Jack and Finn's trip to the estate, when everything had seemed so perfect. Jack and I had woken up together, naked and no longer just friends. We kissed behind the trees while everyone was fishing. At dinner, he reached under the table and ran his finger along the delicate skin behind my knee. I liked planing my hands along his chest. I became greedy for the new rendition of my name that I could elicit from his lips, his look of intense concentration when I climbed onto his lap. There were broken buttons on my shirt and a bloom of colour on his collarbone. And we would always lie there in the aftermath, both of us stripped bare, Jack's hand skimming over my skin. I would watch his face while he did this, curled on my side and unafraid.

But on the last day – the terrible day – the mood had shifted. He and Finn were flying from Aberdeen to London the next day, and then onwards to Australia. Our looming separation didn't seem real to either of us. Jack was quiet at the breakfast table, and I eyed him warily over my teacup.

'So Amira and I are going into town today to go shopping, just the two of us,' Finn said.

He and Amira were now bosom buddies – phone numbers and Instagram handles exchanged, the past forgotten.

'Okay,' I said. 'We might go for a drive. There's something I want to show Jack.'

We borrowed a Range Rover and drove to the outer edge of the estate. There was a cliff out there that had been Mum's favourite place, her retreat from the family as summer dragged on, and old grudges and jealousies started to surface. I would often come along, bouncing in the back of the car as she drove over rough terrain. The cliff was the highest point of the estate, and the view was incomparable. It was a starker beauty out there than the plush pastures along the river. It reminded me of Tasmania.

After a long, wordless drive, I parked the car and we walked among the rocky outcrop to the cliff's edge. Mist had pooled in the valleys and the wind brought more vapour than air. But it was clear enough to see the abundance of my family's lands. Those green hills that rolled all the way to the horizon belonged to us. Jack looked out over everything I would one day own and his eyebrows stitched together.

'This was my mum's favourite place,' I said, my heart uneasy. 'I wanted you to see it.'

He nodded. He was wearing a Barbour jacket bought for him with Mary's palace credit card and he wore it well.

'Lex,' he said finally, 'are you going to be the queen?'

He asked it so freely, so casually. But I could see in his eyes that this question had been humming inside him for as long and as intensely as it had been in me.

'I … have until the end of the year to decide,' I said weakly.

He squinted at me, confused. 'Yeah, but you're meant to be on holiday this month, and Amira said you'll be spending most of it travelling around Scotland to shore up your support here. And she said you're about to shift your office's agenda so it's in line with your philanthropic goals instead of your dad's. It sounds to me like you've already decided and just haven't told anyone. Me included.'

I looked down at my feet. He was right, of course. I had been telling myself that I could go back to Australia at any moment, but as each week passed, I was planting my roots further and further into the familiar soil here.

'I know it's difficult to understand, but I was born into this family, and that means I'm meant to serve. It's just the way it works. The crown is landing on my head and—'

'Lexi, I don't give a shit if you want to be the queen,' he said sharply, running his hands through his hair the way he did when he was stressed. 'I knew you'd made up your mind when we talked about the reception for the African hospital. And I was happy for you. If this is what you want, you should do it.'

'It's not about what I want,' I insisted. 'It's a duty. People find it hard to understand, but—'

'I don't find it hard to understand. I really don't. I may not have all this,' he said, throwing his arm towards the hills around us, 'but I know what family loyalty is. I know what it is to have a legacy. Fixing up the vineyard was all my dad wanted to do, and then he died, and it became mine. I'm keeping those vines alive for him. I get it, Lex, I do.'

'So what are you asking me?'

I could see that I had hurt him then. He looked out at the same timeworn valleys and breathed the same air that used to cleanse my mother.

'I'm asking where I fit in,' he said. 'I haven't wanted to ask for eight months because I didn't want to push you, but I'm here now. I'm wearing the clothes you picked out for me and I'm trying to impress your family. I need to know what you want. Because everyone thinks you're undecided about the crown, but I think maybe you're just undecided about me.'

The wind was starting to pick up and I was grateful for the gusts that gave cover for the tears forming in my eyes.

'Jack,' I said, 'what am I going to do? Ask you to move here? So you can be my consort and follow me around – a few paces behind – for the rest of your life? You know what it would be like for you here, don't you? You'd be shadowed by servants, hosting tea parties and cutting ribbons. The press would be awful to you. You would hate it here. Eventually you'd hate me too. I know you hate the monarchy—'

'I don't *hate* it, Lex,' he said. 'I think it's got some things to answer for, like, I don't know, slavery? And causing so much pain for so many people? But you *agree* with me on that. I know you do.'

'I still have to do this,' I snapped. 'It was meant to be Louis, but now he's gone, and I have to do it for him.'

It was the first time I'd ever said it out loud, and the first time I realised it was true. I would never go back to Tasmania. I would never practise medicine again. The throne was waiting for me, and when my time came, I intended to take it.

Jack walked perilously close to the cliff's edge, breathing deeply with his hands on his hips. Part of me wanted to go back to the trees along the river, where he'd trail his fingertips along my jawline, the real world somewhere else, somewhere very far away.

'I think we should go back,' he said. 'I have to pack for tomorrow.'

'Jack,' I said, 'please don't be angry at me. You said it yourself. You have your father's vineyard, and I think that's so special. But I have to be here and you have to be there. When Georgia asked you to go to New York with her, you wouldn't do it. I'm not going to ask you to do something you can't.'

He turned then and his eyes were blazing. 'I didn't go to New York with Georgia because I was in love with you. After that mess with the photographer, she realised how I felt and that's why she applied for that job. She tested me and I failed.'

I opened my mouth to speak. The whole time he'd been at the estate, I'd been terrified he would say it. I could see it in his face when he kissed me, when we woke up together, when he looked at me across the table through candlelight. I had willed him not to say the words because I had always known that his love would humble me. It would make me soft. It would make me need him. And once the connective tissue that bound us grew so intricate and so fibrous that I could no longer live without him, he would finally see me for who I was, and he would recoil. I refused to trap him inside palace walls with me while I watched that happen, so I turned and started walking back to the car. I wanted to be out of this place. I wanted the granite walls of the palace around me, the endless ticking of the grandfather clock keeping time with my heart. I had to get home.

'Lex,' he called but I kept walking to the car. 'Damn it, Lexi, this is why I've never told you before. I knew you'd do this. Why can't you ever just be honest with me? Why can't you ever just tell me what you're thinking?'

Blinded by my tears, I fumbled for the keys in my pocket and dropped them in the scrub.

'Is this about that guy?' I heard Jack say. I turned to look at him, the keys forgotten at my feet. 'Your uncle said there was something going on. I don't know, something about a library.'

My stomach roiled. Jack and Richard crawling through the heather together two days earlier. I had seen him lean across and whisper in Jack's ear. 'You talked to Richard about me?'

He ran his fingers through his hair again and hesitated. 'He cornered me on the stag hunt. I know what he was up to – I'm not stupid. I was going to ignore it. But ... is that what this is about?'

I thought of Colin, with his titles and his top hats. Granny liked him; the tabloids adored him. Being my consort wouldn't destroy Colin's life, or keep him from his land, or twist his family's history of activism into something shameful. This was what Colin was born for, just as I was born for the throne.

I stooped to pick up the keys. 'We should get back.'

'Lex. I don't—'

'I'm not the girl in the barn anymore.' I wiped my cheeks with my fingertips and shook my head. 'I don't think I ever was. You were wrong about me. You should go home – it's better this way.'

The advancing storm clouds cast us in a low blue light. There were tears in both of our eyes, but neither of us would let them fall. I knew that as long as I lived, the look on his face would never leave me. I desperately wanted to get in the car. And I desperately wanted to stay here on this cliff forever so we never had to say goodbye.

'You were never going to take a risk, were you?' he asked.

The next morning, I hid in my room like a coward. Finn knocked softly on the door and then let himself in. He sat on the foot of the bed.

'Are you okay?' he asked.

'You'll take care of him?'

He dipped his head. 'Who'll take care of you, though?'

Tears spilled over my cheeks. I had lain awake all night and now I had a drilling headache.

'Oh, doll,' Finn soothed, 'are you really sure about this? I know it's complicated, but I've been living with you two for seven years now. What you have, I don't think it's easy to find.'

'You know I'd ruin it,' I said, though I was speaking to myself. I sat up and gathered him in my arms. 'You're going to make a really good surgeon.'

He smiled, but he looked mournful. 'We're going to stay friends, though, right?'

'Of course.'

He looked down at his hands. 'I know I've always got people around me. And maybe it didn't start that way … but you're the first real friend I ever had.'

I smiled. 'I really do love you.'

He held me again, kissed my forehead and then hopped off the bed. He was dressed in the clothes Mary had bought for him, as well as the Barbour jacket that was meant for Jack.

'Okay, we're going to head out.' At the doorway he stopped and smiled. 'And if you can't find anyone, I'll marry you. It'd be fun.'

I managed to laugh. 'Honestly, though, maybe. It's not such a bad idea.'

After he left, I lay back in the pillows and counted the rippling folds in the canopy above me. Then my heart surged, and I ripped back the blankets and ran down the hallway in my pyjamas. From the window on the stairs, I watched as a footman packed their luggage into a Range Rover while they stood together on the gravel driveway. Their backs were to me and I saw Finn rest a hand on Jack's shoulder. When they climbed into the car, Jack looked up and saw me standing there, hiding in a tartan drape. Our eyes met for one last moment, that old charge still coursing between us. He dropped his head and I couldn't tell if it was a bow or an admission of defeat. Then he was gone.

Going over it with Amira now, I told her as much of this as I could bear. She listened in silence, stroking Chino's fur. She knew me well enough to keep her eyes averted while I told her my story. When I was done, she propped her head on one hand and gazed at me.

'I really am sorry,' she said. 'I know you're hurting, but I think you did the right thing. It sounds like he would have come here if you asked him. But it probably would have been a disaster.'

I nodded at the ceiling.

She checked the time on her phone. 'Come on, let's go have some dinner and then we can get drunk on the couch and watch *Love Island*.'

*

The day after the hospital visit, I rose early and went to the pond for the first time in months. The sun was yet to rise, and I was the first one through the gates and onto the frosted deck. I sat down and dipped my feet in the dark water, trying to work up the courage to lower myself into it. Scotland Yard had reassigned Rita to other duties when I stopped swimming, and I had managed to slip out through Cumberland's gates undetected. For the first time in a very long time, I was alone.

I had not told Amira everything about that day in Scotland. I had told no one that after Jack's car had disappeared down the drive, I turned from the window and found Richard standing on the landing. He was in a suit – strange, I thought, even for our family – and his hands were clasped together over his belly as he waited for me to see him. He raised his eyebrows and grinned. Feeling self-conscious in my pyjamas, I wrapped my arms around my chest.

'What do you want?' I asked.

'Has your chap gone already?' he asked. 'Such a shame. I thought you almost had him on the hook there, but alas, he wriggled away. It was a problem poor Isla had too, I suppose.'

More than anything, I was afraid. I could see in his eyes that whatever he had been planning, the time was now. An ambush predator will lie motionless in the sand, it will change its skin to mimic leaves, it will burrow into the earth for as long as it takes for its prey to walk blindly into its lair. He had been waiting for me, I knew it. I could see it, I had sensed it for eight months. I wanted my father, but he wasn't here anymore. No one was. I attempted to pass him so I could flee down the hallway, but he caught me by the elbow with one large hand.

'Don't run off just now,' he said calmly. 'You and I have barely had a chance to chat since we got here.'

'I don't want to talk to you,' I said, shaking his hand off my arm. 'I know what you said to him.'

He briefly looked confused and then smiled. 'Oh, dear, are you upset about that? I must say, I really am surprised at your naivety sometimes. Did you think you could dress him up like your little doll and prop him on the sofa with the Queen and we'd all be one happy family? Lexi, do think logically for once. Do you truly believe he was invited to *this* place because we were all so keen to meet your Australian boyfriend?'

I looked up and down the hallways, desperate for a servant or a valet to appear, but we were alone.

'You know,' he said, putting a finger to his chin as if a novel thought had just occurred to him. He was enjoying himself immensely. I wondered how long he had spent plotting this conversation. 'I always thought your biggest flaw was that you were your mother's daughter. But I'm starting to see that you truly are Freddy's girl. Gosh, he was just the same − hopelessly gaga for Annabelle, who was, despite her good breeding, nothing but a divorced stable girl. We invited your mother up here that summer so your father would understand what needed to be done. Anyway, I suppose there are people in this family who still believe in your accession. But in the end, they didn't even need to put that much effort into running your farmer off, did they? You did that all on your own.'

Trembling, I stepped forward. My hopelessness had combusted into rage, and I was no longer afraid of him. I was the heir apparent, the sole surviving descendant of the Prince of Scotland, the tip of the great Villiers spear.

'I want you to stay away from me,' I said in a low voice. 'If there's not a camera on us, I don't want you anywhere near me. If I read one more lie about myself in the paper, I am going straight to the tabloids to tell them everything I know about you − and my father liked to talk, so I know *quite* a lot. And then I'm going to Granny and telling her everything.'

His lips quivered into a smile, revealing his mismatched teeth. 'But if you did that, I'd have to tell her about David Rossi. It didn't take all that long for the private investigator to track him down, you know.'

I shook my head. 'Who the fuck is David Rossi?'

Again, that smile as he stepped into my space. He was drenched in a Tom Ford cologne that burned the back of my throat. 'I think you know who David Rossi is. And if you really don't, I'm sure it'll come back to you. Give it time.'

The name meant nothing to me, but it meant something to him. I stepped past him, and this time he let me go. Whatever trap he had laid for me, he was confident that its steel teeth were now deep in my flesh.

'Lexi,' he called after me. 'Once you remember, you come see me. You have until the end of the year – obviously.'

*

David Rossi, David Rossi.

Ten weeks on and it still meant nothing. I studied it so closely that it had lost all meaning. It was a jumble of letters and nothing else.

At the deck's edge in the predawn, I lowered my feet into the water and turned the name over in my mind, again and again. Nothing surfaced.

I pushed the coat off my shoulders and slid into the black water. My breath came out of me in steaming billows as I swam forward. Once I was at the pond's still centre, I let myself sink. It was so cold down there that it burned. I felt obliterated, suspended in nothing. It was like the darkest hour of night. I allowed myself to descend deeper, raising my arms over my head like fifth position in ballet. It wasn't what I thought it would be like down there. Had she fought to the end? Had she splashed and screamed until her strength gave out? Or had it been like this – a slow, silent descent to the unknown. I knew it would hurt, that she had felt the agony of water rushing into the lungs. But only for a moment. Then it was just like drifting on the outer edges of sleep.

Underwater reeds wove their slimy fingers around my ankles and I jolted, remembering Mum's face that last time I had seen her. I hadn't known it would be the last time and I had barely taken her in. Suddenly back in my body, desperate for air, I kicked and struggled. By the time I broke the surface, gasping and coughing, I remembered. Of course I remembered. I had always known. From the moment he said it, I'd known. The letters in the name came sharply into focus, like the perfect twist of the microscope that revealed the flourishing bacteria on the petri dish.

Davide Rossi, there you are, I thought.

Not David, as Richard had pronounced it, but *Davide*, with that sharp first syllable, the curt vee sound, and then the floating vowel at the end, almost impossible for any English speaker to get right. Exhausted, I swam back and heaved myself onto the deck. My lungs burned. I was spent; I was done.

'You alright, love?' the lifeguard called. 'I was about to jump in after you.'

Lying there, I nodded, gasping like a sailor who'd survived the wreck and made it to shore. Once the lifeguard was gone, I pulled my coat back on with numb fingers and sat there for a long time, listening to the morning birds as the sky brightened into dawn. There was nothing left to do. I pulled my phone from my pocket and dialled the number. I imagined him on the other side of the planet, the sun setting over Tasmania as he looked at the screen, surprised to see my name, hesitating as he decided whether to answer. Finally, he picked up.

'Lexi?'

I took a deep, shaky breath. My teeth were chattering. 'Uncle James, I'm so sorry.'

'Lexi, what happened?'

'I have to tell you what I did.'

CHAPTER TWENTY-TWO

25 July 2011

I gripped the door handle of the Fiat as Louis veered into a sharp turn on the strada provinciale out of Portofino. An alarmingly wide lorry honked as it approached. I squeezed my eyes shut until it whooshed past.

'Fuck,' I whispered.

'Sorry.' Louis laughed. 'These roads are insane.'

We hit a straight stretch of coastline and I started to relax again. We had the windows rolled down so we could taste the salt air. Cheerful blue beach umbrellas fluttered in the breeze. Bougainvillea heaved itself over walls. Girls on Vespas wove through traffic effortlessly.

'I wish we were staying in Portofino,' Louis said. He was wearing a crisp white shirt that made the caramel tan he'd picked up in the few days we'd been here seem even deeper. 'Bit more going on than in Rapallo.'

'I don't know if security would allow it,' I said.

'Didn't you hear?' he asked, looking at me over his Ray-Bans. 'They had big problems with the villa we're in. A private mooring always freaks them out because anyone can hire a boat and float right up to us. Papa almost called the whole thing off, but Mum agreed to hire that guy to stand on the dock.'

I hadn't heard. All I knew was that the Rapallo villa was on loan from one of Mum's post-divorce friends – a jewellery designer perhaps? A film director? Hiring a place in Portofino for £15,000 a week wasn't an option. The private security guard to top up our royal protection detail was already going to blow out the budget for the trip, and money was becoming a sensitive issue. The divorce settlement had come through, but for a woman like Isla Kilchurn, £18 million was not a lifetime's supply. Round-the-clock private security had swiftly robbed her of her nest egg, so that she was relying on monthly child support payments to get by. They were due to stop the day we turned eighteen, which was only five months away.

The easiest way to make money would be to shop her story to a New York publishing house. But she was bound by Stewart's NDA in perpetuity, which meant that one day she would have to choose. She could find an American investment banker, or a Scottish earl, or a tech billionaire ten years her junior. Or she could become a brand ambassador for luxury watches and mass-produced coffee pods. Both prospects seemed to terrify her. And so that summer, we stayed with rich friends, we accepted free meals at buzzy restaurants, and we paid £5000 for a man to stand guard on our little stone ledge overlooking the marina.

'Don't tell her you don't like the villa,' I said to Louis. 'She really wants us to like it.'

'I won't,' he said. Then he sniggered. 'Is it not the craziest place you've ever seen, though?'

I smiled. 'Yeah.'

The villa had been built by an Italian contessa in the seventies and left to rot and crumble when her marriage broke down. It was considered a monstrosity by the locals in Rapallo, but Mum's friend (a celebrity chef? an art dealer?) had bought it in the nineties and restored it to its strange and decadent former glory. There wasn't a single straight line in the place. Everything was arched and curved. At the centre of the house was a sunken living room – a 'conversation pit', Mum called it – filled with velvet cushions and ashtrays. Instead of hanging artworks, the owner had simply placed paintings on the floor and leaned them against the walls. Every piece was a graphic nude. I thought it was delightful – far more interesting than the usual places to which we were invited. And anyway, who cared what the interior looked like when it hung so precariously over the sea? The villa seemed to open right onto the glittering Rapallo marina. Down some steep steps, you could reach the boat dock and a stone shore.

'Oh, you're home!' Mum called when we walked through the front door. She was wearing a pair of Louis's boardshorts and an old vest knotted at her waist, and she still looked great. 'How was Portofino?'

'Yeah, fine,' Louis said, stretching. She wrapped an arm around his head and kissed his sideburn while he grimaced. They both moved through the world with the ease of the long-limbed and beautiful.

'Now, please be honest, dearest,' she said to him. 'You didn't have a drink in town, did you?'

'We didn't drink, Mum – we got gelato.'

'You know I don't care. Have all the Aperol spritzes you want. But if a photographer catches you and *he* sees, there'll be hell to pay.'

Mum lived in fear of a change to the custody arrangement, even though we were just months from our eighteenth birthday.

'I might get a swim in before dinner,' I said, padding down the hall towards my bedroom. 'Can we really have spritzes with dinner?'

'Yes, alright,' she called.

I took my book and towel down to the water. The paparazzi knew we were travelling around Italy, but they were yet to track us down to Rapallo, so I lay on the hot rock in my bikini, the Ligurian Sea washing up my pale, exposed thighs. There's a feeling you get when you're being watched. I don't know if I was more attuned to it because being observed was my entire purpose, but I opened my eyes and saw a man leaning against the railing on the boat dock. He was wearing aviators and smoking a cigarette. He nodded his head and smiled, and I waved back uncertainly. I hadn't seen the Italian security guard yet, but I supposed that was him. The protection officers who joined us from England were far more discreet, and I felt this man's eyes as I tried to go back to my sunbaking. Eventually, I rolled onto my stomach to hide my body and pretended to read. But the more natural I attempted to be, the more I felt the prickling discomfort of his gaze. From the corner of my eye, I saw the puff of smoke leave his lips as he stood sentry on the dock. How strange to be repulsed by a man's scrutiny, and yet still perform for it. If I walked back to the villa immediately, it would be obvious I was trying to avoid him, and even though this man worked for my mother and I didn't know him at all, I was deeply concerned about hurting his feelings. Instead, I closed my book, got up and leapt off the rocks into the tepid sea. Still, he watched. After a few moments bobbing around in the water, I climbed out, wrapped myself in my towel and headed for the rocky steps.

'Goodbye, *carina*,' he called after me.

I gave him another small wave, emitted a choked squeak meant to be a farewell and hurried up the steps.

'That security guy's a bit creepy,' I said at dinner. We were eating on the deck, watching the sun sink in the sorbet sky. None of us knew how to cook, so Louis had gone into town for pizza.

'Who, Davide?' Mum asked, pronouncing it the correct Italian way, with three distinct syllables. Like me, she was mostly picking at the toppings and leaving behind the cheese and dough. 'He's lovely. He calls me "*Bellezza*".'

Louis scowled. 'Where'd you find this guy?'

Mum shrugged. 'He was recommended by a friend. My options are limited, you know. The number of photographers chasing me has probably doubled in the last year and I'm out there completely alone.'

'You could always go out a bit less,' Louis muttered.

A wave slapped the rocks and a salty mist landed on our bare skin. I sipped my Aperol spritz in silence. Mum was staring at Louis.

'Could I?' she asked coldly.

'I'm not saying ... you know, I'm just ... if you go on people's yachts and into nightclubs, it's part of the territory.'

'And what places would you deem acceptable?' she asked. 'Given that I was cut out of my own life with absolutely no protection, and all my old friends and relatives stopped speaking to me?'

Louis and I stared at our plates.

'Sorry, Mum,' he said. 'I just worry about you sometimes, that's all.'

'Yes, well, you can hold your father responsible for that,' she sniffed. 'He wasn't always quite so cruel, but the closer he gets to the crown, the more vicious he becomes.'

We started eating again and I hoped that was the end of it.

'You're not exactly making it easy for him either,' Louis said softly.

There was a clattering of cutlery and the scrape of a chair. The table shuddered and the drinks slopped out of their glasses as Mum stood up and stalked back into the villa. We sat in silence as the horizon glowed and then blazed behind us.

'Sorry, Lexi,' he murmured.

The year before, Mum had travelled to Haiti to raise money for earthquake victims. Separated from us over Christmas, she had spent a week at a rape crisis centre in the Democratic Republic of Congo instead. A month before we went to Italy, she had been on the Turkish–Syrian border to draw attention to the growing refugee crisis. But she also went to movie premieres and fashion shows, and so all I heard from the people around me was how she was bringing the monarchy into disrepute.

Eventually Louis and I gave up on the evening and parted ways. He was on the top floor of the villa facing the gardens, while I was on the bottom floor overlooking the sea. I have no idea what time it was when Mum woke me up. Later, I would piece together every moment of what happened next, and it's likely I hadn't been asleep for long. I felt her warm hands on my cheeks and when I opened my eyes, she was already dressed in a sweatshirt and jeans.

'What is it?' I whispered.

She smiled at me. 'Let's go on a raft, for real this time.'

I looked out the window. The ocean was like mercury under a sliver of moon. 'Now?'

'We'll take the boat out into the gulf and watch the sun rise,' she said. She didn't seem quite herself, her eyes glassy in a way that should have given me pause, although I dismissed it as a trick of the moonlight. 'I can't believe we've never done it before. My father would sometimes take me and James out on the loch at night. It was the only time we really spent with him. It's magical out there.'

What I really wanted to do was go back to sleep. I will forever wonder what would have happened if I did. But until the end, I followed her. If she was the only one dancing at a reception, I would join her. If she gamely ate the goat testicles floating in stew during a trip to Mongolia, I picked up a spoon. If she wanted to take a boat into unfamiliar waters on a near moonless night, it took very little convincing for me to agree. My eighteenth birthday loomed. Soon I would be travelling the world, and then I would be at St Andrews, and she would be unmoored from the last ties to her old life.

'Do you even know how to drive that boat?' I asked.

'Of course I do,' she said and pulled back my blankets.

It was chillier than I expected on the dock, but Mum strode confidently ahead of me. Davide, who had been leaning against a pole, stood straight when he saw us.

'*Bellezza*,' he said. He had the gravelly voice of a pack-a-day smoker. 'What are you doing up so late?'

'Davide, we're going to take the boat out so we can watch the sun rise. We'll be back at six-thirty at the latest.'

He looked between us. 'I'll come, yes?'

'No, darling,' she said kindly. 'It's a mother–daughter outing. But don't worry. You'll be able to see us the whole time. We won't go far.'

Again, he hesitated. '*Bellezza*, I must be with the boy and the girl, that's what the Englishmen said.'

She gripped his arm and leaned in as if they had a secret. 'They're so strict, aren't they? Don't worry, I won't tell anyone. I spent my whole childhood sailing, I know what I'm doing.'

Finally, he relented and helped us onto the boat. It was a motor yacht that was small enough for me to assume the owner rarely did anything but anchor it in the Tigullio Gulf to day-drink. There were two tiny cabins below deck. At the stern was a flat lounging area in white leather, with a diving board attached so you could jump straight from the yacht into the sparkling sea. As Davide untied the boat and tossed us the ropes, Mum pressed buttons, inserted the key and used the gear stick to lower the motors into the water. As she moved confidently around the cockpit, I started to relax.

'Have you driven this boat before?' I asked.

'Last summer,' she said. 'I was here for about a week, and I got a quick lesson, although they're all pretty much the same. This one's a beauty, isn't she?'

The smell of boat fuel rose up, and the engines shuddered to life. Then Davide was waving to us from the dock as we pulled into the night. I sat on the narrow couch in the cockpit and wrapped myself in one of the blankets Mum had brought with us. She stood at the helm, looking out at the water, and I lay down on the white leather. I don't think I really slept. I just dozed as the boat churned across the glossy surface of the Ligurian Sea. By the time Mum killed the engine, I was unsure how much time had passed. I sat up and looked starboard and saw the lights of the Italian Riviera blinking like distant stars.

'Are we kind of far out?' I asked.

She turned to me, surprised. 'Oh, you're awake. No, not that far. See that lighthouse over there? That's the very tip of Portofino. As long as we don't go past that point, we're still in the gulf.'

I squinted into the dark and saw a pulse of silvery light. Mum dug through the tote bag she'd brought with us and pulled out a bottle of champagne.

'I just thought, why not? You're practically eighteen and this is our last summer together,' she said, pulling off the foil from its neck.

We moved to the leather lounging area and lay down, huddled under the blanket. I was groggy with sleep and didn't much feel like champagne, but I took a sip every time she passed me the bottle. It was cosy lying together under the stars. The water sloshed gently against the boat's hull, and I pulled the blanket tightly around myself.

'Are you alright, Mum?' I asked.

'Of course,' she said. 'I'm going to watch the sunrise with my girl. What more could I want?'

I hesitated. The lighthouse flickered faintly again in the distance. 'I know, but … are you okay?'

She was quiet. Then she took a long draw of the champagne bottle and passed it to me. 'I worry about your brother. I worry about you, too. But it's your brother who worries me the most.'

'He was just in a bad mood tonight,' I said. 'He didn't mean it.'

'I'm not talking about tonight.' She was lying beside me on the lounge, our feet tangled together, looking so young with her bare face and her unkempt hair that she could have passed for my sister. 'You know what I'm talking about.'

'No, I don't.'

She smiled. 'Dearest, do you really think I don't know about Louis and Kris?'

I froze, trying to recall a time when they might have given themselves away in her presence. Once Mum and Papa had separated, Louis and I didn't burden her so much with our own problems, but I wondered now what she had quietly observed.

'Did Louis say something?' I asked.

'No.'

'How do you know then?'

'Because I'm his mother. I've always known.'

I lay back and looked up at the cold stars scattered over our heads, thinking of my brother. I sometimes worried that as we got older I was losing him to Papa and Granny. They were three people bound by fate, and an invisible curtain separated them from the rest of us. Louis was disappearing behind it more and more as he grew up, even though it meant whole parts of himself had to remain concealed. But they were the parts that Mum and I loved, the parts that made him Louis.

'He and Kris really love each other,' I said.

'I'm glad.'

I rolled over. 'I'm sorry I kept it a secret from you.'

She smiled again. 'I understand the honour code between twins. I haven't brought it up with him because I know he's not ready to talk about it, but I'm glad he has you. You two must always be brother and sister first, you know. You must always take care of him.'

'I know,' I paused. 'Why are you worried about me?'

Her eyes were roaming my face with so much love, it clenched my heart.

'Because,' she said, 'you never want anyone to worry about you.'

I was surprised that tears pricked my eyes. I thought again of my brother vanishing behind the curtain, leaving me alone in this world, even though we had arrived here together.

'Sometimes I wonder,' I whispered, 'what's the point of me?'

'Oh, dearest,' she cried softly and brushed my wet cheeks with her fingers. She took my face in her hands. 'You are my brilliant, kind, funny girl. You are here for no other reason than to be yourself. I don't want you to ever make the same mistake I did.'

'What was your mistake?'

She sighed and wiped her eyes.

'I wasn't much older than you when I met your father,' she said. 'We were both ... desperate for something. He was heartbroken over *her*. I just wanted a family – any family, really. And I think we believed that we could offer each other a semblance of what we were missing.'

I had never heard her talk this way. She always discussed the catastrophic breakdown of their marriage as a betrayal. Papa was the arch villain disguised as a handsome prince. She was the innocent maiden who had entered the castle seeking love, only to find herself trapped by writhing dragons and swooping condors.

'Do you think he loved you?' I asked, but I really meant us.

'In his way.' She sighed. 'I don't know. He loved me for giving him Louis – and you. I just didn't think the love would drain away quite so soon. I never expected to be thirty-nine and out on my own again.'

She took the champagne bottle from me and brought it to her lips. She drank for a long time.

'My mistake was believing that the only reason I was put on this Earth was to give birth to a king,' she said. 'So after I had you and Louis, and your father was done with me, I found myself thinking, *What's the point of me now?*'

She put the bottle down so she could find my hands.

'You were born to your position, and that is a privilege. But that is not all you are. Never forget that.'

She pulled me into her warm arms and held me for a long time. The stars flickered above us and we swayed on a placid wave. I fought to keep my eyes open.

'I might fall asleep.'

I felt her lips against the crown of my head. 'Why don't you go down to the berth and sleep where it's warm? It's alright, I'll wake you when the sun's coming up.'

I took the narrow steps below deck and collapsed onto the first bed I found. The pillows were flat and musty, but it was as dark as a tomb down there. I listened to the thump of the water on the hull, and let my champagne-fuzzed head and the gentle rocking of the boat lull me to sleep.

I'm not sure why I snapped awake when I did. No sound roused me. The boat undulated on a rippling tide. Nothing seemed amiss. But when I sat up in bed and listened for something I couldn't name, all I heard was the creaking and settling of the hull. I climbed the stairs to the deck and found it was still night, with the crescent moon now high overhead. I walked past the cockpit towards the stern, expecting to find Mum asleep on the lounge. But no one was there, only the blanket twisted in a heap where she had been.

'Mum?' I said.

When she didn't answer, I figured she must have gone to the other cabin below deck. I climbed back down the steps and pushed the door slightly ajar. I could see nothing in the black.

'Mum?' I whispered.

I didn't want to wake her. She was a poor sleeper and I knew she would be annoyed, but I skimmed my hands along the wall until I found a switch. The yellow light revealed two sets of bunks, every bed empty. Perhaps she had crawled in with me in the other cabin and I hadn't noticed. I walked through the galley, flicking on every light switch I found. My bed was a crumpled mess.

'Mum,' I said sharply, as if perhaps she would stir among the bulk of blankets. When nothing happened, I pulled back all the bedclothes, just to be safe.

I was more furious than frightened as I checked the bathroom and snapped back the shower curtain. Who gets lost on the world's smallest yacht? I went back to the deck, as if we'd missed each other before. The lounging area was still empty, so I climbed onto the dining table and looked through a gap in the fibreglass canopy, wondering if she'd gone up there for a better view. I saw nothing but stars and I stood there listening to my own breath. There was only one place left to check, and there she must be. Trembling a little in the crispy air, I hung onto the metal grab rails that ran along the canopy, placing one bare foot after another as I shimmied myself towards the boat's pointed bow. The guardrails at my feet barely passed my ankles. I was determined not to look down into the shimmering water or give in to the vessel's delicate roll, which, up there, felt like I was lurching on the crest of a towering wave.

I was sure I'd find Mum sitting on the cushions at the bow. The lounging area was too enclosed. She'd want to be right at the tip of the yacht, where she would be under the night sky like she was floating through it. When I found it empty, I sank down into the leather and felt the low thud of my heart. The ocean suddenly looked infinite, a colossal, wrinkling body with no end in sight. I could hear nothing but my ragged breaths and the lapping of water on the metal hull. I could see nothing but the slow, relentless flutter of light in the darkness.

I was alone, and I knew it.

I screamed for her, once, and then swallowed my gasps so I could listen. The breeze brought me nothing in return. I sat there frozen. Surely I was wrong. I scrambled back to the cockpit and checked every inch of the boat again. I even opened cupboards in the galley, as if she would be hiding there. Finally I found my phone and went back to the lounging area at the stern.

With trembling fingers, I dialled the number. It was 3 am in Italy, which meant it was 2 am in London. He barely answered my calls as it was, but his was the only voice I wanted to hear. When it rang out, I sat down on the deck and sobbed into my hands. I would have to call Louis next or the Italian police. I would have to press the panic button that would alert my security detail back at the villa. I would have to switch all the dials in the cockpit and somehow careen the boat back towards Rapallo.

In my lap, my phone chirped and I half-believed it was Mum calling to tell me where she had gone, why she had left me alone on a boat in the middle of the sea. But it wasn't her.

'Papa,' I whimpered.

'Lexi, what on Earth?' he said, his voice rough with sleep. 'What's going on?'

'I can't find her, she's disappeared. We got on the boat and went out so we could watch the sunrise, and I fell asleep, and when I woke up, she was gone. I've checked everywhere.'

He was silent for a moment and I thought the line might have gone dead. 'Wake the captain up right now and put me on to him.'

'No, you don't understand,' I wept. 'It's just us. She drove the boat herself. And now I can't find her. I don't know where I am, and I think I might be out here alone. Should I press my panic button, Papa?'

'No, wait … just give me a moment to think,' he said. I could hear him rustling down a hallway and shutting a door. The line went very quiet.

'Papa?'

'I'm here, Lexi, just give me a minute,' he said sharply. 'Was she acting strangely at all when you last saw her? Was she drinking?'

'I mean, we had some champagne, but—'

'Oh, Lexi,' he groaned. It was the same tone he used when I was a child and stuck my tongue out at the photographers or shoved Louis at an event when we were bickering. The same hot prickle of shame rushed up my throat now. 'Does your brother know? Have you called anyone else?'

'No,' I said. 'Only the Italian security guy knows we're out here. The others didn't see us leave. Should I call the police?'

'No,' he said. 'You and I are going to hang up. I've got the location of your phone, so I'm going to send someone to come get you. It might take a couple of hours, so you'll have to be strong for me, can you do that? While you're waiting, I want you to get all the things that belong to you and pack them up. Did you say you slept in a bed? Go and make it. Get everything on board the way it was, just as you found it.'

'Papa,' I said. 'Shouldn't I look for her?'

'You need to do exactly as I say and nothing more. Do not answer this phone to anyone but me, do you understand?'

'Please don't hang up.'

'I have to, mignonette. I have to make some phone calls now. Do as I say and everything will be alright.'

The line went dead and I was on my own again, floating through black nothingness. The quiet became too much, and I ran through the boat, closing cupboard doors and remaking the bed and switching off all the lights. I looked everywhere for the champagne bottle, but it was gone. Mum's tote bag was still slumped on the floor of the cockpit and my eyes blurred with tears as I stuffed the blanket back inside it. I sensed Papa's plan more than I was willing to acknowledge it. It was like I could glimpse it from the corner of my eye but would not turn to face it. When everything was as it should be, I climbed back to the bow to wait and screamed her name over and over until my throat burned. There was nothing but silence and water.

Distantly, I heard the low rumbling of a boat. It occurred to me then that if a cruiseliner came barrelling through, I was incapable of turning over the yacht's engine and moving out of danger. But instead, a small fishing boat was gliding through the water with its lights off. I clambered back to the stern. I had no idea who was out there, but I knew I had less than a minute before everything changed.

There was a lifebuoy hanging near the cockpit, and I took it and flung it into the dark. If she was alive out there, maybe it would drift towards her. Maybe I could undo this with one final offering to the black night. For the conspiracy theorists who obsessed over my mother's death, this tiny detail would transfix them for years. It had its own subreddits, its own amateur podcasts, its own Wikipedia page. If Princess Isla was really alone on that yacht, who threw the lifebuoy into the water? Some speculated that there was no flotation device on the vessel in the first place. But two months after it went into the water, it washed up on a beach in Cavalaire-sur-Mer, bearing the faded but legible name of the vessel. By then, Italian police had closed the case, and the discovery was shrugged off by everyone who didn't dwell at the internet's hard edges.

The approaching boat slowed to a thudding crawl, and then there was a great flood of light. Blinded, I held my hand up to shield my eyes.

'*Carina?*' a man called.

'Who's there?'

'It's your mother's guard, Davide. Your papa sent me. We have to go now.'

'I can't find her,' I sobbed. 'I woke up and she was gone.'

He was tying his fishing boat to the yacht's swim step. He didn't seem to understand the urgency of the situation. Once he was satisfied with his knot, he held out a hand to me. 'Please, *carina*, we must go now.'

I shook my head and the tears slipped down my neck. 'I can't leave her.'

He looked around at the black night. 'I'll take you to the villa, and then I come back here and search for your mama.'

I hesitated.

'Please, you cannot stay out here. This is what your papa wants.'

It was the kind of walk I thought only possible in a nightmare. I staggered down to the swim step on legs that were feeble and unsteady. Everything was moving too slowly, everyone was taking this catastrophe in their stride, including me. Once I was on board, he began to untie his knots and pull in his ropes.

'Do you think,' I asked, 'that we should check the boat one more time?'

He looked at me impatiently. 'I don't think she is here, but when I drop you off, I will come right back and check again.'

From the stern of the fishing boat, I watched the yacht grow smaller and smaller on the horizon. It bobbed on the waves, receding from view, until finally it was swallowed by the dark. I sat numbly as the engine roared below my wooden seat. The ocean spray stung my face. The stench of boat fuel burned my eyes. As the lights of Rapallo grew closer, Davide Rossi turned the motor down to a purr. He threw me a blanket.

'Lie on the floor and hide under this until I tell you it's safe,' he said.

Compliant, I pressed my cheek against the rough wooden floor of the boat and covered myself with the dusty blanket. We puttered along slowly, and I waited for the wail of police sirens that never came. At some point, Davide turned the engine off completely, and I heard the boom and splash of an oar hitting the water. He was rowing us towards the villa's dock. A scraping of wood against stone meant that we had arrived. I felt the blanket pulled from my face and I looked up to see that the night sky was softening into dawn.

'Okay, *carina*,' Davide said. Shadows pooled in the hollows of his face. 'Go inside, do nothing. Your papa will call you.'

Inside the villa, Louis was sitting in the conversation pit with his fingers pressed together as if in prayer. He did not turn to acknowledge me as I slid open the glass door.

'Louis,' I whispered. My voice sounded foreign and rough, and I realised it must be from the screaming. The floor lurched under me like I was still at sea.

He didn't look at me. He didn't move at all. He sat on the sofa as I stood there with my chattering teeth and shaky legs. I realised that one of Papa's phone calls must have been to Louis to tell him what had happened and what must happen next.

'Louis, I—'

'What the fuck did you do, Lexi?'

'I'm sorry, I don't know. She was just ... gone.'

He put his face into his palms and shook his head. Then he looked up at me with his fierce eyes. 'What were you thinking, going out there with her?'

'I'm sorry.'

'Stop saying *sorry!*' he shouted, and his rage was like a thunderclap. He surged up out of his seat, climbed out of the pit and stalked towards me. 'She's out there alone, do you realise that? She might have done this to herself. And because of *you*, I can't go out there and find her.'

'The security guard is going there now,' I rasped.

Louis shook his head and looked at me with his heartbroken eyes. 'No, he's not. When the police eventually ask us, we're to say he didn't work here last night, he went home sick yesterday afternoon. No one's looking for Mum right now. Everyone's cleaning up your mess.'

I shook my head and staggered on my sea legs. 'He's going out there right now, he told me.'

Louis put his hands on my shoulders. 'He said what Papa told him to say. Do you really think he let Mum hire some random guy to protect us without checking him out? He's probably been paying him this whole time to keep tabs on her. I don't know where he got that boat, but he's taking it back now and then he's going straight home.'

Someone was screaming, and I realised it was me. Louis put his hand over my mouth, and I beat my fists against his chest until my legs could no longer support me. Somehow, we were on the floor and Louis was holding me in his arms and rocking me while we wept. We stayed that way until the red light of dawn slid through the glass and announced that the rest of our lives was about to begin.

At 7 am, Louis went to the villa gates and told our security officers that Mum and the yacht were gone. She wasn't answering her phone either. From there, one domino seemed to crash down upon the next. The coastguard was sceptical – she was an experienced sailor who was allowed to take her boat to sea without informing anyone – but when they radioed the yacht and received no response, they agreed to send someone out to check. By ten-thirty that morning, they found the yacht three nautical miles from Rapallo's marina, with no one on board.

A search and rescue team was deployed. Helicopters droned over the Tigullio Gulf. Papa and Stewart boarded a private plane to Genoa at 11 am, and they were sitting in the villa's living room three hours later.

By then, someone in the coastguard had leaked that Princess Isla was missing, and a huge flotilla of photographers gathered in the marina near our dock. By sundown, Stewart produced his bottle of liquid Valium, and I woke up the next morning in a luxury resort in Portofino. Our security officers had decided the villa was unfit for two future kings and moved us to safer quarters while I slumped unconscious against Louis's shoulder in the back of a town car.

It would take three days to find Mum. Like the lifebuoy, she drifted westward. At some point, she became tangled in sargassum, which kept her from sinking to the depths and being fed upon by larger predators. A chopper hired by a French tabloid spotted her trapped among the swirling brown mess. Before they radioed it in, they flew low enough to get pictures of her floating there, bloated and decayed. No one dared publish them, but they still managed to find their way onto the internet, where they replicated like a virus that had found the perfect host. Blogs started to speculate that she had been assassinated by Papa, who wanted her out of the way so he could marry Annabelle.

But four weeks after she went into the water, a toxicology report revealed she had a blood alcohol reading of 0.12 and had taken benzodiazepine as prescribed by her doctor for anxiety. A coroner concluded that she was likely unsteady on her feet from the combination of drugs and alcohol and had toppled into the water by accident. Disoriented, she would have been unable to haul herself back into the boat and, as she struggled, she was pulled helplessly into the black night by a strong current.

The Italian police, the coroner and the palace were eager to move on, and the mainstream media accepted the obvious narrative of an ex-princess taking a stupid risk while champagne and Xanax fizzed in her bloodstream.

The day after Mum disappeared, a young Rapallo police officer scrawled the name *Davide Rossi* in his notebook. He went to Davide's house in Zoagli to confirm he was off sick the night Mum took the yacht out into the bay. And that was the end of it. No one ever asked our protection officers if they saw Davide Rossi go home. And for reasons I can only guess, they never told anyone that, as far as they were aware, he was standing on the dock the whole night.

A month after Mum's body was found, a large sum of money passed through a Panama shell company and slipped into a Genoa bank account. Davide Rossi was never called as a witness in any coronial inquest and the police never publicly mentioned his name.

But twelve years later, the Duke of Clarence had hired a team of private investigators to dig into my past. One went to the Jennings vineyard and came back with nothing. Another went to interview everyone involved in the search for my mother. The police officer who had scrawled *Davide Rossi* in his notepad was the type of man who kept all his papers from every case he worked on. With the PI's help, he searched his garage for a box marked *2011 – Principessa*. A week later, the investigator tracked Davide Rossi down to a rather nice villa in Porto Venere.

And why would Rossi stay quiet? The man who had bought his silence was gone – buried in ice, he heard – and here was his brother with another deal, another promise of another cheque. Who was he to say no to these feckless people with their fat wallets?

CHAPTER TWENTY-THREE

5 November 2023

I could hardly recognise the woman I saw in the mirror anymore. She was a stranger, someone called Princess Alexandrina, a sleek creature who had absolutely nothing to do with me.

Mary had commissioned Erdem to make me a bespoke skirt suit, black and sculptural, with an exaggerated flared blazer that reminded me of a Victorian-era bustle. I suspected she picked this silhouette to obscure my vanishing hips, which I thought was very clever, even if it did alarm the doctor buried somewhere inside me. And, after months of training, I was finally able to walk in Louboutin So Kates – as slutty as they were expensive – so that I teetered on 120-millimetre black-patent spikes during my very first investiture ceremony.

The honours were dispensed in a Watford Castle reception room, and afterwards I took photographs with the recipients, and then lingered to chat while light refreshments were served. I liked investitures, pinning medals to the lapels of people who did brave and interesting things, like canoe across the Irish Sea to raise money for wounded veterans, or discover a new species of wasp on a nature reserve in Kent. It didn't make much sense for any of these fine people to kneel before me. But it was nice to see them in their best suits and specially purchased hats, serene in the knowledge that they had done one good thing with their lives.

After a polite forty-five minutes, I slipped from the reception room for some air and wandered down the hall until I found myself in the Wellington Chamber. It was a colossal space designed to intimidate whoever entered it, with a portrait of Barbara Villiers on the furthest wall. I went to see her and found that she was gazing down at me with disappointment, ermine robes around her creamy shoulders, rubies in the hollow of her neck.

What would you do? I wished to ask her.

But her violet eyes told me the answer. The House of Villiers was a ramshackle thing when she took possession of it, and she had turned our family into a stone tower that had stood for hundreds of years. You didn't pull that off without getting a little blood on your hands. She didn't flirt and fuck, scheme and conquer, just for me to ruin it all a few centuries later.

The doors boomed, and I flinched.

'There you are.' Mary continued to tap at her phone screen as she crossed the floor.

'Sorry,' I said. 'Just needed a minute.'

Gleefully, she showed me every Instagram post and tabloid story covering the investiture. '*Vogue* says you're a fashion icon,' she said.

'Cool.'

My own phone buzzed, and when I glanced down, I saw that it was James again. He texted me every day at noon, and I imagined him standing in his dark kitchen in Oatlands performing this last task before he went to bed.

Checking in, he wrote.

I angled the screen away, typing out a quick response before Mary caught a glimpse: *All fine.*

I was still stunned that James had found it possible to forgive me. When I called him at the pond, he'd listened to my story in silence. As soon as I'd finished, I apologised over and over.

'You can say sorry one more time, and then I never want to hear it from you again,' he said.

James had always suspected there was more to the story of how his sister died. He knew in his soul that we weren't telling the whole truth. But he said that I was a child who did what children do when they're frightened and alone. I knew he blamed Papa entirely, and he would not allow me to share the responsibility, no matter how much I'd insisted.

'Oh,' Mary said, still staring at her screen. 'I found those contact details you were after – for the Italian man. Phone number and home address. No email. I'll send them through now.'

My phone shivered in my hands, and there he was: Davide Rossi. He had left Rapallo and moved south for the Gulf of Poets, a crescent-shaped coastal inlet once beloved by all the creatives, from Dante to Lord Byron. Percy Shelley had drowned there when his sailboat capsized during a storm. His decomposed body had washed ashore weeks later, and they were only certain it was him because he had a Keats poem folded up in his breast pocket.

'Thank you,' I murmured. 'You were discreet?'

'Yes, of course.'

'He's an old friend of my parents. I might need to go visit him – I'm not quite sure yet.'

Mary glanced at me sideways and then returned to her phone, opening up the calendar that ruthlessly governed both of our lives.

'When? For how long? You don't really have any time off until ... March. Unless you intend to go for the day, but—'

'I haven't decided yet,' I snapped.

She looked me up and down, a new habit she'd developed, perhaps wondering if this mystery man was the reason I'd been quiet and unreliable for months, dropping weight and spacing out during engagements, threatening everything she'd worked so hard to achieve for us both.

'I'm sorry,' I said. 'My father sort of … looked after him, and now that he's gone, I might need to take over. It's not something I've ever discussed with Stewart or the Queen – so if I need to go to Italy, it must be off the books.'

The vaulted ceiling was rimmed with lantern windows, letting in the drowsy autumn sunlight. Dust motes twirled and danced between us.

'Alright,' Mary said cautiously. 'But you can't go anywhere without your protection detail. And I'll have to tell Stewart. He has your passport.'

I closed my eyes. I'd forgotten about that. After Mum went to Darfur to tell the truth about the genocide unfolding there, her philanthropic activities had been heavily curtailed by the palace. For the remainder of her marriage, she had no choice but to stand prettily at flower shows and yacht races, her passport locked in Stewart's desk. *Never, ever let them take your passport or your phone,* she once told me. *You're a person, not a pet.* Stewart had had my passport in his pocket by the end of the very first day.

'Fuck,' I breathed.

'It's not a big deal,' Mary said. 'When you need it, I'll ask him for it.'

I looked up towards Barbara and found that her soft, knowing smile had tightened into a sneer. In almost every portrait of her, she had posed with her chin resting in her white hand, making her look wanton but powerful. Now she just looked exasperated.

'Ma'am, are you alright?'

I met Mary's watchful eyes. 'Yes, of course. I'll let you know what I need to do soon. Are we done? Can we go home?'

We drove back to London in silence, and I dozed most of the way, my cheek against the glass as I listened to the tap of Mary's fingertips on her phone and the endless grind of city traffic. When I woke up, the wrought-iron gates of Cumberland Palace were coming into view, and I saw that there was a swarm of tourists lingering by the boom gate. I fixed my hat and sat up straight, waving benevolently as they peered at me through the dark glass.

Outside Cumberland 1, the driver opened my door, but I hesitated. 'Thank you for today, Mary.'

'Did you want me to come in? We can go over the notes for the blood-drive appearance tomorrow.'

'No,' I said and slid out of the car, wincing as I stood up in my evil high heels. 'I want you to take the rest of the day off. Go to the pub with your friends or something. We can chat tomorrow.'

She nodded uncertainly, and I knew she probably wouldn't go home, or phone a friend, or book a last-minute spot in a yoga class. She'd return to the office and stay there until the autumn gloaming descended into night.

'Yes ma'am.' She looked me up and down appraisingly. 'I love that outfit.'

'You did an incredible job. I'll see you in the morning.'

I was relieved to find the house silent and still, even Chino's favourite afternoon nap spot by the fire empty. Amira must have taken him for a walk. I eased myself onto the bottom step of the staircase and wrenched off my shoes, easing my aching feet into ugg boots, knowing the searing pain that awaited once I stood. I sat for a while, thinking of the weeks ahead, the decisions I must make, the lies I must tell.

I wondered what Jack was doing at that very moment. It was the early hours in Hobart, so he was probably in bed, his face gone boyish and soft with sleep. Or maybe he was out somewhere meeting girls, moving on with his life, hating me more as each day passed. I knew that as the weeks turned to months, he would think of me less and less, and eventually he would be nothing but relieved.

I wondered if Papa would be proud of me, or if he'd despair of me. I wished that Louis were around, as I did dozens of times a day.

I just want my mum, I thought – the old, ceaseless whisper inside me.

I hurled my left Louboutin hard at the wall, leaving a jagged line in the sage-green paint. I froze, as if Mum herself would look around the corner and gape at what I had done to her Farrow & Ball walls. Then I remembered she'd never reappear to scold me or hug me or save me ever again, so I tossed the other shoe in the same direction.

'Good heavens,' came a voice from above.

I flinched and turned to see Vikki at the top of the staircase.

'Oh,' I said guiltily, 'I didn't realise anyone was home.'

Vikki was in her athleisure wear, which meant she was probably there dropping Amira off after Pilates. She descended the stairs, stopping on the last step to stare at the mess I'd made of the wall.

'It was an accident,' I said in a small voice.

Vikki nodded and sat down next to me with a heavy sigh. 'Not to worry. The staff keep a few extra tins of paint for touch-ups. I'll contact them this afternoon.'

'Thank you. Where's Amira?'

'At the park, giving Chino a runaround. Madhav is with her,' she said. 'He's been talking to her about coming to work for the company.'

I looked at Vikki. 'Really?'

She leaned back and propped her elbows on the step behind us. 'Yes, well, it was once the plan that she work there after university. Madhav always said she had more of a head for business than Kris ever did.'

I'd never known that. Our career aspirations were not something Amira and I had ever discussed in school, both our futures already laid out before us, not a single twist or deviation from the path allowed. She was meant to marry up. I had no higher to rise, so I was to marry someone with a respectable name and a face that looked nice on a tea towel.

'What do you think?' I asked.

Vikki smiled sadly. 'I've learned to stay out of the lives of my children.'

Gingerly, I put my feet flat on the floorboards, testing my sore arches. But the pain was so great that I groaned, remembering how it felt to come back down to Earth after a day spent *en pointe* during my ballet years.

Vikki jutted her chin at the So Kates lying on the floor. 'If you want to wear those, you need to get your lady-in-waiting to buy you some numbing spray from the chemist. Then you'll be able to stay up that high as long as you like.'

'Doesn't that just delay the pain?'

She shrugged. 'Yes, I suppose so. But the more you do it, the less you feel it.'

We were quiet again. She seemed to sense that I had something to say.

'Vikki.'

'Yes, darling.'

'Can I ask you something? And it stays between us?'

'Of course, darling.'

My heart was making a low, heavy thud in my chest. 'I might need to ... that is to say, I haven't decided yet ... but I might need to give someone money. I'm not sure he'll take it. I'm not even sure this would work. But I might have to try.'

It had occurred to me during one of my many late-night ruminations that Davide Rossi would not be willing to reveal what happened the night Mum died unless he was being paid handsomely for his story. He had been silent for twelve years. Going public now could only mean photographers pressed up against the gates of his home in an apocalyptic swarm, coronial inquiries reopened, death threats in his mailbox. Whatever Richard was offering him had to make it worth it. But I was fairly certain that money was the one thing Richard didn't have. There were whispers about loans from arms dealers and tycoons, suitcases stuffed with cash that were meant to be charitable donations. All of it was rumoured to be spent on lavish holidays, private jets and designer clothes in a matter of months, so that he was continually seeking more. If Richard was yet to deliver on his promise to Davide Rossi, I had an opportunity to get in first.

'Lexi,' Vikki said carefully, 'are you in trouble?'

'Yes.'

'Can you tell me what kind of trouble you're in?'

'No, I'd rather not,' I murmured. 'All I can say is that someone knows something about me. And I thought, maybe, I could go to him and ask that it remain a secret.'

'How much money do you need?'

'I have no idea.'

'How much time do you have?'

'I'm not sure.' I remembered Richard's face on the stairs in Scotland as I'd stumbled away from him. 'I think until the end of the year?'

'Good,' she said. 'Well, in a situation like this, I recommend going in quite hard. Perhaps £1 million would do it. Don't ask them for a number, and don't try to low-ball them. Just have it done with.'

I looked at her, but she was still lounging against the staircase. Vikki was a certain breed of woman, like Barbara, who knew what needed to be done and didn't hesitate to act.

'You realise, Lexi,' she said, 'that you'll need an emissary. You can't just walk up to this man with a cheque and ask if he'd mind staying quiet.'

I hadn't given much thought to the logistics, although I'd assumed Davide and I were pair-bonded by that awful night, and that if he saw me, he might take pity on me again.

Vikki sat up and took my hands. 'I know you don't like to ask for help, but this isn't the kind of thing one can do alone. *Especially* you.'

I wished suddenly for another So Kate to toss, but I was out of shoes. 'I don't want to involve you in this any more than I already have.'

She winked at me. 'Too late for that.'

We sat for a while in familial silence, her fingers still holding mine, but her face grew sombre.

'You know, if you'd come to me with a problem like this a year ago, I would have *made* you take a cheque and sort this out. I want you to be queen, Lexi, and not just because it would mean that you could always protect Amira. And not even because it would be, well … advantageous for me.' She waited until I met her eyes. 'I want you to be queen because I know you'd be very good at it.'

It was the nicest thing she'd ever said to me, even if I didn't see how it could possibly be true.

'There was a time when all I wanted was to be where I am,' she went on. 'But I didn't quite realise the sacrifice that it would require. I didn't realise I'd lose my baby. I didn't realise what it would be like – living on a landfill of secrets, the stench of it making me sick all the time, making it impossible to sleep.'

Her eyes grew wet, and I squeezed her hands. She had lowered her children into the whirlpool and watched as they were both sucked into its gaping black centre. Only Amira had emerged, like flotsam on a tide.

'If you want to do this, I will help you,' she said. 'We never have to tell Amira, or Madhav, or anyone else. Say the word, and I'll write you a cheque, or put it all into a crypto account, or however these things are handled these days. But once you do something like this, there'll be no turning back. You must understand that.'

She kissed my knuckles and got off the stairs, stooping to collect my So Kates from the floor.

'I'll have the staff take these to the cobbler as well,' she said.

The needle-like heel on the right shoe was now hopelessly askew. Vikki looked at me as I sat at the bottom of the steps like a broken-down doll in my couture and ugg boots. She smiled at me sadly.

'I don't think you're ready to be up this high, do you?'

'No,' I said. 'Not yet. Maybe soon.'

CHAPTER TWENTY-FOUR

15 November 2023

My phone buzzed in my lap and I reached for my napkin so I could surreptitiously look at the screen.

All okay? James had written.

Mary had told me before the Edinburgh Agricultural Society luncheon that if she caught me playing with my phone again, she was going to confiscate it. I typed quickly before anyone saw: *All fine. Will call you later.*

I slipped my phone back into my lap and engaged the man next to me in conversation. His Charolais bull had been declared the pedigree champion at the last Spring Show, but he was worried about his chances next year. I seemed to be constantly in Scotland these days, visiting aged care homes and art exhibitions and agriculture shows and shaking hands with MPs and schoolchildren.

Granny and Stewart had begun discussing plans for an investiture ceremony in Edinburgh the next summer. She would announce that I had decided to wear the crown during her televised Christmas address. No one bothered to ask me if I intended to stay. The fact that I had lasted this long was taken as confirmation that I would.

But first I needed to secure the Scottish coronet. I had been looking at photos of Papa's own investiture when he was twenty-two. *How young he looked*, I thought. Young and doomed. He had designed his coronet for the ceremony – a sparsely decorated modern brushed-gold headpiece that sat slightly off-kilter on his head, no matter how much he adjusted it. I had no idea if it would make its way to me next. Richard was spending as much time in Scotland as I was, his office finding every excuse possible to send him northward.

When the luncheon was done, Mary pulled me aside. 'A bit of a problem, ma'am. Have you looked outside lately?'

'No, I've been looking at photos of bulls and their giant balls.'

'Yes, well, there's a storm. It was meant to blow out over the North Sea by now, but it hasn't. All flights are cancelled because of the winds.'

'Okay.' I shrugged. 'So, we stay here tonight?'

'Unfortunately, yes. But we may struggle to find suitable accommodation.'

I walked over to the window of the city chambers so I could look outside. The red flowers in the window box were blown sideways by the wind. A violent spatter of rain landed on the glass. I realised that if I was going to do this, now might be my only chance.

'Why don't we just go to the estate? We're an hour away. I'm sure the Queen won't mind.'

Mary was already tapping on her phone. 'I'll clear it with Stewart now.'

With the palace's approval, our trio of Range Rovers headed inland. The billowing winds made the cars shudder on the road and our windscreen wipers worked frenziedly against the onslaught of rain. An hour later, we were pulling through the castle gates. I had absolutely no desire to be there again, to walk the halls I had walked with Jack a few months earlier. I asked for my things to be placed in the bedroom Louis had favoured so I wouldn't have to see mine and remember how I'd sneaked Jack in late one night. That had been the last time. His eyes were shining in the firelight, and he'd sunk to his knees and pressed his sandpaper cheek against my abdomen while I threaded my fingers through his hair.

We still hadn't spoken since that last awful day. The only way I could keep going forward was to never let my mind go back there.

Downstairs, I sent Mary and the others to the staff quarters for the night and then lingered in the drawing room for ten minutes, giving them time to cross the lawn and get settled. I rarely hid things from Mary. For nearly a year, she had sat beside me in town cars, waited by the sinks while I peed in the stall, held my purse when I shook an endless row of hands. But this was one mission I needed to complete alone. Once I was sure she would be settled for the night, I pulled my coat and boots back on and asked for a car to be brought around.

As I stepped out into the wild storm, Rita opened the car door for me.

'Where to, ma'am?' she asked. She had to shout over the keening wind to be heard.

'I'd like to go see my stepmother at Candacraig.'

We drove down the narrow country road under an ashen sky. I had been to Candacraig House precisely twice before. It had been a wedding gift for Papa from his grandmother, who told him every married man needed a place of his own. He retreated there often, especially during summer holidays, and forbade us visiting. Like everything that was Papa's, it was elegantly appointed. Not a single tartan print or antler trophy had made its way inside.

The servant who answered the door looked stunned to see me, but she took my drenched raincoat and showed me to a drawing room. I sat on the cream linen sofa closest to the fire, craning my neck as I took in as many details as possible. A few of Papa's lithographs hung on the walls. One of his beloved orchids stood on a table, a spray bottle by its side. On the mantel was a framed photograph of Annabelle and Papa on the front steps of the house. In it, Papa was laughing with abandon, and I realised I'd never seen him look so happy.

'Your Highness,' came a voice behind me.

I turned to watch her come into the room. She was dressed in jeans and a cardigan, with fuzzy pink slippers on her feet.

'Hi,' I said. 'Sorry to drop in unannounced.'

Annabelle didn't curtsy and I didn't expect her to. She sat on the sofa opposite me and ran her hands over her knees. 'Well, I assumed you'd turn up here at one point or another.'

The same servant who had opened the door to me came in with a tray of tea and shortbread. Annabelle and I studied each other silently while the woman poured out our cups and fussed with napkins.

'You should have some shortbread,' Annabelle said when the servant closed the door behind her. 'You're looking thin.'

I took a piece and put it on my plate, though the idea of it sliding down my throat in gritty clumps was enough to make me want to gag.

'I'm here because I have some problems.'

She smiled sadly. 'I'm sorry to hear that, though it's not unexpected.'

'Why? Because you don't think I'm cut out for this?' I snapped and then silently admonished myself.

She took a sip of her tea. 'No. Because you've been swimming in shark–infested waters.'

With a shaky breath, I told her about Richard, Davide Rossi and the private investigator. It was the second time I had unburdened myself in a month, and it still had the same effect. I felt like I had pulled up my skirt and revealed an oozing, gangrenous limb. I was hideous and should be shunned. But there was something about exposing this horror that was like salt water, a salve to the wound.

When I stopped talking, Annabelle had a strange expression on her face. She poured more tea for both of us, taking her time. We both drank. 'This would be most upsetting for your father,' she finally said.

'Yes, well …'

'Perhaps you should know that in the month before your father died, he was extremely distressed. It seems that Richard had come into some information and was threatening to use it against him. We never found out how, but I suppose a private investigator makes the most sense. All they'd have had to do was wait outside Sherbourne House and follow Louis to know where he was spending his nights,' she said.

My chest began to ache. 'Richard knew about Louis and Kris?'

'I'm afraid so. We tried rather hard to keep it under wraps over the years. The Queen doesn't know – though I'm sure she suspected. But we never felt we could trust the family to keep the secret, and unfortunately we were right.' She took a long sip of tea. 'The Duke of Clarence has always enjoyed a certain lifestyle. I'm sure you've heard about the jets and the helicopters and the chateaus. Over the years, he has overextended himself – debts that are much too large to ask the Queen to step in and deal with. She does adore him, but we're talking serious money – and not all of it was borrowed from what you'd call legitimate sources.'

I thought of Papa's strange behaviour in those final days, a certain recklessness that pushed him off the trail and down the mountain that would kill him. 'Was Papa going to pay him?'

'Yes, I think so,' she said. 'I wasn't happy about it, to be honest. Not because I wanted Louis exposed. But my fear was that Richard would simply come back for more. He knew about your father and me in the nineties, and he wielded that over Freddy too. I worried if we gave in, we'd forever have him shadowing our doorstep. It was a very tense Christmas last year.'

This problem of mine was like a puzzle box I'd been trying to solve for months. Now, I'd finally figured out the correct sequence of twists and movements, so that it clicked and sprang open in my hands.

'When Richard and I talked in August, he gave me until the end of the year to decide what I'm going to do,' I said.

'I've always thought that was strange. If he wants what I have so badly, why wait?'

'Why do you think?'

'Davide Rossi won't come forward for free, I'm sure of it. But where would Richard get the money? Papa died before he could pay him. Maybe he needs time to raise the funds — or maybe he thinks the threat is enough to make me leave.'

A pine cone popped in the fire and its forest-floor scent rose up. Annabelle clasped her hands in her lap.

'Richard used to have a lot of friends in London, a lot of benefactors who liked being around royalty,' she said. 'But when the war in Ukraine began, they all left, and his situation became … precarious. His friends' assets are frozen or hidden, and they're in no position to help him. Do you know what I'm talking about?'

I nodded. The UK had once flung open its doors to wealthy foreigners — no questions asked — as long as they were willing to invest in British companies. Belgravia was nicknamed 'the Red Square' for its sudden influx of wealthy Russians. The palace had implored the family to be careful around outsiders, but suddenly there were oligarchs everywhere, and they were all so friendly and magnanimous and charming. For working royals, the line between 'official' gifts and 'personal' ones had always been murky at best and, for Richard, easily ignored. But then came the invasion of Ukraine, and his friends fled while they could, off to new lives in Istanbul and Monaco. Once they were gone, the upper classes simply pretended they hadn't spent the past decade drinking champagne paid for with looted Russian funds.

'I've heard the rumours,' I said.

'Cash is the one thing Richard doesn't have right now,' Annabelle said. 'I'm sure he's promised to pay this Italian man once he's the heir and he's got access to the Duchy of Exeter's funds.'

'I have money.' I cleared my throat, my voice failing me. 'Or, at least, I can borrow some. A lot.'

She raised an eyebrow. 'Well, I believe you have your solution then.'

The fire was making me hot. Or maybe it was the fear of what I was about to become.

'Annabelle,' I asked, 'what do you think I should do?'

She smiled kindly at me. I could see why Papa had been drawn to her. She was grounded and maternal and womanly.

'I'm not sure, dear. Money's one thing, but the crown is quite another. That's everything. That's power, that's your bloodline, that's being told you're God's representative on Earth,' she said. 'The question you need to ask yourself is whether you want it more than he does. If you do, act quickly. Remind this Italian man he's bound by a non-disclosure agreement that Freddy's estate would have no qualms about enforcing. Pay him as a gesture of goodwill for his continued silence. And then put it all behind you.'

'But then wouldn't Richard shadow my doorstep forever?' I asked.

She looked sad. 'Yes, dear, he would.'

We sipped our tea in silence for a while, listening to the snap and hiss of the fire, the wind outside rattling the windows.

'I actually have something for you – wait here,' Annabelle said, rising from her chair. She vanished from the room, and I sat in stunned silence until she returned with a Tesco bag. She pushed it across the coffee table to me and sank back down. 'I'm sorry I didn't give this to you sooner. I did go to get it from Elton Park as soon as he died, but then … I don't know, I couldn't part with it.'

I opened the bag and found a plank of wood inside. It was old and rough, and I held it up to the dim light from the window so I could see the lines scratched into one side. I ran my finger over it, remembering when I was three years old, and we sat on the bed while he pointed them out.

'I think I've violated a few laws dealing with the preservation of artefacts by ripping it out of what's now government property,' she said. 'But he did always say that when he went, he wanted you to have the witch marks from the bedroom floor.'

I held the wood in my hands and let the tears sting my eyes. I wanted it to hurt. I'd spent my life aching for his love. The reserves he had saved for his children were so meagre that I'd run away to punish him. I wondered about all the things I had done – fleeing to Australia, and now trying to be the princess he wanted. How much had I done in pursuit of his wholly inadequate love?

'He tried his best,' Annabelle said, as if reading my thoughts. 'He did love you both very much. He just ... didn't always know how to show you.'

'Thank you,' I managed.

At the doorway, she watched as I buttoned myself back into my raincoat and pulled on my boots. I tucked the Tesco bag into my pocket. The storm had scattered slightly, and the sky reminded me of being underwater, watching from below as a great wave crashed against the surface.

'Are you sure you want to drive in this?' she asked. 'You're welcome to stay the night.'

I shook my head. 'I should go. We're on the first flight tomorrow. But thank you, really.'

She nodded and wrapped her cardigan around herself. 'Everything will work out. This family will always protect its own. It's different for Amira and me. But you're a princess of the blood. The Queen wants it to be you. She knows what the monarchy needs right now is a pretty young woman, not an old man. You'll look lovely on the front page of the papers, and you'll have a wedding one day and then royal babies. That's what the people want.'

I smiled and began to walk down the steps towards the car. But then I stopped. She wasn't at all what I had thought she was.

'Annabelle, can I ask you one more thing?'

She nodded.

'The last time we spoke, you told me to watch out for Mary, my private secretary. What did you mean?'

Again, she swaddled herself in her cardigan and looked down at her feet. 'I was angry then – I shouldn't have said that.'

'But you must have had a reason.'

She sighed and leaned against the doorjamb. 'From the outside looking in, she appears to be doing a good job for you, and that's all that matters. But she was *chosen* for you. The day of the avalanche, the Queen needed a plan to get you back and to keep you here. Amira suggested Mary go with Stewart when he fetched you from Australia. She knew you'd like her.'

An icy raindrop fell on my neck and slid down into the collar of my coat. 'Amira?'

'Yes, well, she knew Mary from school, I think. She got her a job in Wolseley House writing press releases for Freddy. She is fine, I suppose. I just worry she's a little too taken with the family – a bit of a superfan.'

Rita drove me back to the estate in the beating rain, and I ate toast and boiled eggs from a tray balanced on my lap. When I was done, I walked alone through the dark castle halls with the Tesco bag and climbed into Louis's bed, where I held the wooden plank to my chest. I imagined the witch marks casting their wing of light above me. But I couldn't rely on superstitions, or magic, or even my own father to keep me safe any longer, so I reached for my phone on the bedside table.

The number was already saved into my contacts. I hit the button before I could reconsider, and it rang for a long time. But then came a click, an intake of breath, and the quickening of my heart.

'Pronto,' the man said.

His sonorous voice had been hidden in the folds of my memory for twelve long years. Suddenly, the rancid stench of bilge filled my room, and for one frightening moment, the bed lurched on an invisible sea.

'Davide Rossi?' I breathed.

He paused. 'Si.'

'Mr Rossi, my name is Alexandrina, but you used to call me "*carina*". Do you have a moment to talk?'

CHAPTER TWENTY-FIVE

16 November 2023

Colin sat down beside me on the sofa and handed me a whisky.

'I'm glad you called. It's been a while.'

I took the heavy crystal glass and sipped. It was so expensive, it didn't even burn as it went down.

'Yes, sorry about that.'

'Being the heir is a full-time job,' he said and pulled my bare feet into his lap.

Everything about his apartment was beige. It looked like one of the first-class lounges at Doha Airport. Colin was the type of man who had a single drumstick framed on the wall, no doubt a collector's item from some rocker I didn't know. In his closet was a special velvet drawer for his watch collection. There was a leather squash bag in the entrance that never seemed to move from its position leaned against a limestone console.

That morning, I had climbed into the Range Rover next to Mary and we rode silently to Aberdeen International Airport for our flight home. As she dozed beside me in the blue light, I studied her face and tried to conjure memories of her, but none came. At first I thought it was unfathomable that Amira would know someone I didn't at Astley, but by our last year I had lost Mum and thought of nothing else. I had always sensed that Mary and I shared a past she preferred not to discuss. I thought perhaps she'd had a hand in the leaks that came from Wolseley House when it belonged to Papa, but maybe I was wrong. Maybe our past stretched further back than I ever realised.

Once we'd landed in Heathrow, I texted Colin and asked if I could come over. He was still at work, so I had my driver drop me off at his flat, where his concierge let me in. Colin worked at his father's company that managed the family's real estate holdings and investments. I had a bath in his enormous clawfoot tub, and he had come home a few hours later, dressed in his flawless suit, with a bottle of whisky tucked under one arm.

'Can I ask you a slightly illegal question?' I said now as the peat turned to vapour on my tongue.

Colin laughed and dug his knuckle into the arch of my foot. 'Well, that's the most interesting thing anyone's asked me in a while.'

'This is all extremely hypothetical,' I said, my head swimming. 'But imagine that you have to give money to someone. And you couldn't personally do it because they live in another country. And you would need to get them the money without ever being found out.'

He looked at me seriously, but he didn't stop kneading my feet. 'Finding an intermediary would be simple – there's three people I could call now whom I'd trust to do it. I'd ask them to make the deal and then I'd do the exchange with Bitcoin. Or you'd put all the cash on a private jet and have it flown over – that's not a bad option either.'

I stared into the glow of his minimalist fireplace and wondered about myself.

'Hypothetically speaking,' he said, lowering my foot into his lap, 'if you were ever to need something like that, I could help.'

I said nothing. When he crawled towards me on the sofa, I let him kiss me. He pushed me into the cushions, and I wondered if I could succumb to this life. Tomorrow, I could ask Vikki to write a cheque, and Colin would funnel the money into a

Bitcoin wallet for Davide Rossi. Next summer Colin could stand in the esplanade of Edinburgh Castle and watch while Granny placed the coronet on my head. His presence would be enough to divert the press's attention from the inevitable Scottish independence protests I had no hope of snuffing out.

But when he wove his fingers into my hair, it was Jack's face that surfaced in my mind. I thought of the way his eyes crinkled when he smiled at me, the way the early sunlight had caught in his hair on New Year's Day. A great panic rushed through me, and I squirmed out of Colin's arms.

'Sorry,' I said, covering my lips.

'You alright?'

'Yes,' I breathed, though I wanted out of the prison of his heavy limbs. I sat up and let my chest heave. 'I've been having these dizzy spells. Sorry, I'm not sure I'm up for anything tonight.'

He tentatively rubbed my back. 'That's okay. Want to just order a takeaway and go to sleep?'

We slid into his gargantuan bed, and I listened to his rhythmic breaths while I soothed myself by naming in my mind all the bones in the human hand. When I was done, I moved on to the foot, then all the signs of pneumonia, then every step to insert a central line without causing an infection. I lay there, steering my mind through black waters until finally, just before dawn, I sank into sleep.

In the morning, I woke to the smell of coffee. I came into the kitchen and found Colin sipping an espresso, already dressed for work and reading his iPad.

'You're up.' He smiled. 'Would you like a coffee?'

'Yes, please.'

I sat on one of the stools lined against his marble island and watched as he ground coffee beans, measured them on a scale and then brushed off the excess with a tiny brush. He submerged a cup in hot water before pouring in the espresso.

'Can you make designs in the froth?' I asked.

'I actually can.' He laughed.

I drank, and the coffee was as perfect as everything else in his apartment.

'So,' he said. 'Tonight. Why don't we go out? I know it's tricky, but we can go to Oswald's. It's private there. Members only. No one will bother us or take pictures.'

'I've got a reception at the palace tonight,' I said. 'I organised it myself. It's for a clinic in Nairobi that treats obstetric fistula.'

'What's that?'

'It's a serious childbirth injury. It mostly happens to girls who are too young to be pregnant. Prolonged labour can seriously damage the wall of the birth canal and—'

He grimaced and laughed, waving a hand in front of his face. 'I get the picture.'

While I had become something of a derelict princess in recent months, I still cared deeply about my patronages, so I'd thrown myself headlong into planning the reception. The clinic's board members were already in London ahead of the event, and the city's wealthiest and most powerful residents had RSVPed yes. There was one person who would not be there, though. Six weeks earlier, Mary had asked me to go over the guest list one more time before we sent out the invitations. I drew my finger down her leather binder, slowing to a stop when I reached Jack's name. I tried to imagine what would happen if I let it slip through so that the stiff cream invite made its way around the world, landing in the pile of mail on the kitchen bench back home. Would he see it as an entreaty? A cruel tease? I picked up a pencil and crossed him out.

'Mr Jennings is no longer able to attend,' I said.

'Yes, ma'am.'

Afterwards, I locked myself in a stall in the ladies' room and silently wept into my hands. Just for a moment. It was all I would allow myself.

Colin was polishing the steel of his coffee machine until it glowed. 'Come here after the reception if you like.'

I smiled thinly. 'I would, I just haven't seen my dog in a few days, and I think I should.'

'Lou's pointer? Bring him round.'

'That dog in *this* apartment? I'm sweating just imagining him on all these neutral furnishings.'

He laughed, but it was a hollow sound. 'Well, I won't presume to invite myself to Cumberland. I'm not sure Amira would want me hanging around her house anyway.'

I felt a familiar twinge of something I had not been able to name for months. I was beginning to see that for the duration of my time in London, everyone around me had been cloaking themselves in falsehoods, giving me only a fraction of the truth, so that I was no longer sure who to believe.

'What's the problem between you two?'

There was a strange expression on his face. 'I don't have a problem with her. I'm not sure she really liked any of Louis's friends, to be honest.'

'She told me she invited you to a dinner party at their house and you showed up with a new girlfriend, but you hadn't broken up with the old one yet, and she was there too, and it was very awkward.'

'What?' He looked startled, and then rolled his eyes. 'That's not ... I didn't do that. That's not how it went down.'

I shrugged. 'I'm not judging. But maybe that's why she's ... I don't know, ambivalent.'

He studied my face. 'Has she warned you off me?'

'No,' I said. I wasn't quite sure what Amira wanted for me anymore. She was frighteningly unsentimental when it came to marriage and repeatedly insisted there was no better match for me than Colin. But the possibility that I might go through with it seemed to leave her bereft.

'Look, she's your friend, but ... I don't know,' he said, throwing up his hands. 'There's people like us and there's people like her.'

'Sorry?'

He rolled his eyes again, clearly frustrated with me. 'I'm not talking about skin colour. It's just ... you've met her parents. Her mother engineered that whole thing with Lou. She dug her claws into him, and she pushed them together. I don't know if Amira even wanted him. I mean, she wasn't faithful to him, that's for sure.'

I sat very still on my stool while Colin pinched the bridge of his nose. I thought of her simmering resentment, the way she seemed to know everything about him, how quiet she had been on the drive home from our weekend at Lutton Hall.

'That's just what I heard,' he muttered. 'Anyway, let's drop it.'

'It was Amira,' I said slowly. 'The girl at the dinner party who had to sit across the table from you and your new girlfriend. You and Amira were together.'

The howl of an ambulance filled the apartment as it careened past. Once it faded, we sat in the yawning silence. His arms were folded over his chest as he stared at the floor.

'Yes.'

'What happened?'

He looked at me sideways. 'Do you really want to know?'

I shrugged again. When he said nothing, I pushed back my stool and stood up to leave.

'Look,' he said firmly. 'It was a mistake, obviously. I shouldn't have done it. We got a little caught up in things for a while, but I certainly wasn't trying to break up their marriage. But then she started talking about leaving him, and the thing is, Lou was like a brother to me. I would never do that to him, ever, and I wouldn't want to put your family through that. I knew I had to end it. And the way I did it ... yeah, that wasn't great. But I had to shock her out of this fantasy she had. I did it for Louis.'

I nodded. I was dressed only in a t-shirt and suddenly felt exposed. 'I should let you get to work.'

In the bedroom, I started searching for my clothes on the floor. She had kept secrets from me, and she'd been involved in some sort of scheme I didn't quite understand, and yet all I wanted to do was get home to her. Colin appeared at the door and watched me stuff things in my suitcase.

'I know you're upset,' he said.

I didn't look up as I pulled my dress back on. 'It's really fine. I just need to go be with my friend.'

'She's not your friend,' he said. 'That family – those people – have never been your friends. I invited her to Lutton Hall over the summer because I knew you wouldn't come up without her, but it was only you I wanted to see. I'm done with her. It was nothing.'

I pulled my coat off the hook and slung it over my shoulders. 'You're wrong about the Shankars. I can't get into it, but you're wrong. Amira was a good wife to Louis. They both tried their best.'

He shook his head, looking confused. 'Okay.'

'Thank you for letting me stay here last night.'

I made it to the entrance with my suitcase before he caught up to me and grabbed my wrist.

'Lexi,' he said. 'Cards on the table here: I like you. I've liked you since we were kids. And sure, it makes a certain sense for us to be together – I'm not saying I've never thought about that side of things. If everything worked out, our first son would be the heir to the throne. And then we could arrange things so his younger brother becomes the Duke of Hereford and manages the land holdings. That's a powerful pair of siblings. It would solve every problem your family has ever had with the second-born child.'

He saw my face go dark and looked briefly up at the ceiling.

'Sorry, but you know what I mean. All I'm saying is, if you stopped rushing off every time we got closer, you might find that you like me too. I know there's some other guy, some … Australian. Demelza told me about it. But I just think this' – he gestured between us – 'this makes sense.'

He took my hand in his, and I thought suddenly of the last time I'd been standing in a man's apartment this way. *You'd be incapable of living a real life*, Ben had said to me. I could never explain to myself why this had hurt so much, but I understood now what he meant. It was not the world's rabid interest in my private life that I feared. It was being truly known by the person standing in front of me.

Colin and I could merge power bases and call that a family. We could also have our own private dalliances and never ask each other probing questions. And during the decades we spent together, waving from balconies, posing for pictures and keeping our secrets, we would never really get to know each other at all.

Gently, I withdrew my fingers from his grasp and grabbed the handle of my suitcase.

'I really am sorry,' I said.

I took the lift down, and when I hit street level I walked out into the cold November air where I could finally breathe.

CHAPTER TWENTY-SIX

17 November 2023

The reception to raise awareness about obstetric fistula was held in the palace's picture gallery, a long narrow room with an arched skylight that showed off the night sky. Dr Esther Miloyo, the CEO and chief surgeon at the Miloyo Fistula Clinic in Nairobi, was our guest of honour. Surrounded by people, she was explaining that a donation of just £350 covered the cost of one reconstructive surgery, which would forever change the trajectory of a patient's life. Granny and I stood by the fireplace so that guests could pay their respects, Stewart and Mary lingering nearby in case we forgot a name or a face.

That morning, when I left Colin's apartment, I had gone back to Cumberland, but Amira wasn't there. I took Chino to the park so he could chase squirrels among the trees. When he was spent, we sat under the bare arms of an oak and watched people rushing past in pursuit of their lives.

By the time Chino and I had returned to the house, Mary was there with the makeup artist and a silver dress on a hanger.

'Altuzarra,' she said. 'The tiny cutouts at the front are a bit racy, but it's ankle-length, so it still honours the dress code. Just.'

'It looks like armour,' I said as she zipped me into it. 'Do you know where Amira is?'

'She's getting ready at her parents' house. The Shankars will arrive at the reception together.'

From the car window, I watched the first signs of Christmas burgeoning on the streets of London. Soon the city would live under a net of twinkling lights. There would be markets and mulled wine, children gliding around ice skating rinks and carollers on doorsteps. The Earth was approaching perihelion, the closest we get to the sun in our annual loop through space. I had almost made it through the year.

'I was thinking, ma'am,' Mary said from the seat next to me. 'Perhaps next year we should discuss my role.'

I looked across at her, but her face was caught in shadow. 'What do you mean?'

'I just thought once you're the Princess of Scotland, I should focus more on shaping your overall strategy. Perhaps we could bring on a professional for your styling.'

I smiled at her. 'You've always been too clever for this, Mary.'

'Oh, I don't mean that I feel it's beneath me – I do enjoy it,' she said quickly. 'I just think I'd be of more use to you by starting to think about the future.'

I turned back to the window and found that it had fogged over in the cold. With my fingertip, I drew two stars in the glass. 'We would be unstoppable, Mary, I have no doubt.'

As the crowd mingled in the gallery, Jenny approached with her teenage son, and they bowed before us. Granny had a trick of lavishing attention on a VIP's plus one, so while she chatted to Harley, I pulled Jenny aside. The palace videographer was lurking nearby, and this was one guest who would make the final cut of every social media video and television news package. Aware of this, Jenny and I smiled at each other.

'You alright, Lexi?' she whispered.

I nodded, smiled brightly, and then offered her a formal handshake for the cameras.

'Yes, I'm fine, Prime Minister. Thank you for coming.'

When I finally let go of her hand, Jenny receded into the

crowd with her son a few steps behind her, eyes brightening as people saw her, powerful men stepping forward, hoping for her favour. She hated every single one of them, but she had waded into their world in the hope of changing it.

When I turned back, Richard stood before me. We hadn't seen each other since that August morning on the stairs in Scotland. Now, he bared his wolfish teeth in a grin before sliding his eyes over to Granny.

'Looking splendid, Mummy,' he said and dropped his chin to his chest in a bow. 'As always.'

'Oh, do go on.' She sighed. 'Where's Florence this evening?'

'Laid up with a migraine, poor love,' he said, pouting. 'She sends her apologies, of course – she's absolutely devastated to miss an evening dedicated entirely to women's plumbing.'

I was calm as he turned back to me. We looked at each other levelly, neither attempting to smile for the cameras. It struck me then that in many ways, we were the same: two royal babies born too late, forever outshone by our brothers. Our life's purpose was to stay alive if tragedy befell them. Now they were both gone, and it was the two of us in the arena. Richard and I both knew that the crown didn't always float benevolently into your open palms. Sometimes, you had to wrench it away from the gods and plant it on your own head.

'Isn't this year going so fast?' he said quietly.

'Very.'

'That's the thing about getting older. Time starts speeding up. I find that these days, I can barely remember what I did yesterday, though my memories of the past are clearer than ever.'

'Yes,' I said coolly. 'I'm the same.'

He smiled, surprised. 'I see.'

We both glanced over at Granny, who was already occupied by another guest vying for her attention. She had started to wilt a little as she approached her nineties. Soon she wouldn't be able to stand up straight at all. We're all just slowly seeping back into the earth from which we came.

Richard leaned in close enough for me to smell his breath: cigars and milk.

'And what have you decided?' he asked.

I looked around the lively room of doctors, donors and royals, the walls bedecked with paintings of the people who came before us. That was all you could hope for in the end, a place on the wall to watch as the powerful ones shook hands and built empires. Over the mantel was the last portrait of Barbara ever painted. In it, her hair was silver, her sharp chin softening with age, though her neckline remained as scandalous as ever. I met her eyes, and saw that Barbara was waiting to see what I would do.

'Did you really think I would just slink away and let you have it all?' I turned to face Richard. 'Did you think I would let you take what's mine?'

He managed to smile, though a scarlet flush was creeping from the collar of his stiff white shirt. With all cameras trained on us, he leaned forward and put a hand on my shoulder, as if I was his beloved niece, and he was congratulating me for organising this reception all by myself. The tabloids would say he was being paternal. What a good brother to step in when Prince Frederick no longer could, they'd say.

'Remember, I can have Mr Rossi on the front page of the *Post* tomorrow,' he said. 'Don't make me do that to you.'

I shrugged. 'Call him then.'

Richard narrowed his eyes at me, irritated that I wasn't behaving the way he'd expected. But he kept his fingers on my bare skin.

'Perhaps you're hoping the public will forgive you when they find out about your night on the Italian Riviera. But I think you know, deep down, that they won't. You lost their trust forever when you left, and while they're giving you a second chance now, this revelation will confirm that all their suspicions about you were correct. It will sink you. Your reign will be over before it even begins.'

I smiled and eased myself out of his grip. 'Mr Rossi and I spoke a few days ago. He's still waiting for you to deliver on all those promises you made, by the way. Have you been having trouble getting the cash together?'

When a servant appeared with a tray of champagne flutes, I took one, although Richard seemed too stunned to notice he was there. The waiter drifted away to another group of guests nearby. He glanced in Granny's direction, perhaps tempted to tell her everything. He could storm over to the cameras in fury and announce that I had once abandoned my mother in the Ligurian Sea. He could call up the tabloids tomorrow and tell them all that he knew. But Richard was not a man who ever spoke in his own voice. If Davide Rossi was unwilling to speak for him, he knew this was over.

'I know you're wondering how I did it,' I whispered. 'It's simple. Your friends are busy hiding their assets from Western sanctions and trying not to fall out of windows. But *my* friends have demonstrated far more loyalty to this family than you ever have.'

I stepped back, clutching my champagne flute so he wouldn't see the tremor in my fingers. And as if I'd planned it, which I really hadn't, the Shankars appeared in the doorway to the gallery. All three of them were dressed in black. Amira was by her father's side, looking daunted but beautiful. It was Vikki who led the way, striding before her husband and daughter to greet us with a smile.

She gave Granny an elaborate curtsy and then came over to kiss both my cheeks. 'How are you, my darling Royal Highness?'

'I'm very well, Mrs Shankar. Thank you so much for your show of support,' I said. 'You remember my uncle?'

Trapped by the cameras, Richard stood there with the ghost of a smile on his face while Vikki nodded.

'Yes, of course I remember,' she said. 'We once met at the estate in Scotland, I believe. And you called me ... what was it? A trolley dolly? A cart tart? I can't quite remember anymore; it was so long ago.'

Before Richard could form a response, Vikki turned back to me and squeezed my hand.

'If you'll excuse me, I must go find this brilliant doctor and write a great big cheque for her cause.'

Madhav arrived and offered his elbow to Vikki, and we watched as they exchanged the kind of smile that was only possible between two people who were living in the rubble of their old life. But they still found beauty in it, because they still had each other. When they walked away, Richard stood beside me, stunned into silence.

'Why don't you go mingle?' I said to him. 'I'll see you at Christmas.'

He opened his mouth to speak. Then he stalked off in the opposite direction, probably heading upstairs to the private apartments, where he could either sulk or scheme. But I was no longer afraid of him. I would allow no one to shadow my doorstep for the rest of my life.

When Amira came before me, we stared at each other for a moment before she curtsied deeply. It was the first time she had ever done that. In silence, we kissed each other's cheeks, but neither of us could manage a smile. She had always known me better than anyone and, somehow, she knew that I knew.

'Shall we talk later?' I murmured.

'If you like.'

She walked deeper into the gallery until she was swallowed by the crowd. And then it was time to give my toast in honour of Dr Miloyo and her life's work. Mary passed me the cards onto which she had carefully written my speech. We had drafted and submitted my toast to Stewart, who returned it with whole sections crossed out in red pen. I was to make no references to Britain's colonial history in Kenya, only celebrating our countries' 'strong bonds of friendship'. I was forbidden from pointing out that pregnancy was such a perilous endeavour for so many because of the legacy of empire. And I could make no allusions to my own history in medicine. We went back and forth, until I had conceded every point, and he finally permitted me to speak.

At the lectern, I looked into the faces of our guests. Jenny stood with the Shankars. Granny was now seated in a gilt chair, Stewart forever keeping watch by her side. Dr Miloyo and her associates stood at the centre of the room, waiting. So I gave the speech that Stewart had approved, but as I reached the last card, I glanced up one final time to look at Barbara over the mantel. Her DNA might have spiralled down through her descendants so that part of her was still alive within me. I might have had her name and the position she conspired to make mine. But she was just a woman in a painting. She was old bones buried deep beneath the Abbey floor. Her time had passed, and soon mine would too.

I put the card down on the lectern. 'As many of you know, I once dreamed of being a doctor – specifically an obstetrician, after seeing the good work of Dr Miloyo in action when I was a girl on a trip to Nairobi with my mother.'

I could sense more than I saw the lengthening of Mary's spine as she stood in the shadows beside me.

'When choosing a cause for this event, I thought a lot about the good things my family can do with our position,' I went on. 'When we speak, the world sits up and pays attention. But if you choose to speak, you must be as truthful as you know how to be. Otherwise, no one will ever trust your words. And the truth is that the British empire's historical actions in Kenya and elsewhere have a long and terrible legacy. Until we can have a frank conversation about the past and make amends for our sins, we will be unable to move into the future.'

I raised my glass and finished my toast, and when I was done, there was a brief lull before the crowd filled the room with their applause – some of it enthusiastic, some of it merely polite. I noted the exchange of meaningful glances among the guests, the straight line Stewart made of his mouth as he pressed his lips together. But I had no regrets.

After I spent some time chatting to our guests, I slipped away for a moment to stand on the landing of the grand staircase alone. When I looked up, I saw that Amira was sitting on one of the narrower flights of steps that curved up to the palace's third floor. I climbed up, sank down next to her and leaned against the gold-leaf banister. In our silence, we could hear the laughter and voices from the other room.

'So I think we've both been holding out on each other,' I started.

'Colin texted me,' she said. 'He's furious.'

'Why didn't you tell me about that?' I looked at her. She was staring into her empty hands. 'I can't imagine what it's been like for you all these months.'

She twitched as if rejecting the notion that she could feel pain. 'You two make sense. My feelings are irrelevant.'

'Amira,' I said. 'You're my friend. Your feelings are extremely relevant. You were in love with this man, and you had to keep it a secret when it ended, and then you just watched while he carried on with me.'

She brushed at the tears forming in her eyes. 'It doesn't matter anymore.'

'Of course it does. Are we not friends? Because I've heard some things lately that make me wonder. You know Mary and you put her in my path? You have a history with Colin, and you kept pushing him on me to make me forget about Jack.'

She stared at me icily. 'I was doing what I was told.'

'By *who*?'

'Who do you *think*?' she hissed. A servant carrying a tray of empty champagne flutes glided by and we watched quietly until he disappeared down the hall. 'She wanted to keep you here. And I went along with it because this is her family and her institution. And … I wanted you to stay as well. You have no idea what these years have been like for me.'

'Why don't you tell me then?'

*

It wasn't so much that Amira had wanted to marry Louis as it got to a point where turning back would have done more damage than forging on. Before she knew it, she had been Louis's girlfriend for seven years. Louis and Kris still seemed deeply in love, although they would break up for months at a time when the pressure of their secret lives started to smother them, and Amira would wonder if, finally, she might be free. She loved Louis dearly. He treated her better than most of her secondary school boyfriends, taking her to clubs and dinners and buying her gifts.

But she had started to wonder if that was enough for a life – even one as grand as theirs. She hadn't had sex in seven years. No one kissed her or touched her. The tabloids had already started to mock her for her unending patience in waiting for a proposal. At twenty-six, they could break up and it would be humiliating for a while, but then she might be able to start her life anew. If she got any older than this, her prospects would be very grim indeed.

It was then that Louis had raided Mum's safe deposit box for the emerald. He and Vikki had urged her to consider it. Kris refused to be involved. While Amira would be giving up the prospect of romantic love – at least, until they could figure out how to live their lives in private without being discovered – she would get to be the Queen of England. The marriage would not depend on the longevity of Louis's relationship with Kris. This would be forever. And so, she did it. She did it because her mother insisted that marriage was a ladder into the aristocracy. She did it because she saw that Kris and Louis were unable to stay apart and she wanted them to be happy. She did it because every girl in the world is told from the moment she's born that there's nothing finer than being queen.

A few days after his visit to Tasmania, Louis had confided in Amira about the encounter with Finn. There had been others over the years, but never a stranger, never a regular man whose position did not depend on secrecy. Things were too tense at the time for Louis to call and ask me if they could trust Finn. But when Louis had gone to Frederick, wondering if perhaps they should offer to buy Finn's silence, Papa had blamed me for all of it. He had always privately hoped I'd return to London when I finished medical school. After learning from Louis that I had chosen to work at a Tasmanian hospital instead, he was furious, hurt and looking for an excuse to punish me. I was somehow behind this scheme, Papa had declared. I must have got Louis drunk and pushed him and Finn together in the hope of breaking up the wedding. There would be no payout. The only person who would be silenced was me. Exhausted, Louis and Amira had walked down the aisle of Westminster Abbey as Kris and I watched on.

Everything had been fine at first. They had moved to Sherbourne House and found that in Norfolk they could finally breathe. Kris bought a house down the road, and this really was Louis's home. But whether Amira was at a dinner party with Louis's friends or attending an event as the Duchess of Somerset, she felt like she was walking underwater. Everyone thought she was the luckiest girl in the world. She had a large country estate, a handsome husband who was nice to her, and a dazzling future that felt like a life sentence.

She wasn't even sure she liked Colin when he'd started stealing glances at her across the dinner table. He had caused constant sexual drama in their circle, and she had watched with disdain as he dated women and then moved on to their sisters or childhood best friends. She knew he was interested in her for the same reason Louis wanted to surf down a volcano. But it had been so very long since she felt desirable. During a drunken game of hide and seek, she and Colin had shared a delirious moment in a butler's pantry. Then he had repeatedly called her and declared that being away from her was agony. Soon he had started coming over most nights that Louis wasn't there.

Amira hadn't really meant it when she'd told Colin she would leave her marriage for him. By then she thought she loved him – or at least, she'd loved the way he made her feel. The security of the House of Villiers rested entirely on her slim shoulders, and she'd wanted to imagine, just once, what it would be like to run away. But a week later, Colin showed up to dinner at Sherbourne House with a bottle of whisky and the daughter of an earl. Amira sat at the head of her own table and watched as Colin looked into this woman's eyes and held her hand. Amira had realised there would be many more nights like this, a lifetime of dizzying interludes followed by heartbreak, and then she must carry on as if nothing happened.

That was when she had started spending more time in London. At least she had friends there. As an Upper Sixth student at Astley, she'd been a peer support leader, and one of her Shells had got in touch, asking if there were any jobs going at the palace. Amira had always liked Mary, the poor scholarship girl from Brixton with the sick father. Mary was smarter than her meek little face let on, but she was still starstruck by Amira. Using her powers as a duchess, Amira got Mary a job as a media girl in Frederick's office and allowed her to come over to Cumberland now and then to watch her try on gowns for events.

Then the tabloids started to notice that Amira and Louis were going weeks without seeing each other. It hadn't mattered that Amira was an exemplary member of the family; it hadn't mattered that she did twice the charity work of everyone else. The tabloids had been waiting for this day for eight years. With divorce rumours rumbling, Louis and Amira sat down and wondered what they should do. It seemed impossible to go on as they were.

Like so many troubled couples before them, they decided to have a baby. A child could free them both. Once Amira gave the family an heir, they could discuss the possibility of separation. She could move on with her life and Louis would be a bachelor king. They told the IVF specialists they had been trying to conceive without success for more than two years. The egg retrieval process would begin as soon as they got back from Zermatt. For the first time in a long time, Amira and Louis were close again. They went to Switzerland feeling hopeful. They knew this child would be born into a house of love and would be loved in return. Everything was going to be okay.

Then the mountain swept away everything.

As she was driven to the hospital to find out if her husband and her brother were alive, her phone rang. It was Stewart, ready to patch her into a conference call with Granny and Annabelle. Palace aides had finally tracked me down to Maria Island, but my phone was switched off, so the only option was to send someone to fetch me.

'I want her back here as quickly as possible,' the Queen said in a steely voice. 'Once she's here, take her passport and don't let her leave.'

'She won't want to stay,' Amira said. 'She doesn't want to be here. She never has.'

'Then we must change her mind.'

The Queen hadn't reigned for decades without channelling Barbara now and then. Amira was reluctant. Her future was lying on a gurney with a core body temperature of twenty-two degrees. If he died, she would finally have her freedom. But when the golden cage door swung open, she could not make herself step through it. As mother of a future monarch, she might be brave enough. As Amira Shankar, she found that she wasn't ready yet. She looked at the ruins of her life and she realised there had only been one person who predicted this would happen.

'Stewart, take Mary Williams from Wolseley House when you pick up Lexi,' Amira said. 'She will love her. And once she's here, she can move in with me. I'm sure she misses me as much as I've missed her.'

*

When she was done, we sat for a long time. People were starting to leave the reception, and if we kept totally still, they didn't notice us watching them from the stairs. A couple came giggling from the picture gallery, and he twirled her around on the landing and then kissed her. They both looked up at the grand house, but they didn't see us in the shadows. Finally, they left, hand in hand.

'I feel like my life stopped when I went to Patagonia,' Amira said. 'I should have listened to you.'

'I feel like I never got off that boat,' I said. 'I've been drifting out at sea on my own for years. Every time I close my eyes, I'm rocking on the waves in the middle of the night. I should never have left you and Louis on your own.'

She took my hand in hers. 'You're here now.'

I smiled at her – my first true friend, my sister. 'Richard knows what I did. He knows about Kris and Louis. He knows everything. He's been trying to get rid of us for months.'

Her eyes shone in the light from the chandelier, and she lowered her face until her cheek pressed against our intertwined fingers.

'It's going to be okay,' I whispered. 'He's not going to tell anyone. I've made sure of that.' I smoothed her hair from her face. 'But Amira, don't you think it's time you left all this behind?'

She sat up and I saw that her eyes were wet. 'I'm not like you. I won't be able to do it.'

'Yes, you will,' I said. 'You're going to go out there and make yourself a life. You're going to have a career and friends and your own home. And then one day you're going to meet a man, and you two are going to live together and you're going to fight over stupid things and get through rough patches, and you'll be disgustingly happy.'

She rolled her eyes, though tears were now sliding down her face. She smiled at me. 'Like you and Jack.'

His name opened up the sucking chest wound I had been trying to ignore for four months. Even though I'd crossed his name off the guest list, even though I'd given him every reason to hate me for the rest of our lives, I still found myself watching the door all night, wishing he would come through it. My chin began to tremble and I shook my head against the tears.

'No, I ruined that.'

'I don't think that's true,' she said softly.

I wiped my eyes, not caring about my makeup. 'I'm not who he thinks I am. If he knew what I did, he wouldn't want me.'

She pulled me into her arms, our tears dampening the shoulders of our gowns as we both cried. We held each other until the last remaining guests drifted down the stairs, until the staff dimmed the lights in the halls, and a hush fell over the palace. Amira sat back and sighed.

'Let's go home and have a drink,' she said. 'We have a lot to discuss. You need to decide what you're going to do with your life.'

When I looked at her, she smiled and took my hands in hers.

'I want you to forget everything anyone's ever said to you about destiny and service and changing the world. What do you want?'

'I have a duty.'

She nodded. 'Yes. You have a duty to Louis. You have a duty to your parents. You're alive and they're not, so you must live for all three of them. Now, what do *you* want?'

No one had ever really asked me that before – except Jack. I looked up towards the glass dome in the ceiling and found that the stars over London were finally familiar to me again. Maybe I would live in this palace for the rest of my life, my hand sliding up this very banister over thousands of nights as I went upstairs to bed. Maybe I would watch that hand become speckled and frail with age, while the stars over my head would never change. Maybe I would learn to live with my secrets.

When I looked at Amira, another tear traced down my cheek. 'It's an impossible choice.'

CHAPTER TWENTY-SEVEN

25 December 2023

The night had brought a silent snowfall, and when we woke up on Christmas morning, the world was clean again. Demelza, Birdie and I stood in the guest wing of Granny's Norfolk home and looked out the window.

'Christ, I have to change my shoes,' Birdie moaned while pressing her fingers to the glass. 'I'll never be able to walk in these spikes.'

She raced down the hallway towards her bedroom in search of more appropriate footwear while Demelza snorted and flopped into an armchair.

'Only a trollop wears spikes to church.'

She looked regal in her bright white coat and pearl-studded headband, and when I glanced down at my own outfit, I frowned. I'd sent Mary home for Christmas and for the first time in a year, it was up to me to dress myself. I'd pulled on a heavy cream coat that once belonged to Mum and my old black Blundstones. I looked the way I did in years past when I flew to Norfolk for the holidays, slightly dishevelled and relegated to the back row of the church.

Demelza stretched and then studied me with her cool, feline eyes.

'So,' she said, 'are you ever planning to move into Cumberland 3? Or are you and Amira just going to live together forever like old spinsters?'

'I'll be moving very soon.'

She raised an eyebrow. I knew she'd already made a quiet case to Granny that the freshly renovated apartment should be hers since I obviously didn't want it. While I continued to sleep in my childhood home across the square, Cumberland 3 had stood ready and waiting for me for six months. But the time had finally come for me to grow up.

I turned to look out the window, Birdie's oily fingerprints marring the view.

'You know,' I said. 'I've stayed silent about everything that's ever happened in this family. Maybe because I wanted to be part of a family and not a collection of rival courts. I've never leaked anything to the media.'

'Nor have I.'

I looked at her doubtfully, but she shrugged.

'Don't believe me if you don't want to.'

'You told your father about what happened in the library with Colin.'

She groaned. 'Families *gossip*, Lexi. That's what we do. You never read about it in the *Daily Post*, did you?'

I leaned against the cold glass of the window.

'I suppose you're right,' I said. 'But I've come to a decision. Leaking by members of this family will no longer be tolerated. No more backgrounding reporters, no more palace aides doing our dirty work for us. If someone has something to say, they'll say it in their own voice.'

She smirked. 'You're not in charge *yet*, Lexi.'

'No, I'm not, but I can't sit around any longer waiting for my turn to change things.'

She propped her chin in her hand and looked at me, amused. 'Your own father used to talk to the press, you know. *Constantly*. He even leaked against you.'

I nodded. 'And I hope you never know what that feels like – especially with a father like yours. He'd stop at nothing if you ever stood in his way. God help you if he knows any of your secrets.'

She stared at me. 'I'm his *daughter*.'

'Yes, and I'm his niece. Louis was his nephew. My father was his only brother. He betrayed us all.'

I was unsure if Demelza knew what I was talking about. Her face gave nothing away. Maybe Richard had kept her out of his schemes. Perhaps she had no idea that he sheathed information like a blade, keeping it close to his body, until it was time to hold our secrets against our throats.

'Don't ever forget that you're a very pretty girl, and the tabloids are always going to prefer you over him,' I said. 'And when he feels overshadowed – which he will – he'll turn against you like he did almost everyone else in this family.'

She narrowed her eyes at me. 'Whatever. You've always been a mess.'

'Lexi!' Birdie called from her bedroom. 'Can you help me pick a shoe?'

'Coming, Birds.'

I started down the hallway, but when I stopped and looked back at Demelza, I saw that she had been watching me walk away.

'I'll always be your cousin – I hope you know that,' I said.

'I'm not going to side with *you* over my own father.'

I shook my head. 'I'm not asking you to side with anyone but yourself. You're much smarter than anyone gives you credit for. You see more than any of us realise. Personally, I think you act the way you do because you're bored. So, my only question for you is this: don't you think you have a bigger role to play in this family than just being someone's pretty little daughter?'

Something passed over Demelza's face, like the shadow of a winged predator flying above.

'Yes, I do,' she said.

In every portrait of Barbara, there is always a shadow behind her gaze: the dark bird of ambition that guided her extraordinary life. I saw now that Demelza might also possess the ability to train this wild thing.

I gave her one more nod before I walked away.

Every Christmas, villagers and camera crews lined the gravel path to watch us make the 300-metre journey to the church at the edge of Granny's property. We'd hold on to each other, smiling and chatting, as if Stewart hadn't meticulously planned every step of the way, drawing up charts to show us exactly where in the pack we must walk. Granny was driven in one of her Land Rovers, and this year she'd asked Florence to ride in the car with her, a great honour she had not bestowed upon her daughter-in-law for decades.

Richard and I were left to lead the family along the path through the snow-dusted trees. We waited at the gates of the house for our security team to give us the all-clear to begin. Stewart appeared in his overcoat with a clipboard under his arm, looking stony-faced.

'Happy Christmas,' I said.

'Happy Christmas, ma'am.'

I could tell he was still angry with me for going off-script during the reception, the fallout dominating the front pages of the tabloids for weeks. The *Daily Post* had taken to calling me the 'woke princess'. In response, Stewart had banned me from speaking in public, taking back control of my diary from Mary to ensure that I only appeared at carol services and Christmas craft fairs until the end of the year.

'To reiterate,' he said, 'you and Prince Richard will lead the way, followed by princesses Demelza and Birdie, and then—'

'For god's *sake*, old man,' Richard snapped. 'We know how to walk down a garden path without instruction.'

At precisely ten-thirty, the gates parted, and Richard and I set off for church, crunching through the snow as a group of cousins and lower-ranked royals trailed behind us. In the distance, I could see the press pack and all the people who came out to watch this strange tradition of ours. The crowd broke into applause as we passed them.

'Don't forget to smile, Richard,' I said. 'These are the most important family photos of the year.'

He said nothing.

I glanced at him. 'You might be surprised to know that I've decided to forgive you for threatening me. But my forgiveness is conditional. If I ever hear of you hiring private investigators, or talking to the press ever again, I will be done with you. And I think we both know I can make your life very hard.'

Still he said nothing, glowering as we walked. The faces in the crowd were beaming at the sight of us. We were meant to be the ideal family, though we had failed more than most. The least we could do was give the people one photo to which they could aspire.

'You really are a stupid little girl,' he finally muttered.

'Not so stupid that I couldn't outwit you.'

'You're just like Freddy,' he went on. 'You haven't a clue what it was like to grow up with your father. He was always so weak, so shy. Every time we had to do this walk as children, he'd cry because he was scared of strangers. It never made sense to me that he was meant to be king when he couldn't even wave at a couple of photographers without blubbering.'

I held my smile in place, thinking about the time I once wept on the palace balcony because I was afraid of the crowd below.

'When he grew older, he fell in love with that woman, and he wouldn't give her up,' Richard said. 'He wanted her more than he wanted the crown. It was like being in the back seat of a car careening towards a cliff, and Freddy was behind the wheel, wailing like a fool that he'd never wanted to be the driver in the first place.'

The church appeared ahead of us, and Richard and I both gave a friendly wave to the reverend, who was waiting on the steps.

'You might think you have what it takes to do this now,' Richard continued, 'but I know better. You're spoilt and you're selfish, and you will make yourself unhappy, because that's what you do. And even if you manage to keep your dirty little secret under wraps, the people will always sense this weakness in you, just as they sensed it in your father.'

I stopped suddenly, and Richard stopped as well. It was an odd moment – one wrong note in the flawless symphony Stewart had conducted – and I could sense the photographers taking notice. Usually, we all went straight up the church steps and greeted the reverend before heading indoors. But I was standing in the snow with my uncle, and a sizzle of camera shutters filled the silence as the crowds watched to see what I would do. I smiled at Richard and put a hand on his arm.

'You're not half the man my father was,' I murmured. 'Now stay one step behind me. Remember who I am.'

After the church service, we went home for lunch, where Granny was waiting for us. As her heir, I came into the dining room first, followed by Richard and Florence, then Demelza and Birdie. A flock of distant relations streamed through the door last. There was always too much food on the table – ham and lobster, freshly baked rolls, stuffing and sprouts, pudding with brandy butter.

'Is Amira not joining us this year, Lexi?' a second cousin asked as we sat down at the table.

'No,' I said. 'She and her parents have gone to South Africa for the holidays.'

'Next year then.'

I nodded and smiled, though I knew it would be a very long time before Amira set foot in a royal household again. Once her bags were packed, and the car idled outside Cumberland 1 to take her to the airport, Amira and I held each other for a long time, promising to call each other every day.

When I went back to my bedroom, which had once been Mum's office, and was meant to be a nursery for Louis and

Amira's child, I found a black velvet box on my pillow. Inside was the emerald, glimmering with monstrous beauty. For both the women who wore it, the ring was meant to be a shield. The stone had once been a brooch gifted by my great-grandfather to his wife. Papa had it reset on a gold band, hoping their love might inspire his own. Instead, it hung like an albatross from Mum's delicate hand. Louis hoped the ring on Amira's finger would evoke the fairytale our parents' marriage was once supposed to be. I held it up to the light, just once, and remembered the way Mum would absentmindedly twist it on her knuckle, the way it would dwarf Amira's small hand. I had no desire to try it on. I would cherish it, but I would never wear it. It would stay with me for the rest of my life, along with the witch marks and the polaroid of Louis and Kris – hard evidence of my family's often hidden capacity for love.

After lunch, we moved to the drawing room to watch Granny's pre-recorded Christmas address. The Clarences tended to elbow everyone out of the way so they could squeeze in beside her on the lounge. I took my usual seat in the bay window at the back. For half a century, Granny had appeared on our screens at exactly three o'clock every Christmas afternoon, standing in front of a twinkling tree to reflect on the year almost past.

'This Christmas season, I have been pondering the act of service, the gift a person gives in dedicating their life to others,' Granny said on the television. 'Service can take many forms. For some, it leads to accolades and fame. For others, it is as simple but sacrosanct as caring for the ill.'

As Granny spoke, I sensed that I was being watched. Richard was staring at me across the drawing room, his dark eyes burning, his mouth set in a bitter frown. Neither of us looked away. I wondered if he might take my forgiveness or if he would succumb to his worst impulses, forcing me to invoke the second part of my plan. It was his choice. I already knew what my future held, while Richard didn't have a clue what lay ahead of him.

I looked back at the TV screen as it faded to black, and the room burst into applause.

'Well done, Granny,' Florence said. 'I think that might be your best one yet.'

'Yes, well,' Granny said as she rose from her chair, forcing everyone else to their feet, 'you do fifty in a row, you get pretty good at it.' She looked around until she found me sitting in the bay window alone. Papa had always resembled her, and for one fleeting moment, he was in the room with us.

'Lexi,' she said. 'Get that ill-behaved dog of yours. We're going for a walk around the grounds.'

So I followed my grandmother down the hall and out into the snow, knowing Richard was watching my every move, deciding what he might do next.

28 December 2023

On the morning of my thirtieth birthday, I woke to find £3 million in my bank account. I lay in bed for a long time, staring at my phone screen. Then I called Antony Eastaughffe, the trustee in charge of Mum's estate. He was Papa's only friend from their days in the bleak boarding house in the Scottish Highlands. They would often laugh together about how older boys whipped them with frozen willow stems and forced them to crawl across the muddy rugby oval before dawn.

'I thought my portion of the estate came to £5000,' I said.

'Yes, when your mother died, she left £10,000 to be divided equally between her children.' I heard the rustling of papers as he looked for something on his desk. 'Louis's portion remains £5000 – your father expected that he would one day inherit the Duchy of Exeter, of course, and saw no reason to give him any more. But when it came to your trust, Freddy added a substantial amount of his own money. We've been investing it for you over the years, so most of it is tied up in stocks. This £3 million lump sum is in honour of your thirtieth birthday. I am happy to liquidate the rest if you wish – the terms of the trust allow you to do so – but it was Freddy's hope you'd live off the quarterly distributions instead.'

'Wait,' I said. 'How much money do I have?'

More papers rustled on his desk. 'Just over £12.7 million.'

I looked at the string of numbers in my banking app again. 'Papa did this?'

'Yes, ma'am. I'm sorry ... I thought he would have told you. He always said that if you could make it to thirty without needing his help, he knew you would be alright. But he still wanted you to be comfortable.'

I felt a familiar twinge in my heart, one I had spent my life struggling to identify. I understood now that I was angry with Papa for being so proud, that I loved him and yearned for him, and always would. We had waited too long and there was nowhere left for that love to go. But I was grateful that I finally got to know him, even if it had to happen after he died.

'Okay,' I said to Mr Eastaughffe, not bothering to disguise the tears that had thickened my voice. 'Let's do as he wished and stick with quarterly distributions.'

I glanced one more time at Papa's birthday gift. It was enough to change the trajectory of someone's life forever.

'There's a hospital in Nairobi,' I said. 'I'd like to make an anonymous donation – perhaps half? And there's something I'd like to do with the rest.'

'It's your money to spend as you wish.'

We made an appointment for later in the morning. After breakfast, I left the house and walked to Mr Eastaughffe's office in Earl's Court, trailed by Rita. Once I was finished and had the cheque, I wandered into a park and sat on a bench. The air was charged with the electrical current that signalled snow was coming, and I found myself holding my breath as I waited for the first flake to fall. Rita stood under a tree nearby; as the year drew to a close, my security detail hovered even closer. No more sneaking out to the pond on my own.

My phone buzzed in my pocket and I knew it must be noon.

'Hello, James,' I said.

'Happy birthday.'

'Thank you.'

He paused. 'The first one without your twin is the hardest.'

For the final years of his life, Louis and I had communicated only on this day. *Hey happy bday*, one of us would type out in a fit of resentful obligation. There would be hours of silence and then, finally, the other would respond: *Thx u too*. On the last birthday we shared, we didn't even bother to do that much.

'Does it ever get easier?' I asked.

'Not really. You just learn to live without the rest of you.'

We kept the line open as I sat on my park bench, and he stood in his dark hallway at the bottom of the world. We were two incomplete halves that would never make a full set, but he was all I had left.

'Do you remember the last time you and Mum spoke?'

'Yes,' he said quietly. 'Although we didn't really speak. It was our birthday, and she called in the middle of the night. She must have been touring through Scotland, and someone was singing "The Parting Glass" for her. They were singing it beautifully – just them, no instruments – and she held up the phone so I could hear it.'

Both the Irish and the Scots claim the old song, but it doesn't really matter who it belongs to, because we all like to sing it at the end of the night – one more drink before friends part. From the heavy white sky, the first flurry spun into view, and I breathed against my aching chest.

'I'm sorry,' I said. 'I know you don't want to hear that, but I am. I'm so sorry.'

'Lexi,' he said, 'you've spent the last year chasing the approval of a bunch of strangers, people who don't know you and never will. But at some point, you need to forgive yourself. Otherwise, you'll never be able to accept it from anyone else.'

A family went past, bundled in mittens and coats. I watched as they hurried under the steady snowfall.

'What if ...' I said, my heart racing as the question of my life finally dared itself to be asked. 'What if she could have been saved? What if I'd called the coastguard instead of him? What if she died out there because of me?'

James said nothing for a long time. 'I've read everything there is to read about what happened. I don't think she could have been saved.'

The snow burned my throat as I breathed in. 'But we don't know.'

'We don't,' he said. 'What I do know is that she loved you. And she didn't want to leave you that night.'

The park emptied out as people vanished into the city. A light sifting of snow was accumulating on my coat, flakes caught on the tips of my eyelashes and in my hair. I remembered that I had a cheque for £1.5 million in my pocket that I probably shouldn't get wet.

'I'll talk to you in a couple of days,' I said softly.

'Stay in touch. Let me know when you're safe.'

I made it back to Cumberland with Rita a few paces behind before the snow started to descend in a silent storm. It was three days after Christmas, so those who hadn't stayed in Norfolk for the week would be watching from their windows. At exactly 2 pm, the car rolled into view, a white van with WILLIAMS CARPET CLEANING written in bright red letters on the side. The older relatives didn't like it when servicemen clogged up the quadrangle, but I would need to endure their disappointment one more time for this to work. When the bell rang, I found a young man, no older than nineteen, with Mary's slight features and narrow shoulders. He had the same fierce eyes that seemed to see everything. Across the square, a lace curtain shifted in a second-storey window.

The boy patted Chino, who appeared at the door to greet this stranger, and then smiled at me. 'Hey. I'm Charlie.'

He rolled a carpet cleaner and a heavy plastic trolley into the living room, and we shut the door behind him. My suitcase and backpack stood by the stairs.

'So ... I can actually clean some carpets while I'm here since you're paying me and all,' he said. 'The noise will kind of add to the whole thing.'

'Oh,' I said. 'If you want? I'm moving out of a room upstairs, so maybe it'll be nice for the owner if it's all clean.'

His machines droned so loudly upstairs that I almost missed the knock at the door. I edged closer and saw Stewart through the windows. When he spotted me, he waved, leaving me no choice but to open the door to him. The trolley stood in front of my suitcase and backpack, and I hoped Stewart wouldn't try to come into the house in case he saw them. Luckily Chino leapt forward, whining with excitement and pawing at his pressed grey suit.

'Forgive the intrusion, Your Highness,' he said, trying to politely push Chino's nose out of his crotch. 'I saw the workman's van, so I assumed you were home.'

I could never recall an aide dropping by uninvited. He must have seen Charlie's van and come prowling over to check on me. The moment called for me to be irritated. If I looked as terrified as I felt, his suspicion would be confirmed.

'What do you need?' I asked brusquely. 'I'm trying to get the house in order before I move out.'

He dropped his head. 'Yes, of course, apologies. I have some documents for you to review. They're not the kind I can just email to your office.'

I took the manila envelope from his hands but made no move to open it.

'Okay,' I said.

We looked at each other. When I was small, I would sometimes flee the tears and shouting at Cumberland 1, cross the quadrangle and find Stewart's door among the row of staff apartments over the garage. Reluctantly, he would let me in, and I would sprawl on his living-room floor to watch TV in peace. A bowl of crisps would appear by my side, but he otherwise left me alone until, eventually, he looked at the clock and sent me home.

He hesitated. I wondered if he too remembered he had once been the only stable adult in my life.

'I do wish you had come to me, ma'am,' he said finally. 'I think you know that I'm fond of you. If you were having trouble, I would have been able to help you.'

I nodded, remembering all the small kindnesses he had shown me – so that by the time he had asked me to open my mouth and placed the dropper of sedative under my tongue, I complied.

'It's strange, isn't it?' I said. 'When I was a child, I loved you. I used to pretend you were my father. But when I needed you, I didn't go to you for help.'

He opened his mouth, hesitating again. After a pause, he bowed slightly and said, 'Review that document and we can discuss it in a few days.'

He walked back down the steps, careful of the snow.

'Stewart,' I called and he turned. 'I don't remember much of the days after my mother died – you made sure of that – but my body never forgot it. That's why I didn't go to you. I couldn't make myself do it.'

He had the decency to look ashamed, but I knew drugging me into submission was the least he would do in service of the monarchy; perhaps he even told himself he had done it to protect me.

Again, he bowed – deeply this time – and walked back to his tiny apartment, an old man dressed in a suit three days after Christmas. Chino watched him mournfully as he left us.

'Come on,' I said, and he cocked his head. 'It's almost time.'

An hour later, Charlie trotted down the stairs and started packing up his equipment. He heaved my bags into his trolley and swung the lid over the top. I watched from the window as he loaded them into the back of his van. When he came back, his brows were furrowed, the way Mary's were when she was concentrating.

'Are you ready?'

I nodded, suddenly nervous. When I looked back at the drawing room, I remembered that it was the place Louis and I once built forts out of sheets and fought over the remote, it was where Mum tried to teach herself the guitar, and Amira and I had curled up together almost every night for a year. This house was my first home, and I was certain I would never see it again. I looked at Charlie and nodded again.

'Okay,' I said.

Together we lifted a wriggling, unhappy Chino into the trolley and then I climbed in after him. Inside, it smelled like cleaning solvents and wet towels.

'I'll close you in now,' Charlie said as pulled the lid up. 'Don't worry, it'll only be for a minute.'

We were in the dark. The plastic drum wobbled on its wheels as Charlie steered us over the carpet, across the floorboards and out the front door. When we skittered through some gravel, Chino let out a yelp and I pulled him to my chest to soothe him. For a moment everything was still. But a great shove threw us backwards, like the ascent of a rollercoaster, and I knew Charlie was pushing us up the ramp and into the van. There was a metallic thunk as the doors shut us inside.

'Everything okay back there?' he said as he buckled himself into his seat. 'Let's get through the gate and then I'll park around the block and let you out.'

'All fine,' I said.

The van shook to life and soon we were crunching through the gravel of the quadrangle before the tyres gained traction on the sealed road. There would be two police officers standing sentry at the gates. I'd emailed them that morning to let the carpet cleaner in, and now all they had to do was sign him out. The air in the trolley was becoming moist from our quick breaths and I tried to stay quiet as the van slowed to a stop. Burying my face in Chino's fur, I silently pleaded with him not to make a sound.

'Hey,' Charlie called in an affable voice. 'All done in there – thanks, mate.'

'Right then, one moment,' I heard one of the officers reply. 'Happy Christmas.'

The iron gates groaned against their frozen hinges, and then the van was rolling forward. Soon we were moving at speed, just another workman's car on the streets of London. It was the week before New Year's, when time seems endless, and no one leaves the house if they can help it. By the time Stewart realised I was gone, it would be too late. The quadrangle would be scandalised by my escape. All my older relatives would stand around whispering, trying to figure out how I had done it.

It was the second time that I had slipped away from them undetected. But this time, I didn't plan to return.

*

Two weeks before Christmas, Mary had called Stewart to ask that the Queen's speech no longer announce my forthcoming investiture as the Princess of Scotland. The public shouldn't be promised something that would never occur. Over a series of fraught, clandestine meetings at Amira's dining table, Stewart had made clear that if I intended to give up the crown, I would be giving it all up. My titles, my name and my privileges would all be taken away so that I didn't overshadow Richard's future reign. No one had ever willingly removed themselves from the line before, so if I did this, I would be choosing a life in exile.

'I know what I'm giving up,' I said.

I was not permitted to speak to the Queen directly about my decision. Instead, Stewart spoke to her himself. She sent a message back, saying that I was to take the fortnight before Christmas to make sure that I was sure. Her speech would become a meditation on the meaning of service. If, by the time it was broadcast, my case of cold feet had passed, we would pretend it had never happened. No one would ever know how close Richard had come to wearing the crown, least of all Richard himself. But if I searched my soul and found that it was not fit for a queen, I would be shown the door.

374

On Christmas afternoon, with her speech aired and our family taking tea in the drawing room, Granny and I went for a walk around her estate. Chino and Pud raced ahead of us into the fading afternoon sun, while she held on to my arm gingerly to navigate the muddy snowmelt.

'You know, there were many times when I was your age that I wanted to give this up,' she said. 'Your grandfather and I had our hardships early on and I wondered if perhaps it was best for my family if I handed it over to Beatrix. She always wanted it more than I did.'

'I never knew that.'

We stopped by the old water fountain that had been drained and covered for the winter. Granny's blonde hair glowed like a corona in the setting sun.

'I hope you're not reconsidering because of the furore over last month's reception,' she said. 'It's been my view for quite some time that you are being poorly advised. The people around you have been filling your head with dangerous ideas about what this role can be. I did consider intervening earlier, but it's a lesson we must all learn the hard way.'

'What is the lesson?'

'That this role is not a platform for your ideas.' She looked at me. 'What did you say at the reception? When we speak, the world sits up and pays attention? That is not the role of a monarch.'

'What is the role, then?'

'You should hardly speak at all. We are meant to be solid and stable as the nation shifts around us. We're the thing they grasp on to. I know some people think we're a relic of the past, but everyone needs steadying now and then.'

I looked back at the house. I knew that Richard would be watching from one of the many windows that overlooked the gardens. I could feel his eyes on me.

'So a more appropriate monarch is a man who hires private investigators to stalk his own family? A man who blackmails the people he's supposed to love? Richard has been threatening me for months. He said that if I didn't leave, he would expose something that Papa and I did years ago. I know you prefer to stay out of these things, but perhaps it's best if you know what's happening in your own home.'

A huge skein of geese came twisting and undulating through the skies, their call so loud that we had no choice but to wait until they passed. It was a frighteningly beautiful sight, but I realised Granny wasn't looking at the birds. She was staring at me. When the geese vanished into the horizon, she turned back to the open lawns of the estate and kept walking.

'Freddy had a strange attraction to secrecy,' she said quietly. 'His first instinct was always to lie, to cover things up, rather than just confront them and move on. I told him as much at the time, although by then it was too late – he'd already paid that Italian man to get you off the boat.'

Of course he had told her what happened in Italy. He hadn't been able to keep a secret from her in his life.

'I had no idea you knew.'

'Things reach me one way or another,' she said. 'It was a foolish thing to do, but I think he just couldn't bear to be at the centre of another scandal.'

'Maybe he thought he was protecting me,' I said, suddenly desperate to defend my father.

'Maybe,' she said, sighing out a foggy breath.

The dogs ran in circles around our feet and shot off again towards the trees.

'If you're worried about the truth coming out, I do think it's possible for you to survive this. Your mother was extraordinarily irresponsible that night. Many people have wondered what her intentions were. We could very easily give the impression that your father merely sought to protect her reputation after she made a reckless decision in the throes of a great crisis.'

I looked at her, stunned. 'No, I can't do that.'

It was a theory I could never entertain. She would not have taken me out there just to leave me alone.

Granny gave no sign that she had heard me. As we approached the forest, she turned and leaned against the craggy trunk of a Scots pine. Then she pulled a handkerchief from her pocket, unfolded it and scattered bits of roast ham from lunch on the forest floor for the dogs.

'Richard has always wanted this desperately. It must be a terrible misfortune to be born second,' she said. 'Did you ever resent your brother?'

'No, it was always meant to be him.'

She smiled to herself. 'Yes, he was special.'

'Richard knew things about him. He was going to expose Louis,' I said, staring at her, desperate for a sign that she could hear me. 'When they went up the mountain that day, they were scared, and they weren't thinking clearly.'

She shook the last of the meat from her handkerchief and dusted her hands. When she finally looked up, her eyes were shining with tears.

'This entire year, all I've heard is how much you wanted it to be me,' I said, remembering how she once taught me to handfeed a horse with an open palm, how to curtsy, how to prune roses without taking the bud eye.

'Yes.'

'I would have done anything you asked me. I was willing to change my life, I was willing to give up—' I faltered, unable to say his name. Tears came, but I held them back. 'I was willing to give it all up for this duty. But I know now that the only way for me to do this is to keep burying all these secrets inside myself, and I can't do that anymore.'

She looked sad but unruffled. 'I understand.'

'Do you?'

Delicately, she pressed a gloved fingertip to her cheek to absorb the tear before it slid any further. Then she waved her hand over her face, as if commanding herself not to shed a single tear more. When she looked at me again, my grandmother was gone, and Queen Eleanor had returned.

'For some monarchs, the moment the crown is placed on their heads feels like a death, as if they have lost themselves forever,' she said. 'For others, it is the moment the crown lands that we are finally, *finally* our true selves. It's not always easy. But we would never give it up, no matter how much we might be tempted, because that would be giving up who we really are. You, my dear girl, don't want it enough. Richard does.'

'Everyone says he could be the end of this thing.'

'He won't,' she said and crossed her arms across her chest. 'He won't. People are reluctant to give up their traditions. He'll be the one who stayed, and you'll be the one who left. You'll be shocked by how they cling to him.'

I shook my head. 'You think that little of them?'

She held her hands open, palms up, nothing left for me. 'Quite the opposite. I just know them better than they know themselves.'

I saw then that she would always choose the crown over her family. It was the pact you made for the honour of wearing it, and it was not a weight I could bear. I looked back towards the house again. A servant was turning on the lights one by one, making the manor glow in the winter dusk. Inside, Richard stalked the halls. He had spent his life methodically removing every obstacle until, finally, it was only the Queen standing in his way.

'I should get you inside,' I said to my grandmother. 'It's getting cold.'

*

When we reached a snowy street in Brixton, Charlie parked his van and led me to a narrow terrace with a red door. Mary, unfamiliar in jeans and a sweatshirt, pulled us into the claustrophobic hallway. She and Charlie wore identical pinched expressions as Chino pushed past their legs and ran into the house.

'How did it go?' she asked.

'Yeah, fine,' I said in a breathy voice that failed to sound cheerful. 'Thanks to Charlie.'

'It was pretty cool, actually.' He laughed. 'But now I need a pint to take the edge off.'

I'd seen how his hands had trembled on the steering wheel for the entire journey home.

'I'm just at the pub on the corner if you need me,' he told Mary, then gave me a nod. 'Good luck, ma'am.'

As he slipped through the front door, Mary led me down the hall to a kitchen overlooking an empty courtyard. Everything about the terrace was small. A rooster-themed wallpaper border curled at its edges. Faded curtains hung limply in the window. This was a woman's space, once carefully curated, but since abandoned. At the table, Jenny Walsh and a man I didn't recognise sat together sipping tea. They rose from their chairs when I came into the room, and I knew this was the last time anyone would do this for me.

'Your Highness,' Jenny said. 'Did it all go to plan?'

A month earlier, when I had reached forward to shake Jenny's hand at the palace reception, I had pressed a note into her palm. '*I need your help*,' it read. She had called me the next morning, and when I told her I wished to leave, she had engaged the services of Emmanuel Mensah, a constitutional scholar she knew from law school. He had quietly agreed to represent me as I relinquished my claim to the throne. When Mary and I sat down, he pulled a piece of paper and a fountain pen from his bag and placed them on the scratched table.

After long and careful consideration, I have decided to renounce my claim as heir apparent, it began, though I didn't bother to read the rest. I knew how it went. I would ask parliament to strip me of my titles, withdraw me from the line of succession and bar any of my future descendants from a claim to the throne.

'Are we sure this will work?' I asked, the pen poised over the page. 'The Queen doesn't need to be here to make it legal?'

'Quite the opposite,' Emmanuel said. 'Only parliament can bring an act to remove you from the line. Everything they've planned for next week is just theatre.'

I had left the manila envelope containing Stewart's letter on the dining table in Cumberland 1. In his version, I claimed to be temperamentally unfit to wear the crown and that I therefore had no choice but to pass it to my beloved uncle. Granny and Richard were supposed to stand behind me while a palace photographer captured the moment I signed everything away. There had been talk of an interview with the BBC, but someone had clearly baulked at the idea, no longer trusting me in front of cameras. By the time I was meant to board the jet at Northolt a week from now, the Queen would be giving a televised address, reassuring her subjects that while the line had curved in recent years, it would never be broken.

I would give Richard the crown, but I was not willing to say he was worthy of wearing it. I had told the world enough lies as it was. With my passport hidden somewhere in Stewart's apartment, and my security detail under strict instruction to follow my every move, it had been Mary's idea to slip me out in the back of a van.

I lowered the heavy fountain pen to the letter and signed my name. Ink dripped from the nib and left a constellation around my signature. Mary fanned the wet spatter with her hand and then signed the document as my witness. Gingerly, she passed it to Emmanuel. Everyone was very quiet as we watched the ink dry.

'So that's it?' I asked.

'Once everything's public, I'll ask the opposition leader to join me in bringing an act to parliament that recognises and ratifies your decision and passes succession to your uncle,' Jenny said.

Emmanuel left with the letter and a promise to stay in touch. Jenny, Mary and I sat back down at the table in silence and listened to the monotonous ticking of a rooster clock wedged into a pine hutch. Chino draped himself across my lap and fell asleep with one hindleg still balancing on the linoleum floor. After no one made a move to leave, Mary went to the kitchen and returned with a small white box. Inside was one cupcake lathered in pink icing. She stuck a candle in it and lit it with a match.

'Happy birthday, ma'am,' she said.

We stared as the candle started to dribble, until finally I leaned forward and blew it out. Mary took over, cutting the cake into quarters and handing a piece to each of us.

'I know the risks you're taking to help me,' I started.

'Don't,' Mary said sharply, and Jenny looked up from her cake. 'You don't have to say that.'

'I just wanted to say how grateful I am.'

Jenny popped a piece of cake into her mouth. 'It shouldn't have been this way.'

'Still,' I said, eating icing and a smatter of candle wax, the taste of childhood. 'I don't know where I'd be without you both.'

When we were done, Jenny packed up her bag and we walked to the front door. Outside, she signalled to her officer, who was loitering further up the street. She smiled and then reached into her pocket and handed me a navy-blue passport.

'Fresh from the printers,' she said.

I opened it to the photo page and saw for the first time my new name. No HRH, no title. Only *Alexandrina Anne Barbara Mary Villiers*. It was grand by any measure – overstuffed with Christian names and far too many syllables. But to me it felt as stark as the snow that blanketed the road.

I looked up at Jenny. 'Are you going to get into trouble for all this?'

She smiled at me wearily. 'Privately? Probably a little bit. Publicly? No. I don't think they'll want it out there that I had to help you slip out of the country like a fugitive.'

We hugged for a long time, and then I watched as she walked briskly down the street towards her waiting car. When they drove away, I stood under a foggy streetlight and breathed in the cold night air.

Inside, I found Mary at the kitchen sink, Chino lying at her feet.

'Is it just you and Charlie living here?' I asked.

She nodded as she scraped the cupcake liner and the melted candle into the bin. Mary was one of those people who seemed a different creature outside her professional environment. She was softer in her own domain. 'Our mum left when we were kids and our dad's in care. Alzheimer's. Early onset.'

'I'm sorry.'

'Thank you.' She picked up the folder I had brought with me from the van. 'So, this is all of Chino's stuff?'

'Yes,' I said. 'Louis brought him over from Bulgaria last year, so his vaccinations were already up to date. I've done the paperwork, so you just need to take him to that address in a few days, and they'll fly him to Australia. I'll be there to collect him when his quarantine is done.'

She nodded.

'He might be a bit of a terror,' I said, looking around at their slight home.

She smiled again. 'Chino was actually a gift from Prince Frederick to Prince Louis. Your brother was always talking about how much he loved your dog in Australia, so your father decided to get him a pointer for his birthday. I helped pick him out from the breeder's website and I went to fetch him when he landed at Heathrow. It'll be nice to spend time with him again.'

The rooster clock crowed to herald the new hour. Mary and I smiled awkwardly at each other.

'Did we ever meet at Astley, Mary?' I asked.

She wiped down the counters with a sponge. 'A few times. The Dowager Duchess of Somerset would occasionally let me into your suite while she was getting ready for dances. I'd help pick her shoes. You were pretty quiet.'

'I'm sorry I don't remember,' I said. 'I was a bit of a zombie then.'

She shrugged. 'You won three prizes that year. Chemistry, biology and maths – the most of any upperclassman. And at the ceremony, I came onto the stage and gave you three bunches of flowers from the student body.'

The blue delphiniums, the gerbera daisies and the white lilies wrapped in squeaky cellophane. Two small arms struggling around the arrangements. A swell of applause. Papa was in the audience, although he left before the ceremony was over.

'Of course,' I said. 'I remember you.'

Her smile quickly faded. 'I'm sorry I didn't mention it sooner. The Queen asked me not to. And I was worried you'd think I was some kind of stalker. But it's not like that. I just always looked up to you. The royal family used to give me so much hope when I was a kid. And that's how it should be. The institution just needs to address its past so it can move forward. I thought leaving the way you did was amazing. It was the shock they needed. So when you came back, I jumped at the chance to work for you.'

I shook my head. 'I'm just sorry I've made it impossible for you to keep working at the palace.'

She tossed the sponge into the sink and leaned against the counter. 'It's fine. You're right. I'm too smart for all that.'

'Yes, you are.'

Her eyes flicked towards the rooster clock. 'We should get going. Your flight leaves in a few hours.'

'Oh, wait,' I said and pulled the envelope from the pocket of my hoodie. I handed it to her. 'This is for you.'

She used two fingers to spread open the envelope, looked at the cheque inside and then snapped it shut. 'Your Highness, no.'

'Firstly,' I said gently, 'it's Lexi. And secondly, yes. Buy a house. Turn Williams Carpet Cleaning into a franchise. Use it to get your father into a nicer place. Personally, I think you should start your own crisis communications firm or something. But it's your money to do with as you please.'

Her eyes brimmed and she shook her head until she finally stopped and clutched the envelope to her chest. She smiled through her tears. 'I'll need my first client.'

'Well, I'm about to blow up my life and turn everyone against me, so I'm in desperate need of help.'

We embraced in the dim light of her mother's kitchen. Then we went out into the street with Chino and hopped into the van. I held the solid weight of him in my lap as we cruised towards Heathrow, wondering if I would ever return to the seat of my family's power. Three centuries ago, my ancestor Barbara Villiers had transformed herself from impoverished noblewoman to concubine to de facto monarch. Her line had looped and whirled through decades of war and advancement, through pandemics and famines, through weak monarchs and towering ones. As London rippled outwards and its buildings grew taller, the crown had been slowly, slowly inching towards me. I did not expect it; I did not desire it. And when it spun into view and hovered above my hands, I found that I couldn't do what needed to be done for it to be mine.

My name could have been Alexandrina, by the Grace of God of Great Britain, Northern Ireland and the British Dominions beyond the Seas, Queen, Defender of the Faith. I could have worn gold and had my face etched into coins and believed myself to be divine. But it would have been a lie. What made me special was that I was Isla and Frederick's daughter and Louis's twin.

It was time for me to become Lexi Villiers.

29 December 2023

I had always liked the anonymity of airports, all that humanity packed in together, the terminals humming with stress and possibility. As long as I didn't hold up the security line, no one ever gave me a second look. So I walked through Hong Kong International Airport in a hoodie that was as good as an invisibility cloak, feeling lonely and displaced, but perhaps finally free.

When I switched my phone back on, there was a message from James: *How was the flight?*

Good, I wrote back. *One leg down, two to go.*

I'll be there to pick you up when you get home.

Once I landed in Hobart, James would take me to his farm so I could lie low for a couple of weeks. Then I would need to find myself a flat so I could resume my residency in the new year. Ben, terse but efficient over email, had quietly settled things with the hospital so that I could return. I couldn't wait to wear scrubs, my hair frizzy and tied in a knot at the crown of my head, my well-trained hands finally occupied again.

I wandered the terminal for a while. When I passed a food court, I was surprised to find that I was famished. For months I'd been so nauseous and panicked that I couldn't bear the thought of eating, but the scent of dumplings and barbecued pork was so dizzying that I immediately walked up to a stall and ordered a wonton soup, an egg tart and a milk tea.

I sat and ate my meal while people rushed around me. Not since I woke up on the boat all those years ago had I felt quite so alone. But this time, I was unafraid.

I wondered what would happen if I called Jack. I had considered making contact over the last few weeks as things fell apart. I had typed out, and then deleted, countless apologies for everything I had done – the lies I had told, the truths I had withheld, the way I'd concealed my heart for fear he might refuse it. But it had been five months since we last spoke and, if he'd moved on, I knew the most loving thing I could do was to leave him alone.

As I finished my soup and pushed back the bowl, my phone rang, and it was Mary. Only a handful of people had my new number, and she was one of them.

'Did you get in okay?' she asked.

'All fine. Any updates at your end?'

She hesitated. 'Yes. I'm afraid so. Richard's been calling journalists again,' Mary said. 'I'm not sure if you remember Posey Habsburg-Mollard from the *Post*? She was a favourite of your father's.'

'How could I forget?'

'Yes, well, she called me this morning to say she'd received the most bizarre tip about you,' Mary said. 'It sounds like Richard called her very late last night, sounding worse for wear, and told her she should be digging into the death of Princess Isla. He gave her Davide Rossi's name and said he holds the key to everything.'

I sighed and leaned back in my chair. 'Oh, Richard.'

'Yes,' Mary said. 'You did warn him. But men like him simply must have the last word, I suppose.'

I looked around the terminal at the weary travellers. Some were staring into their steaming bowls of soup, others were gazing out the windows while a plane trundled down the runway.

'So we go with plan B then?' I said quietly.

Mary and I had spoken in code as we plotted my escape. Plan A would see me divulge my own secrets as I excised myself from the line. Plan B was something else altogether.

'Yes.' Mary paused again. 'Are you scared?'

I thought for a while. 'I was. But I don't think I am anymore.'

After I visited Annabelle, I had determined that the only way I could fix my life was to go back to the moment when everything broke. Davide Rossi's voice had haunted me for more than a decade, so I called him up from my bed in Scotland, gripping the witch marks to my chest with trembling fingers.

He had seemed utterly unsurprised to hear from me, chatting as if we were old friends. He told me there were too many tourists in Rapallo now, so he had moved further south, where he planned to spend the rest of his days fishing in the Gulf of Poets and watching his grandchildren grow up.

'Do you ever think about that night?' I asked.

'Sometimes,' he said. 'I see you in the magazines, and I remember when I found you on that boat, looking at me with your big eyes – so young, so afraid, just a girl who lost her mama.'

Tears had blurred my vision as I remembered how it felt to be caught in the bright white beam of his navigation lights.

'The agreement you signed with my father is still binding, you know. If you speak, the lawyers for his estate could sue you.'

'I see,' he said in a way that suggested he saw but didn't particularly care. He knew he'd caught a big fish, and now he had me wriggling and gasping in the belly of his boat. Richard would pay him to speak, or I would pay him to stay quiet. Either way, he stood to benefit.

'Aren't you worried that everyone will be angry with you if they find out?' I asked. 'They'll blame me and my father, but they'll blame you too. They'll reopen investigations. Journalists will follow you and your family everywhere. You'll have money, yes, but you'll have a lot of troubles as well.'

I heard the flinty scrape of a cigarette lighter before he sighed. 'I don't look forward to losing my quiet life. But it seems to me, *carina*, that no one knows what you did and yet you still have many troubles, don't you?'

I needed a couple of days to decide what to do, so I had promised to call him back. All it would take was a cash donation from Vikki and a fresh non-disclosure agreement in my name, and then Davide Rossi could recede to the dark edges of my subconscious forever. But on the night of my reception at the palace, I had finally understood that my secrets would always find a way of resurfacing. It would be a matter of months or years, and then I would be gripped by panic again, engaging lawyers and writing cheques, desperately trying to push everything back down. When Amira and I returned to Cumberland 1 that night, we had crawled into my bed and whispered in the dark about what we should do with our lives.

'I want to be a doctor, not a queen.'

'Good,' she said. There was something scrappy in her tone. It reminded me of when she was young and bold. 'What else?'

'I don't want to spend my life wondering when the past is coming back for me. I don't want to cut deals and pay people off. I don't want to live like that anymore.'

She felt around the blankets until she found my hand. 'Then don't.'

The next day, I called Davide Rossi and told him that I had no interest in buying his silence.

'I'm going to speak,' I said. 'I'm going to tell people what I did, so I can finally be free of it.'

The line between us went very quiet.

'Maybe you'll call Richard now, and tell him what I'm going to do,' I went on. 'But I think the smarter option is to wait. Wait until I tell my story, because if you do, I'll tell everyone that a very kind security guard helped me when I needed him. I was a child out at sea alone, and you were a good man who shouldn't be blamed for any of it. And then, if you wish, you can sell your own story to a tabloid. My father's lawyers won't take you to court, I'll make sure of it. But this is the only way you'll ever get money out of this family again.'

He was silent for so long that I wondered if he had hung up. Then he wheezed with laughter.

'You're not a little girl anymore, are you, *carina?*'

Soon, everyone in the world would know my secret. They would know that I once woke in the middle of the night and chose the crown over my own mother. But most importantly, Richard's power over me would evaporate. I would be the one who allowed him to be king. I would be the one who stepped out of the way so he could complete his relentless climb to the throne. But I had meant what I said to him on our walk through the snow on Christmas morning. My benevolence depended on his good behaviour, and he hadn't even made it four days before he disappointed me.

A woman with a trolley came along and gathered up my empty bowl and teacup, and I pulled my hood up so she wouldn't see my face. It was unlikely that I'd be recognised in Hong Kong, but all it would take was one sharp-eyed traveller or airport cleaner to take my photo, and weeks of careful planning would be ruined.

'I'll get in touch with Annabelle and Amira and let them know we're going with plan B,' Mary said. 'You should go to the hotel now. The reporter is waiting for you.'

I got off my chair, slung my backpack over my shoulder and headed for the airport hotel, which was tucked away at the back of the terminal.

After deciding to speak, I had texted Annabelle to ask for her blessing. I was going to reveal something that would forever change the way Papa was perceived. No matter how staunchly I defended him, his legacy would suffer.

At first, Annabelle didn't respond. But a few days later, my phone lit up my bedroom at 3 am.

You shouldn't do this alone, she wrote. *If you go with plan A, I will speak in support of you and your father. If you go with plan B, I will tell them everything I know, and everything Richard has done. Either way, I am with you.*

I expected Amira to try to talk us out of it. She was the practical one; she would remind me of the dangers of turning powerful friends into enemies. Instead, something ferocious shone in her eyes.

'Me too,' she said. 'I want to speak as well.'

We chose the newspaper in New York not just for its reputation, but because the American courts would never intervene on the palace's behalf. If we exposed Richard, no injunction could stop us, no defamation suit was likely to succeed. The paper had a team of reporters travelling the world in pursuit of the story. One was heading to India to talk to Annabelle; another was going to South Africa to see Amira. And I was due to meet with Dee, a fearsome Pulitzer winner who knew little about the royal family but everything about secrets and power.

In the hotel lobby, I kept my hood pulled over my face as I walked past the bored-looking staff at the check-in desk. When we'd agreed to meet here for our interview, Dee sent me a list of instructions over Signal so I could slip into her room without being recognised. Between two elevators stood a plastic palm tree. I casually reached into the pot and found a key card taped to the inside, just as she'd said I would.

At room 1207, I knocked twice and swiped the card. Inside, I found a woman sitting at a table by the window with a voice recorder before her. She looked at me with shrewd, pale eyes, a leather jacket draped over her shoulders.

She rose to her feet and hesitated, unsure what to do next. How does one greet a soon-to-be-ex-royal who was briefly the heir to the British throne before tumbling back down to Earth?

'Hi,' I said. I reached out my hand. 'I'm Lexi Villiers.'

'I'm Dee.'

We stood awkwardly for a moment in the rundown little room, stains on the carpet and the distant roar of a plane outside.

'I'm sorry about all the subterfuge involved in meeting up today,' I said. 'I'm just trying to get through this without being recognised. My family still thinks I'm in London.'

She put a gentle hand on my arm, and I saw that she was used to being in charge of every space she occupied, a queen in her own right, who ruled over newsrooms and granted mercy to nervous interviewees.

'It's fine. Come sit down,' she said.

I sank into a plastic chair and looked warily at the recorder before me. Once I spoke into it, there would be no going back.

I looked at Dee. 'I'm here to talk about the night my mother died, and I want to explain why I am unable to wear the crown,' I said. 'But there's something else I need to tell you. It's time the British people knew who their future king really is.'

CHAPTER THIRTY

31 December 2023

I woke up as the plane glided over Boomer Bay, sparkling in the summer sun, and then landed among the pine forests that surrounded the airport.

It was a perfect Hobart day. Despite the heat, I walked across the tarmac in my hoodie, breathing in the pure Southern Ocean air. I knew I was home when I watched, bleary-eyed, as a fibreglass seal statue glided past on the baggage carousel. Children with Australian accents dodged me as they ran around my feet. Sniffer dogs inspected my backpack for illicit apples.

I felt Jack's proximity like a cosmic tug. He was down the road, across a few paddocks, and behind the gates of the Jennings vineyard. But I knew I couldn't think about that. I pulled my hood forward so it nearly covered my eyes. No one had recognised me yet, not in the hotel where I spent twelve hours with Dee, and not on the two subsequent flights to get home. But Hobart was a small town, where it was common to run into old friends at the airport, so I kept my eyes on the floor.

As soon as I turned my phone back on, it rang.

'Hey,' I said quietly.

'Last leg okay?'

'Yep, all fine.' I peered at the hole in the wall where bags were starting to emerge. 'Any more updates?'

'Well,' Mary said, sounding pleased, 'Dee called Davide Rossi, and he agreed to give her an interview.'

My stomach lurched, and I looked at the people around me. Their eyes remained on the carousel as they waited for their bags.

'But Dee won't pay him,' I said. 'She's not that kind of journalist – she works for a paper of record, not a tabloid.'

'I know. She was as surprised as you are.'

A couple jostled to the front so they could pull a suitcase from the conveyor belt. Their little girl peered up at me curiously, and I turned, wandering further down the carousel where I would be away from the crowd.

'I don't understand why he'd do it.'

'She gave him a call, expecting he would just hang up. But she said he agreed to an interview on the spot. He wasn't looking for payment, he just wanted to be truthful about what happened,' Mary said. 'According to Dee, he said he'd never seen a mother and daughter who loved each other more. He called you "*bellezza* and *carina*".'

I let out a shaky breath and closed my eyes against the pain at the core of me. It was difficult to imagine that anyone could forgive me. But maybe James was right. Maybe I needed to forgive myself first.

'What happens now?' I asked Mary.

My bag finally appeared, and I struggled to drag it to my feet.

'Annabelle's and Amira's interviews are done, so Rossi is the last piece of the puzzle,' she said. 'The paper will have to talk to their legal team and then give Richard adequate time to respond, so I imagine the story will be out in about a week.'

I heard her hesitate.

'The palace will come after you hard. You know that, right? Their only option will be to try to discredit you.'

'I know.'

It felt like I had slowly edged the pin from my old life. Now I was watching the spring-loaded striker smashing against the fuse, lighting a tiny unstoppable spark. In a week's time, I would be stripped of my titles by parliament. But as Richard stepped over me, I was ready for him – I would be the explosive rolled at just the right moment, at just the right angle, detonating beneath his foot.

Soon everyone would know that he had tried to blackmail me. They would know that Papa and Annabelle spent years living in fear of Richard. And while Amira had spoken in support of Annabelle and me, she had shared no secrets of her own. The truth of Louis and Kris's relationship wasn't our story to tell. Maybe one day everyone would know how happy they were – after we were all gone.

'Why are you doing this?' Dee had asked me in the hotel room, her pen poised over a scribble-filled notepad. 'Are you trying to topple the monarchy?'

I was silent for a while, unsure of the answer. I had once believed I could change things from the inside. But if Granny was right, the crown had already decided whose head it was destined to land upon. There was a reason it briefly floated towards me – if only so I could nudge it away from Richard and towards Demelza.

'I'm doing this because I can't live with the lies anymore,' I said to Dee. 'My only option is to be honest about everything I've done and everything my uncle has done. The people of Britain and the Commonwealth deserve the truth. What happens next is up to them.'

Outside the airport, the heat was dry and stifling. I pulled off the hoodie I'd used to hide my face.

'Do you think this is going to work?' I asked Mary.

'Do I think three women can take on a powerful institution and force it to change? Probably not. But what's the alternative? Staying silent forever?'

I walked towards the pick-up lane. Ahead of me, I could see James leaning against the back of his LandCruiser with his hands in his pockets.

'I should go, my ride's here,' I said.

'Okay, I'll call with updates when I have them,' she said. 'Oh, and happy new year. For tomorrow.'

I wheeled my bag up to James's car and we stood staring at each other, neither of us able to smile. I was struck by how much he looked like Mum, though his hair was starting to go silver around his temples, the grooves in his face more pronounced. It was hard not to look at him and see her face if she had been allowed to age.

'Oh, dearest,' he said kindly, 'you look like hell.'

As he wrapped his arms around me, the tears finally came. I wept silently against his chest. I cried for my family and the mess I had made of my life. I cried for our twins who were lost to us. In all the years I had known him, James had never held me before, but he rubbed my back awkwardly and kissed the top of my head.

'It's alright. You're home now.'

We drove out of the airport and I looked from the window at the dry hills shimmering under a blue sky. Everything was the same as it always was – parched and spare and beautiful – and I could almost believe my lost year had never really happened. London felt very far away. Soon the real world would encroach again, but for now I was home, and no one knew where to find me.

'When do you start back at the hospital?' James asked as we turned onto the road towards Richmond.

The route would take us past the vineyard, and I braced myself for the sight of it.

'In two weeks,' I said.

'Do you think you'll be ready for that?'

I would be a third-year resident while all my colleagues had already moved onto their specialties. Every patient would know exactly who I was and what I had done. My face would be in their gossip magazines, and they would whisper about me behind their hands. I would be followed by photographers for months until the world moved on to the next scandal.

'I need to get back to my life,' I said, and it was true.

I could see the bright-red gates of the Jennings vineyard ahead of us, the neat rows of the pinot vines already fluttering by my window. I was wondering whether I should avert my eyes when I realised James was pulling the car over.

'What are we doing?' I asked, alarmed.

He turned the engine off and looked at me levelly. 'I think we should go in.'

My eyes blurred with hot tears. Even in the midst of my distress, I wondered if I was ever going to get hold of myself again. I had once been a girl who hadn't cried in years, who couldn't force the tears to come even when I needed them to. Now I couldn't seem to stop.

'No,' I said, shaking my head. 'Please, you don't understand—'

'Lexi,' James said, 'Jack knows everything. Amira called him a few weeks ago and told him what was happening. She told him what Richard was doing to you. She told him about the boat. She told him you've been miserable ever since he left Scotland.'

When I turned to look at him, he brushed a tear off my cheek.

'Then she had to call *me* because it was all she could do to stop him getting on a plane to London to go rescue you himself. I had to drive down here in the middle of the night and promise him I would get you home safe.'

I hid my face in my palms and wept. Distantly, I felt James's hand on my back again.

'I won't make you go in,' he said. 'But he knows I'm picking you up today and he wants to see you.'

'Amira told him?' I managed.

James nodded. 'All of it. Now, what do you want to do?

Should we keep driving? Or do you want to go tell this man how you feel?'

We drove through the gates and up the long gravel path, through the thick vines that would soon be ready to harvest, and past the old house. Among the poplars, I could just glimpse our cottage. It was New Year's Eve, so Paula would be camping down on the peninsula. Finn, I knew, was on shift at the hospital. We rumbled through the cluster of sheds and out towards the back field where Jack had once told me he planned to experiment with a dark-skinned terret noir.

Between two young budding vines, he stood with his back to us. But when he heard the car, he turned, shading his eyes against the afternoon sun. There he was, all of him exactly the same, still too wonderful to contemplate.

James wrenched up the handbrake and looked at me.

'Go on,' he said. 'It'll be alright.'

On unsteady legs, I got out of the car. Jack stood there waiting, the stretch of field between us somehow several furlongs, and also just a few shaky steps if either of us cared to measure. *If he comes towards me,* I thought, *maybe he can forgive me. If he meets me halfway, maybe everything will be alright.* I had spent the last five months banishing any thought of him from my mind, convinced I could forget him if I tried hard enough. With one glimpse of his warm eyes, I understood that all of it was a lie, the surge of feeling, all feelings, like a wellspring inside me.

I walked down the vine row, and he came towards me until we met in the middle.

'Hi,' I rasped, astonished by his face all over again.

He smiled at me sadly. 'Are you okay?'

'Yeah,' I said. Then I took a deep breath; I had nothing left to give him but the truth. 'I mean, no. I've actually been a bit of a mess.'

He reached forward then, tentatively putting his hands on my shoulders.

'Amira told me what happened,' he said. He laughed and shook his head. 'I bought a plane ticket. I was going to go over there to make sure you were okay. But Amira and James were worried I'd blow your cover. They said you needed to get yourself home.'

A family of magpies carrolled in the trees and his thumb stroked the curve of my shoulder.

'She told me about your mum too. I'm so sorry, Lex. I wish I'd known.'

I was determined to pluck out my secrets like they were thorns hidden in my flesh. But even as I had found a journalist and told her my story, I still couldn't allow myself to think of the moment Jack read it and learned the truth about me. It made me hot with shame to imagine him discovering how completely I could fail the people I loved. But, I supposed, he'd already learned that about me when I walked away from him on that cliff in Scotland.

'I used to be terrified that you'd find out,' I said. 'I was scared of anyone knowing, but you especially.'

'Why?'

'Because ...' I dipped my head, unable to cope with his eyes on me. 'I always thought Mum and I were different from the others, but when it really counted, I chose them. I thought if you knew that about me, you'd never ...'

My voice began to fail me. Throughout our history as dogged, dysfunctional friends, I was occasionally possessed by the desire to tell him. We'd be on one of our long walks through the Tasmanian bush when I'd suddenly turn, heady with the possibility of confession. But one glance at his face had always been enough to convince me to swallow the truth back down.

'I wouldn't what?' Jack asked softly.

'You wouldn't ... look at me the same.'

'You were just a kid. You were in trouble, and you called your dad. Amira said you thought I wouldn't want you if I knew, and Lex ...'

I was still staring at my feet, but he put a finger under my chin so I would meet his gaze. There was a fierce expression on his face that I could barely take.

'Am I looking at you differently?'

He wasn't, and it was more than I deserved. A tear slipped down my cheek. 'I don't understand – you should hate me.'

His brows came together, his eyes shining.

'Lex, I could never hate you,' he said. 'And I don't really know what you want or how you feel, but you're always going to be my best friend, okay? Always.'

We looked at each other in the beating summer sun. I'd been granted the gift of one final chance, and I would not let the only thing I really wanted slip through my fingers.

'I'm so sorry I sent you away,' I said, short-breathed. 'I just … I was so scared of what would happen if you really knew me. And then I was scared I was never going to see you again. Because I love you – of course I do, I always have. I loved you right from the start.'

How easily the words came, even though they'd been lodged inside me for years. Sometimes they were buried safe in my gut; sometimes they grew like saplings in my chest. But they had always been there, no matter how much I tried to ignore them, until I finally dared to speak, and they bloomed from my parted lips.

Jack took my fingers in his and then he pressed them, interwoven, against his chest. The hammer of his heart matched mine.

'When are you going to understand that I've always known you, Lex? And I'm never going to stop loving you. I tried. I tried for five months, and every day felt like it was going to kill me. I couldn't give you up.'

This was the second time I'd crossed a field for him, and the second time I had looked into his face and known my life was about to change. I reached for him, my hands on his chest, my tremulous breaths on his cheek, and he pulled me into his arms and covered my mouth with his.

I wondered if I would ruin this, or if I might find myself more capable than I imagined. We could unpack my bags and put the treasures I'd brought home from London in new, permanent locations around the cottage. Maybe I would hide the polaroid of Louis and Kris between the pages of a book, watching the edges curl, their beautiful faces fading as the years passed. I could jimmy a plank out of the barn floor and replace it with the witch marks Papa left for me, knowing it was always underfoot, always protecting me. Then, finally, I could dig a hole in the cottage garden and return Mum's ring to the earth – the gold and the emerald back where they belonged. Maybe I would stay on this vineyard, surrounded by the remnants of my family, for the rest of my days.

Wrapped in his arms, I looked at Jack, my weary heart daring to hope.

'Everything's about to get really bad,' I whispered.

He smiled and shook his head. Then he kissed my temple and put his mouth to my ear.

'You're wrong,' he said. 'Everything's about to get really good.'

*

I'm drifting on a black sea under an explosion of stars. This time, Mum is beside me. She looks over and smiles and I see that she's no longer young. She never fell from the boat, but she lived and she aged and she stayed in the world. We hold hands and look up so we can marvel at the sky above us.

These days, I'm no longer afraid of sleep.

Jack kisses my bare shoulder to wake me. It might be the morning after I came home from London. It might be a decade later. For the rest of our lives, we would wake up every New Year's Day to greet the sun.

'Hey,' he whispers. 'Time to wake up.'

I groan, not quite ready to let Mum go. 'Now?'

He kisses my neck and I turn so I can pull him into my embrace. It's so warm that I can feel him starting to sink back into sleep, but he stirs again.

'Now,' he says. 'Come on. First sunrise of the year.'

I blink awake and see him lying there, his cheek against the pillow next to mine. He smiles that slow smile of his.

'There you are,' he whispers and presses his lips to mine. 'Time to go.'

We pull on our clothes and, with our hands intertwined, we walk among the vines towards the slightest arc of light on the horizon. The sun is slowly dying, burning through its fire and its vim. One day it will go dark and everything will be cold. But for now, as we make another orbit around the sun, it all feels new. Anything feels possible.

AUTHOR'S ACKNOWLEDGEMENTS

The Heir Apparent was written in lutruwita and I pay my respects to the Tasmanian Aboriginal people as the traditional and original owners of this land. This is a story about monarchy and colonialism, forces that brought unimaginable horrors to this island. I honour the true custodians of this beautiful place, and acknowledge their sovereignty over land, river and sky, none of which was ever ceded.

While writing a novel is a solitary experience, releasing it into the world is a community effort. You wouldn't be holding it in your hands (or listening to the audiobook version if that's more your speed) if not for an incredible group of people who found me, rallied around me, and turned *The Heir Apparent* into something finer than I could ever have been capable of achieving alone.

My biggest thanks go to my agent Gaby Naher, who is easily the coolest woman in the world. She plucked me from obscurity and made all my dreams come true in a matter of days. Your belief in me changed everything. Without you, none of this would have happened. My heartfelt gratitude also goes to Victoria Hobbs and everyone at the AM Heath team, Kim Witherspoon at Inkwell, and Mary Pender at WME.

It has been an honour and a pleasure to work with publishers Catherine Milne, Reagan Arthur and Priyal Agrawal. I am in awe of all of you. Your brilliant ideas and creativity blew open all the doors and windows in my mind. Your faith in me has been transformative. Thank you for this opportunity.

Thank you to Dr Norman Swan for your wise counsel and for changing Will's and my lives several times over. You have always been unfailingly generous to both of us, and even though you don't like a fuss, please know that we love you.

A big teary thank you to Tim Ayliffe, who was a mentor to me when I was a young producer and then transitioned seamlessly into becoming my writing mentor when I decided to follow in his footsteps and attempt to write a book. Thank you for taking all my slightly panicked phone calls throughout this journey and letting me send way too many pages to your house.

I was lucky enough to be able to ask three very smart women, Yasmin Parry, Emily Clark and Laura McCusker, to read a rough draft of this manuscript, and their encouragement and very smart feedback made *The Heir Apparent* what it is today. Thank you for being my very first readers, as well as invaluable friends.

There are so many people working behind the scenes in publishing who support writers, who love books and want stories to be the best versions they could be. Huge thanks to everyone at HarperCollins Australia, freelance editor Jo Lyons, everyone at Hachette/Grand Central and Cardinal including Gideon Pine and Emily Chen, and the team at HQ UK.

Thank you to the family of journalists, producers and editors who taught me how to write, who honed my storytelling skills, put up with me, honoured me with their friendship, and raised me over the last twenty years: Zahed Cachalia, Edmond Roy, Gavin Fang, Lisa Whitby, Roscoe Whalan, Sophie Scott, James Thomas, Jake Sturmer, Tom Joyner, Carrington Clarke, Lucy Sweeney, Danielle Cronin, Ben Atherton, Leigh Tonkin and Wing Kuang. Thank you to Dee Porter – none of this would have happened without your belief in me. You retired on a Friday, and by Monday, I was on this publishing journey, and I truly believe that was the universe looking out for me. And thank you to my work wife and byline bestie, Lucia Stein. There is nothing better than yapping to you all day on Teams about which juicy mystery or royal scandal we will tackle next.

Thank you to my parents, Noel and Lynda, who have always supported me, let me read anything I wanted, kept every silly thing I wrote as a child, and allowed me to drop maths in high school, even though it made them very nervous. Thank you to Sarah for being my very first friend in this world. Thank you to Oz, Rose, Oli and Nica. Thank you to my grandmother, Anne Jackson, who is the family's original storyteller and our own queen. Thank you to Chino and Ragu for being good boys.

Thank you to Clive and Angela Ockenden for being dreamy in-laws who always offer me a glass of wine whenever I walk through the door, and who made the vineyard sections of this book sound about right. Thank you to Andy Philpott and Lucy Ockenden for letting me pick your brains about the medical profession, and for being wonderful friends.

Thank you to Will for being my love and my champion. Thank you for bringing me a coffee in bed every morning and for supporting me on every step of this journey. Thank you for believing this was possible.

This novel is one big love letter to lutruwita/Tasmania, whose ravishing beauty finally inspired me to stop thinking about *The Heir Apparent* and just write it down. Thank you for being wild, pristine and chilly enough that I could plonk myself by the fire and finally get this done. Thank you to the creative, kind-hearted people of lutruwita/Tasmania, half of whom seemed to know I was writing a book before I'd even told anyone, and offered nothing but encouragement and love.

*

I would also like to acknowledge a few specific sources. To create my semi-fictional version of Barbara Villiers, I often consulted the diaries of English writer Samuel Pepys. When Jenny Walsh says the three rights of the modern sovereign are to consult, to encourage and to warn, she is quoting *The English Constitution* by Walter Bagehot. And when Lexi and Stewart discuss the aftermath of Isla's death, Lexi paraphrases a famous quote by psychiatrist JL Moreno: 'The body remembers what the mind forgets.'

Finally, I'd like to acknowledge that the seal statue no longer rides the baggage carousel at Hobart Airport and note that *The Heir Apparent* takes place in a better world where it was never removed.

All errors in this book are unfortunately mine – or, perhaps, Barbara Villiers changed some of the rules of British monarchy during her fictional regency.

ONE PLACE. MANY STORIES

Bold, innovative and
empowering publishing.

FOLLOW US ON:

@HQStories